The Caves of Steel

The Rest of the Robots

D1810364

Isaac Asimov

HarperCollins*Publishers*

Voyager
An Imprint of HarperCollins*Publishers*
77-85 Fulham Palace Road
Hammersmith, London W6 8JB

www.voyager-books.com

This omnibus edition 2006

Caves of Steel © Isaac Asimov 1954
The Rest of the Robots © Isaac Asimov 1964

ISBN 0007777701

Printed and bound in Great Britain by
Bookmarque Ltd, Croydon, Surrey

Isaac Asimov

Isaac Asimov, world maestro of science fiction, was born in Russia near Smolensk in 1920 and brought to the United States by his parents three years later. He grew up in Brooklyn where he went to grammar school and at the age of eight he gained his citizen papers. A remarkable memory helped him finish high school before he was sixteen. He then went on to Columbia University and resolved to become a chemist rather than follow the medical career his father had in mind for him. He graduated in chemistry and after a short spell in the Army he gained his doctorate in 1949 and qualified as an instructor in biochemistry at Boston University School of Medicine where he became Associate Professor in 1955, doing research in nucleic acid. Increasingly, however, the pressures of chemical research conflicted with his aspirations in the literary field, and in 1958 he retired to full-time authorship while retaining his connection with the University.

Asimov's fantastic career as a science fiction writer began in 1939 with the appearance of a short story, *Marooned Off Vesta*, in *Amazing Stories*. Thereafter he became a regular contributor to the leading SF magazines of the day including *Astounding*, *Astonishing Stories*, *Super Science Stories* and *Galaxy*. He won the Hugo Award four times and the Nebula Award once. With nearly five hundred books to his credit and several hundred articles, Asimov's output was prolific by any standards. Apart from his many world-famous science fiction works, Asimov also wrote highly successful detective mystery stories, a four-volume *History of North America*, a two-volume *Guide to the Bible*, a biographical dictionary, encyclopaedias, textbooks and an impressive list of books on many aspects of science, as well as two volumes of autobiography.

Isaac Asimov died in 1992 at the age of 72.

BY THE SAME AUTHOR

The Caves of Steel

To My Wife
GERTRUDE
and My Son
DAVID

Contents

CHAPTER ONE

CONVERSATION WITH A COMMISSIONER

Lije Baley had just reached his desk when he became aware of R. Sammy watching him expectantly.

The dour lines of his long face hardened. "What do you want?"

"The boss wants you, Lije. Right away. Soon as you come in."

"All right."

R. Sammy stood there blankly.

Baley said, "I said, all right. Go away!"

R. Sammy turned on his heel and left to go about his duties. Baley wondered irritably why those same duties couldn't be done by a man.

He paused to examine the contents of his tobacco pouch and make a mental calculation. At two pipefuls a day, he could stretch it to next quota day.

Then he stepped out from behind his railing (he'd rated a railed corner two years ago) and walked the length of the common room.

Simpson looked up from a merc-pool file as he passed. "Boss wants you, Lije."

"I know. R. Sammy told me."

A closely coded tape reeled out of the merc-pool's vitals as the small instrument searched and analyzed its "memory" for the desired information stored in the tiny vibration patterns of the gleaming mercury surface within.

"I'd kick R. Sammy's behind if I weren't afraid I'd break a leg," said Simpson. "I saw Vince Barrett the other day."

"Oh?"

"He was looking for his job back. Or any job in the Department. The poor kid's desperate, but what could I tell him. R. Sammy's doing his job and that's all. The kid has to work a delivery tread on the yeast farms now. He was a bright boy, too. Everyone liked him."

Baley shrugged and said in a manner stiffer than he intended or felt, "It's a thing we're all living through."

The boss rated a private office. It said JULIUS ENDERBY on the clouded glass. Nice letters. Carefully etched into the fabric of the glass. Underneath, it said COMMISSIONER OF POLICE, CITY OF NEW YORK.

Baley stepped in and said, "You want to see me, Commissioner?"

Enderby looked up. He wore spectacles because his eyes were sensitive and couldn't take the usual contact lenses. It was only after one got used to the sight of them that one could take in the rest of the face, which was quite undistinguished. Baley had a strong notion that the Commissioner valued his glasses for the personality they lent him and suspected that his eyeballs weren't as sensitive as all that.

The Commissioner looked definitely nervous. He straightened his cuffs, leaned back, and said, too heartily, "Sit down, Lije. Sit down."

Baley sat down stiffly and waited.

Enderby said, "How's Jessie? And the boy?"

"Fine," said Baley, hollowly. "Just fine. And your family?"

"Fine," echoed Enderby. "Just fine."

It had been a false start.

Baley thought: Something's wrong with his face.

Aloud, he said, "Commissioner, I wish you wouldn't send R. Sammy out after me."

"Well, you know how I feel about those things, Lije. But he's been put here and I've got to use him for something."

"It's uncomfortable, Commissioner. He tells me you want me and then he stands there. You know what I mean. I have to tell him to go or he just keeps on standing there."

"Oh, that's my fault, Lije. I gave him the message to deliver and forgot to tell him specifically to get back to his job when he was through."

Baley sighed. The fine wrinkles about his intensely brown eyes grew more pronounced. "Anyway, you wanted to see me."

"Yes, Lije," said the Commissioner, "but not for anything easy."

He stood up, turned away, and walked to the wall behind his desk. He touched an inconspicuous contact switch and a section of the wall grew transparent.

Baley blinked at the unexpected insurge of grayish light.

The Commissioner smiled. "I had this arranged specially last year, Lije. I don't think I've showed it to you before. Come over here and take a look. In the old days, all rooms had things like this. They were called 'windows.' Did you know that?"

Baley knew that very well, having viewed many historical novels.

"I've heard of them," he said.

"Come here."

Baley squirmed a bit, but did as he was told. There was something indecent about the exposure of the privacy of a room to the outside world. Sometimes the Commissioner carried his affectation of Medievalism to a rather foolish extreme.

Like his glasses, Baley thought.

That was it! That was what made him look wrong!

Baley said, "Pardon me, Commissioner, but you're wearing new glasses, aren't you?"

The Commissioner stared at him in mild surprise, took off his glasses, looked at them and then at Baley. Without his glasses, his round face seemed rounder and his chin a trifle more pronounced. He looked vaguer, too, as his eyes failed to focus properly.

He said, "Yes."

He put his glasses back on his nose, then added with real anger, "I broke my old ones three days ago. What with one thing or another I wasn't able to replace them till this morning. Lije, those three days were hell."

"On account of the glasses?"

"And other things, too. I'm getting to that."

He turned to the window and so did Baley. With mild shock, Baley realized it was raining. For a minute, he was lost in the spectacle of water dropping from the sky, while the Commissioner exuded a kind of pride as though the phenomenon were a matter of his own arranging.

"This is the third time this month I've watched it rain. Quite a sight, don't you think?"

Against his will, Baley had to admit to himself that it was impressive. In his forty-two years he had rarely seen rain, or any of the phenomena of nature, for that matter.

He said, "It always seems a waste for all that water to come down on the city. It should restrict itself to the reservoirs."

"Lije," said the Commissioner, "you're a modernist. That's your trouble. In Medieval times, people lived in the open. I don't mean on the farms only. I mean in the cities, too. Even in New York. When it rained, they didn't think of it as waste. They gloried in it. They lived close to nature. It's healthier, better. The troubles of modern life come from being divorced from nature. Read up on the Coal Century, sometimes."

Baley had. He had heard many people moaning about the invention of the atomic pile. He moaned about it himself when things went wrong, or when he got tired. Moaning like that was a built-in facet of human nature. Back in the Coal Century, people moaned about the invention of the steam engine. In one of Shakespeare's plays, a character moaned about the invention of gunpowder. A thousand years in the future, they'd be moaning about the invention of the positronic brain.

The hell with it.

He said, grimly, "Look, Julius." (It wasn't his habit to get friendly with the Commissioner during office hours, however many 'Lijes' the Commissioner threw at him, but something special seemed called for here.) "Look, Julius, you're talking about everything except what I came in here for, and it's worrying me. What is it?"

The Commissioner said, "I'll get to it, Lije. Let me do it my way. It's – it's trouble."

"Sure. What isn't on this planet? More trouble with the R's?"

"In a way, yes, Lije. I stand here and wonder how much more trouble the old world can take. When I put in this window, I wasn't just letting in the sky once in a while. I let in the City. I look at it and I wonder what will become of it in another century."

Baley felt repelled by the other's sentimentality, but he found himself staring outward in fascination. Even dimmed by the weather, the City was a tremendous thing to see. The Police Department was in the upper levels of City Hall, and City Hall reached high. From the Commissioner's window, the neighboring towers fell short and the tops were visible. They were so many fingers, groping upward. Their walls were blank, featureless. They were the outer shells of human hives.

"In a way," said the Commissioner, "I'm sorry it's raining.

We can't see Spacetown."

Baley looked westward, but it was as the Commissioner said. The horizon closed down. New York's towers grew misty and came to an end against blank whiteness.

"I know what Spacetown is like," said Baley.

"I like the picture from here," said the Commissioner. "It can just be made out in the gap between the two Brunswick Sectors. Low domes spread out. It's the difference between us and the Spacers. We reach high and crowd close. With them, each family has a dome for itself. One family: one house. And land between each dome. Have you ever spoken to any of the Spacers, Lije?"

"A few times. About a month ago, I spoke to one right here on your intercom," Baley said, patiently.

"Yes, I remember. But then I'm getting philosophical. We and they. Different ways of life."

Baley's stomach was beginning to constrict a little. The more devious the Commissioner's approach, the deadlier he thought might be the conclusion.

He said, "All right. But what's so surprising about it? You can't spread eight million people over Earth in little domes. They've got space on their worlds, so let them live their way."

The Commissioner walked to his chair and sat down. His eyes looked unblinkingly at Baley, shrunken a bit by the concave lenses in his spectacles. He said, "Not everyone is that tolerant about differences in culture. Either among us or among the Spacers."

"All right. So what?"

"So three days ago, a Spacer died."

Now it was coming. The corners of Baley's thin lips raised a trifle, but the effect upon his long, sad face was unnoticeable. He said, "Too bad. Something contagious, I hope. A virus. A cold, perhaps."

The Commissioner looked startled, "What are you talking about?"

Baley didn't care to explain. The precision with which the Spacers had bred disease out of their societies was well known. The care with which they avoided, as far as possible, contact with disease-riddled Earthmen was even better known. But then, sarcasm was lost on the Commissioner.

Baley said, "I'm just talking. What did he die of?" He turned back to the window.

The Commissioner said, "He died of a missing chest. Someone had used a blaster on him."

Baley's back grew rigid. He said, without turning, "What are *you* talking about?"

"I'm talking about murder," said the Commissioner, softly. "You're a plain-clothes man. You know what murder is."

And now Baley turned. "But a Spacer! Three days ago?"

"Yes."

"But who did it? How?"

"The Spacers say it was an Earthman."

"It can't be."

"Why not? You don't like the Spacers. I don't. Who on Earth does? Someone didn't like them a little too much, that's all."

"Sure, but –"

"There was the fire at the Los Angeles factories. There was the Berlin R-smashing. There were the riots in Shanghai."

"All right."

"It all points to rising discontent. Maybe to some sort of organization."

Baley said, "Commissioner, I don't get this. Are you testing me for some reason?"

"What?" The Commissioner looked honestly bewildered.

Baley watched him. "Three days ago a Spacer was murdered and the Spacers think the murderer is an Earthman. Till now," his finger tapped the desk, "nothing's come out. Is that right? Commissioner, that's unbelievable. Jehoshaphat, Commissioner, a thing like this would blow New York off the face of the planet if it really happened."

The Commissioner shook his head. "It's not as simple as that. Look, Lije, I've been out three days. I've been in conference with the Mayor. I've been out to Spacetown. I've been down in Washington, talking to the Terrestrial Bureau of Investigation."

"Oh? And what do the Terries have to say?"

"They say it's our baby. It's inside city limits. Spacetown is under New York jurisdiction."

"But *with* extraterritorial rights."

"I know. I'm coming to that." The Commissioner's eyes fell away from Baley's flinty stare. He seemed to regard himself

as having been rudely demoted to the position of Baley's under-
ling, and Baley behaved as though he accepted the fact.

"The Spacers can run the show," said Baley.

"Wait a minute, Lije," pleaded the Commissioner. "Don't
rush me. I'm trying to talk this over, friend to friend. I want you
to know my position. I was there when the news broke. I had an
appointment with him – with Roj Nemennuh Sarton."

"The victim?"

"The victim." The Commissioner groaned. "Five minutes
more and I, myself, would have discovered the body. What a
shock that would have been. As it was, it was brutal, brutal. They
met me and told me. It started a three-day nightmare, Lije. That
on top of having everything blur on me and having no time to
replace my glasses for days. *That* won't happen again, at least.
I've ordered three pairs."

Baley considered the picture he conjured up of the event. He
could see the tall, fair figures of the Spacers approaching the
Commissioner with the news and breaking it to him in their un-
varnished emotionless way. Julius would remove his glasses and
polish them. Inevitably, under the impact of the event, he would
drop them, then look down at the broken remnants with a
quiver of his soft, full lips. Baley was quite certain that, for five
minutes anyway, the Commissioner was much more disturbed
over his glasses than over the murder.

The Commissioner was saying, "It's a devil of a position. As
you say, the Spacers have extraterritorial rights. They *can* insist
on their own investigation, make whatever report they wish to
their home governments. The Outer Worlds could use this as an
excuse to pile on indemnity charges. You know how *that* would
sit with the population."

"It would be political suicide for the White House to agree to
pay."

"And another kind of suicide not to pay."

"You don't have to draw me a picture," said Baley. He had
been a small boy when the gleaming cruisers from outer space
last sent down their soldiers into Washington, New York, and
Moscow to collect what they claimed was theirs.

"Then you see. Pay or not pay, it's trouble. The only way out
is to find the murderer on our own and hand him over to the
Spacers. It's up to us."

"Why not give it to the TBI? Even if it is our jurisdiction from a legalistic viewpoint, there's the question of interstellar relations –"

"The TBI won't touch it. This is *hot* and it's in our lap." For a moment, he lifted his head and gazed keenly at his subordinate. "And it's not good, Lije. Every one of us stands the chance of being out of a job."

Baley said, "Replace us all? Nuts. The trained men to do it with don't exist."

"R's," said the Commissioner. "*They* exist."

"What?"

"R. Sammy is just a beginning. He runs errands. Others can patrol the expressways. Damn it, man, I know the Spacers better than you do, and I know what they're doing. There are R's that can do your work and mine. We can be declassified. Don't think differently. And at our age, to hit the labor pool . . ."

Baley said, gruffly, "All right."

The Commissioner looked abashed. "Sorry, Lije."

Baley nodded and tried not to think of his father. The Commissioner knew the story, of course.

Baley said, "When did all this replacement business come up?"

"Look, you're being naïve, Lije. It's been happening all along. It's been happening for twenty-five years, ever since the Spacers came. You know that. It's just beginning to reach higher, that's all. If we muff this case, it's a big, long step toward the point where we can stop looking forward to collecting our pension-tab booklets. On the other hand, Lije, if we handle the matter well, it can shove that point far into the future. And it would be a particular break for you."

"For me?" said Baley.

"You'll be the operative in charge, Lije."

"I don't rate it, Commissioner. I'm a C—5, that's all."

"You want a C—6 rating, don't you?"

Did he? Baley knew the privileges a C—6 rating carried. A seat on the expressway in the rush hour, not just from ten to four. Higher up on the list-of-choice at the Section kitchens. Maybe even a chance at a better apartment and a quota ticket to the Solarium levels for Jessie.

"I want it," he said. "Sure. Why wouldn't I? But what would I get if I couldn't break the case?"

"Why wouldn't you break it, Lije?" the Commissioner wheedled. "You're a good man. You're one of the best we have."

"But there are half a dozen men with higher ratings in my department section. Why should they be passed over?"

Baley did not say out loud, though his bearing implied it strongly, that the Commissioner did not move outside protocol in this fashion except in cases of wild emergency.

The Commissioner folded his hands. "Two reasons. You're not just another detective to me, Lije. We're friends, too. I'm not forgetting we were in college together. Sometimes it may look as though I have forgotten, but that's the fault of rating. I'm Commissioner, and you know what that means. But I'm still your friend and this is a tremendous chance for the right person. I want you to have it."

"That's one reason," said Baley, without warmth.

"The second reason is that I think you're my friend. I need a favor."

"What sort of favor?"

"I want you to take on a Spacer partner in this deal. That was the condition the Spacers made. They've agreed not to report the murder; they've agreed to leave the investigation in our hands. In return, they insist one of their own agents be in on the deal, the whole deal."

"It sounds like they don't trust us altogether."

"Surely you see their point. If this is mishandled, a number of them will be in trouble with their own governments. I'll give them the benefit of the doubt, Lije. I'm willing to believe they mean well."

"I'm sure they do, Commissioner. That's the trouble with them."

The Commissioner looked blank at that, but went on. "Are you willing to take on a Spacer partner, Lije?"

"You're asking that as a favor?"

"Yes, I'm asking you to take the job with all the conditions the Spacers have set up."

"I'll take a Spacer partner, Commissioner."

"Thanks, Lije. He'll have to live with you."

"Oh, now, hold on."

"I know. I know. But you've got a large apartment, Lije. Three rooms. Only one child. You can put him up. He'll be no trouble. No trouble at all. And it's necessary."

"Jessie won't like it. I know that."

"You tell Jessie," the Commissioner was earnest, so earnest that his eyes seemed to bore holes through the glass discs blocking his stare, "that if you do this for me, I'll do what I can when this is all over to jump you a grade. C—7, Lije. C—7!"

"All right, Commissioner, it's a deal."

Baley half rose from his chair, caught the look on Enderby's face, and sat down again.

"There's something else?"

Slowly, the Commissioner nodded. "One more item."

"Which is?"

"The name of your partner."

"What difference does that make?"

"The Spacers," said the Commissioner, "have peculiar ways. The partner they're supplying isn't – isn't . . ."

Baley's eyes opened wide. "Just a minute!"

"You've got to, Lije. You've *got* to. There's no way out."

"Stay at my apartment? A thing like that?"

"As a friend, please!"

"No. *No!*"

"Lije, I can't trust anyone else in this. Do I have to spell it out for you? We've got to work with the Spacers. We've got to succeed, if we're to keep the indemnity ships away from Earth. But we can't succeed just any old way. You'll be partnered with one of their R's. If *he* breaks the case, if he can report that we're incompetent, we're ruined, anyway. We, as a department. You see that, don't you? So you've got a delicate job on your hands. You've got to work with him, but see to it that *you* solve the case and not he. Understand?"

"You mean co-operate with him 100 per cent, except that I cut his throat? Pat him on the back with a knife in my hand?"

"What else can we do? There's no other way out."

Lije Baley stood irresolute. "I don't know what Jessie will say."

"I'll talk to her, if you want me to."

"No, Commissioner." He drew a deep, sighing breath. "What's my partner's name?"

"R. Daneel Olivaw."

Baley said, sadly, "This isn't a time for euphemism, Commissioner. I'm taking the job, so let's use his full name. *Robot* Daneel Olivaw."

CHAPTER TWO
ROUND TRIP ON AN EXPRESSWAY

There was the usual, entirely normal crowd on the expressway: the standees on the lower level and those with seat privileges above. A continuous trickle of humanity filtered off the expressway, across the decelerating strips to localways or into the stationaries that led under arches or over bridges into the endless mazes of the City Sections. Another trickle, just as continuous, worked inward from the other side, across the accelerating strips and onto the expressway.

There were the infinite lights: the luminous walls and ceilings that seemed to drip cool, even phospherescence; the flashing advertisements screaming for attention: the harsh, steady gleam of the "light-worms" that directed THIS WAY TO JERSEY SECTIONS, FOLLOW ARROWS TO EAST RIVER SHUTTLE, UPPER LEVEL FOR ALL WAYS TO LONG ISLAND SECTIONS.

Most of all there was the noise that was inseparable from life: the sound of millions talking, laughing, coughing, calling, humming, breathing.

No directions anywhere to Spacetown, thought Baley.

He stepped from strip to strip with the ease of a lifetime's practice. Children learned to "hop the strips" as soon as they learned to walk. Baley scarcely felt the jerk of acceleration as his velocity increased with each step. He was not even aware that he leaned forward against the force. In thirty seconds he had reached the final sixty-mile-an-hour strip and could step aboard the railed and glassed-in moving platform that was the expressway.

No directions to Spacetown, he thought.

No need for directions. If you've business there, you know the way. If you don't know the way, you've no business there. When Spacetown was first established some twenty-five years earlier, there was a strong tendency to make a showplace out of it. The hordes of the City herded in that direction.

The Spacers put a stop to that. Politely (they were always polite), but without any compromise with tact, they put up a force barrier between themselves and the City. They established a combination Immigration Service and Customs Inspection. If you had business, you identified yourself, allowed yourself to be searched, and submitted to a medical examination and a routine disinfection.

It gave rise to dissatisfaction. Naturally. More dissatisfaction than it deserved. Enough dissatisfaction to put a serious spoke in the program of modernization. Baley remembered the Barrier Riots. He had been part of the mob that had suspended itself from the rails of the expressways, crowded onto the seats in disregard of their rating privileges, run recklessly along and across the strips at the risk of a broken body, and remained just outside the Spacetown barrier for two days, shouting slogans and destroying City property out of sheer frustration.

Baley could still sing the chants of the time if he put his mind to it. There was "Man Was Born on Mother Earth, Do You Hear?" to an old folk tune with the gibberish refrain, "Hinky-dinky-parley-voo."

> *"Man was born on Mother Earth, do you hear?*
> *Earth's the world that gave him birth, do you hear?*
> *Spacer, get off the face*
> *Of Mother Earth and into space.*
> *Dirty Spacer, do you hear?"*

There were hundreds of verses. A few were witty, most were stupid, many were obscene. Every one, however, ended with "Dirty Spacer, do you hear?" Dirty, dirty. It was the futile throwing back in the face of the Spacers their most keenly felt insult: their insistence on considering the natives of Earth as disgustingly diseased.

The Spacers didn't leave, of course. It wasn't even necessary for them to bring any of their offensive weapons into play. Earth's outmoded fleet had long since learned that it was suicide to venture near any Outer World ship. Earth planes that had ventured over the Spacetown area in the very early days of its establishment had simply disappeared. At the most, a shredded wing tip might tumble down to Earth.

And no mob could be so maddened as to forget the effect of the subetheric hand disruptors used on Earthmen in the wars of a century ago.

So the Spacers sat behind their barrier, which itself was the product of their own advanced science, and that no method existed on Earth of breaking. They just waited stolidly on the other side of the barrier until the City quieted the mob with somno vapor and retch gas. The below-level penitentiaries rattled afterward with ringleaders, malcontents, and people who had been picked up simply because they were nearest at hand. After a while they were all set free.

After a proper interva', the Spacers eased their restrictions. The barrier was removed and the City Police entrusted with the protection of Spacetown's isolation. Most important of all, the medical examination was more unobtrusive.

Now, thought Baley, things might take a reverse trend. If the Spacers seriously thought that an Earthman had entered Spacetown and committed murder, the barrier might go up again. It would be bad.

He lifted himself onto the expressway platform, made his way through the standees to the tight spiral ramp that led to the upper level, and there sat down. He didn't put his rating ticket in his hatband till they passed the last of the Hudson Sections. A C—5 had no seat rights east of the Hudson and west of Long Island, and although there was ample seating available at the moment, one of the way guards would have automatically ousted him. People were increasingly petty about rating privileges and in all honesty, Baley lumped himself in with "people."

The air made the characteristic whistling noise as it frictioned off the curved windshields set up above the back of every seat. It made talking a chore, but it was no bar to thinking when you were used to it.

Most Earthmen were Medievalists in one way or another. It was an easy thing to be when it meant looking back to a time when Earth was *the* world and not just one of fifty. The misfit one of fifty at that.

Baley's head snapped to the right at the sound of a female shriek. A woman had dropped her handbag; he saw it for an instant, a pastel pink blob against the dull gray of the strips. A passenger hurrying from the expressway must inadvertently have kicked it in the direction of deceleration and now the owner was whirling away from her property.

A corner of Baley's mouth quirked. She might catch up with it, if she were clever enough to hurry to a strip that moved slower still and if other feet did not kick it this way or that. He would never know whether she would or not. The scene was half a mile to the rear, already.

Chances were she wouldn't. It had been calculated that, on the average, something was dropped on the strips every three minutes somewhere in the City and not recovered. The Lost and Found Department was a huge proposition. It was just one more complication of modern life.

Baley thought: It was simpler once. Everything was simpler. That's what makes Medievalists.

Medievalism took different forms. To the unimaginative Julius Enderby, it means the adoption of archaisms. Spectacles! Windows!

To Baley, it was a study of history. Particularly the history of folkways.

The City now! New York City in which he lived and had his being. Larger than any City but Los Angeles. More populous than any but Shanghai. It was only three centuries old.

To be sure, something had existed in the same geographic area before then that had been *called* New York City. That primitive gathering of population had existed for three thousand years, not three hundred, but it hadn't been a *City*.

There were no Cities then. There were just huddles of dwelling places large and small, open to the air. They were something like the Spacer's Domes, only much different, of course. These huddles (the largest barely reached ten million in population and most never reached one million) were scattered all over Earth by the thousands. By modern standards, they had been completely inefficient, economically.

Efficiency had been forced on Earth with increasing population. Two billion people, three billion, even five billion could be supported by the planet by progressive lowering of the standard of living. When the population reaches eight billion, however, semistarvation becomes too much like the real thing. A radical change had to take place in man's culture, particularly when it turned out that the Outer World's (which had merely been Earth's colonies a thousand years before) were tremendously serious in their immigration restrictions.

The radical change had been the gradual formation of the Cities over a thousand years of Earth's history. Efficiency implied bigness. Even in Medieval times that had been realized, perhaps unconsciously. Home industry gave way to factories and factories to continental industries.

Think of the inefficiency of a hundred thousand houses for a hundred thousand families as compared with a hundred-thousand-unit Section; a book-film collection in each house as compared with a Section film concentrate; independent video for each family as compared with video-piping systems.

For that matter, take the simple folly of endless duplication of kitchens and bathrooms as compared with the thoroughly efficient diners and shower rooms made possible by City culture.

More and more the villages, towns, and "cities" of Earth died and were swallowed by the Cities. Even the early prospects of atomic war only slowed the trend. With the invention of the force shield, the trend became a headlong race.

City culture meant optimum distribution of food, increasing utilization of yeasts and hydroponics. New York City spread over two thousand square miles and at the last census its population was well over twenty million. There were some eight hundred Cities on Earth, average population, ten million.

Each City became a semiautonomous unit, economically all but self-sufficient. It could roof itself in, gird itself about, burrow itself under. It became a steel cave, a tremendous, self-contained cave of steel and concrete.

It could lay itself out scientifically. At the centre was the enormous complex of administrative offices. In careful orientation to one another and to the whole were the large residential Sections connected and interlaced by the expressway and the localways. Toward the outskirts were the factories, the hydroponic plants, the yeast-culture vats, the power plants. Through all the melee were the water pipes and sewage ducts, schools, prisons and shops, power lines and communication beams.

There was no doubt about it: the City was the culmination of man's mastery over the environment. Not space travel, not the fifty colonized worlds that were now so haughtily independent, but the City.

Practically none of Earth's population lived outside the Cities. Outside was the wilderness, the open sky that few men could face with anything like equanimity. To be sure, the open space was necessary. It held the water that men must have, the coal and the wood that were the ultimate raw materials for plastics and for the eternally growing yeast. (Petroleum had long since gone, but oil-rich strains of yeast were an adequate substitute.) The land between the Cities still held the mines, and was still used to a larger extent than most men realized for growing food and grazing stock. It was inefficient, but beef, pork, and grain always found a luxury market and could be used for export purposes.

But few humans were required to run the mines and ranches, to exploit the farms and pipe the water, and these supervised at long distance. Robots did the work better and required less.

Robots! That was the one huge irony. It was on Earth that the positronic brain was invented and on Earth that robots had first been put to productive use.

Not on the Outer Worlds. Of course, the Outer Worlds always acted as though robots had been born of their culture.

In a way, of course, the culmination of robot economy had taken place on the Outer Worlds. Here on Earth, robots had always been restricted to the mines and farmlands. Only in the last quarter century, under the urgings of the Spacers, had robots filtered their slow way into the Cities.

The Cities were good. Everyone but the Medievalists knew that there was no substitute, no reasonable substitute. The only trouble was that they wouldn't stay good. Earth's population was still rising. Some day, with all that the Cities could do, the available calories per person would simply fall below basic subsistence level.

It was all the worse because of the existence of the Spacers, the descendants of the early emigrants from Earth, living in luxury on their underpopulated robot-ridden worlds out in space. They were coolly determined to keep the comfort that grew out of the emptiness of their worlds and for that purpose they kept their birth rate down and immigrants from teeming Earth out. And this –

Spacetown coming up!

A nudge at Baley's unconscious warned him that he was approaching the Newark Section. If he stayed where he was much longer, he'd find himself speeding southwestward to the Trenton Section turning of the way, through the heart of the warm and musty-odored yeast country.

It was a matter of timing. It took so long to shinny down the ramp, so long to squirm through the grunting standees, so long to slip along the railing and out an opening, so long to hop across the decelerating strips.

When he was done, he was precisely at the off-shooting of the proper stationary. At no time did he time his steps consciously. If he had, he would probably have missed.

Baley found himself in unusual semi-isolation. Only a policeman was with him inside the stationary and, except for the whirring of the expressway, there was an almost uncomfortable silence.

The policeman approached, and Baley flashed his badge impatiently. The policeman lifted his hand in permission to pass on.

The passage narrowed and curved sharply three or four times. That was obviously purposeful. Mobs of Earthmen couldn't gather in it with any degree of comfort and direct charges were impossible.

Baley was thankful that the arrangements were for him to meet his partner this side of Spacetown. He didn't like the thought of a medical examination any better for its reputed politeness.

A Spacer was standing at the point where a series of doors marked the opening to the open air and the domes of Spacetown. He was dressed in the Earth fashion, trousers tight at the waist, loose at the ankle, and color-striped down the seam of each leg. He wore an ordinary Textron shirt, open collar, seam-zipped, and ruffled at the wrist, but he was a Spacer. There was something about the way he stood, the way he held his head, the calm and unemotional lines of his broad, high-cheekboned face, the careful set of his short, bronze hair lying flatly backward and without a part, that marked him off from the native Earthman.

Baley approached woodenly and said in a monotone, "I am Plain-clothes Man Elijah Baley, Police Department, City of New York, Rating C—5."

He showed his credentials and went on, "I have been instructed to meet R. Daneel Olivaw at Spacetown Approachway." He looked at his watch. "I am a little early. May I request the announcement of my presence?"

He felt more than a little cold inside. He was used, after a fashion, to the Earth-model robots. The Spacer models would be different. He had never met one, but there was nothing more common on Earth than the horrid whispered stories about the tremendous and formidable robots that worked in superhuman fashion on the far-off, glittering Outer Worlds. He found himself gritting his teeth.

The Spacer, who had listened politely, said, "It will not be necessary. I have been waiting for you."

Baley's hand went up automatically, then dropped. So did his long chin, looking longer in the process. He didn't quite manage to say anything. The words froze.

The Spacer said, "I shall introduce myself. I am R. Daneel Olivaw."

"Yes? Am I making a mistake? I thought the first initial –"

"Quite so. I am a robot. Were you not told?"

"I was told." Baley put a damp hand to his hair and smoothed it back unnecessarily. Then he held it out. "I'm sorry, Mr. Olivaw. I don't know what I was thinking of. Good day. I am Elijah Baley, your partner."

"Good." The robot's hand closed on his with a smoothly increasing pressure that reached a comfortably friendly peak, then declined. "Yet I seem to detect disturbance. May I ask that you be frank with me? It is best to have as many relevant facts as possible in a relationship such as ours. And it is customary on my world for partners to call one another by the familiar name. I trust that that is not counter to your own customs."

"It's just, you see, that you don't look like a robot," said Baley, desperately.

"And that disturbs you?"

"It shouldn't, I suppose, Da – Daneel. Are they all like you on your world?"

"There are individual differences, Elijah, as with men."

"Our own robots . . . Well, you can tell they're robots, you understand. You look like a Spacer."

"Oh, I see. You expected a rather crude model and were surprised. Yet it is only logical that our people use a robot of pronounced humanoid characteristics in this case if we expect to avoid unpleasantness. Is that not so?"

It was certainly so. An obvious robot roaming the City would be in quick trouble.

Baley said, "Yes."

"Then let us leave now, Elijah."

They made their way back to the expressway. R. Daneel caught the purpose of the accelerating strips and maneuvered along them with a quick proficiency. Baley, who had begun by moderating his speed, ended by hastening it in annoyance.

The robot kept pace. He showed no awareness of any difficulty. Baley wondered if R. Daneel were not deliberately moving slower than he might. He reached the endless cars of expressway and scrambled aboard with what amounted to outright recklessness. The robot followed easily.

Baley was red. He swallowed twice and said, "I'll stay down here with you."

"Down here?" The robot, apparently oblivious to both the noise and the rhythmic swaying of the platform said, "Is my information wrong? I was told that a rating of C—5 entitled one to a seat on the upper level under certain conditions."

"You're right. I can go up there, but you can't."

"Why can I not go up with you?"

"It takes a C—5, Daneel."

"I am aware of that."

"You're not a C—5." Talking was difficult. The hiss of frictioning air was louder on the less shielded lower level and Baley was understandably anxious to keep his voice low.

R. Daneel said, "Why should I not be a C—5? I am your partner and, consequently, of equal rank. I was given this."

From an inner shirt pocket he produced a rectangular credential card, quite genuine. The name given was Daneel Olivaw, without the all-important initial. The rating was C—5.

"Come on up," said Baley, woodenly.

Baley looked straight ahead, once seated, angry with himself, very conscious of the robot sitting next to him. He had been caught twice. First he had not recognized R. Daneel as a robot; secondly, he had not guessed the logic that demanded R. Daneel be given C—5 rating.

The trouble was, of course, that he was not the plainclothes man of popular myth. He was not incapable of surprise, imperturbable of appearance, infinite of adaptability, and lightning of mental grasp. He had never supposed he was, but he had never regretted the lack before.

What made him regret it was that, to all appearances, R. Daneel Olivaw *was* that very myth, embodied.

He had to be. He was a robot.

Baley began to find excuses for himself. He was accustomed to the robots like R. Sammy at the office. He had expected a creature with a skin of a hard and glossy plastic, nearly dead white in color. He had expected an expression fixed at an unreal level of inane good humor. He had expected jerky, faintly uncertain motions.

R. Daneel was none of it.

Baley risked a quick side glance at the robot. R. Daneel turned simultaneously to meet his eyes and nod gravely. His lips moved naturally when he had spoken and did not simply remain parted as those of Earth robots did. There had been glimpses of an articulating tongue.

Baley thought: Why does he have to sit there so calmly? This must be something completely new to him. Noise, lights, crowds!

Baley got up, brushed past R. Daneel, and said, "Follow me!"

Off the expressway, down the decelerating strips.

Baley thought: "Good Lord, what do I tell Jessie, anyway?

The coming of the robot had rattled that thought out of his head, but it was coming back with sickening urgency now that they were heading down the localway that led into the very jaws of the Lower Bronx Section.

He said, "This is all one building, you know, Daneel; everything you see, the whole City. Twenty million people live in it. The expressways go continuously, night and day, at sixty miles an hour. There are two hundred and fifty miles of it altogether and hundreds of miles of localways."

Any minute now, Baley thought, I'll be figuring out how many tons of yeast product New York eats per day and how many cubic feet of water we drink and how many megawatts of power the atomic piles deliver per hour.

Daneel said, "I was informed of this and other similar data in my briefing."

Baley thought: Well, that covers the food, drink, and power situation, too, I suppose. Why try to impress a robot?

They were at East 182nd Street and in not more than two hundred yards they would be at the elevator banks that fed those steel and concrete layers of apartments that included his own.

He was on the point of saying, "This way," when he was stopped by a knot of people gathering outside the brilliantly lighted force door of one of the many retail departments that lined the ground levels solidly in this Section.

He asked of the nearest person in an automatic tone of authority, "What's going on?"

The man he addressed, who was standing on tiptoe, said, "Damned if I know. I just got here."

Someone else said, excitedly, "They got those lousy R's in there. I think maybe they'll throw them out here. Boy, I'd like to take them apart."

Baley looked nervously at Daneel, but, if the latter caught the significance of the words or even heard them, he did not show it by any outward sign.

Baley plunged into the crowd. "Let me through. Let me through. Police!"

They made way, Baley caught words behind him.

". . . take them apart. Nut by nut. Split them down the seams slowlike . . ." And someone else laughed.

Baley turned a little cold. The City was the acme of efficiency, but it made demands of its inhabitants. It asked them to live in a tight routine and order their lives under a strict and scientific control. Occasionally, built-up inhibitions exploded.

He remembered the Barrier Riots.

Reasons for anti-robot rioting certainly existed. Men who found themselves faced with the prospect of the desperate minimum involved in declassification, after half a lifetime of effort, could not decide cold-bloodedly that individual robots were not to blame. Individual robots could at least be struck at.

One could not strike at something called "governmental policy" or at a slogan like "Higher production with robot labour."

The government called it growing pains. It shook its collective head sorrowfully and assured everyone that after a necessary period of adjustment, a new and better life would exist for all.

But the Medievalist movement expanded along with the de-classification process. Men grew desperate and the border between bitter frustration and wild destruction is sometimes easily crossed.

At this moment, minutes could be separating the pent-up hostility of the crowd from a flashing orgy of blood and smash.

Baley writhed his way desperately to the force door.

CHAPTER THREE

INCIDENT AT A SHOE COUNTER

The interior of the store was emptier than the street outside. The manager, with commendable foresight, had thrown the force door early in the game, preventing potential troublemakers from entering. It also kept the principals in the argument from leaving, but that was minor.

Baley got through the force door by using his officer's neutralizer. Unexpectedly, he found R. Daneel still behind him. The robot was pocketing a neutralizer of his own, a slim one, smaller and neater than the standard police model.

The manager ran to them instantly, talking loudly. "Officers, my clerks have been assigned me by the City. I am perfectly within my rights."

There were three robots standing rodlike at the rear of the department. Six humans were standing near the force door. They were all women.

"All right, now," said Baley, crisply. "What's going on? What's all the fuss about?"

One of the women said, shrilly, "I came in for shoes. Why can't I have a decent clerk? Ain't I respectable?" Her clothing, especially her hat, were just sufficiently extreme to make it more than a rhetorical question. The angry flush that covered her face masked imperfectly her overdone makeup.

The manager said, "I'll wait on her myself if I have to, but I can't wait on all of them, Officer. There's nothing wrong with my men. They're registered clerks. I have their spec charts and guarantee slips –"

"Spec charts," screamed the woman. She laughed shrilly,

turning to the rest. "Listen to him. He calls them men! What's the matter with you anyway? They ain't men. They're ro-bots!" She stretched out the syllables. "And I tell you what they do, in case you don't know. They steal jobs from men. That's why the government always protects them. They work for nothin' and, on account o' that, families gotta live out in the barracks and eat raw yeast mush. Decent hard-working families. We'd smash up all the ro-bots, if *I* was boss. I tell you that!"

The others talked confusedly and there was always the growing rumble from the crowd just beyond the force door.

Baley was conscious, brutally conscious, of R. Daneel Olivaw standing at his elbow. He looked at the clerks. They were Earth-made, and even on that scale, relatively inexpensive models. They were just robots made to know a few simple things. They would know all the style numbers, their prices, the sizes available in each. They could keep track of stock fluctuations, probably better than humans could, since they would have no outside interests. They could compute the proper orders for the next week. They could measure the customer's foot.—

In themselves, harmless. As a group, incredibly dangerous.

Baley could sympathize with the woman more deeply than he would have believed possible the day before. No, two hours before. He could feel R. Daneel's nearness and he wondered if R. Daneel could not replace an ordinary plainclothes man C—5. He could see the barracks, as he thought that. He could taste the yeast mush. He could remember his father.

His father had been a nuclear physicist, with a rating that had put him in the top percentile of the City. There had been an accident at the power plant and his father had borne the blame. He had been declassified. Baley did not know the details: it had happened when he was a year old.

But he remembered the barracks of his childhood; the grinding communal existence just this side of the edge of bearability. He remembered his mother not at all; she had not survived long. His father he recalled well, a sodden man, morose and lost, speaking sometimes of the past in hoarse, broken sentences.

His father died, still declassified, when Lije was eight. Young Baley and his two older sisters moved into the Section orphanage. Children's Level, they called it. His mother's brother, Uncle Boris, was himself too poor to prevent that.

So it continued hard. And it was hard going through school, with no father-derived status privileges to smooth the way.

And now he had to stand in the middle of a growing riot and beat down men and women who, after all, only feared declassification for themselves and those they loved, as he himself did.

Tonelessly, he said to the woman who had already spoken, "Let's not have any trouble, lady. The clerks aren't doing you any harm."

"Sure they ain't done me no harm," sopranoed the woman. "They ain't gonna, either. Think I'll let their cold, greasy fingers touch me? I came in here expecting to get treated like a human being. I'm a citizen. I got a right to have human beings wait on me. And listen, I got two kids waiting for supper. They can't go to the Section kitchen without me, like they was orphans. I gotta get out of here."

"Well, now," said Baley, feeling his temper slipping, "if you had let yourself be waited on, you'd have been out of here by now. You're just making trouble for nothing. Come on now."

"Well!" The woman registered shock. "Maybe you think you can talk to me like I was dirt. Maybe it's time the gov'min' reelized robots ain't the only things on Earth. I'm a hard-working woman and I've got rights." She went on and on and on.

Baley felt harassed and caught. The situation was out of hand. Even if the woman would consent to be waited on, the waiting crowd was ugly enough for anything.

There must be a hundred crammed outside the display window now. In the few minutes since the plain-clothes men had entered the store, the crowd had doubled.

"What is the usual procedure in such a case?" asked R. Daneel Olivaw, suddenly.

Baley nearly jumped. He said, "This is an unusual case in the first place."

"What is the law?"

"The R's have been duly assigned here. They're registered clerks. There's nothing illegal about that."

They were speaking in whispers. Baley tried to look official and threatening. Olivaw's expression, as always, meant nothing at all.

"In that case," said R. Daneel, "order the woman to let herself be waited on or to leave."

Baley lifted a corner of his lip briefly. "It's a mob we have to deal with, not a woman. There's nothing to do but call a riot squad."

"It should not be necessary for citizens to require more than one officer of the law to direct what should be done," said Daneel.

He turned his broad face to the store manager. "Open the force door, sir."

Baley's arm shot forward to seize R. Daneel's shoulder, swing him about. He arrested the motion. If, at this moment, two law men quarreled openly, it would mean the end of all chance for a peaceful solution.

The manager protested, looked at Baley. Baley did not meet his eye.

R. Daneel said, unmoved, "I order you with the authority of the law."

The manager bleated, "I'll hold the City responsible for any damage to the goods or fixtures. I serve notice that I'm doing this under orders."

The barrier went down; men and women crowded in. There was a happy roar from them. They sensed victory.

Baley had heard of similar riots. He had even witnessed one. He had seen robots being lifted by a dozen hands, their heavy unresisting bodies carried backward from straining arm to straining arm. Men yanked and twisted at the metal mimicry of men. They used hammers, force knives, needle guns. They finally reduced the miserable objects to shredded metal and wire. Expensive positronic brains, the most intricate creation of the human mind, were thrown from hand to hand like footballs and mashed to uselessness in a trifle of time.

Then, with the genius of destruction so merrily let loose, the mobs turned on anything else that could be taken apart.

The robot clerks could have no knowledge of any of this, but they squealed as the crowd flooded inward and lifted their arms before their faces as though in a primitive effort at hiding. The woman who had started the fuss, frightened at seeing it grow suddenly so far beyond what she had expected, gasped, "Here, now. Here, now."

Her hat was shoved down over her face and her voice became only a meaningless shrillness.

The manager was shrieking, "Stop them, Officer. Stop them!"

R. Daneel spoke. Without apparent effort, his voice was suddenly decibels higher than a human's voice had a right to.be. Of course, thought Baley for the tenth time, he's not –

R. Daneel said, "The next man who moves will be shot."

Someone well in the back yelled, "Get him!"

But for a moment, no one moved.

R. Daneel stepped nimbly upon a chair and from that to the top of a Transtex display case. The colored fluoresence gleaming through the slits of polarized molecular film turned his cool, smooth face into something unearthly.

Unearthly, thought Baley.

The tableau held as R. Daneel waited, a quietly formidable person.

R. Daneel said crisply, "You are saying, This man is holding a neuronic whip, or a tickler. If we all rush forward, we will bear him down and at most one or two of us will be hurt and even they will recover. Meanwhile, we will do just as we wish and to space with law and order."

His voice was neither harsh nor angry, but it carried authority. It had the tone of confident command. He went on, "You are mistaken. What I hold is not a neuronic whip, nor is it a tickler. It is a blaster and very deadly. I will use it and I will not aim over your heads. I will kill many of you before you seize me, perhaps most of you. I am serious. I look serious, do I not?"

There was motion at the outskirts, but the crowd no longer grew. If newcomers still stopped out of curiosity, others were hurrying away. Those nearest R. Daneel were holding their breath, trying desperately not to sway forward in response to the mass pressure of the bodies behind them.

The woman with the hat broke the spell. In a sudden whirlpool of sobbing, she yelled, "He's gonna kill us. I ain't done nothing. Oh, lemme outta here."

She turned, but faced an immovable wall of crammed men and women. She sank to her knees. The backward motion in the silent crowd grew more pronounced.

R. Daneel jumped down from the display counter and said, "I will now walk to the door. I will shoot the man or woman who touches me. When I reach the door, I will shoot any man or woman who is not moving about his business. This woman here –"

"No, no," yelled the woman with the hat, "I tell ya I didn't do nothing. I didn't mean no harm. I don't want no shoes. I just wanta go home."

"This woman here," went on Daneel, "will remain. She will be waited on."

He stepped forward.

The mob faced him dumbly. Baley closed his eyes. It wasn't his fault, he thought desperately. There'll be murder done and the worst mess in the world, but *they* forced a robot on me as partner. *They* gave him equal status.

It wouldn't do. He didn't believe himself. He might have stopped R. Daneel at the start. He might at any moment have put in the call for a squad car. He had let R. Daneel take responsibility, instead, and had felt a cowardly relief. When he tried to tell himself that R. Daneel's personality simply dominated the situation, he was filled with a sudden self-loathing. A *robot* dominating . . .

There was no unusual noise, no shouting and cursing, no groans, no yells. He opened his eyes.

They were dispersing.

The manager of the store was cooling down, adjusting his twisted jacket, smoothing his hair, muttering angry threats at the vanishing crowd.

The smooth, fading whistle of a squad car came to a halt just outside. Baley thought: Sure, when it's all over.

The manager plucked his sleeve. "Let's have no more trouble, Officer."

Baley said, "There won't be any trouble."

It was easy to get rid of the squad-car police. They had come to response to reports of a crowd in the street. They knew no details and could see for themselves that the street was clear. R. Daneel stepped aside and showed no sign of interest as Baley explained to the men in the squad car, minimizing the event and completely burying R. Daneel's part in it.

Afterward, he pulled R. Daneel to one side, against the steel and concrete of one of the building shafts.

"Listen," he said, "I'm not trying to steal your show, you understand."

"Steal my show? Is it one of your Earth idioms?"

"I didn't report your part in this."

"I do not know all your customs. On my world, a complete report is usual, but perhaps it is not so on your world. In any case, civil rebellion was averted. That is the important thing, is it not?"

"Is it? Now you look here." Baley tried to sound as forceful as possible under the necessity of speaking in an angry whisper. "Don't you ever do it again."

"Never again insist on the observance of law? If I am not to do that, what then is my purpose?"

"Don't ever threaten a human being with a blaster again."

"I would not have fired under any circumstances, Elijah, as you know very well. I am incapable of hurting a human. But, as you see, I did not have to fire. I did not expect to have to."

"That was the purest luck, your not having to fire. Don't take that kind of chance again. I could have pulled the grandstand stunt you did –"

"Grandstand stunt? What is that?"

"Never mind. Get the sense from what I'm saying. I could have pulled a blaster on the crowd myself. I had a blaster to do it with. But it isn't the kind of gamble I am justified in taking, or you, either. It was safer to call squad cars to the scene than to try one-man heroics."

R. Daneel considered. He shook his head. "I think you are wrong, partner Elijah. My briefing on human characteristics here among the people of Earth includes the information that, unlike the men of the Outer Worlds, they are trained from birth to accept authority. Apparently this is the result of your way of living. One man, representing authority firmly enough, was quite sufficient, as I proved. Your own desire for a squad car was only an expression, really, of your almost instinctive wish for superior authority to take responsibility out of your hands. On my own world, I admit that what I did would have been most unjustified."

Baley's long face was red with anger. "If they had recognized you as a robot –"

"I was sure they wouldn't."

"In any case, remember that you *are* a robot. Nothing more than a robot. Just a robot. Like those clerks in the shoe store."

"But this is obvious."

"And you're *not* human.". Baley felt himself being driven into cruelty against his will.

R. Daneel seemed to consider that. He said, "The division between human and robot is perhaps not as significant as that between intelligence and nonintelligence."

"Maybe on your world," said Baley, "but not on Earth."

He looked at his watch and could scarcely make out that he was an hour and a quarter late. His throat was dry and raw with the thought that R. Daneel had won the first round, had won when he himself had stood by helpless.

He thought of the youngster, Vince Barrett, the teen-ager whom R. Sammy had replaced. And of himself, Elijah Baley, whom R. Daneel could replace. Jehoshaphat, at least his father had been thrown out because of an accident that had done damage, that had killed people. Maybe it *was* his fault; Baley didn't know. Suppose he had been eased out to make room for a mechanical physicist. Just for that. For no other reason. Nothing he could do about it.

He said, curtly, "Let's go now. I've got to get you home."

R. Daneel said, "You see, it is not proper to make any distinction of lesser meaning than the fact of intel—"

Baley's voice rose. "All *right*. The subject is closed. Jessie is waiting for us." He walked in the direction of the nearest intrasection communo-tube. "I'd better call and tell her we're on our way up."

"Jessie?"

"My wife."

Jehoshaphat, thought Baley, I'm in a fine mood to face Jessie.

CHAPTER FOUR

INTRODUCTION TO A FAMILY

It had been her name that had first made Elijah Baley really conscious of Jessie. He had met her at the Section Christmas party back in '02, over a bowl of punch. He had just finished his schooling, just taken his first job with the City, just moved into the Section. He was living in one of the bachelor alcoves of Common Room 122A. Not bad for a bachelor alcove.

She was handing out the punch. "I'm Jessie," she said. "Jessie Navodny. I don't know you."

'Baley," he said, "Lije Baley. I've just moved into the Section."

He took his glass of punch and smiled mechanically. She impressed him as a cheerful and friendly person, so he stayed near her. He was new and it is a lonely feeling to be at a party where you find yourself watching people standing about in cliques of which you aren't a part. Later, when enough alcohol had trickled down throats, it might be better.

Meanwhile, he remained at the punch bowl, watching the folks come and go and sipping thoughtfully.

"I helped make the punch." The girl's voice broke in upon him. "I can guarantee it. Do you want more?"

Baley realized his little glass was empty. He smiled and said, "Yes."

The girl's face was oval and not precisely pretty, mostly because of a slightly overlarge nose. Her dress was demure and she wore her light brown hair in a series of ringlets over her forehead.

She joined him in the next punch and he felt better.

"Jessie," he said, feeling the name with his tongue. "It's nice. Do you mind if I use it when I'm talking to you?"

"Certainly. If you want to. Do you know what it's short for?"

"Jessica?"

"You'll never guess."

"I can't think of anything else."

She laughed and said archly, "My full name is Jezebel."

That was when his interest flared. He put his punch glass down and said, intently, "No, really?"

"Honestly. I'm not kidding. Jezebel. It's my real-for-true name on all my records. My parents liked the sound of it."

She was quite proud of it, even though there was never a less likely Jezebel in the world.

Baley said, seriously, "My name is Elijah, you know. My full name, I mean."

It didn't register with her.

He said, "Elijah was Jezebel's great enemy."

"He was?"

"Why, sure. In the Bible."

"Oh? I didn't know that. Now isn't that *funny*? I hope that doesn't mean you'll have to be my enemy in real life."

From the very beginning there was no question of that. It was the coincidence of names at first that made her more than just a pleasant girl at the punch bowl. But afterward he had grown to find her cheerful, tender-hearted, and, finally, even pretty. He appreciated her cheerfulness particularly. His own sardonic view of life needed the antidote.

But Jessie never seemed to mind his long grave face.

"Oh, goodness," she said, "what if you do look like an awful lemon? I know you're not really, and I guess if you were always grinning away like clockwork, the way I do, we'd just explode when we got together. You stay the way you are, Lije, and keep me from floating away."

And she kept Lije Baley from sinking down. He applied for a small Couples apartment and got a contingent admission pending marriage. He showed it to her and said, "Will you fix it so I can get out of Bachelor's, Jessie? I don't like it there."

Maybe it wasn't the most romantic proposal in the world, but Jessie liked it.

Baley could only remember one occasion on which Jessie's habitual cheer deserted her completely and that, too, had involved her name. It was in their first year of marriage, and their baby had not yet come. In fact, it had been the very month in which Bentley was conceived. (Their I.Q. rating, Genetic Values status, and his position in the Department entitled him to two children, of which the first might be conceived during the first year.) Maybe, as Baley thought back upon it, Bentley's beginnings might explain part of her unusual skittishness.

Jessie had been drooping a bit because of Baley's consistent overtime.

She said, "It's embarrassing to eat alone at the kitchen every night."

Baley was tired and out of sorts. He said, "Why should it be? You can meet some nice single fellows there."

And of course she promptly fired up. "Do you think I can't make an impression on them, Lije Baley?"

Maybe it was just because he was tired; maybe because Julius Enderby, a classmate of his, had moved up another notch on the C-scale rating while he himself had not. Maybe it was simply because he was a little tired of having her try to act up to the name she bore when she was nothing of the sort and never could be anything of the sort.

In any case, he said bitingly, "I suppose you can, but I don't think you'll try. I wish you'd forget your name and be yourself."

"I'll be just what I please."

"Trying to be Jezebel won't get you anywhere. If you must know the truth, the name doesn't mean what you think, anyway. The Jezebel of the Bible was a faithful wife and a good one according to her lights. She had no lovers that we know of, cut no high jinks, and took no moral liberties at all."

Jessie stared angrily at him. "That isn't so. I've heard the phrase, 'a painted Jezebel.' I know what that means."

"Maybe you think you do, but listen. After Jezebel's husband, King Ahab died, her son, Jehoram, became king. One of the captains of his army, Jehu, rebelled against him and assassinated him. Jehu then rode to Jezreel where the old queen-mother, Jezebel, was residing. Jezebel heard of his coming and knew that he could only mean to kill her. In her pride and courage, she painted her face and dressed herself in her best clothes so that she could meet him as a haughty and defiant queen. He had her thrown from the window of the palace and killed, but she made a good end, according to my notions. And that's what people refer to when they speak of 'a painted Jezebel,' whether they know it or not."

The next evening Jessie said in a small voice, "I've been reading the Bible, Lije."

"What?" For a moment, Baley was honestly bewildered.

"The parts about Jezebel."

"Oh! Jessie, I'm sorry if I hurt your feelings. I was being childish."

"No. No." She pushed his hand from her waist and sat on the couch, cool and upright, with a definite space between them. "It's good to know the truth. I don't want to be fooled by not knowing. So I read about her. She *was* a wicked woman, Lije."

"Well, her enemies wrote those chapters. We don't know her side."

"She killed all the prophets of the Lord she could lay her hands on."

"So they say she did." Baley felt about in his pocket for a stick of chewing gum. (In later years he abandoned that habit because Jessie said that with his long face and sad, brown eyes, it made him look like an old cow stuck with an unpleasant wad of grass it couldn't swallow and wouldn't spit out.) He said, "If you want her side, I could think of some arguments for you. She valued the religion of her ancestors who had been in the land long before the Hebrews came. The Hebrews had their own God, and, what's more, it was an exclusive God. They weren't content to worship Him themselves; they wanted everyone in reach to worship Him as well.

"Jezebel was a conservative, sticking to the old beliefs against the new ones. After all, if the new beliefs had a higher moral content, the old ones were more emotionally satisfying. The fact that she killed priests just marks her as a child of her times. It was the usual method of proselytization in those days. If you read I Kings, you must remember that Elijah (*my* namesake this time) had a contest with 850 prophets of Baal to see which could bring down fire from heaven. Elijah won and promptly ordered the crowd of onlookers to kill the 850 Baalites. And they did."

Jessie bit her lip. "What about Naboth's vineyard, Lije. Here was this Naboth not bothering anybody, except that he refused to sell the King his vineyard. So Jezebel arranged to have people perjure themselves and say that Naboth had committed blasphemy or something."

"He was supposed to have 'blasphemed God and the king,'" said Baley.

"Yes. So they confiscated his property after they executed him."

"That was wrong. Of course, in modern times, Naboth would have been handled quite easily. If the City wanted his property or even if one of the Medieval nations had wanted his property, the courts would have ordered him off, had him removed by force if necessary, and paid him whatever they considered a fair price. King Ahab didn't have that way out. Still, Jezebel's solution was wrong. The only excuse for her is that Ahab was sick and unhappy over the situation and she felt that her love for her husband came ahead of Naboth's welfare. I keep telling you, she was the model of a faithful wi—"

Jessie flung herself away from him, red-faced and angry. "I think you're mean and spiteful."

He looked at her with complete dismay. "What have I done? What's the matter with you?"

She left the apartment without answering and spent the evening and half the night at the subetheric video levels, traveling petulantly from showing to showing and using up a two-month supply of her quota allowance (and her husband's, to boot).

When she came back to a still wakeful Lije Baley, she had nothing further to say to him.

It occurred to Baley later, much later, that he had utterly smashed an important part of Jessie's life. Her name had signified something intriguingly wicked to her. It was a delightful makeweight for her prim, overrespectable past. It gave her an aroma of licentiousness, and she adored that.

But it was gone. She never mentioned her full name again, not to Lije, not to her friends, and maybe, for all Baley knew, not even to herself. She was Jessie and took to signing her name so.

As the days passed she began speaking to him again, and after a week or so their relationship was on the old footing and, with all subsequent quarrels, nothing ever reached that one bad spot of intensity.

Only once was there even an indirect reference to the matter. It was in her eighth month of pregnancy. She had left her own position as dietitian's assistant in Section Kitchen A-23 and with unaccustomed time on her hands was amusing herself in speculation and preparation for the baby's birth.

She said, one evening, "What about Bentley?"

"Pardon me, dear?" said Baley, looking up from a sheaf of work he had brought home with him. (With an additional mouth soon to feed and Jessie's pay stopped and his own promotions to the nonclerical levels as far off, seemingly, as ever, extra work was necessary.)

"I mean if the baby's a boy. What about Bentley as a name?"

Baley pulled down the corners of his mouth. "Bentley Baley? Don't you think the names are too similar?"

"I don't know. It has a swing, I think. Besides, the child

can always pick out a middle name to suit himself when he gets older."

"Well, it's all right with me."

"Are you sure? I mean.... Maybe you wanted him to be named Elijah?"

"And be called Junior? I don't think that's a good idea. He can name his son Elijah, if he wants to."

Then Jessie said, "There's just one thing," and stopped.

After an interval, he looked up. "What one thing?"

She did not quite meet his eye, but she said, forcefully enough, "Bentley isn't a Bible name, is it?"

"No," said Baley, "I'm quite sure it isn't."

"All right, then. I don't want any Bible names."

And that was the only harking back that took place from that time to the day when Elijah Baley was coming home with Robot Daneel Olivaw, when he had been married for more than eighteen years and when his son Bentley Baley (middle name still unchosen) was past sixteen.

Baley paused before the large double door on which there glowed in large letters PERSONAL – MEN. In smaller letters were written SUB-SECTION 1A—1E. In still smaller letters, just above the key slit, it stated: "In case of loss of key, communicate at once with 27—101—51."

A man inched past them, inserted an aluminum sliver into the key slit, and walked in. He closed the door behind him, making no attempt to hold it open for Baley. Had he done so, Baley would have been seriously offended. By strong custom men disregarded one another's presence entirely either within or just outside the Personals. Baley remembered one of the more interesting marital confidences to have been Jessie's telling him that the situation was quite different at Women's Personals.

She was always saying, "I met Josephine Greely at Personal and she said . . ."

It was one of the penalties of civic advancement that when the Baleys were granted, permission for the activation of the small wash-bowl in their bedroom, Jessie's social life suffered.

Baley said, without completely masking his embarrassment, "Please wait out here, Daneel."

"Do you intend washing?" asked R. Daneel.

Baley squirmed and thought: Damned robot! If they were briefing him on everything under steel, why didn't they teach him manners? I'll be responsible if he ever says anything like this to anyone else.

He said, "I'll shower. It gets crowded evenings. I'll lose time then. If I get it done now we'll have the whole evening before us."

R. Daneel's face maintained its repose. "Is it part of the social custom that I wait outside?"

Baley's embarrassment deepened. "Why need you go in for — for no purpose."

"Oh, I understand you. Yes, of course. Nevertheless, Elijah, my hands grow dirty, too, and I will wash them."

He indicated his palms, holding them out before him. They were pink and plump, with the proper creases. They bore every mark of excellent and meticulous workmanship and were as clean as need be.

Baley said, "We have a washbasin in the apartment, you know." He said it casually. Snobbery would be lost on a robot.

"Thank you for your kindness. On the whole, however, I think it would be preferable to make use of this place. If I am to live with you men of Earth, it is best that I adopt as many of your customs and attitudes as I can."

"Come on in, then."

The bright cheerfulness of the interior was a sharp contrast to the busy utilitarianism of most of the rest of the City, but this time the effect was lost on Baley's consciousness.

He whispered to Daneel, "I may take up to half an hour or so. Wait for me." He started away, then returned to add, "And listen, don't talk to anybody and don't look at anybody. Not a word, not a glance! It's a custom."

He looked hurriedly about to make certain that his own small conversation had not been noted, was not being met by shocked glances. Nobody, fortunately, was in the antecorridor, and after all it *was* only the antecorridor.

He hurried down it, feeling vaguely dirty, past the common chambers to the private stalls. It had been five years now since he had been awarded one — large enough to contain a shower, a small laundry, and other necessities. It even had a small projector that could be keyed in for the news films.

"A home away from home," he had joked when it was first

made available to him. But now, he often wondered how he would bear the adjustment back to the more Spartan existence of the common chambers if his stall privileges were ever canceled.

He pressed the button that activated the laundry and the smooth face of the meter lighted.

R. Daneel was waiting patiently when Baley returned with a scrubbed body, clean underwear, a freshened shirt, and, generally, a feeling of greater comfort.

"No trouble?" Baley asked, when they were well outside the door and able to talk.

"None at all, Elijah," said R. Daneel.

Jessie was at the door, smiling nervously. Baley kissed her.

"Jessie," he mumbled, "this is my new partner, Daneel Olivaw."

Jessie held out a hand, which R. Daneel took and released. She turned to her husband, then looked timidly at R. Daneel.

She said, "Won't you sit down, Mr. Olivaw? I must talk to my husband on family matters. It'll take just a minute. I hope you won't mind."

Her hand was on Baley's sleeve. He followed her into the next room.

She said, in a hurried whisper, "You aren't hurt, are you? I've been so worried ever since the broadcast."

"What broadcast?"

"It came through nearly an hour ago. About the riot at the shoe counter. They said two plain-clothes men stopped it. I knew you were coming home with a partner and this was right in our subsection and right when you were coming home and I thought they were making it better than it was and you were –"

"*Please*, Jessie. You see I'm perfectly all right."

Jessie caught hold of herself with an effort. She said, shakily, "Your partner isn't from your division, is he?"

"No," replied Baley miserably. "He's – a complete stranger."

"How do I treat him?"

"Like anybody else. He's just my partner, that's all."

He said it so unconvincingly, that Jessie's quick eyes narrowed. "What's wrong?"

"Nothing. Come, let's go back into the living room. It'll begin to look queer."

Lije Baley felt a little uncertain about the apartment now. Until this very moment, he had felt no qualms. In fact, he had always been proud of it. It had three large rooms; the living room, for instance, was an ample fifteen feet by eighteen. There was a closet in each room. One of the main ventilation ducts passed directly by. It meant a little rumbling noise on rare occasions, but, on the other hand, assured first-rate temperature control and well-conditioned air. Nor was it too far from either Personal, which was a prime convenience.

But with the creature from worlds beyond space sitting in the midst of it, Baley was suddenly uncertain. The apartment seemed mean and cramped.

Jessie said, with a gaiety that was slightly synthetic, "Have you and Mr. Olivaw eaten, Lije?"

"As a matter of fact," said Baley, quickly, "Daneel will not be eating with us. I'll eat, though."

Jessie accepted the situation without trouble. With food supplies so narrowly controlled and rationing tighter than ever, it was good form to refuse another's hospitality.

She said, "I hope you won't mind our eating, Mr. Olivaw. Lije, Bentley, and I generally eat at the Community kitchen. It's much more convenient and there's more variety, you see, and just between you and me, bigger helpings, too. But then, Lije and I *do* have permission to eat in our apartment three times a week if we want to – Lije is quite successful at the Bureau and we have very nice status – and I thought that just for this occasion, if you wanted to join us, we would have a little private feast of our own, though I do think that people who overdo their privacy privileges are just a bit anti-social, you know."

R. Daneel listened politely.

Baley said, with an undercover "shushing" wiggle of his fingers, "Jessie, I'm hungry."

R. Daneel said, "Would I be breaking a custom, Mrs. Baley, if I addressed you by your given name?"

"Why no, of course not." Jessie folded a table out of the wall and plugged the plate warmer into the central depression on the table top. "You just go right ahead and call me Jessie all you feel like – uh – Daneel." She giggled.

Baley felt savage. The situation was getting rapidly more uncomfortable. Jessie thought R. Daneel a man. The thing would be someone to boast of and talk about in Women's Personal. He was good-looking in a wooden way, too, and Jessie was pleased with his deference. Anyone could see that.

Baley wondered about R. Daneel's impression of Jessie. She hadn't changed much in eighteen years, or at least not to Lije Baley. She was heavier, of course, and her figure had lost much of its youthful vigor. There were lines at the angles of the mouth and a trace of heaviness about her cheeks. Her hair was more conservatively styled and a dimmer brown than it had once been.

But that's all beside the point, thought Baley, somberly. On the Outer Worlds the women were tall and as slim and regal as the men. Or, at least, the book-films had them so and that must be the kind of women R. Daneel was used to.

But R. Daneel seemed quite unperturbed by Jessie's conversation, her appearance, or her appropriation of his name. He said, "Are you sure that is proper? The name, Jessie, seems to be a diminutive. Perhaps its use is restricted to members of your immediate circle and I would be more proper if I used your full given name."

Jessie, who was breaking open the insulating wrapper surrounding the dinner ration, bent her head over the task in sudden concentration.

"Just Jessie," she said, tightly. "Everyone calls me that. There's nothing else."

"Very well, Jessie."

The door opened and a youngster entered cautiously. His eyes found R. Daneel almost at once.

"Dad?" said the boy, uncertainly.

"My son, Bentley," said Baley, in a low voice. "This is Mr. Olivaw, Ben."

"He's your partner, huh, Dad? How d'ya do, Mr. Olivaw." Ben's eyes grew large and luminous. "Say, Dad, what happened down in the shoe place? The newscast said –"

"Don't ask any questions now, Ben," interposed Baley sharply.

Bentley's face fell and he looked toward his mother, who motioned him to a seat.

"Did you do what I told you, Bentley?" she asked, when he sat down. Her hands moved caressingly over his hair. It was as dark as his father's and he was going to have his father's height, but all the rest of him was hers. He had Jessie's oval face, her hazel eyes, her light-hearted way of looking at life.

"Sure, Mom," said Bentley, hitching himself forward a bit to look into the double dish from which savory vapours were already rising. "What we got to eat? Not zymoveal again, Mom? Huh, Mom?"

"There's nothing wrong with zymoveal," said Jessie, her lips pressing together. "Now, you just eat what's put before you and let's not have any comments."

It was quite obvious they *were* having zymoveal.

Baley took his own seat. He himself would have preferred something other than zymoveal, with its sharp flavor and definite aftertaste, but Jessie had explained her problem before this.

"Well, I just can't, Lije," she had said. "I live right here on these levels all day and I can't make enemies or life wouldn't be bearable. They know I used to be assistant dietitian and if I just walked off with steak or chicken every other week when there's hardly anyone else on the floor that has private eating privileges even on Sunday, they'd say it was pull or friends in the prep room. It would be talk, talk, talk, and I wouldn't be able to put my nose out the door or visit Personal in peace. As it is, zymoveal and protoveg are very good. They're well-balanced nourishment with no waste and, as a matter of fact, they're full of vitamins and minerals and everything anyone needs and we can have all the chicken we want when we eat in Community on the chicken Tuesdays."

Baley gave in easily. It was as Jessie said; the first problem of living is to minimize friction with the crowds that surround you on all sides. Bentley was a little harder to convince.

On this occasion, he said, "Gee, Mom, why can't I use Dad's ticket and eat in Community myself? I'd just as soon."

Jessie shook her head in annoyance and said, "I'm surprised at you, Bentley. What would people say if they saw you eating by yourself as though your own family weren't good enough for you or had thrown you out of the apartment?"

"Well, gosh, it's none of people's business."

Baley said, with a nervous edge in his voice, "Do as your mother tells you, Bentley."

Bentley shrugged, unhappily.

R. Daneel said, suddenly, from the other side of the room, "Have I the family's permission to view these book-films during your meal?"

"Oh, sure," said Bentley, slipping away from the table, a look of instant interest upon his face. "They're mine. I got them from the library on special school permit. I'll get you my viewer. It's a pretty good one. Dad gave it to me for my last birthday."

He brought it to R. Daneel and said, "Are you interested in robots, Mr. Olivaw?"

Baley dropped his spoon and bent to pick it up.

R. Daneel said, "Yes, Bentley. I am quite interested."

"Then you'll like these. They're all about robots. I've got to write an essay on them for school, so I'm doing research. It's quite a complicated subject," he said importantly. "I'm against them myself."

"Sit down, Bentley," said Baley, desperately, "and don't bother Mr. Olivaw."

"He's not bothering me, Elijah. I'd like to talk to you about the problem, Bentley, another time. Your father and I will be very busy tonight."

"Thanks, Mr. Olivaw." Bentley took his seat and, with a look of distaste in his mother's direction, broke off a portion of the crumbly pink zymoveal with his fork.

Baley thought: Busy tonight?

Then, with a resounding shock, he remembered his job. He thought of a Spacer lying dead in Spacetown and realized that for hours he had been so involved with his own dilemma that he had forgotten the cold fact of murder.

CHAPTER FIVE

ANALYSIS OF A MURDER

Jessie said good-bye to them. She was wearing a formal hat and a little jacket of keratofiber as she said, "I hope you'll excuse me, Mr. Olivaw. I know you have a great deal to discuss with Lije."

She pushed her son ahead of her as she opened the door.

"When will you be back, Jessie?" asked Baley.

She paused. "When do you want me to be back?"

"Well. . . . No use staying out all night. Why don't you come back your usual time? Midnight or so." He looked doubtfully at R. Daneel.

R. Daneel nodded. "I regret having to drive you from your home."

"Don't worry about *that*, Mr. Olivaw. You're not driving me out at all. This is my usual evening out with the girls anyway. Come on, Ben."

The youngster was rebellious. "Aw, why the dickens do I have to go, anyway. I'm not going to bother them. Nuts!"

"Now, do as I say."

"Well, why can't I got to the etherics along with you?"

"Because I'm going with some friends and you've got other things –" The door closed behind them.

And now the moment had come. Baley had put it off in his mind. He had thought: First let's meet the robot and see what he's like. Then it was: Let's get him home. And then: Let's eat.

But now it was all over and there was no room for further delay. It was down at last to the question of murder, of interstellar complications, of possible raises in ratings, of possible disgrace. And he had no way of even beginning except to turn to the robot for help.

His fingernails moved aimlessly on the table, which had not been returned to its wall recess.

R. Daneel said, "How secure are we against being overheard?"

Baley looked up, surprised. "No one would listen to what's proceeding in another man's apartment."

"It is not your custom to eavesdrop?"

"It just isn't done, Daneel. You might as well suppose they'd – I don't know – that they'd look in your plate while you're eating."

"Or that they would commit murder?"

"What?"

"It is against your customs to kill, is it not, Elijah?"

Baley felt anger rising. "See here, if we're going to be partners, don't try to imitate Spacer arrogance. There's no room for it in you, R. Daneel." He could not resist emphasizing the "R."

"I am sorry if I have hurt your feelings, Elijah. My intention was only to indicate that, since human beings are occasionally capable of murder in defiance of custom, they may be able to violate custom for the smaller impropriety of eavesdropping."

"The apartment is adequately insulated," said Baley, still frowning. "You haven't heard anything from the apartments on any side of us, have you? Well, they won't hear us, either. Besides, why should anyone think anything of importance is going on here?"

"Let us not underestimate the enemy."

Baley shrugged. "Let's get started. My information is sketchy, so I can spread out my hand without much trouble. I know that a man named Roj Nemennuh Sarton, a citizen of the planet Aurora, and a resident of Spacetown, has been murdered by person or persons unknown. I understand that it is the opinion of the Spacers that this is not an isolated event. Am I right?"

"You are quite right, Elijah."

"They tie it up with recent attempts to sabotage the Spacer-sponsored project of converting us to an integrated human/robot society on the model of the Outer Worlds, and assume the murder was the product of a well-organized terrorist group."

"Yes."

"All right. Then to begin with, is this Spacer assumption necessarily true? Why can't the murder have been the work of an isolated fanatic? There is strong anti-robot sentiment on Earth, but there are no organized parties advocating violence of this sort."

"Not openly, perhaps. No."

"Even a secret organization dedicated to the destruction of robots and robot factories would have the common sense to realize that the worst thing they could do would be to murder a Spacer. It seems much more likely to have been the work of an unbalanced mind."

R. Daneel listened carefully, then said, "I think the weight of probability is against the 'fanatic' theory. The person killed was too well chosen and the time of the murder too appropriate for anything but deliberate planning on the part of an organized group."

"Well, then, you've got more information than I have. Spill it!"

"Your phraseology is obscure, but I think I understand. I will have to explain some of the background to you. As seen from Spacetown, Elijah, relations with Earth are unsatisfactory."

"Tough," muttered Baley.

"I have been told that when Spacetown was first established, it was taken for granted by most of our people that Earth would be willing to adopt the integrated society that has worked so well on the Outer Worlds. Even after the first riots, we thought that it was only a matter of your people getting over the first shock of novelty.

"That has not proven to be the case. Even with the co-operation of the Terrestrial government and of most of the various City governments, resistance has been continuous and progress has been very slow. Naturally, this has been a matter of great concern to our people."

"Out of altruism, I suppose," said Baley.

"Not entirely," said R. Daneel, "although it is good of you to attribute worthy motives to them. It is our common belief that a healthy and modernized Earth would be of great benefit to the whole Galaxy. At least, it is the common belief among our people at Spacetown. I must admit that there are strong elements opposed to them on the Outer Worlds."

"What? Disagreement among the Spacers?"

"Certainly. There are some who think that a modernized Earth will be a dangerous and an imperialistic Earth. This is particularly true among the populations of those older worlds which are closer to Earth and have greater reason to remember the first few centuries of interstellar travel when their worlds were controlled, politically and economically, by Earth."

Baley sighed. "Ancient history. Are they really worried? Are they still kicking at us for things that happened a thousand years ago?"

"Humans," said R. Daneel, "have their own peculiar make-up. They are not as reasonable, in many ways, as we robots, since their circuits are not as preplanned. I am told that this, too, has its advantages."

"Perhaps it may," said Baley, dryly.

"You are in a better position to know," said R. Daneel. "In

any case, continuing failure on Earth has strengthened the Nationalist parties on the Outer Worlds. They say that it is obvious that Earthmen are different from Spacers and cannot be fitted into the same traditions. They say that if we imposed robots on Earth by superior force, we would be loosing destruction on the Galaxy. One thing they never forget, you see, is that Earth's population is eight billions, while the total population of the fifty Outer Worlds combined is scarcely more than five and a half billions. Our people here, particularly Dr. Sarton –"

"He was a doctor?"

"A Doctor of Sociology, specializing in robotics, and a very brilliant man."

"I see. Go on."

"As I said, Dr. Sarton and the others realized that Spacetown and all it meant would not exist much longer if such sentiments on the Outer Worlds were allowed to grow by feeding on our continued failure. Dr. Sarton felt that the time had come to make a supreme effort to understand the psychology of the Earthman. It is easy to say that the Earth people are innately conservative and to speak tritely of 'the unchanging Earth' and 'the inscrutable Terrestrial mind,' but that is only evading the problem.

"Dr. Sarton said it was ignorance speaking and that we could not dismiss the Earthman with a proverb or a bromide. He said the Spacers who were trying to remake Earth must abandon the isolation of Spacetown and mingle with Earthmen. They must live as they, think as they, be as they."

Baley said, "The Spacers? Impossible."

"You are quite right," said R. Daneel. "Despite his views, Dr. Sarton himself could not have brought himself to enter any of the Cities, and he knew it. He would have been unable to bear the hugeness and the crowds. Even if he had been forced inside at the point of a blaster, the externals would have weighed him down so that he could never have penetrated the inner truths for which he sought."

"What about the way they're always worrying about disease?" demanded Baley. "Don't forget that. I don't think there's one of them that would risk entering a City on that account alone."

"There is that, too. Disease in the Earthly sense is unknown on the Outer Worlds and the fear of the unknown is always morbid. Dr. Sarton appreciated all of this, but nevertheless, he insisted on the necessity of growing to know the Earthman and his way of life intimately."

"He seems to have worked himself into a corner."

"Not quite. The objections to entering the City hold for human Spacers. Robot Spacers are another thing entirely."

Baley thought: I keep forgetting, damn it. Aloud, he said, "Oh?"

"Yes," said R. Daneel. "We are more flexible, naturally. At least in this respect. We can be designed for adaptation to an Earthly life. By being built into a particularly close similarity to the human externals, we could be accepted by Earthmen and allowed a closer view of their life."

"And you yourself –" began Baley in sudden enlightenment.

"Am just such a robot. For a year, Dr. Sarton had been working upon the design and construction of such robots. I was the first of his robots and so far the only one. Unfortunately, my education is not yet complete. I have been hurried into my role prematurely as a result of the murder."

"Then not all Spacer robots are like you? I mean, some look more like robots and less like humans. Right?"

"Why, naturally. The outward appearance is dependent on a robot's function. My own function requires a very manlike appearance, and I have it. Others are different, although all are humanoid. Certainly they are more humanoid than the distressingly primitive models I saw at the shoe counter. Are all your robots like that?"

"More or less," said Baley. "You don't approve?"

"Of course not. It is difficult to accept a gross parody of the human form as an intellectual equal. Can your factories do no better?"

"I'm sure they can, Daneel. I think we just prefer to know when we're dealing with a robot and when we're not." He stared directly into the robot's eyes as he said that. They were bright and moist, as a human's would be, but it seemed to Baley that their gaze was steady and did not flicker slightly from point to point as a man's would.

R. Daneel said, "I am hopeful that in time I will grow to understand that point of view."

For a moment, Baley thought there was sarcasm in the sentence, then dismissed the possibility.

"In any case," said R. Daneel, "Dr. Sarton saw clearly the fact that it was a case for C/Fe."

"See fee? What's that?"

"Just the chemical symbols for the elements carbon and iron, Elijah. Carbon is the basis of human life and iron of robot life. It becomes easy to speak of C/Fe when you wish to express a culture that combines the best of the two on an equal but parallel basis."

"See fee. Do you write it with a hyphen? Or how?"

"No, Elijah. A diagonal line between the two is the accepted way. It symbolizes neither one nor the other, but a mixture of the two, without priority."

Against his will, Baley found himself interested. Formal education on Earth included virtually no information on Outer World history or sociology after the Great Rebellion that made them independent of the mother planet. The popular book-film romances, to be sure, had their stock Outer World characters: the visiting tycoon, choleric and eccentric; the beautiful heiress, invariably smitten by the Earthman's charms and drowning disdain in love; the arrogant Spacer rival, wicked and forever beaten. These were worthless pictures, since they denied even the most elementary and well-known truths: the Spacers never entered Cities and Spacer women virtually never visited Earth.

For the first time in his life, Baley was stirred by an odd curiosity. What was Spacer life really like?

He brought his mind back to the issue at hand with something of an effort. He said, "I think I get what you're driving at. Your Dr. Sarton was attacking the problem of Earth's conversion to C/Fe from a new and promising angle. Our conservative groups or Medievalists, as they call themselves, were perturbed. They were afraid he might succeed. So they killed him. That's the motivation that makes it an organized plot and not an isolated outrage. Right?"

"I would put it about like that, Elijah. Yes."

Baley whistled thoughtfully under his breath. His long fingers tapped lightly against the table. Then he shook his head. "It won't wash. It won't wash at all."

"Pardon me. I do not understand you."

"I'm trying to get the picture. An Earthman walks into Spacetown, walks up to Dr. Sarton, blasts him, and walks out. I just don't see it. Surely the entrance to Spacetown is guarded."

R. Daneel nodded. "I think it is safe to say that no Earthman can possibly have passed through the entrance illegally."

"Then where does that leave you?"

"It would leave us in a confusing position, Elijah, if the entrance were the only way of reaching Spacetown from New York City."

Baley watched his partner thoughtfully. "I don't get you. It's the only connection between the two."

"Directly between the two, yes." R. Daneel waited a moment, then said, "You do not follow me. Is that not so?"

"That *is* so. I don't get you at all."

"Well, if it will not offend you, I will try to explain myself. May I have a piece of paper and a writer? Thank you. Look here, partner Elijah. I will draw a big circle and label it 'New York City.' Now, tangent to it, I will draw a small circle and label it 'Spacetown.' Here, where they touch, I draw an arrowhead and label it 'Barrier.' Now do you see no other connection?"

Baley said, "Of course not. There is no other connection."

"In a way," said the robot, "I am glad to hear you say this. It is in accordance with what I have been taught about Terrestrial ways of thinking. The barrier is the only *direct* connection. But both the City and Spacetown are open to the countryside in all directions. It is possible for a Terrestrial to leave the City at any of numerous exits and strike out cross country to Spacetown, where no barrier will stop him."

The tip of Baley's tongue touched his upper lip and for a moment stayed there. Then he said, "Cross country?"

"Yes."

"Cross *country*! Alone?"

"Why not?"

"Walking?"

"Undoubtedly walking. Walking would offer the least chance of detection. The murder took place early in the working day and the trip was undoubtedly negotiated in the hours before dawn."

"Impossible! There isn't a man in the City who would do it. Leave the City? Alone?"

"Ordinarily, it would seem unlikely. Yes. We Spacers know that. It is why we guard only the entrance. Even in the Great Riot, your people attacked only at the barrier that then protected the entrance. Not one left the City."

"Well, then?"

"But now we are dealing with an unusual situation. It is not the blind attack of a mob following the line of least resistance, but the organized attempt of a small group to strike, deliberately, at the unguarded point. It explains why, as you say, a Terrestrial could enter Spacetown, walk up to his victim, kill him, and walk away. The man attacked through a complete blind spot on our part."

Baley shook his head. "It's too unlikely. Have your people done anything to check that theory?"

"Yes, we have. Your Commissioner of Police was present almost at the time of the murder –"

"I know. He told me so."

"That, Elijah, is another example of the timeliness of the murder. Your Commissioner has co-operated with Dr. Sarton in the past and he was the Earthman with whom Dr. Sarton planned to make initial arrangements concerning the infiltration of your city by R's such as myself. The appointment for that morning was to concern that. The murder, of course, stopped those plans, at least temporarily, and the fact that it happened when your own Commissioner of Police was actually within Spacetown made the entire situation more difficult and embarrassing for Earth, and for our own people, too.

"But that is not what I started to say. Your Commissioner was present. We said to him, 'The man must have come cross country.' Like you, he said, 'Impossible,' or perhaps, 'Unthinkable.' He was quite disturbed, of course, and perhaps that may have made it difficult for him to see the essential point. Nevertheless, we forced him to begin checking that possibility almost at once."

Baley thought of the Commissioner's broken glasses and, even in the middle of somber thoughts, a corner of his mouth twitched. Poor Julius! Yes, he *would* be disturbed. Of course, there would be no way for Enderby to have explained the situation to the lofty Spacers, who looked upon physical disability as a peculiarly disgusting attribute of the non-genetically selected Earthmen. At least, he couldn't without losing face, and face was valuable to Police Commissioner Julius Enderby. Well, Earthmen had to stick together in some respects. The robot would never find out about Enderby's nearsightedness from Baley.

R. Daneel continued, "One by one, the various exit points from the City were investigated. Do you know how many there are, Elijah?"

Baley shook his head, then hazarded, "Twenty?"

"Five hundred and two."

"What?"

"Originally, there were many more. Five hundred and two are all that remain functional. Your City represents a slow growth, Elijah. It was once open to the sky and people crossed from City to country freely."

"Of course. I know that."

"Well, when it was first enclosed, there were many exits left. Five hundred and two still remain. The rest are built over or blocked up. We are not counting, of course, the entrance points for air freight."

"Well, what of the exit points?"

"It was hopeless. They are unguarded. We could find no official who was in charge or who considered them under his jurisdiction. It seemed as though no one even knew they existed. A man could have walked out of any of them at any time and returned at will. He would never have been detected."

"Anything else? The weapon was gone, I suppose."

"Oh, yes."

"Any clues of any sort?"

"None. We have investigated the grounds surrounding Space-town thoroughly. The robots on the truck farms were quite useless as possible witnesses. They are little more than automatic farm machinery, scarcely humanoid. And there were no humans."

"Uh-huh. What next?"

"Having failed, so far, at one end, Spacetown, we will work

at the other, New York City. It will be our duty to track down all possible subversive groups, to sift all dissident organizations –"

"How much time do you intend to spend?" interrupted Baley.

"As little as possible, as much as necessary."

"Well," said Baley, thoughtfully, "I wish you had another partner in this mess."

"I do not," said R. Daneel. "The Commissioner spoke very highly of your loyalty and ability."

"It was nice of him," said Baley sardonically. He thought: Poor Julius. I'm on his conscience and he tries hard.

"We didn't rely entirely on him," said R. Daneel. "We checked your records. You have expressed yourself openly against the use of robots in your department."

"Oh? Do you object?"

"Not at all. Your opinions are, obviously, your own. But it made it necessary for us to check your psychological profile very closely. We know that, although you dislike R's intensely, you *will* work with one if you conceive it to be your duty. You have an extraordinarily high loyalty aptitude and a respect for legitimate authority. It is what we need. Commissioner Enderby judged you well."

"You have no personal resentment toward my anti-robot sentiments?"

R. Daneel said, "If they do not prevent you from working with me and helping me do what is required of me, how can they matter?"

Baley felt stopped. He said, belligerently, "Well, then, if I pass the test, how about you? What makes you a detective?"

"I do not understand you."

"You were designed as an information-gathering machine. A man-imitation to record the facts of human life for the Spacers."

"That is a good beginning for an investigator, is it not? To be an information-gathering machine?"

"A beginning, maybe. But it's not all there is, by a long shot."

"To be sure, there has been a final adjustment of my circuits."

"I'd be curious to hear the details of that, Daneel."

"That is easy enough. A particularly strong drive has been inserted into my motivation banks; a desire for justice."

"*Justice!*" cried Baley. The irony faded from his face and was replaced by a look of the most earnest distrust.

But R. Daneel turned swiftly in his chair and stared at the door. "Someone is out there."

Someone was. The door opened and Jessie, pale and thin-lipped, walked in.

Baley was startled. "Why, Jessie! Is anything wrong?"

She stood there, eyes not meeting his. "I'm sorry. I had to . . ." Her voice trailed off.

"Where's Bentley?"

"He's to stay the night in the Youth Hall."

Baley said, "Why? I didn't tell you to do that."

"You said your partner would stay the night. I felt he would need Bentley's room."

R. Daneel said, "There was no necessity, Jessie."

Jessie lifted her eyes to R. Daneel's face, staring at it earnestly. Baley looked at his fingertips, sick at what might follow, somehow unable to interpose. The momentary silence pressed thickly on his eardrums and then, far away, as through folds of plastex, he heard his wife say, "I think you are a robot, Daneel."

And R. Daneel replied, in a voice as calm as ever, "I am."

CHAPTER SIX

WHISPERS IN A BEDROOM

On the uppermost levels of some of the wealthiest sub-sections of the City are the natural Solariums, where a partition of quartz with a movable metal shield excludes the air but lets in the sunlight. There the wives and daughters of the City's highest administrators and executives may tan themselves. There a unique thing happens every evening.

Night falls.

In the rest of the City (including the UV-Solariums, where the millions, in strict sequence of allotted time, may occasionally expose themselves to the artificial wavelengths of arc lights) there are only the arbitrary cycles of hours.

The business of the City might easily continue in three eight-hour or four six-hour shifts, by "day" and "night" alike. Light and work could easily proceed endlessly. There are always civic reformers who periodically suggest such a thing in the interests of economy and efficiency.

The notion is never accepted.

Much of the earlier habits of Earthly society have been given up in the interests of that same economy and efficiency; space, privacy, even much of free will. They are the products of civilization, however, and not more than ten thousand years old.

The adjustment of sleep to night, however, is as old as man: a million years. The habit is not easy to give up. Although the evening is unseen, apartment lights dim as the hours of darkness pass and the City's pulse sinks. Though no one can tell noon from midnight by any cosmic phenomenon along the enclosed avenues of the City, mankind follows the mute partitionings of the hour hand.

The expressways empty, the noise of life sinks, the moving mob among the colossal alleys melts away; New York City lies in Earth's unnoticed shadow, and its population sleeps.

Elijah Baley did not sleep. He lay in bed and there was no light in his apartment, but that was as far as it went.

Jessie lay next to him, motionless in the darkness. He had not felt nor heard her move.

On the other side of the wall sat, stood, lay (Baley wondered which) R. Daneel Olivaw.

Baley whispered, "Jessie!" Then again, "Jessie!"

The dark figure beside him stirred slightly under the sheet. "What do you want?"

"Jessie, don't make it worse for me."

"You might have told me."

"How could I? I was planning to, when I could think of a way. Jehoshaphat, Jessie –"

"Sh!"

Baley's voice returned to its whisper. "How did you find out? Won't you tell me?"

"Lije." Her voice was scarcely more than a stirring of air. "Can he hear us? That thing?"

"Not if we whisper."

"How do you know? Maybe he has special ears to pick up tiny sounds. Spacer robots can do all sorts of things."

Baley knew that. The prorobot propaganda was forever stressing the miraculous feats of the Spacer robots, their endurance, their extra senses, their service to humanity in a hundred novel ways. Personally, he thought that approach defeated itself. Earthmen hated the robots all the more for their superiority.

He whispered, "Not Daneel. They made him human-type on purpose. They wanted him to be accepted as a human being, so he must have only human senses."

"How do you know?"

"If he had extra senses, there would be too much danger of his giving himself away as non-human by accident. He would do too much, know too much."

"Well, maybe."

Silence fell again.

A minute passed and Baley tried a second time. "Jessie, if you'll just let things be until – until. . . . Look, dear, it's unfair of you to be angry."

"Angry? Oh, Lije, you fool, I'm not angry. I'm scared; I'm scared clean to death."

She made a gulping sound and clutched at the neck of his pajamas. For a while, they clung together, and Baley's growing sense of injury evaporated into a troubled concern.

"Why, Jessie? There's nothing to be worried about. He's harmless. I swear he is."

"Can't you get rid of him, Lije?"

"You know I can't. It's Department business. How can I?"

"What kind of business, Lije? Tell me."

"Now, Jessie, I'm surprised at you." He groped for her cheek in the darkness and patted it. It was wet. Using his pajama sleeve, he carefully wiped her eyes.

"Now, look," he said tenderly, "you're being a baby."

"Tell them at the Department to have someone else do it, whatever it is. Please, Lije."

Baley's voice hardened a bit. "Jessie, you've been a policeman's wife long enough to know an assignment is an assignment."

"Well, why did it have to be you?"

"Julius Enderby –"

She stiffened in his arms. "I might have known. Why can't you tell Julius Enderby to have someone else do the dirty work just once. You stand for too much, Lije, and this is just –"

"All right, all right," he said, soothingly.

She subsided, quivering.

Baley thought: She'll never understand.

Julius Enderby had been a fighting word with them since their engagement. Enderby had been two classes ahead of Baley at the City School of Administrative Studies. They had been friends. When Baley had taken his battery of aptitude tests and neuroanalysis and found himself in line for the police force, he found Enderby there ahead of him. Enderby had already moved into the plain-clothes division.

Baley followed Enderby, but at a continually greater distance. It was no one's fault, precisely. Baley was capable enough, efficient enough, but he lacked something that Enderby had. Enderby fit the administrative machine perfectly. He was one of those persons who was born for a hierarchy, who was just naturally comfortable in a bureaucracy.

The Commissioner wasn't a great brain, and Baley knew it. He had his childish peculiarities, his intermittent rash of ostentatious Medievalism, for instance. But he was smooth with others; he offended no one; he took orders gracefully; he gave them with the proper mixture of gentleness and firmness. He even got along with the Spacers. He was perhaps over-obsequious to them (Baley himself could never have dealt with them for half a day without getting into a state of bristle; he was sure of that, even though he had never really spoken to a Spacer), but they trusted him, and that made him extremely useful to the City.

So, in a Civil Service where smooth and sociable performance was more useful than an individualistic competence, Enderby went up the scale quickly, and was at the Commissioner level when Baley himself was nothing more than a C—5. Baley did not resent the contrast, though he was human enough to regret it. Enderby did not forget their earlier friendship and, in his queer way, tried to make up for his success by doing what he could for Baley.

The assignment of partnership with R. Daneel was an example of it. It was tough and unpleasant, but there was no question that it carried within it the germs of tremendous advance. The Commissioner might have given the chance to someone else. His own talk, that morning, of needing a favor masked but did not hide that fact.

Jessie never saw things that way. On similar occasions in the past, she had said, "It's your silly loyalty index. I'm so tired of hearing everyone praise you for being so full of a sense of duty. Think of yourself once in a while. I notice the ones on top don't bring up the topic of their *own* loyalty index."

Baley lay in bed in a state of stiff wakefulness, letting Jessie calm down. He had to *think*. He had to be certain of his suspicions. Little things chased one another and fitted together in his mind. Slowly, they were building into a pattern.

He felt the mattress give as Jessie stirred.

"Lije?" Her lips were at his ear.

"What?"

"Why don't you resign?"

"Don't be crazy."

"Why not?" She was suddenly almost eager. "You can get rid of that horrible robot that way. Just walk in and tell Enderby you're through."

Baley said coldly, "I can't resign in the middle of an important case. I can't throw the whole thing down the disposal tube just any time I feel like it. A trick like that means declassification for cause."

"Even so. You can work your way up again. You can do it, Lije. There are a dozen places where you'd fit into Service."

"Civil Service doesn't take men who are declassified for cause. Manual labor is the only thing I can do; the only thing you could do. Bentley would lose all inherited status. For God's sake, Jessie, you don't know what it's like."

"I've read about it. I'm not afraid of it," she mumbled.

"You're crazy. You're plain crazy." Baley could feel himself trembling. There was a familiar, flashing picture of his father in his mind's eye. His father, moldering away toward death.

Jessie sighed heavily.

Baley's mind turned savagely away from her. In desperation, it returned to the pattern it was constructing.

He said, tightly, "Jessie, you've got to tell me. How did you find out Daneel was a robot? What made you decide that?"

She began, "Well..." and just ran down. It was the third time she had begun to explain and failed.

He crushed her hand in his, willing her to speak. "Please, Jessie. What's frightening you?"

She said, "I just guessed he was a robot, Lije."

He said, "There wasn't anything to make you guess that, Jessie. You didn't think he was a robot before you left, now did you?"

"No-o, but I got to thinking..."

"Come on, Jessie. What was it?"

"Well. . . . Look, Lije, the girls were talking in the Personal. You know how they are. Just talking about everything."

Women! thought Baley.

"Anyway," said Jessie. "The rumor is all over town. It must be."

"All over town?" Baley felt a quick and savage touch of triumph, or nearly that. Another piece in place!

"It was the way they sounded. They said there was talk about a Spacer robot loose in the City. He was supposed to look just like a man and to be working with the police. They even asked *me* about it. They laughed and said, 'Does your Lije know anything about it, Jessie?' and I laughed, and said, 'Don't be silly!'

"Then we went to the etherics and I got to thinking about your new partner. Do you remember those pictures you brought home, the ones Julius Enderby took in Spacetown, to show me what Spacers looked like? Well, I got to thinking that's what your partner looked like. It just came to me that that's what he looked like and I said to myself, oh, my God, someone must've recognized him in the shoe department and he's with Lije and I just said I had a headache and I ran –"

Baley said, "Now, Jessie, stop, stop. Get hold of yourself. Now why are you afraid? You're not afraid of Daneel himself. You faced up to him when you came home. You faced up to him fine. So –"

He stopped speaking. He sat up in bed, eyes uselessly wide in the darkness.

He felt his wife move against his side. His hand leaped, found her lips and pressed against them. She heaved against his grip, her hands grasping his wrist and wrenching, but he leaned down against her the more heavily.

Then, suddenly, he released her. She whimpered.

He said, huskily, "Sorry, Jessie. I was listening."

He was getting out of bed, pulling warm Plastofilm over the soles of his feet.

"Lije, where are you going? Don't leave me."

"It's all right. I'm just going to the door."

The Plastofilm made a soft, shuffling noise as he circled the bed. He cracked the door to the living room and waited a long moment. Nothing happened. It was so quiet, he could hear the thin whistle of Jessie's breath from their bed. He could hear the dull rhythm of blood in his ears.

Baley's hand crept through the opening of the door, snaking out to the spot he needed no light to find. His fingers closed upon the knob that controlled the ceiling illumination. He exerted the smallest pressure he could and the ceiling gleamed dimly, so dimly that the lower half of the living room remained in semidusk.

He saw enough, however. The main door was closed and the living room lay lifeless and quiet.

He turned the knob back into the off position and moved back to bed.

It was all he needed. The pieces fit. The pattern was complete.

Jessie pleaded with him. "Lije, what's wrong?"

"Nothing's wrong, Jessie. Everything's all right. He's not here."

"The robot? Do you mean he's gone? For good?"

"No, no. He'll be back. And before he does, answer my question."

"What question?"

"What are you afraid of?"

Jessie said nothing.

Baley grew more insistent. "You said you were scared to death."

"Of him."

"No, we went through that. You weren't afraid of him and, besides, you know quite well a robot cannot hurt a human being."

Her words came slowly. "I thought if everyone knew he was a robot there might be a riot. We'd be killed."

"Why kill us?"

"You know what riots are like."

"They don't even know where the robot is, do they?"

"They might find out."

"And that's what you're afraid of, a riot?"

"Well —"

"Sh!" He pressed Jessie down to the pillow.

Then he put his lips to her ear. "He's come back. Now listen and don't say a word. Everything's fine. He'll be gone in the morning and he won't be back. There'll be no riot, nothing."

He was almost contented as he said that, almost completely contented. He felt he could sleep.

He thought again: No riot, nothing. And no declassification.

And just before he actually fell asleep, he thought: Not even a murder investigation. Not even that. The whole thing's solved. . . .

He slept.

CHAPTER SEVEN

EXCURSION INTO SPACETOWN

Police Commissioner Julius Enderby polished his glasses with exquisite care and placed them upon the bridge of his nose.

Baley thought: It's a good trick. Keeps you busy while you're thinking what to say, and it doesn't cost money the way lighting up a pipe does.

And because the thought had entered his mind, he drew out his pipe and dipped into his pinchéd store of rough-cut. One of the few luxury crops still grown on Earth was tobacco, and its end was visibly approaching. Prices had gone up, never down, in Baley's lifetime; quotas down, never up.

Enderby, having adjusted his glasses, felt for the switch at one end of his desk and flicked his door into one-way transparency for a moment. "Where is he now, by the way?"

"He told me he wanted to be shown through the Department, and I let Jack Tobin do the honors." Baley lit his pipe and tightened its baffle carefully. The Commissioner, like most non-indulgers, was petty about tobacco smoke.

"I hope you didn't tell him Daneel was a robot."

"Of course I didn't."

The Commissioner did not relax. One hand remained aimlessly busy with the automatic calendar on his desk.

"How is it?" he asked, without looking at Baley.

"Middling rough."

"I'm sorry, Lije."

Baley said, firmly, "You might have warned me that he looked completely human."

The Commissioner looked surprised. "I didn't?" Then, with sudden petulance, "Damn it, you should have known. I wouldn't have asked you to have him stay at your house if he looked like R. Sammy. Now would I?"

"I know, Commissioner, but I'd never seen a robot like that and you had. I didn't even know such things were possible. I just wish you'd mentioned it, that's all."

"Look, Lije, I'm sorry. I should have told you. You're right. It's just that this job, this whole deal, has me so on edge that half the time I'm just snapping at people for no reason. He, I mean this Daneel thing, is a new-type robot. It's still in the experimental stage."

"So he explained himself."

"Oh. Well, that's it, then."

Baley tensed a little. This was it, now. He said, casually, teeth clenched on pipestem, "R. Daneel has arranged a trip to Spacetown for me."

"To Spacetown!" Enderby looked up with instant indignation.

"Yes. It's the logical next move, Commissioner. I'd like to see the scene of the crime, ask a few questions."

Enderby shook his head decidedly. "I don't think that's a good idea, Lije. We've gone over the ground. I doubt there's anything new to be learned. And they're strange people. Kid gloves! They've got to be handled with kid gloves. You don't have the experience."

He put a plump hand to his forehead and added, with unexpected fervor, "I hate them."

Baley inserted hostility into his voice. "Damn it, the robot came here and I should go there. It's bad enough sharing a front seat with a robot; I hate to take a back seat. Of course, if you don't think I'm capable of running this investigation, Commissioner –"

"It isn't that, Lije. It's not you, it's the Spacers. You don't know what they're like."

Baley deepened his frown. "Well, then, Commissioner, suppose you come along." His right hand rested on his knee, and two of his fingers crossed automatically as he said that.

The Commissioner's eyes widened. "No, Lije. I won't go there. Don't ask me to." He seemed visibly to catch hold of his runaway words. More quietly, he said, with an unconvincing smile, "Lots of work here, you know. I'm days behind."

Baley regarded him thoughtfully. "I tell you what then. Why not get into it by trimension later on. Just for a while, you understand. In case I need help."

"Well, yes. I suppose I can do that." He sounded unenthusiastic.

"Good." Baley looked at the wall clock, nodded, and got up. "I'll be in touch with you."

Baley looked back as he left the office, keeping the door open for part of an additional second. He saw the Commissioner's head begin bending down toward the crook of one elbow as it rested on the desk. The plain-clothes man could almost swear he heard a sob.

Jehoshaphat! he thought, in outright shock.

He paused in the common room and sat on the corner of a nearby desk, ignoring its occupant, who looked up, murmured a casual greeting, and returned to his work.

Baley unclipped the baffle from the bowl of the pipe and blew into it. He inverted the pipe itself over the desk's small ash vacuum and let the powdery white tobacco ash vanish. He looked regretfully at the empty pipe, readjusted the baffle, and put it away. Another pipeful gone forever!

He reconsidered what had just taken place. In one way, Enderby had not surprised him. He had expected resistance to any attempt on his own part to enter Spacetown. He had heard the Commissioner talk often enough about the difficulties of dealing with Spacers, about the dangers of allowing any but experienced negotiators to have anything to do with them, even over trifles.

He had not expected, however, to have the Commissioner give in so easily. He had supposed, at the very least, that Enderby would have insisted on accompanying him. The pressure of other work was meaningless in the face of the importance of this problem.

And that was not what Baley wanted. He wanted exactly what he had gotten. He wanted the Commissioner to be present by trimensional personification so that he could witness the proceedings from a point of safety.

Safety was the key word. Baley would need a witness that could not be put out of the way immediately. He needed that much as the minimum guarantee of his own safety.

The Commissioner had agreed to that at once. Baley remembered the parting sob, or ghost of one, and thought: Jehoshaphat, the man's into this past his depth.

A cheerful, slurring voice sounded just at Baley's shoulder and Baley started.

"What the devil do you want?" he demanded savagely.

The smile on R. Sammy's face remained foolishly fixed. "Jack says to tell you Daneel is ready, Lije."

"All right. Now get out of here."

He frowned at the robot's departing back. There was nothing so irritating as having that clumsy metal contraption forever making free with your front name. He'd complained about that when R. Sammy first arrived and the Commissioner had shrugged his shoulders and said, "You can't have it both ways, Lije. The public insists that City robots be built with a strong friendship circuit. All right, then. He is drawn to you. He calls you by the friendliest name he knows."

Friendship circuit! No robot built, of any type, could possibly hurt a human being. That was the First Law of Robotics:

"A robot may not injure a human being, or, through inaction, allow a human being to come to harm."

No positronic brain was ever built without that injunction driven so deeply into its basic circuits that no conceivable derangement could displace it. There was no need for specialized friendship circuits.

Yet the Commissioner was right. The Earthman's distrust for

robots was something quite irrational and friendship circuits had to be incorporated, just as all robots had to be made smiling. On Earth, at any rate.

R. Daneel, now, never smiled.

Sighing, Baley rose to his feet. He thought: Spacetown, next stop – or, maybe, last stop!

The police forces of the City, as well as certain high officials, could still make use of individual squad cars along the corridors of the City and even along the ancient underground motorways that were barred to foot traffic. There were perennial demands on the part of the Liberals that these motorways be converted to children's playgrounds, to new shopping areas, or to expressway or localway extensions.

The strong pleas of "Civic safety!" remained unvanquished, however. In cases of fires too large to be handled by local devices, in cases of massive breakdowns in power lines or ventilators, most of all in cases of serious riot, there had to be some means whereby the forces of the City could be mobilized at the stricken point in a hurry. No substitute for the motorways existed or could exist.

Baley had traveled along a motorway several times before in his life, but its indecent emptiness always depressed him. It seemed a million miles from the warm, living pulsation of the City. It stretched out like a blind and hollow worm before his eyes as he sat at the controls of the squad car. It opened continuously into new stretches as he moved around this gentle curve or that. Behind him, he knew without looking, another blind and hollow worm continually contracted and closed. The motorway was well lit, but lighting was meaningless in the silence and emptiness.

R. Daneel did nothing to break that silence or fill that emptiness. He looked straight ahead, as unimpressed by the empty motorway as by the bulging expressway.

In one sounding moment, to the tune of a wild whine of the squad car's siren, they popped out of the motorway and curved gradually into the vehicular lane of a City corridor.

The vehicular lanes were still conscientiously marked down each major corridor in reverence for one vestigial portion of the past. There were no vehicles any longer, except for squad cars, fire engines, and maintenance trucks, and pedestrians used the lanes in complete self-assurance. They scattered in indignant hurry before the advance of Baley's squealing car.

Baley, himself, drew a freer breath as noise surged in about him, but it was an interval only. In less than two hundred yards they turned into the subdued corridors that led to Spacetown Entrance.

They were expected. The guards obviously knew R. Daneel by sight and, although themselves human, nodded to him without the least self-consciousness.

One approached Baley and saluted with perfect, if frigid, military courtesy. He was tall and grave, though not the perfect specimen of Spacer physique that R. Daneel was.

He said, "Your identification card, if you please, sir."

It was inspected quickly but thoroughly. Baley noticed that the guard wore flesh-colored gloves and had an all but unnoticeable filter in each nostril.

The guard saluted again and returned the card. He said, "There is a small Men's Personal here which we would be pleased to have you use if you wish to shower."

It was in Baley's mind to deny the necessity, but R. Daneel plucked gently at his sleeve, as the guard stepped back to his place.

R. Daneel said, "It is customary, partner Elijah, for City dwellers to shower before entering Spacetown. I tell you this since I know you have no desire, through lack of information on this matter, to render yourself or ourselves uncomfortable. It is also advisable for you to attend to any matters of personal hygiene you may think advisable. There will be no facilities within Spacetown for that purpose."

"No facilities!" said Baley, strenuously. "But that's impossible."

"I mean, of course," said R. Daneel, "none for use by City dwellers."

Baley's face filled with a clearly hostile astonishment.

R. Daneel said, "I regret the situation, but it is a matter of custom."

Wordlessly, Baley entered the Personal. He felt, rather than saw, R. Daneel entering behind him.

He thought: Checking on me? Making sure I wash the City dust off myself?

For a furious moment, he reveled in the thought of the shock he was preparing for Spacetown. It seemed to him suddenly minor that he might, in effect, be pointing a blaster at his own chest.

The Personal was small, but it was well appointed and antiseptic in its cleanliness. There was a trace of sharpness in the air. Baley sniffed at it, momentarily puzzled.

Then he thought: Ozone! They've got ultraviolet radiation flooding the place.

A little sign blinked on and off several times, then remained steadily lit. It said, "Visitor will please remove all clothing, including shoes, and place it in the receptacle below."

Baley acquiesced. He unhitched his blaster and blaster strap and recircled it about his naked waist. It felt heavy and uncomfortable.

The receptacle closed and his clothing was gone. The lighted sign blanked out. A new sign flashed ahead.

It said: "Visitor will please tend to personal needs, then make use of the shower indicated by arrow."

Baley felt like a machine tool being shaped by long-distance force edges on an assembly line.

His first act upon entering the small shower cubicle was to draw up the moisture-proof flap on his blaster holster and clip it down firmly all about. He knew by long-standing test that he could still draw and use it in less than five seconds.

There was no knob or hook on which to hang his blaster. There was not even a visible shower head. He placed it in a corner away from the cubicle's entrance door.

Another sign flashed: "Visitor will please hold arms directly out from his body and stand in the central circle with feet in the indicated positions."

As he placed his feet in the small depressions allowed for them, the sign blanked out. As it did so, a stinging, foaming spray hit him from ceiling, floor, and four walls. He felt the water welling up even beneath the soles of his feet. For a full minute it lasted, his skin reddening under the combined force of the heat and pressure and his lungs gasping for air in the warm dampness. There followed another minute of cool, low-

pressure spray, and then finally a minute of warm air that left
him dry and refreshed.

He picked up his blaster and blaster strap and found that
they, too, were dry and warm. He strapped them on and stepped
out of the cubicle in time to see R. Daneel emerge from a neighboring shower. Of course! R. Daneel was not a City dweller, but
he had accumulated City dust.

Quite automatically, Baley looked away. Then, with the
thought that, after all, R. Daneel's customs were not City customs, he forced his unwilling eyes back for one moment. His
lips quirked in a tiny smile. R. Daneel's resemblance to humanity
was not restricted to his face and hands but had been carried
out with painstaking accuracy over the entire body.

Baley stepped forward in the direction he had been traveling
continuously since entering the Personal. He found his clothes
waiting for him, neatly folded. They had a warm, clean odor to
them.

A sign said, "Visitor will please resume his clothing and place
his hand in the indicated depression."

Baley did so. He felt a definite tingling in the ball of his
middle finger as he laid it down upon the clean, milky surface.
He lifted his hand hastily and found a little drop of blood oozing
out. As he watched, it stopped flowing.

He shook it off and pinched the finger. No more blood was
flowing even then.

Obviously, they were analyzing his blood. He felt a definite
pang of anxiety. His own yearly routine examination by Department doctors, he felt sure, was not carried on with the
thoroughness or, perhaps, with the knowledge of these cold
robot-makers from outer space. He was not sure he wanted too
probing an inquiry into the state of his health.

The time of waiting seemed long to Baley, but when the light
flashed again, it said simply, "Visitor will proceed."

Baley drew a long breath of relief. He walked onward and
stepped through an archway. Two metal rods closed in before
him and, written in luminous air, were the words: "Visitor is
warned to proceed no further."

"What the devil —" called out Baley, forgetting in his anger
the fact that he was still in the Personal.

R. Daneel's voice was in his ear. "The sniffers have detected a power source, I imagine. Are you carrying your blaster, Elijah?"

Baley whirled, his face a deep crimson. He tried twice, then managed to croak out, "A police officer has his blaster on him or in easy reach at all times, on duty and off."

It was the first time he had spoken in a Personal, proper, since he was ten years old. That had been in his uncle Boris's presence and had merely been an automatic complaint when he stubbed his toe. Uncle Boris had beaten him well when he reached home and had lectured him strongly on the necessities of public decency.

R. Daneel said, "No visitor may be armed. It is our custom, Elijah. Even your Commissioner leaves his blaster behind on all visits."

Under almost any other circumstances, Baley would have turned on his heel and walked away, away from Spacetown and away from that robot. Now, however, he was almost mad with desire to go through with his exact plan and have his revenge to the brim in that way.

This, he thought, was the unobtrusive medical examination that had replaced the more detailed one of the early days. He could well understand, he could understand to overflowing, the indignation and anger that had led to the Barrier Riots of his youth.

In black anger, Baley unhitched his blaster belt. R. Daneel took it from him and placed it within a recess in the wall. A thin metal plate slithered across it.

"If you will put your thumb in the depression," said R. Daneel, "only your thumb will open it later on."

Baley felt undressed, far more so, in fact, than he had felt in the shower. He stepped across the point at which the rods had lately barred him, and, finally, out of the Personal.

He was back in a corridor again, but there was an element of strangeness about it. Up ahead, the light had an unfamiliar quality to it. He felt a whiff of air against his face and, automatically, he thought a squad car had passed.

R. Daneel must have read his uneasiness in his face. He said, "You are essentially in open air now, Elijah. It is unconditioned."

Baley felt faintly sick. How could the Spacers be so rigidly careful of a human body, merely because it came from the City, and then breathe the dirty air of the open fields? He tightened his nostrils, as though by pulling them together he could the more effectively screen the ingoing air.

R. Daneel said, "I believe you will find that open air is not deleterious to human health."

"All right," said Baley, faintly.

The air currents hit annoyingly against his face. They were gentle enough, but they were erratic. That bothered him.

Worse came. The corridor opened into blueness and as they approached its end, strong white light washed down. Baley had seen sunlight. He had been in a natural Solarium once in the line of duty. But there, protecting glass had enclosed the place and the sun's own image had been refracted into a generalized glow. Here, all was open.

Automatically, he looked up at the sun, then turned away. His dazzled eyes blinked and watered.

A Spacer was approaching. A moment of misgiving struck Baley.

R. Daneel, however, stepped forward to greet the approaching man with a handshake. The Spacer turned to Baley and said, "Won't you come with me, sir? I am Dr. Han Fastolfe."

Things were better inside one of the domes. Baley found himself goggling at the size of the rooms and the way in which space was so carelessly distributed, but was thankful for the feel of the conditioned air.

Fastolfe said, sitting down and crossing his long legs, "I'm assuming that you prefer conditioning to unobstructed wind."

He seemed friendly enough. There were fine wrinkles on his forehead and a certain flabbiness to the skin below his eyes and just under his chin. His hair was thinning, but showed no signs of gray. His large ears stood away from his head, giving him a humorous and homely appearance that comforted Baley.

Early that morning, Baley had looked once again at those pictures of Spacetown that Enderby had taken. R. Daneel had just arranged the Spacetown appointment and Baley was absorbing the notion that he was to meet Spacers in the flesh. Somehow that was considerably different from speaking to them across miles of carrier wave, as he had done on several occasions before.

The Spacers in those pictures had been, generally speaking, like those that were occasionally featured in the book-films: tall, red-headed, grave, coldly handsome. Like R. Daneel Olivaw, for instance.

R. Daneel named the Spacers for Baley and when Baley suddenly pointed and said, in surprise, "That isn't you, is it?" R. Daneel answered, "No, Elijah, that is my designer, Dr. Sarton."

He said it unemotionally.

"You were made in your maker's image?" asked Baley, sardonically, but there was no answer to that and, in truth, Baley scarcely expected one. The Bible, as he knew, circulated only to the most limited extent on the Outer Worlds.

And now Baley looked at Han Fastolfe, a man who deviated very noticeably from the Spacer norm in looks, and the Earthman felt a pronounced gratitude for that fact.

"Won't you accept food?" asked Fastolfe.

He indicated the table that separated himself and R. Daneel from the Earthman. It bore nothing but a bowl of varicolored spheroids. Baley felt vaguely startled. He had taken them for table decorations.

R. Daneel explained. "These are the fruits of natural plant life grown on Aurora. I suggest you try this kind. It is called an apple and is reputed to be pleasant."

Fastolfe smiled. "R. Daneel does not know this by personal experience, of course, but he is quite right."

Baley brought an apple to his mouth. Its surface was red and green. It was cool to the touch and had a faint but pleasant odor. With an effort, he bit into it and the unexpected tartness of the pulpy contents hurt his teeth.

He chewed it gingerly. City dwellers ate natural food, of course, whenever rations allowed it. He himself had eaten natural meat and bread often. But such food had always been processed in some way. It had been cooked or ground, blended or compounded. Fruit, now, properly speaking, should come in the form of sauce or preserve. What he was holding now must have come straight from the dirt of a planet's soil.

He thought: I hope they've washed it at least.

Again he wondered at the spottiness of Spacer notions concerning cleanliness.

Fastolfe said, "Let me introduce myself a bit more specifically. I am in charge of the investigation of the murder of Dr. Sarton at the Spacetown end as Commissioner Enderby is at the City end. If I can help you in any way, I stand ready to do so. We are as eager for a quiet solution of the affair and prevention of future incidents of the sort as any of you City men can be."

"Thank you, Dr. Fastolfe," said Baley. "Your attitude is appreciated."

So much, he thought, for the amenities. He bit into the center of the apple and hard, dark little ovoids popped into his mouth. He spat automatically. They flew out and fell to the ground. One would have struck Fastolfe's leg had not the Spacer moved it hastily.

Baley reddened, started to bend.

Fastolfe said, pleasantly, "It is quite all right, Mr. Baley. Just leave them, please."

Baley straightened again. He put the apple down gingerly. He had the uncomfortable feeling that once he was gone, the lost little objects would be found and picked up by suction; the bowl of fruit would be burnt or discarded far from Spacetown; the very room they were sitting in would be sprayed with viricide.

He covered his embarrassment with brusqueness. He said, "I would like to ask permission to have Commissioner Enderby join our conference by trimensional personification."

Fastolfe's eyebrows raised. "Certainly, if you wish it. Daneel, would you make the connection?"

Baley sat in stiff discomfort until the shiny surface of the large parallelepiped in one corner of the room dissolved away to show Commissioner Julius Enderby and part of his desk. At that moment, the discomfort eased and Baley felt nothing short of love for that familiar figure, and a longing to be safely back in that office with him, or anywhere in the City, for that matter. Even in the least prepossessing portion of the Jersey yeast-vat districts.

Now that he had his witness, Baley saw no reason for delay. He said, "I believe I have penetrated the mystery surrounding the death of Dr. Sarton."

Out of the corner of his eye, he saw Enderby springing to his feet and grabbing wildly (and successfully) at his flying spectacles. By standing, the Commissioner thrust his head out of the limits of the trimensic receiver and was forced to sit down again, red-faced and speechless.

In a much quieter way, Dr. Fastolfe, head inclined to one side, was as startled. Only R. Daneel was unmoved.

"Do you mean," said Fastolfe, "that you know the murderer?"

"No," said Baley, "I mean there was no murder."

"What!" screamed Enderby.

"One moment, Commissioner Enderby," said Fastolfe, raising a hand. His eyes held Baley's and he said, "Do you mean that Dr. Sarton is alive?"

"Yes, sir, and I believe I know where he is."

"Where?"

"Right there," said Baley, and pointed firmly at R. Daneel Olivaw.

CHAPTER EIGHT

DEBATE OVER A ROBOT

At the moment, Baley was most conscious of the thud of his own pulse. He seemed to be living in a moment of suspended time. R. Daneel's expression was, as always, empty of emotion. Han Fastolfe wore a look of well-bred astonishment on his face and nothing more.

It was Commissioner Julius Enderby's reaction that most concerned Baley, however. The trimensic receiver out of which his face stared did not allow of perfect reproduction. There was always that tiny flicker and that not-quite-ideal resolution. Through that imperfection and through the further masking of the Commissioner's spectacles, Enderby's eyes were unreadable.

Baley thought: Don't go to pieces on me, Julius. I need you.

He didn't really think that Fastolfe would act in haste or under emotional impulse. He had read somewhere once that Spacers had no religion, but substituted, instead, a cold and phlegmatic intellectualism raised to the heights of a philosophy. He believed that and counted on it. They would make a point of acting slowly and then only on the basis of reason.

If he were alone among them and had said what he had said,

he was certain that he would never have returned to the City. Cold reason would have dictated that. The Spacers' plans were worth more to them, many times over, than the life of a City dweller. There would be some excuse made to Julius Enderby. Maybe they would present his corpse to the Commissioner, shake their heads, and speak of an Earthman conspiracy having struck again. The Commissioner would believe them. It was the way he was built. If he hated Spacers, it was a hatred based on fear. He wouldn't dare disbelieve them.

That was why he had to be an actual witness of events, a witness, moreover, safely out of reach of the Spacers' calculated safety measures.

The Commissioner said, chokingly, "Lije, you're all wrong. I saw Dr. Sarton's corpse."

"You saw the charred remnants of something you were told was Dr. Sarton's corpse," retorted Baley, boldly. He thought grimly of the Commissioner's broken glasses. That had been an unexpected favor for the Spacers.

"No, no, Lije. I knew Dr. Sarton well and his head was undamaged. It was he." The Commissioner put his hand to his glasses uneasily, as though he, too, remembered, and added, "I looked at him closely, very closely."

"How about this one, Commissioner?" asked Baley, pointing to R. Daneel again. "Doesn't he resemble Dr. Sarton?"

"Yes, the way a statue would."

"An expressionless attitude can be assumed, Commissioner. Suppose that were a robot you had seen blasted to death. You say you looked closely. Did you look closely enough to see whether the charred surface at the edge of the blast was really decomposed organic tissue or a deliberately introduced layer of carbonization over fused metal."

The Commissioner looked revolted. He said, "You're being ridiculous."

Baley turned to the Spacer. "Are you willing to have the body exhumed for examination, Dr. Fastolfe?"

Dr. Fastolfe smiled. "Ordinarily, I would have no objection, Mr. Baley, but I'm afraid we do not bury our dead. Cremation is a universal custom among us."

"Very convenient," said Baley.

"Tell me, Mr. Baley," said Dr. Fastolfe, "just how did you

arrive at this very extraordinary conclusion of yours?"

Baley thought: He isn't giving up. He'll brazen it out, if he can.

He said, "It wasn't difficult. There's more to imitating a robot than just putting on a frozen expression and adopting a stilted style of conversation. The trouble with you men of the Outer Worlds is that you're too used to robots. You've gotten to accept them almost as human beings. You've grown blind to the differences. On Earth, it's different. We're very conscious of what a robot is.

"Now in the first place, R. Daneel is too good a human to be a robot. My first impression of him was that he was a Spacer. It was quite an effort for me to adjust myself to his statement that he was a robot. And of course, the reason for that was that he *was* a Spacer and *wasn't* a robot."

R. Daneel interrupted, without any sign of self-consciousness at being himself so intimately the topic of debate. He said, "As I told you, partner Elijah, I was designed to take a temporary place in a human society. The resemblance to humanity is purposeful."

"Even," asked Baley, "down to the painstaking duplication of those portions of the body which, in the ordinary course of events, would always be covered by clothes? Even to the duplication of organs which, in a robot, would have no conceivable function?"

Enderby said suddenly, "How did you find that out?"

Baley reddened. "I couldn't help noticing in the – in the Personal."

Enderby looked shocked.

Fastolfe said, "Surely you understand that a resemblance must be complete if it is to be useful. For our purposes, half measures are as bad as nothing at all."

Baley asked abruptly, "May I smoke?"

Three pipefuls in one day was a ridiculous extravagance, but he was riding a rolling torrent of recklessness and needed the release of tobacco. After all, he was talking back to Spacers. He was going to force their lies down their own throats.

Fastolfe said, "I'm sorry, but I'd prefer that you didn't."

It was a "preference" that had the force of a command. Baley felt that. He thrust back the pipe, the bowl of which he had already taken into his hand in anticipation of automatic permission.

Of course not, he thought bitterly. Enderby didn't warn me, because he doesn't smoke himself, but it's obvious. It follows. They don't smoke on their hygienic Outer Worlds, or drink, or have any human vices. No wonder they accept robots in their damned – what did R. Daneel call it? – C/Fe society? No wonder R. Daneel can play the robot as well as he does. They're all robots out there to begin with.

He said, "The too complete resemblance is just one point out of a number. There was a near riot in my section as I was taking *him* home." (He had to point. He could not bring himself to say either R. Daneel or Dr. Sarton.) "It was he that stopped the trouble and he did it by pointing a blaster at the potential rioters."

"Good Lord," said Enderby, energetically, "the report stated that it was you –"

"I know, Commissioner," said Baley. "The report was based on information that I gave. I didn't want to have it on the record that a robot had threatened to blast men and women."

"No, no. Of course not." Enderby was quite obviously horrified. He leaned forward to look at something that was out of the range of the trimensic receiver.

Baley could guess what it was. The Commissioner was checking the power gauge to see if the transmitter were being tapped.

"Is that a point in your argument?" asked Fastolfe.

"It certainly is. The First Law of Robotics states that a robot cannot harm a human being."

"But R. Daneel did no harm."

"True. He even stated afterward that he wouldn't have fired under any circumstances. Still, no robot I ever heard of could have violated the spirit of the First Law to the extent of threatening to blast a man, even if he really had no intention to do so."

"I see. Are you a robotics expert, Mr. Baley?"

"No, sir. But I've had a course in general robotics and in positronic analysis. I'm not completely ignorant."

"That's nice," said Fastolfe, agreeably, "but you see, I *am* a robotics expert, and I assure you that the essence of the robot mind lies in a completely literal interpretation of the universe. It recognizes no spirit in the First Law, only the letter. The simple models you have on Earth may have their First Law so overlaid with additional safeguards that, to be sure, they may well be incapable of threatening a human. An advanced model such as R. Daneel is another matter. If I gather the situation correctly, Daneel's threat was necessary to prevent a riot. It was intended then to prevent harm to human beings. He was obeying the First Law, not defying it."

Baley squirmed inwardly, but maintained a tight external calm. It would go hard, but he would match this Spacer at his own game.

He said, "You may counter each point separately, but they add up just the same. Last evening in our discussion of the so-called murder, this alleged robot claimed that he had been converted into a detective by the installation of a new drive into his positronic circuits. A drive, if you please, for justice."

"I'll vouch for that," said Fastolfe. "It was done to him three days ago under my own supervision."

"A drive for *justice*? Justice, Dr. Fàstolfe, is an abstraction. Only a human being can use the term."

"If you define 'justice' in such a way that it is an abstraction, if you say that it is the rendering of each man his due, that it is adhering to the right, or anything of the sort, I grant you your argument, Mr. Baley. A human understanding of abstractions cannot be built into a positronic brain in the present state of our knowledge."

"You admit that, then – as an expert in robotics?"

"Certainly. The question is, what did R. Daneel mean by using the term 'justice'?"

"From the context of our conversation, he meant what you and I and any human being would mean, but what no robot could mean."

"Why don't you ask him, Mr. Baley, to define the term?"

Baley felt a certain loss of confidence. He turned to R. Daneel. "Well?"

"Yes, Elijah?"

"What is your definition of justice?"

"Justice, Elijah, is that which exists when all the laws are enforced."

Fastolfe nodded. "A good definition, Mr. Baley, for a robot. The desire to see all laws enforced has been built into R. Daneel, now. Justice is a very concrete term to him since it is based on law enforcement, which is in turn based upon the existence of specific and definite laws. There is nothing abstract about it. A human being can recognize the fact that, on the basis of an abstract moral code, some laws may be bad ones and their enforcement unjust. What do you say, R. Daneel?"

"An unjust law," said R. Daneel evenly, "is a contradiction in terms."

"To a robot it is, Mr. Baley. So you see, you mustn't confuse your justice and R. Daneel's."

Baley turned to R. Daneel sharply and said, "You left my apartment last night."

R. Daneel replied, "I did. If my leaving disturbed your sleep, I am sorry."

"Where did you go?"

"To the Men's Personal."

For a moment, Baley was staggered. It was the answer he had already decided was the truth, but he had not expected it to be the answer R. Daneel would give. He felt a little more of his certainty oozing away, yet he held firmly on his track. The Commissioner was watching, his lensed eyes flickering from one to the other as they spoke. Baley *couldn't* back down now, no matter what sophistries they used against him. He had to hold to his point.

He said, "On reaching my section, *he* insisted on entering Personal with me. His excuse was a poor one. During the night, he left to visit Personal again as he has just admitted. If he were a man, I'd say he had every reason and right to do so. Obviously. As a robot, however, the trip was meaningless. The conclusion can only be that he is a man."

Fastolfe nodded. He seemed not in the least put out. He said, "This is most interesting. Suppose we ask Daneel why he made his trip to Personal last night."

Commissioner Enderby leaned forward. "Please, Dr. Fastolfe," he muttered, "it is not proper to –"

"You need not be concerned, Commissioner," said Fastolfe, his thin lips curving back in something that looked like a smile but wasn't, "I am certain that Daneel's answer will not offend your sensibilities or those of Mr. Baley. Won't you tell us, Daneel?"

R. Daneel said, "Elijah's wife, Jessie, left the apartment last night on friendly terms with me. It was quite obvious that she had no reason for thinking me to be other than human. She returned to the apartment knowing I was a robot. The obvious conclusion is that the information to that effect exists outside the apartment. It followed that my conversation with Elijah last night had been overheard. In no other way could the secret of my true nature have become common knowledge.

"Elijah told me that the apartments were well insulated. We spoke together in low voices. Ordinary eavesdropping would not do. Still, it was known that Elijah is a policeman. If a conspiracy exists within the City sufficiently well organized to have planned the murder of Dr. Sarton, they may well have been aware that Elijah had been placed in charge of the murder investigation. It would fall within the realm of possibility then, even of probability, that his apartment had been spy-beamed.

"I searched the apartment as well as I could after Elijah and Jessie had gone to bed, but could find no transmitter. This complicated matters. A focused duo-beam could do the trick even in the absence of a transmitter, but that requires rather elaborate equipment.

"Analysis of the situation led to the following conclusion. The one place where a City dweller can do almost anything without being disturbed or questioned is in the Personals. He could even set up a duo-beam. The custom of absolute privacy in the Personals is very strong and other men would not even look at him. The Section Personal is quite close to Elijah's apartment, so that the distance factor is not important. A suitcase model could be used. I went to the Personal to investigate."

"And what did you find?" asked Baley quickly.

"Nothing, Elijah. No sign of a duo-beam."

Dr. Fastolfe said, "Well, Mr. Baley, does this sound reasonable to you?"

But Baley's uncertainty was gone, now. He said, "Reasonable as far as it goes, perhaps, but it stops short of perfection by a hell of a way. What *he* doesn't know is that my wife told me where she got the information and *when*. She learned he was a robot shortly after she left the house. Even then, the rumor had been circulating for hours. So the fact that he was a robot could not have leaked out through spying on our last evening's conversation."

"Nevertheless," said Dr. Fastolfe, "his action last night of going to the Personal stands explained, I think."

"But something is brought up that is *not* explained," retorted Baley, heatedly. "When, where, and how was the leak? How did the news get about that there was a Spacer robot in the City. As far as I know, only two of us knew about the deal, Commissioner Enderby and myself, and we told no one. – Commissioner, did anyone else in the Department know?"

"No," said Enderby, anxiously. "Not even the Mayor. Only we, and Dr. Fastolfe."

"And *he*," added Baley, pointing.

"I?" asked R. Daneel.

"Why not?"

"I was with you at all times, Elijah."

"You were *not*," cried Baley, fiercely. "I was in Personal for half an hour or more before we went to my apartment. During that time, we two were completely out of contact with one another. It was then that you got in touch with your group in the City."

"What group?" asked Fastolfe.

And "What group?" echoed Commissioner Enderby almost simultaneously.

Baley rose from his chair and turned to the trimensic receiver. "Commissioner, I want you to listen closely to this. Tell me if it doesn't fall into a pattern. A murder is reported and by a curious coincidence it happens just as you are entering Spacetown to keep an appointment with the murdered man. You are shown the corpse of something supposed to be human, but the corpse has since been disposed of and is not available for close examination.

"The Spacers insist an Earthman did the killing, even though the only way they can make such an accusation stick is to suppose that a City man had left the City and cut cross-country to Spacetown alone and at night. You know damn well how unlikely that is.

"Next they send a supposed robot into the City; in fact, they insist on sending him. The first thing the robot does is to threaten a crowd of human beings with a blaster. The second is to set in motion the rumor that there is a Spacer robot in the City. In fact, the rumor is so specific that Jessie told me it was known that he was working with the police. That means that before long it will be known that it was the robot who handled the blaster. Maybe even now the rumor is spreading across the yeast-vat country and down the Long Island hydroponic plants that there's a killer robot on the loose."

"This is impossible. Impossible!" groaned Enderby.

"No, it isn't. It's exactly what's happening, Commissioner. Don't you see it? There's a conspiracy in the City, all right, but it's run from Spacetown. The Spacers *want* to be able to report a murder. They *want* riots. They *want* an assault on Spacetown. The worse things get, the better the incident – and Spacer ships come down and occupy the Cities of Earth."

Fastolfe said, mildly, "We had an excuse in the Barrier Riots of twenty-five years ago."

"You weren't ready then. You are now." Baley's heart was pounding madly.

"This is quite a complicated plot you're attributing to us, Mr. Baley. If we wanted to occupy Earth, we could do so in much simpler fashion."

"Maybe not, Dr. Fastolfe. Your so-called robot told me that public opinion concerning Earth is by no means unified on your Outer Worlds. I think he was telling the truth at that time, anyway. Maybe an outright occupation wouldn't sit well with the people at home. Maybe an incident is an absolute necessity. A good shocking incident."

"Like a murder, eh? Is that it? You'll admit it would have to be a pretended murder. You won't suggest, I hope, that we'd really kill one of ourselves for the sake of an incident."

"You built a robot to look like Dr. Sarton, blasted the robot, and showed the remains to Commissioner Enderby."

"And then," said Dr. Fastolfe, "having used R. Daneel to impersonate Dr. Sarton in the false murder, we have to use Dr. Sarton to impersonate R. Daneel in the false investigation of the false murder."

"Exactly. I am telling you this in the presence of a witness who is not here in the flesh and whom you cannot blast out of existence and who is important enough to be believed by the City government and by Washington itself. We will be prepared for you and we know what your intentions are. If necessary, our government will report directly to your people, expose the situation for exactly what it is. I doubt if this sort of interstellar rape will be tolerated."

Fastolfe shook his head. "Please, Mr. Baley, you are being unreasonable. Really, you have the most astonishing notions. Suppose now, just quietly suppose, that R. Daneel is really R. Daneel. Suppose he is actually a robot. Wouldn't it follow that the corpse Commissioner Enderby saw was really Dr. Sarton? It would be scarcely reasonable to believe that the corpse were still another robot. Commissioner Enderby witnessed R. Daneel under construction and can vouch for the fact that only one existed."

"If it comes to that," said Baley, stubbornly, "the Commissioner is not a robotics expert. You might have had a dozen such robots."

"Stick to the point, Mr. Baley. What if R. Daneel is really R. Daneel? Would not the entire structure of your reasoning fall to the ground? Would you have any further basis for your belief in this completely melodramatic and implausible interstellar plot you have constructed?"

"*If* he is a robot! I say he is human."

"Yet you haven't really investigated the problem, Mr. Baley," said Fastolfe. "To differentiate a robot, even a very humanoid robot, from a human being, it isn't necessary to make elaborately shaky deductions from little things he says and does. For instance, have you tried sticking a pin into R. Daneel?"

"What?" Baley's mouth fell open.

"It's a simple experiment. There are others perhaps not quite so simple. His skin and hair look real, but have you tried looking at them under adequate magnification. Then again, he seems to breathe, particularly when he is using air to talk, but have you noticed that his breathing is irregular, that minutes may go by during which he has no breath at all. You might even have trapped some of his expired air and measured the carbon dioxide content. You might have tried to draw a sample of blood. You might have tried to detect a pulse in his wrist, or a heartbeat under his shirt. Do you see what I mean, Mr. Baley?"

"That's just talk," said Baley, uneasily. "I'm not going to be bluffed. I might have tried any of those things, but do you suppose this alleged robot would have let me bring a hypodermic to him, or a stethoscope or a microscope?"

"Of course. I see your point," said Fastolfe. He looked at R. Daneel and gestured slightly.

R. Daneel touched the cuff of his right shirt sleeve and the diamagnetic seam fell apart the entire length of his arm. A smooth, sinewy, and apparently entirely human limb lay exposed. Its short, bronze hairs, both in quantity and distribution, were exactly what one would expect of a human being.

Baley said, "So?"

R. Daneel pinched the ball of his right middle finger with the thumb and forefinger of his left hand. Exactly what the details of the manipulation that followed were, Baley could not see.

But, just as the fabric of the sleeve had fallen in two when the diamagnetic field of its seam had been interrupted, so now the arm itself fell in two.

There, under a thin layer of fleshlike material, was the dull blue gray of stainless steel rods, cords, and joints.

"Would you care to examine Daneel's workings more closely, Mr. Baley?" asked Dr. Fastolfe politely.

Baley could scarcely hear the remark for the buzzing in his ears and for the sudden jarring of the Commissioner's high-pitched and hysterical laughter.

CHAPTER NINE

ELUCIDATION BY A SPACER

The minutes passed and the buzzing grew louder and drowned out the laughter. The dome and all it contained wavered and Baley's time sense wavered, too.

At least, he found himself sitting in an unchanged position but with a definite feeling of lost time. The Commissioner was gone; the trimensic receiver was milky and opaque; and R. Daneel sat at his side, pinching up the skin of Baley's bared upper arm. Baley could see, just beneath the skin, the small thin darkness of a hypo-sliver. It vanished as he watched, soaking and spreading away into the intercellular fluid, from that into the blood stream and the neighboring cells, from that into all the cells of his body.

His grip on reality heightened.

"Do you feel better, partner Elijah?" asked R. Daneel.

Baley did. He pulled at his arm and the robot let him take it away. He rolled down his sleeve and looked about. Dr. Fastolfe sat where he had been, a small smile softening the homeliness of his face.

Baley said, "Did I black out ?"

Dr. Fastolfe said, "In a way, yes. You received a sizable shock, I'm afraid."

It came back to Baley quite clearly. He seized R. Daneel's nearer arm quickly, forcing up the sleeve as far as it would go, exposing the wrist. The robot's flesh felt soft to his fingers, but underneath was the hardness of something more than bone.

R. Daneel let his arm rest easily in the plain-clothes man's grip. Baley stared at it, pinching the skin along the median line. Was there a faint seam?

It was logical, of course, that there should be. A robot, covered with synthetic skin, and deliberately made to look human, could not be repaired in the ordinary fashion. A chest plate could not be unriveted for the purpose. A skull could not be hinged up and outward. Instead, the various parts of the mechanical body would have to be put together along a line of micromagnetic fields. An arm, a head, an entire body, must fall in two at the proper touch, then come together again at a contrary touch.

Baley looked up. "Where's the Commissioner?" he mumbled, hot with mortification.

"Pressing business," said Dr. Fastolfe. "I encouraged him to leave, I'm afraid. I assured him we would take care of you."

"You've taken care of me quite nicely already, thank you," said Baley, grimly. "I think our business is done."

He lifted himself erect on tired joints. He felt an old man, very suddenly. Too old to start over again. He needed no deep insight to foresee that future.

The Commissioner would be half frightened and half furious. He would face Baley whitely, taking his glasses off to wipe them every fifteen seconds. His soft voice (Julius Enderby almost never shouted) would explain carefully that the Spacers had been mortally offended.

"You *can't* talk to Spacers that way, Lije. They won't take it." (Baley could hear Enderby's voice very plainly down to the finest shade of intonation.) "I warned you. No saying how much damage you've done. I can see your point, mind you. I see what you were trying to do. If they were Earthmen, it would be different. I'd say yes, chance it. Run the risk. Smoke them out. But *Spacers*! You might have told me, Lije. You might have consulted me. I know them. I know them inside and out."

And what would Baley be able to say? That Enderby was exactly the man he couldn't tell. That the project was one of tremendous risk and Enderby a man of tremendous caution. That it had been Enderby himself who had pointed up the supreme dangers of either outright failure or of the wrong kind of success. That the one way of defeating declassification was to show that guilt lay in Spacetown itself. . . .

Enderby would say, "There'll have to be a report on this, Lije. There'll be all sorts of repercussions. I know the Spacers. They'll demand your removal from the case, and it'll have to be that way. You understand that, Lije, don't you? I'll try to make it easy for you. You can count on that. I'll protect you as far as I can, Lije."

Baley knew that would be exactly true. The Commissioner would protect him, but only as far as he could, not to the point, for instance, of infuriating further an angry Mayor.

He could hear the Mayor, too. "Damn it. Enderby, what *is* all this? Why wasn't I consulted? Who's running the City? Why was an unauthorized robot allowed inside the City? And just what the devil did this Baley . . ."

If it came to a choice between Baley's future in the Department and the Commissioner's own, what possible result could Baley expect? He could find no reasonable way of blaming Enderby.

The least he could expect was demotion, and that was bad enough. The mere act of living in a modern City insured the bare possibility of existence, even for those entirely declassified. How bare that possibility was he knew only too well.

It was the addition of status that brought the little things: a more comfortable seat here, a better cut of meat there, a shorter wait in line at the other place. To the philosophical mind, these items might seem scarcely worth any great trouble to acquire.

Yet no one, however philosophical, could give up those privileges, *once acquired*, without a pang. That was the point.

What a trifling addition to the convenience of the apartment an activated washbasin was when for thirty years previously the trip to Personal had been an automatic and unregarded one. How useless it was even as a device to prove "status" when it was considered the height of ill form to parade "status." Yet were the washbasin to be deactivated, how humiliating and unbearable would each added trip to Personal be! How yearningly attractive the memory of the bedroom shave! How filled with a sense of lost luxury!

It was fashionable for modern political writers to look back with a smug disapproval at the "fiscalism" of Medieval times, when economy was based on money. The competitive struggle for existence, they said, was brutal. No truly complex society could be maintained because of the strains introduced by the eternal "fight-for-the-buck." (Scholars had varying interpretations of the word "buck," but there was no dispute over the meaning as a whole.)

By contrast, modern "civism" was praised highly as efficient and enlightened.

Maybe so. There were historical novels both in the romantic and the sensational tradition, and the Medievalists thought "fiscalism" had bred such things as individualism and initiative.

Baley wouldn't commit himself, but now he wondered sickly if ever a man fought harder for that buck, whatever it was, or felt its loss more deeply, than a City dweller fought to keep from losing his Sunday night option on a chicken drumstick – a real-flesh drumstick from a once-living bird.

Baley thought: Not me so much. There's Jessie and Ben.

Dr. Fastolfe's voice broke in upon his thoughts. "Mr. Baley, do you hear me?"

Baley blinked. "Yes?" How long had he been standing there like a frozen fool?

"Won't you sit down, sir? Having taken care of the matter on your mind, you may now be interested in some films we have taken of the scene of the crime and of the events immediately following."

"No, thank you. I have business in the City."

"Surely the case of Dr. Sarton comes first."

"Not with me. I imagine I'm off the case already." Suddenly, he boiled over. "Damn it, if you could prove R. Daneel was a robot, why didn't you do it at once? Why did you make such a farce of it all?"

"My dear Mr. Baley, I was very interested in your deductions. As for being off the case, I doubt it. Before the Commissioner left, I made a special point of asking that you be retained. I believe he will co-operate."

Baley sat down, not entirely voluntarily. He said, sharply, "Why?"

Dr. Fastolfe crossed his legs and sighed. "Mr. Baley, in general I have met two kinds of City dwellers, rioters and politicians. Your Commissioner is useful to us, but he is a politician. He tells us what we want to hear. He *handles* us, if you know what I mean. Now you came here and boldly accused us of tremendous crimes and tried to prove your case. I enjoyed the process. I found it a hopeful development."

"How hopeful?" asked Baley sardonically.

"Hopeful enough. You are someone I can deal with frankly. Lsst night, Mr. Baley, R. Daneel reported to me by shielded subether. Some things about you interested me very much. For instance, there was the point concerning the nature of the book-films in your apartment."

"What about them?"

"A good many dealt with historical and archaeological subjects. It makes it appear that you are interested in human society and that you know a little about its evolution."

"Even policemen can spend their free time on book-films, if they so choose."

"Quite. I'm glad of your choice in viewing matter. It will help me in what I am trying to do. In the first place, I want to explain, or try to, the exclusivism of the men of the Outer Worlds. We live here in Spacetown; we don't enter the City; we mingle with you City dwellers only in a very rigidly limited fashion. We breathe the open air, but when we do, we wear filters. I sit here now with filters in my nostrils, gloves on my hands, and a fixed determination to come no closer to you than I can help. Why do you suppose that is?"

Baley said, "There's no point in guessing." Let *him* talk now.

"If you guessed as some of your people do, you would say that it was because we despised the men of Earth and refused to lose caste by allowing their shadow to fall upon us. That is not so. The true answer is really quite obvious. The medical examination you went through, as well as the cleansing procedures, were not matters of ritual. They were dictated by necessity."

"Disease?"

"Yes, disease. My dear Mr. Baley, the Earthmen who colonized the Outer Worlds found themselves on planets entirely free of Terrestrial bacteria and viruses. They brought in their own, of course, but they also brought with them the latest medical and microbiological techniques. They had a small community of micro-organisms to deal with and no intermediate hosts. There were no mosquitoes to spread malaria, no snails to spread schistosomiasis. Disease agents were wiped out and symbiotic bacteria allowed to grow. Gradually, the Outer Worlds became disease-free. Naturally, as time went on, entrance requirements for immigrant Earthmen were made more and more rigorous, since less and less could the Outer Worlds endure the possible introduction of disease."

"You've never been sick, Dr. Fastolfe?"

"Not with a parasitic disease, Mr. Baley. We are all liable to degenerative diseases such as atheroschlerosis, of course, but I have never had what you would call a cold. If I were to contract one, I might die of it. I've built up no resistance to it whatsoever. That's what's wrong with us here in Spacetown. Those of us who come here run a definite risk. Earth is riddled with diseases to which we have no defense, no *natural* defense. You yourself are carrying the germs of almost every known disease. You are not aware of it, since you keep them all under control at almost all times through the antibodies your body has developed over the years. I, myself, lack the antibodies. Do you wonder that I come no closer to you? Believe me, Mr. Baley, I act aloof only in self-defense."

Baley said, "If this is so, why isn't the fact made known on Earth? I mean, that it is not just queasiness on your part, but a defense against an actual physical danger."

The Spacer shook his head. "We are few, Mr. Baley, and are disliked as foreigners anyway. We maintain our own safety on the basis of a rather shaky prestige as a superior class of being. We cannot afford to lose face by admitting that we are *afraid* to approach an Earthman. Not at least until there is a better understanding between Earthmen and Spacers."

"There won't be, on present terms. It's your supposed superiority that we – they hate you for."

"It is a dilemma. Don't think we aren't aware of it."

"Does the Commissioner know of this?"

"We have never explained it to him flatly, as I have just done to you. He may guess it, however. He is quite an intelligent man."

"If he guessed it, he might have told me," Baley said reflectively.

Dr. Fastolfe lifted his eyebrows. "If he had, then you wouldn't have considered the possibility of R. Daneel being a human Spacer. Is that it?"

Baley shrugged slightly, tossing the matter to one side.

But Dr. Fastolfe went on, "That's quite true, you know, Putting the psychological difficulties to one side, the terrible effect of the noise and crowds upon us, the fact remains that for one of us to enter the City is the equivalent of a death sentence. It is why Dr. Sarton initiated his project of humanoid robots. They were substitute men, designed to enter the City instead of us –"

"Yes. R. Daneel explained this to me."

"Do you disapprove?"

"Look," said Baley, "since we're talking to one another so freely, let me ask a question in simple words. Why have you Spacers come to Earth anyway? Why don't you leave us alone?"

Dr. Fastolfe said, with obvious surprise, "Are you *satisfied* with life on Earth?"

"We get along."

"Yes, but how long will that continue? Your population goes up continuously; the available calories meet the needs only as a result of greater and greater effort. Earth is in a blind alley, man."

"We get along," repeated Baley stubbornly.

"Barely. A City like New York must spend every ounce of effort getting water in and waste out. The nuclear power plants are kept going by uranium supplies that are constantly more difficult to obtain even from the other planets of the system, and the supply needed goes up steadily. The life of the City depends every moment on the arrival of wood pulp for the yeast vats and minerals for the hydroponic plants. Air must be circulated unceasingly. The balance is a very delicate one in a hundred directions, and growing more delicate each year. What would happen to New York if the tremendous flow of input and outgo were to be interrupted for even a single hour?"

"It never has been."

"Which is no security for the future. In primitive times, individual population centres were virtually self-supporting, living on the produce of neighboring farms. Nothing but immediate disaster, a flood or a pestilence or crop failure, could harm them. As the centers grew and technology improved, localized disasters could be overcome by drawing on help from distant centers, but at the cost of making even larger areas independent. In Medieval times, the open cities, even the largest, could subsist on food stores and on emergency supplies of all sorts for a week at least. When New York first became a City, it could have lived on itself for a day. Now it cannot do so for an hour. A disaster that would have been uncomfortable ten thousand years ago, merely serious a thousand years ago, and acute a hundred years ago would now be surely fatal."

Baley moved, restlessly in his chair. "I've heard all this before. The Medievalists want an end to Cities. They want us to get back to the soil and to natural agriculture. Well, they're mad; we can't. There are too many of us and you can't go backward in history, only forward. Of course, if emigration to the Outer Worlds were not restricted –"

"You know why it must be restricted."

"Then what is there to do? You're tapping a dead power line."

"What about emigration to new worlds? There are a hundred billion stars in the Galaxy. It is estimated that there are a hundred million planets that are inhabitable or can be made inhabitable."

"That's ridiculous."

"Why?" asked Dr. Fastolfe, with vehemence. "Why is the suggestion ridiculous? Earthmen have colonized planets in the past. Over thirty of the fifty Outer Worlds, including my native Aurora, were directly colonized by Earthmen. Is colonization no longer possible?"

"Well . . ."

"No answer? Let me suggest that if it *is* no longer possible, it is because of the development of City culture on Earth. Before the Cities, human life on Earth wasn't so specialized that they couldn't break loose and start all over on a raw world. They did it thirty times. But now, Earthmen are all so coddled, so enwombed in their imprisoning caves of steel, that they are caught forever. You, Mr. Baley, won't even believe that a City dweller is capable of crossing country to get to Spacetown. Crossing space to get to a new world must represent impossibility squared to you. Civism is ruining Earth, sir."

Baley said angrily, "And if it does? How does it concern you people? It's our problem. We'll solve it. If not, it's our own particular road to hell."

"Better your own road to hell than another's road to heaven, eh? I know how you must feel. It is not pleasant to listen to the preaching of a stranger. Yet I wish your people could preach to us, for we, too, have a problem, one that is quite analogous to yours."

Baley smiled crookedly. "Overpopulation?"

"Analogous, not identical. Ours is underpopulation. How old would you say I was?"

The Earthman considered for a moment and then deliberately overestimated. "Sixty, I'd say."

"A hundred and sixty, you should say."

"What!"

"A hundred and sixty-three next birthday, to be exact. There's no trick to that. I'm using the Standard Earth year as the unit. If I'm fortunate, if I take care of myself, most of all, if I catch no disease on Earth, I may double that age. Men on Aurora have been known to live over three hundred and fifty years. And life expectancy is still increasing."

Baley looked to R. Daneel (who throughout the conversation had been listening in stolid silence), as though he were seeking confirmation.

He said, "How is that possible?"

"In an underpopulated society, it is practical to concentrate study on gerontology, to do research on the aging process. In a world such as yours, a lengthened life expectancy would be disastrous. You couldn't afford the resulting rise in population. On Aurora, there is room for tricentenarians. Then, of course, a long life becomes doubly and triply precious.

"If you were to die now, you would lose perhaps forty years of your life, probably less. If I were to die, I would lose a hundred fifty years, probably more. In a culture such as ours, then, individual life is of prime importance. Our birth rate is low and population increase is rigidly controlled. We maintain a definite robot/man ratio designed to maintain the individual in the greatest comfort. Logically, developing children are carefully screened for physical and mental defects before being allowed to mature."

Baley interrupted. "You mean you kill them if they don't —"

"If they don't measure up. Quite painlessly, I assure you. The notion shocks you, just as the Earthman's uncontrolled breeding shocks us."

"We're controlled, Dr. Fastolfe. Each family is allowed so many children."

Dr. Fastolfe smiled tolerantly. "So many of any kind of children; not so many *healthy* children. And even so, there are many illegitimates and your population increases."

"Who's the judge which children should live?"

"That's rather complicated and not to be answered in a sentence. Some day we may talk it out in detail."

"Well, where's your problem? You sound satisfied with your society."

"It is stable. That's the trouble. It is too stable."

Baley said, "Nothing pleases you. Our civilization is at the ragged edge of chaos, according to you, and your own is too stable."

"It is possible to be too stable. No Outer World has colonized a new planet in two and a half centuries. There is no prospect for colonization in the future. Our lives in the Outer Worlds are too long to risk and too comfortable to upset."

"I don't know about that, Dr. Fastolfe. You've come to Earth. You risk disease."

"Yes, I do. There are some of us, Mr. Baley, who feel that the future of the human race is even worth the possible loss of an extended lifetime. Too few of us, I am sorry to say."

"All right. We're coming to the point. How is Spacetown helping matters?"

"In trying to introduce robots here on Earth, we're doing our best to upset the balance of your City economy."

"That's your way of helping?" Bailey's lips quivered. "You mean you're creating a growing group of displaced and declassified men on purpose?"

"Not out of cruelty or callousness, believe me. A group of displaced men, as you call them, are what we need to serve as a nucleus for colonization. Your ancient America was discovered by ships fitted out with men from the prisons. Don't you see that the City's womb has failed the displaced man. He has nothing to lose and worlds to gain by leaving Earth."

"But it isn't working."

"No, it isn't," said Dr. Fastolfe, sadly. "There is something wrong. The resentment of the Earthman for the robot blocks things. Yet those very robots can accompany humans, smooth the difficulties of initial adjustment to a raw world, make colonization practical."

"Then what? More Outer Worlds?"

"No. The Outer Worlds were established before Civism had spread over Earth, before the Cities. The new colonies will be built by humans who have the City background plus the beginnings of a C/Fe culture. It will be a synthesis, a cross-breeding. As it stands now, Earth's own structure must go rocketing down in the near future, the Outer Worlds will slowly degenerate and decay in a somewhat further future, but the new colonies will be a new and healthy strain, combining the best of both cultures. By their reaction upon the older worlds, including Earth, we ourselves may gain new life."

"I don't know. It's all misty, Dr. Fastolfe."

"It's a dream, yes. Think about it." Abruptly the Spacer rose to his feet. "I have spent more time with you than I intended. In fact, more time than our health ordinances allow. You will excuse me?"

Baley and R. Daneel left the dome. Sunlight, at a different angle, somewhat yellower, washed down upon them once again. In Baley, there was a vague wonder whether sunlight might not seem different on another world. Less harsh and brazen perhaps. More acceptable.

Another world? The ugly Spacer with the prominent ears had filled his mind with queer imaginings. Did the doctors of Aurora once look at the child Fastolfe and wonder if he ought to be allowed to mature? Wasn't he too ugly? Or did their criteria include physical appearance at all? When did ugliness become a deformity and what deformities . . .

But when the sunlight vanished and they entered the first door that led to the Personal, the mood became harder to maintain.

Baley shook his head with exasperation. It was all ridiculous. Forcing Earthmen to emigrate, to set up a new society! It was nonsense! What were these Spacers *really* after?

He thought about it and came to no conclusion.

Slowly, their squad car rolled down the vehicular lane. Reality was surging all about Baley. His blaster was a warm and comfortable weight against his hip. The noise and vibrant life of the City was just as warm, just as comfortable.

For a moment, as the City closed in, his nose tingled to a slight and fugitive pungence.

He thought wonderingly: The City smells.

He thought of the twenty million human beings crammed into the steel walls of the great cave and for the first time in his life he smelled them with nostrils that had been washed clean by outdoor air.

He thought: Would it be different on another world? Less people and more air – cleaner?

But the afternoon roar of the City was all around them, the smell faded and was gone, and he felt a little ashamed of himself.

He let the drive rod in slowly and tapped a larger share of the beamed power. The squad car accelerated sharply as it slanted down into the empty motorway.

"Daneel," he said.

"Yes, Elijah."

"Why was Dr. Fastolfe telling me all he did?"

"It seems probable to me, Elijah, that he wished to impress upon you the importance of the investigation. We are not here just to solve a murder, but to save Spacetown and with it, the future of the human race."

Baley said dryly, "I think he'd have been better off if he'd let me see the scene of the crime and interview the men who first found the body."

"I doubt if you could have added anything, Elijah. We have been quite thorough."

"Have you? You've got nothing. Not a clue. Not a suspect."

"No, you are right. The answer must be in the City. To be accurate, though, we did have one suspect."

"What? You said nothing of this before."

"I did not feel it to be necessary, Elijah. Surely it is obvious to you that one suspect automatically existed."

"Who? In the devil's name, who?"

"The one Earthman who was on the scene. Commissioner Julius Enderby."

CHAPTER TEN

AFTERNOON OF A PLAIN-CLOTHES MAN

The squad car veered to one side, halted against the impersonal concrete wall of the motorway. With the humming of its motor stopped, the silence was dead and thick.

Baley looked at the robot next to him and said in an incongruously quiet voice, "What?"

Time stretched while Baley waited for an answer. A small and lonesome vibration rose and reached a minor peak, then faded. It was the sound of another squad car, boring its way past them on some unknown errand, perhaps a mile away. Or else it was a fire car hurrying along toward its own appointment with combustion.

A detached portion of Baley's mind wondered if any one man any longer knew all the motorways that twisted about in New York City's bowels. At no time in the day or night could the entire motorway system be completely empty, and yet there must be individual passages that no man had entered in years. With sudden, devastating clarity, he remembered a short story he had viewed as a youngster.

It concerned the motorways of London and began, quietly enough, with a murder. The murderer fled toward a prearranged hideout in the corner of a motorway in whose dust his own shoeprints had been the only disturbance for a century. In that abandoned hole, he could wait in complete safety till the search died.

But he took a wrong turning and in the silence and loneness of

those twisting corridors he swore a mad and blaspheming oath
that, in spite of the Trinity and all the saints, he would yet reach
his haven.

From that time on, no turning was right. He wandered through
an unending maze from the Brighton Sector on the Channel to
Norwich and from Coventry to Canterbury. He burrowed endlessly beneath the great City of London from end to end of its
sprawl across the south-eastern corner of Medieval England.
His clothes were rags and his shoes ribbons, his strength wore
down but never left him. He was tired, tired, but unable to stop.
He could only go on and on with only wrong turnings ahead of
him.

Sometimes he heard the sound of passing cars, but they were
always in the next corridor, and however fast he rushed (for he
would gladly have given himself up by then) the corridors he
reached were always empty. Sometimes he saw an exit far ahead
that would lead to the City's life and breath, but it always glim-
mered further away as he approached until he would turn – and
it would be gone.

Occasionally, Londoners on official business through the
underground would see a misty figure limping silently toward
them, a semi-transparent arm lifted in pleading, a mouth open
and moving, but soundless. As it approached, it would waver
and vanish.

It was a story that had lost the attributes of ordinary fiction
and had entered the realm of folklore. The "Wandering Lon-
doner" had become a familiar phrase to all the world.

In the depths of New York City, Baley remembered the story
and stirred uneasily.

R. Daneel spoke and there was a small echo to his voice. He
said, "We may be overheard."

"Down here? Not a chance. Now what about the Commissioner?"

"He was on the scene, Elijah. He is a City dweller. He was
inevitably a suspect."

"Was! Is he still a suspect?"

"No. His innocence was quickly established. For one thing,
there was no blaster in his possession. There could not very well
be one. He had entered Spacetown in the usual fashion; that was

quite certain; and, as you know, blasters are removed as a matter of course."

"Was the murder weapon found at all, by the way?"

"No, Elijah. Every blaster in Spacetown was checked and none had been fired for weeks. A check of the radiation chambers was quite conclusive."

"Then whoever had committed the murder had either hidden the weapon so well —"

"It could not have been hidden anywhere in Spacetown. We were quite thorough."

Baley said impatiently, "I'm trying to consider all possibilities. It was either hidden or it was carried away by the murderer when he left."

"Exactly."

"And if you admit only the second possibility, then the Commissioner is cleared."

"Yes. As a precaution, of course, he was cerebroanalyzed."

"What?"

"By cerebroanalysis, I mean the interpretation of the electromagnetic fields of the living brain cells."

"Oh," said Baley, unenlightened. "And what does that tell you?"

"It gives us information concerning the temperamental and emotional makeup of an individual. In the case of Commissioner Enderby, it told us that he was incapable of killing Dr. Sarton. Quite incapable."

"No," agreed Baley. "He isn't the type. I could have told you that."

"It is better to have objective information. Naturally, all our people in Spacetown allowed themselves to be cerebroanalyzed as well."

"All incapable, I suppose."

"No question. It is why we know that the murderer must be a City dweller."

"Well, then, all we have to do is pass the whole City under your cute little process."

"It would not be very practical, Elijah. There might be millions temperamentally capable of the deed."

"Millions," grunted Baley, thinking of the crowds of that long ago day who had screamed at the dirty Spacers, and of the threatening and slobbering crowds outside the shoe store the night before.

He thought: Poor Julius. A suspect!

He could hear the Commissioner's voice describing the period after the discovery of the body. "It was brutal, brutal." No wonder he broke his glasses in shock and dismay. No wonder he did not want to return to Spacetown. "I hate them," he had ground out between his teeth.

Poor Julius. The man who could handle Spacers. The man whose greatest value to the City lay in his ability to get along with them. How much did that contribute to his rapid promotions?

No wonder the Commissioner had wanted Baley to take over. Good old loyal, close-mouthed Baley. College chum! He would keep quiet if he found out about that little incident. Baley wondered how cerebroanalysis was carried out. He imagined huge electrodes, busy pantographs skidding inklines across graphed paper, self-adjusting gears clicking into place now and then.

Poor Julius. If his state of mind were as appalled as it almost had a right to be, he might already be seeing himself at the end of his career with a forced letter of resignation in the hands of the Mayor.

The squad car slanted up into the sublevels of City Hall.

It was 14:30 when Baley arrived back at his desk. The Commissioner was out. R. Sammy, grinning, did not know where the Commissioner was.

Baley spent some time thinking. The fact that he was hungry didn't register.

At 15:20 R. Sammy came to his desk and said, "The Commissioner is in now, Lije."

Baley said, "Thanks."

For once he listened to R. Sammy without being annoyed. R. Sammy, after all, was a kind of relation to R. Daneel, and R. Daneel obviously wasn't a person — or thing, rather — to get annoyed with. Baley wondered how it would be on a new planet with men and robots starting even in a City culture. He considered the situation quite dispassionately.

The Commissioner was going through some documents, as Baley entered, stopping occasionally to make notations.

He said, "That was a fairly giant-size blooper you pulled out in Spacetown."

It flooded back strongly. The verbal duel with Fastolfe . . .

His long face took on a lugubrious expression of chagrin. "I'll admit I did, Commissioner. I'm sorry."

Enderby looked up. His expression was keen through his glasses. He seemed more himself than at any time these thirty hours. He said, "No real matter. Fastolfe didn't seem to mind, so we'll forget it. Unpredictable, these Spacers. You don't deserve your luck, Lije. Next time you talk it over with me before you make like a one-man subether hero."

Baley nodded. The whole thing rolled off his shoulders. He had tried a grandstand stunt and it hadn't worked. Okay. He was a little surprised that he could be so casual about it, but there it was.

He said, "Look, Commissioner. I want to have a two-man apartment assigned to Daneel and myself. I'm not taking him home tonight."

"What's all this?"

"The news is out that he's a robot. Remember? Maybe nothing will happen, but if there is a riot, I don't want my family in the middle of it."

"Nonsense, Lije. I've had the thing checked. There's no such rumor in the City."

"Jessie got the story somewhere, Commissioner."

"Well, there's no organized rumor. Nothing dangerous. I've been checking this ever since I got off the trimensic at Fastolfe's dome. It was why I left. I had to track it down, naturally, and fast. Anyway, here are the reports. See for yourself. There's Doris Gillid's report. She went through a dozen Women's Personals in different parts of the City. You know Doris. She's a competent girl. Well, nothing showed. Nothing showed anywhere."

"Then how did Jessie get the rumor, Commissioner?"

"It can be explained. R. Daneel made a show of himself in the shoe store. Did he really pull a blaster, Lije, or were you stretching it a little?"

"He really pulled one. Pointed it, too."

Commissioner Enderby shook his head. "All right. Someone recognized him. As a robot, I mean."

"Hold on," said Baley, indignantly. "You can't tell him for a robot."

"Why not?"

"Could you? I couldn't."

"What does that prove? We're no experts. Suppose there was a technician out of the Westchester robot factories in the crowd. A professional. A man who has spent his life building and designing robots. He notices something queer about R. Daneel. Maybe in the way he talks or holds himself. He speculates about it. Maybe he tells his wife. She tells a few friends. Then it dies. It's not too improbable. People don't believe it. Only it got to Jessie before it died."

"Maybe," said Baley, doubtfully. "But how about an assignment to a bachelor room for two, anyway?"

The Commissioner shrugged, lifted the intercom. After a while, he said, "Section Q—27 is all they can do. It's not a very good neighborhood."

"It'll do," said Baley.

"Where's R. Daneel now, by the way?"

"He's at our record files. He's trying to collect information on Medievalist agitators."

"Good Lord, there are millions."

"I know, but it keeps him happy."

Baley was nearly at the door, when he turned, half on impulse, and said, "Commissioner, did Dr. Sarton ever talk to you about Spacetown's program? I mean, about introducing the C/Fe culture?"

"The what?"

"Introducing robots."

"Occasionally." The Commissioner's tone was not one of any particular interest.

"Did he ever explain what Spacetown's point was?"

"Oh, improve health, raise the standard of living. The usual talk; it didn't impress me. Oh, I agreed with him. I nodded my head and all that. What could I do? It's just a matter of humoring them and hoping they'll keep within reason in their notions. Maybe some day . . ."

Baley waited but he didn't say what maybe-some-day might bring.

Baley said, "Did he ever mention anything about emigration?"

"Emigration! Never. Letting an Earthman into an Outer World is like finding a diamond asteroid in the rings of Saturn."

"I mean emigration to new worlds."

But the Commissioner answered that one with a simple stare of incredulousness.

Baley chewed that for a moment, then said with sudden bluntness, "What's cerebroanalysis, Commissioner? Ever hear of it?"

The Commissioner's round face didn't pucker; his eyes didn't blink. He said evenly, "No, what's it supposed to be?"

"Nothing. Just picked it up."

He left the office and at his desk continued thinking. Certainly, the Commissioner wasn't *that* good an actor. Well, then . . .

At 16 : 05 Baley called Jessie and told her he wouldn't be home that night nor probably any night for a while. It took a while after that to disengage her.

"Lije, is there trouble? Are you in danger?"

A policeman is always in a certain amount of danger, he explained lightly. It didn't satisfy her. "Where will you be staying?"

He didn't tell her. "If you're going to be lonely tonight," he said, "stay at your mother's." He broke connections abruptly, which was probably just as well.

At 16:20 he made a call to Washington. It took a certain length of time to reach the man he wanted and an almost equally long time to convince him he ought to make an air trip to New York the next day. By 16 : 40, he had succeeded.

At 16 : 55 the Commissioner left, passing him with an uncertain smile. The day shift left en masse. The sparser population that filled the offices in the evening and through the night made its way in and greeted him in varied tones of surprise.

R. Daneel came to his desk with a sheaf of papers.

"And those are?" asked Baley.

"A list of men and women who might belong to a Medievalist organization."

"How many does the list include?"

"Over a million," said R. Daneel. "These are just part of them."

"Do you expect to check them all, Daneel?"

"Obviously that would be impractical, Elijah."

"You see, Daneel, almost all Earthmen are Medievalists in one way or another. The Commissioner, Jessie, myself. Look at the Commissioner's –" (He almost said, "spectacles," then remembered that Earthmen must stick together and that the Commissioner's face must be protected in the figurative as well as the literal sense.) He concluded, lamely, "eye ornaments."

"Yes," said R. Daneel, "I had noticed them, but thought it indelicate, perhaps, to refer to them. I have not seen such ornaments on other City dwellers."

"It is a very old-fashioned sort of thing."

"Does it serve a purpose of any sort?"

Baley said, abruptly, "How did you get your list?"

"It was a machine that did it for me. Apparently, one sets it for a particular type of offense and it does the rest. I let it scan all disorderly conduct cases involving robots over the last twenty-five years. Another machine scanned all City newspapers over an equal period for the names of those involved in un-favourable statements concerning robots or men of the Outer Worlds. It is amazing what can be done in three hours. The machine even eliminated the names of non-survivors from the lists."

"You are amazed? Surely you've got computers on the Outer Worlds?"

"Of many sorts, certainly. Very advanced ones. Still, none are as massive and complex as the ones here. You must remember, of course, that even the largest Outer World scarcely has the population of one of your Cities and extreme complexity is not necessary."

Baley said, "Have you ever been on Aurora?"

"No," said R. Daneel, "I was assembled here on Earth."

"Then how do you know about Outer World computers?"

"But surely that is obvious, partner Elijah. My data store is drawn from that of the late Dr. Sarton. You may take it for granted that it is rich in factual material concerning the Outer Worlds."

"I see. Can you eat, Daneel?"

"I am nuclear-powered. I had thought you were aware of that."

"I'm perfectly aware of it. I didn't ask if you needed to eat. I asked if you *could* eat. If you could put food in your mouth, chew it, and swallow it. I should think that would be an important item in seeming to be a man."

"I see your point. Yes, I can perform the mechanical operations of chewing and swallowing. My capacity is, of course, quite limited, and I would have to remove the ingested material from what you might call my stomach sooner or later."

"All right. You can regurgitate, or whatever you do, in the quiet of our room tonight. The point is that I'm hungry. I've missed lunch, damn it, and I want you with me when I eat. And you can't sit there and *not* eat without attracting attention. So if you can eat, that's what I want to hear. Let's go!"

Section kitchens were the same all over the City. What's more, Baley had been in Washington, Toronto, Los Angeles, London, and Budapest in the way of business, and they had been the same there, too. Perhaps it had been different in Medieval times when languages had varied and dietaries as well. Nowadays, yeast products were just the same from Shanghai to Tashkent and from Winnipeg to Buenos Aires; and English might not be the "English" of Shakespeare or Churchill, but it was the final potpourri that was current over all the continents and, with some modification, on the Outer Worlds as well.

But language and dietary aside, there were the deeper similarities. There was always that particular odor, undefinable but completely characteristic of "kitchen." There was the waiting triple line moving slowly in, converging at the door and splitting up again, right, left, center. There was the rumble of humanity, speaking and moving, and the sharper clatter of plastic on plastic. There was the gleam of simulated wood, highly polished, highlights on glass, long tables, the touch of steam in the air.

Baley inched slowly forward as the line moved (with all possible staggering of meal hours, a wait of at least ten minutes was almost unavoidable) and said to R. Daneel in sudden curiosity, "Can you smile?"

R. Daneel, who had been gazing at the interior of the kitchen with cool absorption, said, "I beg your pardon, Elijah."

"I'm just wondering, Daneel. Can you smile?" He spoke in a casual whisper.

R. Daneel smiled. The gesture was sudden and surprising. His lips curled back and the skin about either end folded. Only the mouth smiled, however. The rest of the robot's face was untouched.

Baley shook his head. "Don't bother, R. Daneel. It doesn't do a thing for you."

They were at the entrance. Person after person thrust his metal food tag through the appropriate slot and had it scanned. Click – click – click –

Someone once calculated that a smoothly running kitchen could allow the entrance of two hundred persons a minute, the tags of each one being fully scanned to prevent kitchen-jumping, meal-jumping, and ration stretching. They had also calculated how long a waiting line was necessary for maximum efficiency and how much time was lost when any one person required special treatment.

It was therefore always a calamity to interrupt that smooth click-click by stepping to the manual window, as Baley and R. Daneel did, in order to thrust a special-permit pass at the official in charge.

Jessie, filled with knowledge of an assistant dietitian, had explained it once to Baley.

"It upsets things completely," she had said. "It throws off consumption figures and inventory estimates. It means special checks. You have to match slips with all the different Section kitchens to make sure the balance isn't too unbalanced, if you know what I mean. There's a separate balance sheet to be made out each week. Then if anything goes wrong and you're overdrawn, it's always your fault. It's never the fault of the City Government for passing out special tickets to everybody and his kid sister. Oh, no. And when we have to say that free choice is suspended for the meal, don't the people in line make a fuss. It's always the fault of the people behind the counter . . ."

Baley had the story in the fullest detail and so he quite understood the dry and poisonous look he received from the woman behind the window. She made a few hurried notes. Home Section, occupation, reason for meal displacement ("official business," a very irritating reason indeed, but quite irrefutable). Then she folded the slip with firm motions of her fingers and pushed it into a slot. A computer seized it, devoured the contents, and digested the information.

She turned to R. Daneel.

Baley let her have the worst. He said, "My friend is out-of-City."

The woman looked finally and completely outraged. She said, "Home City, please."

Baley intercepted the ball for Daneel once again. "All records are to be credited to the Police Department. No details necessary. Official business."

The woman brought down a pad of slips with a jerk of her arm and filled in the necessary matter in dark-light code with practised pressings of the first two fingers of her right hand.

She said, "How long will you be eating here?"

"Till further notice," said Baley.

"Press fingers here," she said, inverting the information blank.

Baley had a short qualm as R. Daneel's even fingers with their glistening nails pressed downward. Surely, they wouldn't have forgotten to supply him with fingerprints.

The woman took the blank away and fed it into the all-consuming machine at her elbow. It belched nothing back and Baley breathed more easily.

She gave them little metal tags that were in the bright red that meant "temporary."

She said, "No free choices. We're short this week. Take table DF."

They made their way toward DF.

R. Daneel said, "I am under the impression that most of your people eat in kitchens such as these regularly."

"Yes. Of course, it's rather gruesome eating in a strange kitchen. There's no one about whom you know. In your own kitchen, it's quite different. You have your own seat which you occupy all the time. You're with your family, your friends. Especially when you're young, mealtimes are the bright spot of the day." Baley smiled in brief reminiscence.

Table DF was apparently among those reserved for transients. Those already seated watched their plates uneasily and did not talk with one another. They looked with sneaking envy at the laughing crowds at the other tables.

There is no one so uncomfortable, thought Baley, as the man

eating out-of-Section. Be it ever so humble, the old saying went, there's no place like home-kitchen. Even the food tastes better, no matter how many chemists are ready to swear it to be no different from the food in Johannesburg.

He sat down on a stool and R. Daneel sat down next to him.

"No free choice," said Baley, with a wave of his fingers, "so just close the switch there and wait."

It took two minutes. A disc slid back in the table top and a dish lifted.

"Mashed potatoes, zymoveal sauce, and stewed apricots. Oh, well," said Baley.

A fork and two slices of whole yeast bread appeared in a recess just in front of the low railing that went down the long center of the table.

R. Daneel said in a low voice, "You may help yourself to my serving, if you wish."

For a moment, Baley was scandalized. Then he remembered and mumbled. "That's bad manners. Go on. Eat."

Baley ate industriously but without the relaxation that allows complete enjoyment. Carefully, he flicked an occasional glance at R. Daneel. The robot ate with precise motions of his jaws. Too precise. It didn't look quite natural.

Strange! Now that Baley knew for a fact that R. Daneel was in truth a robot, all sorts of little items showed up clearly. For instance, there was no movement in an Adam's apple when R. Daneel swallowed.

Yet he didn't mind so much. Was he getting used to the creature? Suppose people started afresh on a new world (how that ran through his mind ever since Dr. Fastolfe had put it there); suppose Bentley, for instance, were to leave Earth; could he get so he didn't mind working and living alongside robots? Why not? The Spacers themselves did it.

R. Daneel said, "Elijah, is it bad manners to watch another man while he is eating?"

"If you mean stare directly at him, of course. That's only common sense, isn't it? A man has a right to his privacy. Ordinary conversation is entirely in order, but you don't peer at a man while he's swallowing."

"I see. Why is it then that I count eight people watching us closely, very closely?"

Baley put down his fork. He looked about as though he were searching for the salt-pinch dispenser. "I see nothing out of the ordinary."

But he said it without conviction. The mob of diners was only a vast conglomeration of chaos to him. And when R. Daneel turned his impersonal brown eyes upon him, Baley suspected uncomfortably that those were not eyes he saw, but scanners capable of noting, with photographic accuracy and in split seconds of time, the entire panorama.

"I am quite certain," said R. Daneel, calmly.

"Well, then, what of it? It's crude behaviour, but what does it prove?"

"I cannot say, Elijah, but is it coincidence that six of the watchers were in the crowd outside the shoe store last night?"

CHAPTER ELEVEN

ESCAPE ALONG THE STRIPS

Baley's grip tightened convulsively on his fork.

"Are you sure?" he asked automatically, and as he said it, he realized the uselessness of the question. You don't ask a computer if it is sure of the answer it disgorges; not even a computer with arms and legs.

R. Daneel said, "Quite!"

"Are they close to us?"

"Not very. They are scattered."

"All right, then." Baley returned to his meal, his fork moving mechanically. Behind the frown of his long face, his mind worked furiously.

Suppose the incident last night had been organized by a group of anti-robot fanatics, that it had not been the spontaneous trouble it had seemed. Such a group of agitators could easily include men who had studied robots with the intensity born of deep opposition. One of them might have recognized R. Daneel for what he was. (The Commissioner had suggested it, in a way. Damn it, there were surprising depths to that man.)

It worked itself out logically. Granting they had been unable to act in an organized manner on the spur of last evening's moment, they would still have been able to plan for the future. If they could recognize a robot such as R. Daneel, they could certainly realize that Baley himself was a police officer. A police officer in the unusual company of a humanoid robot would very likely be a responsible man in the organization. (With the wisdom of hindsight, Baley followed the line of reasoning with no trouble at all.)

It followed then that observers at City Hall (or perhaps agents within City Hall) would be bound to spot Baley, R. Daneel, or both before too long a time had passed. That they had done so within twenty-four hours was not surprising. They might have done so in less time if so much of Baley's day had not been spent in Spacetown and along the motorway.

R. Daneel had finished his meal. He sat quietly waiting, his perfect hands resting lightly on the end of the table.

"Had we not better do something?" he asked.

"We're safe here in the kitchen," said Baley. "Now leave this to me. Please."

Baley looked about him cautiously and it was as though he saw a kitchen for the first time.

People! Thousands of them. What was the capacity of an average kitchen? He had once seen the figure. Two thousand two hundred, he thought. This one was larger than average.

Suppose the cry, "Robot," were sent out into the air. Suppose it were tossed among the thousands like a . . .

He was at a loss for a comparison, but it didn't matter. It wouldn't happen.

A spontaneous riot could flare anywhere, in the kitchens as easily as in the corridors or in the elevators. More easily, perhaps. There was a lack of inhibition at mealtimes, a sense of horseplay that could degenerate into something more serious at a trifle.

But a planned riot would be different. Here in the kitchen, the planners would themselves be trapped in a large and mob-filled room. Once the dishes went flying and the tables cracking there would be no easy way to escape. Hundreds would certainly die and they themselves might easily be among them.

No, a safe riot would have to be planned in the avenues of the City, in some relatively narrow passageway. Panic and hysteria would travel slowly along the construction and there would be time for the quick, prepared fadeaway along the side passage or the unobtrusive step onto an escalating localway that would move them to a higher level and disappearance.

Baley felt trapped. There were probably others waiting outside. Baley and R. Daneel were to be followed to a proper point and the fuse would be set off.

R. Daneel said, "Why not arrest them?"

"That would only start the trouble sooner. You know their faces, don't you? You won't forget?"

"I am not capable of forgetting."

"Then we'll nab them another time. For now, we'll break their net. Follow me. Do exactly as I do."

He rose, turned his dish carefully upside down, centering it on the movable disc from below which it had risen. He put his fork back in its recess. R. Daneel, watching, matched his action. The dishes and utensils dropped out of sight.

R. Daneel said, "They are getting up, too."

"All right. It's my feeling they won't get too close. Not here."

The two moved into line now, drifting toward an exit where the click-click-click of the tags sounded ritualistically, each click recording the expenditure of a ration unit.

Baley looked back through the steamy haze and the noise and, with incongruous sharpness, thought of a visit to the City Zoo with Ben six or seven years ago. No, eight, because Ben had just passed his eighth birthday then. (Jehoshaphat! Where did the time go?)

It had been Ben's first visit and he had been excited. After all, he had never actually seen a cat or a dog before. Then, on top of that, there was the bird cage! Even Baley himself, who had seen it a dozen times before, was not immune to its fascination.

There is something about the first sight of living objects hurtling through the air that is incomparably startling. It was feeding time in the sparrow cage and an attendant was dumping cracked oats into a long trough (human beings had grown used to yeast substitutes, but animals, more conservative in their way, insisted on real grain).

The sparrows flocked down in what seemed like hundreds. Wing to wing, with an ear-splitting twitter, they lined the trough. . . .

That was it: that was the picture that came to Baley's mind

as he looked back at the kitchen he was leaving. Sparrows at the trough. The thought repelled him.

He thought: Jehoshaphat, there must be a better way.

But what better way? What was wrong with this way? It had never bothered him before.

He said abruptly to R. Daneel, "Ready, Daneel?"

"I am ready, Elijah."

They left the kitchen and escape was now clearly and flatly up to Baley.

There is a game that youngsters know called "running the strips." Its rules vary in trivial fashion from City to City, but its essentials are eternal. A boy from San Francisco can join the game in Cairo with no trouble.

Its object is to get from point A to point B via the City's rapid transit system in such a way that the "leader" manages to lose as many of his followers as possible. A leader who arrives at the destination alone is skillful indeed, as is a follower who refuses to be shaken.

The game is usually conducted during the evening rush hour when the increased density of the commuters makes it at once more hazardous and more complicated. The leader sets off, running up and down the accelerating strips. He does his best to do the unexpected, remaining standing on a given strip as long as possible, then leaping off suddenly in either direction. He will run quickly through several strips, then remain waiting once more.

Pity the follower who incautiously careens forward one strip too far. Before he has caught his mistake, unless he is extraordinarily nimble, he has driven past the leader or fallen behind. The clever leader will compound the error by moving quickly in the appropriate direction.

A move designed to increase the complexity of the task tenfold involves boarding the localways or the expressways themselves, and hurtling off the other side. It is bad form to avoid them completely and also bad form to linger on them.

The attraction of the game is not easy for an adult to understand, particularly for an adult who has never himself been a teenage strip-runner. The players are roughly treated by legitimate travelers into whose path they find themselves inevitably flying. They are persecuted bitterly by the police and punished by their parents. They are denounced in the schools and on the subetherics. No year passes without its four or five teen-agers killed at the game, its dozens hurt, its cases of innocent bystanders meeting tragedy of varying degree.

Yet nothing can be done to wipe out the strip-running gangs. The greater the danger, the more the strip-runners have that most valuable of all prizes, honor in the eyes of their fellows. A successful one may well swagger; a well-known leader is cock-of-the-walk.

Elijah Baley, for instance, remembered with satisfaction even now that he had been a strip-runner once. He had led a gang of twenty from the Concourse Sector to the borders of Queens, crossing three expressways. In two tireless and relentless hours, he had shaken off some of the most agile followers of the Bronx, and arrived at the destination point alone. They talked about that run for months.

Baley was in his forties now, of course. He hadn't run the strips for over twenty years, but he remembered some of the tricks. What he had lost in agility, he made up in another respect. He was a policeman. No one but another policeman as experienced as himself could possibly know the City as well, know where almost every metal-bordered alley began and ended.

He walked away from the kitchen briskly, but not too rapidly. Each moment he expected the cry of "Robot, robot" to ring out behind him. That initial set of moments was the riskiest. He counted the steps until he felt the first accelerating strip moving under him.

He stopped for a moment, while R. Daneel moved smoothly up behind him.

"Are they still behind us, Daneel?" asked Baley in a whisper.

"Yes. They're moving closer."

"That won't last," said Baley confidently. He looked at the strips stretching to either side, with their human cargo whipping to his left more and more rapidly as their distance from him increased. He had felt the strips beneath his feet many times a day almost all the days of his life, but he had not bent his knees in anticipation of running them in seven thousand days and more. He felt the old familiar thrill and his breath grew more rapid.

He quite forgot the one time he had caught Ben at the game. He had lectured him interminably and threatened to have him put under police surveillance.

Lightly, quickly, at double the "safe" rate, he went up the strips. He leaned forward sharply against the acceleration. The localway was humming past. For a moment, it looked as though he would mount, but suddenly he was fading backward, backward, dodging through the crowd to left and right as it thickened on the slower strips.

He stopped, and let himself be carried along at a mere fifteen miles an hour.

"How many are with us, Daneel?"

"Only one, Elijah." The robot was at his side, unruffled, unbreathing.

"He must have been a good one in his day, too, but he won't last either."

Full of self-confidence, he felt a half-remembered sensation of his younger days. It consisted partly of the feeling of immersion in a mystic rite to which others did not belong, partly of the purely physical sensation of wind against hair and face, partly of a tenuous sense of danger.

"They call this the side shuffle," he said to R. Daneel in a low voice.

His long stride ate distance, but he moved along a single strip, dodging the legitimate crowd with a minimum of effort. He kept it up, moving always closer to the strip's edge, until the steady movement of his head through the crowd must have been hypnotic in its constant velocity – as it was intended to be.

And then, without a break in his step, he shifted two inches sideways and was on the adjoining strip. He felt an aching in his thigh muscles as he kept his balance.

He whipped through a cluster of commuters and was on the forty-five-mile strip.

"How is it now, Daneel?" he asked.

"He is still with us," was the calm answer.

Baley's lips tightened. There was nothing for it but to use the moving platforms themselves, and that really required co-ordination; more, perhaps, than he still retained.

He looked about quickly. Exactly where were they now? B-22d Street flashed by. He made rapid calculations and was off. Up the remaining strips, smoothly and steadily, a swing onto the localway platform.

The impersonal faces of men and women, calloused with the ennui of way-riding, were jolted into something like indignation as Baley and R. Daneel clambered aboard and squeezed through the railings.

"Hey, now," called a woman shrilly, clutching at her hat.

"Sorry," said Baley, breathlessly.

He forced his way through the standees and with a wriggle was off on the other side. At the last moment, a jostled passenger thumped his back in anger. He went staggering.

Desperately he tried to regain his footing. He lurched across a strip boundary and the sudden change in velocity forced him to his knees and then over on his side.

He had the sudden, panicky vision of men colliding with him and bowling over, of a spreading confusion on the strips, one of the dreaded "man-jams" that would not fail to put dozens in the hospital with broken limbs.

But R. Daneel's arm was under his back. He felt himself lifted with more than a man's strength.

"Thanks," gasped Baley, and there was no time for more.

Off he went and down the decelerating strips in a complicated pattern so designed that his feet met the V-joint strips of an expressway at the exact point of crossover. Without the loss of rhythm, he was accelerating again, then up and over an expressway.

"Is he with us, Daneel?"

"Not one in sight, Elijah."

"Good. But what a strip-runner you would have been, Daneel! – Oops, now, now!"

Off onto another localway in a whirl and down the strips with a clatter to a doorway, large and official in appearance. A guard rose to his feet.

Baley flashed his identification. "Official business."

They were inside.

"Power plant," said Baley, curtly. "This breaks our tracks completely."

He had been in power plants before, including this one. Familiarity did not lessen his feeling of uncomfortable awe. The feeling was heightened by the haunting thought that once his father had been high in the hierarchy of a plant such as this. That is, before . . .

There was the surrounding hum of the tremendous generators hidden in the central well of the plant, the faint sharpness of ozone in the air, the grim and silent threat of the red lines that marked the limits beyond which no one could pass without protective clothing.

Somewhere in the plant (Bayley had no idea exactly where) a pound of fissionable material was consumed each day. Every so often, the radioactive fission products, the so-called "hot ash," were forced by air pressure through the leaden pipes to distant caverns ten miles out in the ocean and a half mile below the ocean floor. Baley sometimes wondered what would happen when the caverns were filled.

He said to R. Daneel with sudden gruffness, "Stay away from the red lines." Then, he bethought himself and added sheepishly, "But I suppose it doesn't matter to you."

"Is it a question of radioactivity?" asked Daneel.

"Yes."

"Then it does matter to me. Gamma radiation destroys the delicate balance of a positronic brain. It would affect me much sooner than it would affect you."

"You mean it would *kill* you?"

"I would require a new positronic brain. Since no two can be alike, I would be a new individual. The Daneel you now speak to would be, in a manner of speaking, dead."

Baley looked at the other doubtfully. "I never knew that — Up these ramps."

"The point isn't stressed. Spacetown wishes to convince Earthmen of the usefulness of such as myself, not of our weaknesses."

"Then why tell me?"

R. Daneel turned his eyes full on his human companion. "You are my partner, Elijah. It is well that you know my weaknesses and shortcomings."

Baley cleared his throat and had nothing more to say on the subject.

"Out in this direction," he said a moment later, "and we're a quarter of a mile from our apartment."

It was a grim, lower-class apartment. One small room and

two beds. Two fold-in chairs and a closet. A built-in subetheric screen that allowed no manual adjustment, and would be working only at stated hours, but *would* be working then. No washbasin, not even an unactivated one, and no facilities for cooking or even boiling water. A small trash-disposal pipe was in one corner of the room, an ugly, unadorned, unpleasantly functional object.

Baley shrugged. "This is it, I guess we can stand it."

R. Daneel walked to the trash-disposal pipe. His shirt unseamed at a touch, revealing a smooth and, to all appearances, well-muscled chest.

"What are you doing?" asked Baley.

"Getting rid of the food I ingested. If I were to leave it, it would putrefy and I would become an object of distaste."

R. Daneel placed two fingers carefully under one nipple and pushed in a definite pattern of pressure. His chest opened longitudinally. R. Daneel reached in and from a welter of gleaming metal withdrew a thin, translucent sac, partly distended. He opened it while Baley watched with a kind of horror.

R. Daneel hesitated. He said, "The food is perfectly clean. I do not salivate or chew. It was drawn in through the gullet by suction, you know. It is edible."

"That's all right," said Baley, gently. "I'm not hungry. You just get rid of it."

R. Daneel's food sac was of fluorocarbon plastic, Baley decided. At least the food did not cling to it. It came out smoothly and was placed little by little into the pipe. A waste of good food at that, he thought.

He sat down on one bed and removed his shirt. He said, "I suggest an early start tomorrow."

"For a specific reason?"

"The location of this apartment isn't known to our friends yet. Or at least I hope not. If we leave early, we are that much safer. Once in City Hall, we will have to decide whether our partnership is any longer practical."

"You think it is perhaps not?"

Baley shrugged and said dourly. "We can't go through this sort of thing every day."

"But it seems to me –"

R. Daneel was interrupted by the sharp scarlet sliver of the door signal.

Baley rose silently to his feet and unlimbered his blaster. The door signal flashed once more.

He moved silently to the door, put his thumb on the blaster contact while he threw the switch that activated the one-way transparency patch. It wasn't a good view-patch; it was small and had a distorting effect, but it was quite good enough to show Baley's youngster, Ben, outside the door.

Baley acted quickly. He flung the door open, snatched brutally at Ben's wrist as the boy raised his hand to signal a third time, and pulled him in.

The look of fright and bewilderment faded only slowly from Ben's eyes as he leaned breathlessly against the wall toward which he had been hurled. He rubbed his wrist.

"Dad!" he said in grieved tones. "You didn't have to grab me like that."

Baley was staring through the view-patch of the once-again-closed door. As nearly as he could tell, the corridor was empty.

"Did you see anyone out there, Ben?"

"No. Gee, Dad, I just came to see if you were all right,"

"Why shouldn't I be all right?"

"I don't know. It was Mom. She was crying and all like that. She said I had to find out. If I didn't go, she said she would go herself, and then she didn't know what would happen. She *made* me go, Dad."

Baley said, "How did you find me? Did your mother know where I was?"

"No, she didn't. I called up your office."

"And they told you?"

Ben looked startled at his father's vehemence. He said, in a low voice, "Sure. Weren't they supposed to?"

Baley and Daneel looked at one another.

Baley rose heavily to his feet. He said, "Where's your mother now, Ben? At the apartment?"

"No, we went to Grandma's for dinner and stayed there. I'm supposed to go back there now. I mean, as long as you're all right, Dad."

"You'll stay here. Daneel, did you notice the exact location of the floor communo?"

The robot said, "Yes. Do you intend leaving the room to use it?"

"I've got to. I've got to get in touch with Jessie."

"Might I suggest that it would be more logical to let Bentley do that. It is a form of risk and he is less valuable."

Baley stared. "Why, you –"

He thought: Jehoshaphat, what am I getting angry about?

He went on more calmly, "You don't understand, Daneel. Among us, it is not customary for a man to send his young son into possible danger, even if it is logical to do so."

"Danger!" squeaked Ben in a sort of horrified pleasure. "What's going on, Dad? Huh, Dad?"

"Nothing, Ben. Now, this isn't any of your business. Understand? Get ready for bed. I want you in bed when I get back. You hear me?"

"Aw, gosh. You could tell a fellow. I won't say anything."

"In bed!"

"Gosh!"

Baley hitched his jacket back as he stood at the floor communo, so that his blaster butt was ready for snatching. He spoke his personal number into the mouthpiece and waited while a computer fifteen miles away checked it to make sure the call was permissible. It was a very short wait that was involved, since a plain-clothes man had no limit on the number of his business calls. He spoke the code number of his mother-in-law's apartment.

The small screen at the base of the instrument lit up, and her face looked out at him.

He said, in a low voice, "Mother, put on Jessie."

Jessie must have been waiting for him. She was on at once. Baley looked at her face and then darkened the screen deliberately.

"All right, Jessie. Ben's here. Now, what's the matter?" His eyes roved from side to side continuously, watching.

"Are you all right? You aren't in trouble?"

"I'm obviously all right, Jessie. Now stop it."

"Oh, Lije, I've been so worried."

"What about?" he asked tightly.

"You know. Your friend."

"What about him?"

"I told you last night. There'll be trouble."

"Now, that's nonsense. I'm keeping Ben with me for tonight and you go to bed. Good-by, dear."

He broke connections and waited for two breaths before starting back. His face was gray with apprehension and fear.

Ben was standing in the middle of the room when Baley returned. One of his contact lenses was neatly pocketed in a little suction cup. The other was still in his eye.

Ben said, "Gosh, Dad, isn't there any water in the place? Mr. Olivaw says I can't go to the Personal."

"He's right. You can't. Put that thing back in your eye, Ben. It won't hurt you to sleep with them for one night."

"All right." Ben put it back, put away his suction cup and climbed into bed. "Boy, what a mattress!"

Baley said to R. Daneel, "I suppose you won't mind sitting up."

"Of course not. I was interested, by the way, in the queer glass Bentley wears close to his eyes. Do all Earthmen wear them?"

"No. Just some," said Baley, absently. "I don't, for instance."

"For what reason is it worn?"

Baley was too absorbed with his own thoughts to answer. His own uneasy thoughts.

The lights were out.

Baley remained wakeful. He was dimly aware of Ben's breathing as it turned deep and regular and became a bit rough. When he turned his head, he grew somehow conscious of R. Daneel, sitting in a chair with grave immobility, face turned toward the door.

Then he fell asleep, and when he slept, he dreamed.

He dreamed Jessie was falling into the fission chamber of a nuclear power plant, falling and falling. She held out her arms to him, shrieking, but he could only stand frozenly just outside a scarlet line and watch her distorted figure turn as it fell, growing smaller until it was only a dot.

He could only watch her, in the dream, knowing that it was he, himself, who had pushed her.

CHAPTER TWELVE

WORDS FROM AN EXPERT

Elijah Baley looked up as Commissioner Julius Enderby entered the office. He nodded wearily.

The Commissioner looked at the clock and grunted, "Don't tell me you've been here all night!"

Baley said, "I won't."

The Commissioner said in a low voice, "Any trouble last night?"

Baley shook his head.

The Commissioner said, "I've been thinking that I could be minimizing the possibility of riots. If there's anything to – "

Baley said tightly, "For God's sake, Commissioner, if anything happened, I'd tell you. There was no trouble of any sort."

"All right." The Commissioner moved away, passing beyond the door that marked off the unusual privacy that became his exalted position.

Baley looked after him and thought: *He* must have slept last night.

Baley bent to the routine report he was trying to write as a cover-up for the real activities of the last two days, but the words he had tapped out by finger touch blurred and danced. Slowly, he became aware of an object standing by his desk.

He lifted his head. "What do you want?"

It was R. Sammy. Baley thought: Julius's private flunky. It pays to be a Commissioner.

R. Sammy said through his fatuous grin, "The Commissioner wants to see you, Lije. He says right away."

Baley waved his hand. "He just saw me. Tell him I'll be in later."

R. Sammy said, "He says right away."

"All right. All right. Go away."

The robot backed away, saying, "The Commissioner wants to see you right away, Lije. He says right away."

"Jehoshaphat," said Baley between his teeth. "I'm going.

I'm going." He got up from his desk, headed for the office, and R. Sammy was silent.

Baley said as he entered, "Damn it, Commissioner, *don't* send that thing after me, will you?"

But the Commissioner only said, "Sit down, Lije. Sit down."

Baley sat down and stared. Perhaps he had done old Julius an injustice. Perhaps the man hadn't slept after all. He looked fairly beat.

The Commissioner was tapping the paper before him. "There's a record of a call you made to a Dr. Gerrigel at Washington by insulated beam."

"That's right, Commissioner."

"There's no record of the conversation, naturally, since it was insulated. What's it all about?"

"I'm after background information."

"He's a roboticist, isn't he?"

"That's right."

The Commissioner put out a lower lip and suddenly looked like a child about to pout. "But what's the point? What kind of information are you after?"

"I'm not sure, Commissioner. I just have a feeling that in a case like this, information on robots might help." Baley clamped his mouth shut after that. He wasn't going to be specific, and that was that.

"I wouldn't, Lije. I wouldn't. I don't think it's wise."

"What's your objection, Commissioner?"

"The fewer the people who know about all this, the better."

"I'll tell him as little as I can. Naturally."

"I still don't think it's wise."

Baley was feeling just sufficiently wretched to lose patience. He said, "Are you ordering me not to see him?"

"No. No. You do as you see fit. You're heading this investigation. Only . . ."

"Only what?"

The Commissioner shook his head. "Nothing. – Where is *he*? You know who I mean."

Baley did. He said, "Daneel's still at the files."

The Commissioner paused a long moment, then said, "We're not making much progress, you know."

"We're not making any so far. Still, things may change."

"All right, then," said the Commissioner, but he didn't look as though he really thought it were all right.

R. Daneel was at Baley's desk, when the latter returned.

"Well, and what have *you* got?" Baley asked gruffly.

"I have completed my first, rather hasty, search through the files, partner Elijah, and I have located two of the people who tried to track us last night and who, moreover, were at the shoe store during the former incident."

"Let's see."

R. Daneel placed the small, stamp-size cards before Baley. They were mottled with the small dots that served as code. The robot also produced a portable decoder and placed one of the cards into an appropriate slot. The dots possessed electrical conduction properties different from that of the card as a whole. The electric field passing through the card was therefore distorted in a highly specific manner and in response to that specification the three-by-six screen above the decoder was filled with words. Words which, uncoded, would have filled several sheets of standard size report paper. Words, moreover, which could not possibly be interpreted by anyone not in possession of an official police decoder.

Baley read through the material stolidly. The first person was Francis Clousarr, age thirty-three at time of arrest two years before; cause of arrest, inciting to riot; employee at New York Yeast; home address, so-and-so; parentage, so-and-so; hair, eyes, distinguishing marks, educational history, employment history, psychoanalytic profile, physical profile, data here, data there, and finally reference to tri-photo in the rogues' gallery.

"You checked the photograph?" asked Baley.

"Yes, Elijah."

The second person was Gerhard Paul. Baley glanced at the material on that card and said, "This is all no good."

R. Daneel said, "I am sure that cannot be so. If there is an organization of Earthmen who are capable of the crime we are investigating, these are members. Is that not an obvious likelihood? Should they then not be questioned?"

"We'd get nothing out of them."

"They were there, both at the shoe store and in the kitchen. They cannot deny it."

"Just being there's no crime. Besides which, they *can* deny it. They can just say they weren't there. It's as simple as that. How can we prove they're lying?"

"I saw them."

"That's no proof," said Baley, savagely. "No court, if it ever came to that, would believe that you could remember two faces in a blur of a million."

"It is obvious that *I* can."

"Sure. Tell them what you are. As soon as you do that, you're no witness. Your kind have no status in any court of law on Earth."

R. Daneel said, "I take it, then, that you have changed your mind."

"What do you mean?"

"Yesterday, in the kitchen, you said there was no need to arrest them. You said that as long as I remembered their faces, we could arrest them at any time."

"Well, I didn't think it through," said Baley. "I was crazy. It can't be done."

"Not even for psychological reasons? They would not know we had no legal proof of their complicity in conspiracy."

Baley said, tensely, "Look, I am expecting Dr. Gerrigel of Washington in half an hour. Do you mind waiting till he's been here and gone? Do you mind?"

"I will wait," said R. Daneel.

Anthony Gerrigel was a precise and very polite man of middle height, who looked far from being one of the most erudite roboticists on Earth. He was nearly twenty minutes late, it turned out, and quite apologetic about it. Baley, white with an anger born of apprehension, shrugged off the apologies gracelessly. He checked his reservation on Conference Room D, repeated his instructions that they were not to be disturbed on any account for an hour, and led Dr. Gerrigel and R. Daneel down the corridor, up a ramp, and through the door that led to one of the spy-beam-insulated chambers.

Baley checked the walls carefully before sitting down, listening to the soft burr of the pulsometer in his hand, waiting for any fading of the steady sound which would indicate a break, even a small one, in the insulation. He turned it on the ceiling, floor, and, with particular care, on the door. There was no break.

Dr. Gerrigel smiled a little. He looked like a man who never smiled more than a little. He was dressed with a neatness that could only be described as fussy. His iron-gray hair was smoothed carefully back and his face looked pink and freshly washed. He sat with a posture of prim stiffness as though repeated maternal advice in his younger years concerning the desirability of good posture had rigidified his spine forever.

He said to Baley, "You make this all seem very formidable."

"It's quite important, Doctor. I need information about robots that only you can give me, perhaps. Anything we say here, of course, is top secret and the City will expect you to forget it all when you leave." Baley looked at his watch.

The little smile on the roboticist's face winked away. He said, "Let me explain why I am late." The matter obviously weighed upon him. "I decided not to go by air. I get airsick."

"That's too bad," said Baley. He put away the pulsometer, after checking its standard settings to make last-minute certain that there was nothing wrong with *it*, and sat down.

"Or at least not exactly airsick, but nervous. A mild agoraphobia. It's nothing particularly abnormal, but there it is. So I took the expressways."

Baley felt a sudden sharp interest. "Agoraphobia?"

"I make it sound worse than it is," the roboticist said at once. "It's just the feeling you get in a plane. Have you ever been in one, Mr. Baley?"

"Several times."

"Then you must know what I mean. It's that feeling of being surrounded by nothing; of being separated from – from empty air by a mere inch of metal. It's very uncomfortable."

"So you took the expressway?"

"Yes."

"All the way from Washington to New York?"

"Oh, I've done it before. Since they built the Baltimore-Philadelphia tunnel, it's quite simple."

So it was. Baley had never made the trip himself, but he was perfectly aware that it was possible. Washington, Baltimore, Philadelphia, and New York had grown, in the last two centuries, to the point where all nearly touched. The Four-City Area was almost the official name for the entire stretch of coast, and there was a considerable number of people who favored administrational consolidation and the formation of a single super-City. Baley disagreed with that, himself. New York City by itself was almost too large to be handled by a centralized government. A larger City, with over fifty million population, would break down under its own weight.

"The trouble was," Dr. Gerrigel was saying, "that I missed a connection in Chester Sector, Philadelphia, and lost time. That, and a little difficulty in getting a transient room assignment, ended by making me late."

"Don't worry about that, Doctor. What you say, though, is interesting. In view of your dislike for planes, what would you say to going outside City limits on foot, Dr. Gerrigel?"

"For what reason?" He looked startled and more than a little apprehensive.

"It's just a rhetorical question. I'm not suggesting that you really should. I want to know how the notion strikes you, that's all."

"It strikes me very unpleasantly."

"Suppose you had to leave the City at night and walk cross country for half a mile or more."

"I – I don't think I could be persuaded to."

"No matter how important the necessity?"

"If it were to save my life or the lives of my family, I might try. . . ." He looked embarrassed. "May I ask the point of these questions, Mr. Baley?"

"I'll tell you. A serious crime has been committed, a particularly disturbing murder. I'm not at liberty to give you the details. There is a theory, however, that the murderer in order to commit the crime, did just what we were discussing; he crossed open country at night and alone. I was just wondering what kind of man could do that."

Dr. Gerrigel shuddered. "No one I know. Certainly not I. Of course, among millions I suppose you could find a few hardy individuals."

"But you wouldn't say it was a very likely thing for a human being to do?"

"No. Certainly not likely."

"In fact, if there's any other explanation for the crime, any other *conceivable* explanation, it should be considered."

Dr. Gerrigel looked more uncomfortable than ever as he sat bolt upright with his well-kept hands precisely folded in his lap. "Do you have an alternative explanation in mind?"

"Yes. It occurs to me that a robot, for instance, would have no difficulty at all in crossing open country."

Dr. Gerrigel stood up. "Oh, my dear sir!"

"What's wrong?"

"You mean a robot may have committed the crime?"

"Why not?"

"Murder? Of a human being?"

"Yes. Please sit down, Doctor."

The roboticist did as he was told. He said, "Mr. Baley, there are two acts involved: walking cross country, and murder. A human being could commit the latter easily, but would find difficulty in doing the former. A robot could do the former easily, but the latter act would be completely impossible. If you're going to replace an unlikely theory by an impossible one –"

"Impossible is a hell of a strong word, Doctor."

"You've heard of the first Law of Robotics, Mr. Baley?"

"Sure. I can even quote it: A robot may not injure a human being, or, through inaction, allow a human being to come to harm." Baley suddenly pointed a finger at the roboticist and went on, "Why can't a robot be built without the First Law? What's so sacred about it?"

Dr. Gerrigel looked startled, then tittered, "Oh, Mr. Baley."

"Well, what's the answer?"

"Surely, Mr. Baley, if you even know a little about robotics, you must know the gigantic task involved, both mathematically and electronically, in building a positronic brain."

"I have an idea," said Baley. He remembered well his visit to a robot factory once in the way of business. He had seen their library of book-films, long ones, each of which contained the mathematical analysis of a single type of positronic brain. It took more than an hour for the average such film to be viewed at standard scanning speed, condensed though its symbolisms were. And no two brains were alike, even when prepared according to the most rigid specifications. That, Baley understood, was a consequence of Heisenberg's Uncertainty Principle. This meant that each film had to be supplemented by appendices involving possible variations.

Oh, it was a job, all right. Baley wouldn't deny that.

Dr. Gerrigel said, "Well, then, you must understand that a design for a new type of positronic brain, even one where only minor innovations are involved, is not the matter of a night's work. It usually involves the entire research staff of a moderately sized factory and takes anywhere up to a year of time. Even this large expenditure of work would not be nearly enough if it were not that the basic theory of such circuits has already been standardized and may be used as a foundation for further elaboration. The standard basic theory involves the Three Laws of Robotics: the First Law, which you've quoted; the Second Law, which states, 'A robot must obey the orders given it by human beings except where such orders would conflict with the First Law,' and the Third Law, which states, 'A robot must protect its own existence as long as such protection does not conflict with the First or Second Law.' Do you understand?"

R. Daneel, who, to all appearances, had been following the conversation with close attention, broke in. "If you will excuse me, Elijah, I would like to see if I follow Dr. Gerrigel. What you imply, sir, is that any attempt to build a robot, the working of whose positronic brain is not oriented about the Three Laws, would require first the setting up of a new basic theory and that this, in turn, would take many years."

The roboticist looked very gratified. "That is exactly what I mean, Mr. . . ."

Baley waited a moment, then carefully introduced R. Daneel: "This is Daneel Olivaw, Dr. Gerrigel."

"Good day, Mr. Olivaw." Dr. Gerrigel extended his hand and shook Daneel's. He went on, "It is my estimation that it would take fifty years to develop the basic theory of a non-Asenion positronic brain – that is, one in which the basic assumptions of the Three Laws are disallowed – and bring it to the point where robots similar to modern models could be constructed."

"And this has never been done?" asked Baley. "I mean, Doctor, that we've been building robots for several thousand years. In all that time, hasn't anybody or any group had fifty years to spare?"

"Certainly," said the roboticist, "but it is not the sort of work that anyone would care to do."

"I find that hard to believe. Human curiosity will undertake anything."

"It hasn't undertaken the non-Asenion robot. The human race, Mr. Baley, has a strong Frankenstein complex."

"A what?"

"That's a popular name derived from a Medieval novel describing a robot that turned on its creator. I never read the novel myself. But that's beside the point. What I wish to say is that robots without the First Law are simply not built."

"And no theory for it even exists?"

"Not to my knowledge, and my knowledge," he smiled self-consciously, "is rather extensive."

"And a robot with a First Law built in could not kill a man?"

"Never. Unless such killing were completely accidental or unless it were necessary to save the lives of two or more men. In either case, the positronic potential built up would ruin the brain past recovery."

"All right," said Baley. "All this represents the situation on Earth. Right?"

"Yes. Certainly."

"What about the Outer Worlds?"

Some of Dr. Gerrigel's self-assurance seemed to ooze away. "Oh dear, Mr. Baley, I couldn't say of my own knowledge, but I'm sure that if non-Asenion positronic brains were ever designed or if the mathematical theory were worked out, we'd hear of it."

"Would we? Well, let me follow up another thought in my mind, Dr. Gerrigel. I hope you don't mind."

"No. Not at all." He looked helplessly first at Baley, then at R. Daneel. "After all, if it is as important as you say, I'm glad to do all I can."

"Thank you, Doctor. My question is, why humanoid robots? I mean that I've been taking them for granted all my life, but now it occurs to me that I don't know the reason for their existence. Why should a robot have a head and four limbs? Why should he look more or less like a man?"

"You mean, why shouldn't he be built functionally, like any other machine?"

"Right," said Baley. "Why not?"

Dr. Gerrigel smiled a little. "Really, Mr. Baley, you are born too late. The early literature of robotics is riddled with a discussion of that very matter and the polemics involved were something frightful. If you would like a very good reference to the disputations among the functionalists and anti-functionalists, I can recommend Handford's 'History of Robotics.' Mathematics is kept to a minimum. I think you'd find it very interesting."

"I'll look it up," said Baley, patiently. "Meanwhile, could you give me an idea?"

"The decision was made on the basis of economics. Look here, Mr. Baley, if you were supervising a farm, would you care to buy a tractor with a positronic brain, a reaper, a harrow, a milker, an automobile, and so on, each with a positronic brain; or would you rather have ordinary unbrained machinery with a single positronic robot to run them all. I warn you that the second alternative represents only a fiftieth or a hundredth the expense."

"But why the human form?"

"Because the human form is the most successful generalized form in all nature. We are not a specialized animal, Mr. Baley, except for our nervous systems and a few odd items. If you want a design capable of doing a great many widely various things, all fairly well, you could do no better than to imitate the human form. Besides that, our entire technology is based on the human form. An automobile, for instance, has its controls so made as to be grasped and manipulated most easily by human hands and feet of a certain size and shape, attached to the body by limbs of a certain length and joints of a certain type. Even such simple objects as chairs and tables or knives and forks are designed to meet the requirements of human measurements and manner of working. It is easier to have robots imitate the human shape than to redesign radically the very philosophy of our tools."

"I see. That makes sense. Now isn't it true, Doctor, that the roboticists of the Outer World manufacture robots that are much more humanoid than our own?"

"I believe that is true."

"Could they manufacture a robot so humanoid that it would pass for human under ordinary conditions?"

Dr. Gerrigel lifted his eyebrows and considered that. "I think they could, Mr. Baley. It would be terribly expensive. I doubt that the return could be profitable."

"Do you suppose," went on Baley, relentlessly, "that they could make a robot that would fool *you* into thinking it was human?"

The roboticist tittered. "Oh, my dear Mr. Baley. I doubt that. Really. There's more to a robot than just his appear—"

Dr. Gerrigel froze in the middle of the word. Slowly, he turned to R. Daneel, and his pink face went very pale.

"Oh, dear me," he whispered. "Oh, dear me."

He reached out one hand and touched R. Daneel's cheek gingerly. R. Daneel did not move away but gazed at the roboticist calmly.

"Dear me," said Dr. Gerrigel, with what was almost a sob in his voice, "you *are* a robot."

"It took you a long time to realize that," said Baley, dryly.

"I wasn't expecting it. I never saw one like this. Outer World manufacture?"

"Yes," said Baley.

"It's obvious now. The way he holds himself. The manner of his speaking. It is not a perfect imitation, Mr. Baley."

"It's pretty good though, isn't it?"

"Oh, it's marvelous. I doubt that anyone could recognize the imposture at sight. I am very grateful to you for having me brought face to face with him. May I examine him?" The roboticist was on his feet, eager.

Baley put out a hand. "Please, Doctor. In a moment. First, the matter of the murder, you know."

"Is that real then?" Dr. Gerrigel was bitterly disappointed and showed it. "I thought perhaps that was just a device to keep my mind engaged and to see how long I could be fooled by —"

"It is not a device, Dr. Gerrigel. Tell me, now, in constructing a robot as humanoid as this one, with the deliberate purpose of having it pass as human, is it not necessary to make its brain possess properties as close to that of the human brain as possible?"

"Certainly."

"Very well. Could not such a humanoid brain lack the First Law? Perhaps it is left out accidentally. You say the theory is unknown. The very fact that it is unknown means that the constructors might set up a brain without the First Law. They would not know what to avoid."

Dr. Gerrigel was shaking his head vigorously. "No. No. Impossible."

"Are you sure? We can test the Second Law, of course. – Daneel, let me have your blaster."

Baley's eyes never left the robot. His own hand, well to one side, gripped his own blaster tightly.

R. Daneel said calmly, "Here it is, Elijah," and held it out, butt first.

Baley said, "A plain-clothes man must never abandon his blaster, but a robot has no choice but to obey a human."

"Except, Mr. Baley," said Dr. Gerrigel, "when obedience involves breaking the First Law."

"Do you know, Doctor, that Daneel drew his blaster on an unarmed group of men and women and threatened to shoot?"

"But I did not shoot," said R. Daneel.

"Granted, but the threat was unusual in itself, wasn't it, Doctor?"

Dr. Gerrigel bit his lip. "I'd need to know the exact circumstances to judge. It sounds unusual."

"Consider this, then. R. Daneel was on the scene at the time of the murder, and if you omit the possibility of an Earthman having moved across open country, carrying a weapon with him, Daneel and Daneel alone of all the persons on the scene could have hidden the weapon."

"Hidden the weapon?" asked Dr. Gerrigel.

"Let me explain. The blaster that did the killing was not found. The scene of the murder was searched minutely and it was not found. Yet it could not have vanished like smoke. There is only one place it could have been, only one place they would not have thought to look."

"Where, Elijah?" asked R. Daneel.

Baley brought his blaster into view, held its barrel firmly in the robot's direction.

"In your food sac," he said. "In your food sac, Daneel!"

CHAPTER THIRTEEN

SHIFT TO THE MACHINE

"That is not so," said R. Daneel, quietly.

"Yes? We'll let the Doctor decide. Dr. Gerrigel?"

"Mr. Baley?" The roboticist, whose glance had been alternating wildly between the plain-clothes man and the robot as they spoke, let it come to rest upon the human being.

"I've asked you here for an authoritative analysis of this robot. I can arrange to have you use the laboratories of the City Bureau of Standards. If you need any piece of equipment they don't have, I'll get it for you. What I want is a quick and definite answer and hang the expense and trouble."

Baley rose. His words had emerged calmly enough, but he felt a rising hysteria behind them. At the moment, he felt that if he could only seize Dr. Gerrigel by the throat and choke the necessary statements out of him, he would forgo all science.

He said, "Well, Dr. Gerrigel?"

Dr. Gerrigel tittered nervously and said, "My dear Mr. Baley, I won't need a laboratory."

"Why not?" asked Baley apprehensively. He stood there, muscles tense, feeling himself twitch.

"It's not difficult to test the First Law. I've never had to, you understand, but it's simple enough."

Baley pulled air in through his mouth and let it out slowly. He said, "Would you explain what you mean? Are you saying that you can test him here?"

"Yes, of course. Look, Mr. Baley, I'll give you an analogy. If I were a Doctor of Medicine and had to test a patient's blood sugar, I'd need a chemical laboratory. If I needed to measure his basal metabolic rate, or test his cortical function, or check his genes to pinpoint a congenital malfunction, I'd need elaborate equipment. On the other hand, I could check whether he were blind by merely passing my hand before his eyes and I could test whether he were dead by merely feeling for his pulse.

"What I'm getting at is that the more important and fundamental the property being tested, the simpler the needed equipment. It's the same in a robot. The First Law is fundamental. It affects everything. If it were absent, the robot could not react properly in two dozen obvious ways."

As he spoke, he took out a flat, black object which expanded into a small book-viewer. He inserted a well-worn spool into the receptacle. He then took out a stop watch and a series of white, plastic slivers that fitted together to form something that looked like a slide rule with three independent movable scales. The notations upon it struck no chord of familiarity to Baley.

Dr. Gerrigel tapped his book-viewer and smiled a little, as though the prospect of a bit of field work cheered him.

He said, "It's my *Handbook of Robotics*. I never go anywhere without it. It's part of my clothes." He giggled self-consciously.

He put the eyepiece of the viewer to his eyes and his finger dealt delicately with the controls. The viewer whirred and stopped.

"Built-in index," the roboticist said, proudly, his voice a little muffled because of the way in which the viewer covered his mouth. "I constructed it myself. It saves a great deal of time. But then, that's not the point now, is it? Let's see. Umm, won't you move your chair near me, Daneel."

R. Daneel did so. During the roboticist's preparations, he had watched closely and unemotionally.

Baley shifted his blaster.

What followed confused and disappointed him. Dr. Gerrigel proceeded to ask questions and perform actions that seemed without meaning, punctuated by references to his triple slide rule and occasionally to the viewer.

At one time, he asked, "If I have two cousins, five years apart in age, and the younger is a girl, what sex is the older?"

Daneel answered (inevitably, Baley thought), "It is impossible to say on the information given."

To which Dr. Gerrigel's only response, aside from a glance at his stop watch, was to extend his right hand as far as he could sideways and to say, "Would you touch the tip of my middle finger with the tip of the third finger of your left hand?"

Daneel did that promptly and easily.

In fifteen minutes, not more, Dr. Gerrigel was finished. He used his slide rule for a last silent calculation, then disassembled it with a series of snaps. He put away his stop watch, withdrew the *Handbook* from the viewer, and collapsed the latter.

"Is that all?" said Baley, frowning.

"That's all."

"But it's ridiculous. You've asked nothing that pertains to the First Law."

"Oh, my dear Mr. Baley, when a doctor hits your knee with a little rubber mallet and it jerks, don't you accept the fact that it gives information concerning the presence or absence of some degenerative nerve disease? When he looks closely at your eyes and considers the reaction of your iris to light, are you surprised that he can tell you something concerning your possible addiction to the use of certain alkaloids?"

Baley said, "Well, then? What's your decision?"

"Daneel is fully equipped with the First Law!" The roboticist jerked his head in a sharp affirmative.

"You can't be right," said Baley huskily.

Baley would not have thought that Dr. Gerrigel could stiffen into a rigidity that was greater than his usual position. He did so, however, visibly. The man's eyes grew narrow and hard.

"Are you teaching me my job?"

"I don't mean you're incompetent," said Baley. He put out a large, pleading hand. "But couldn't you be mistaken? You've said yourself nobody knows anything about the theory of non-Asenion robots. A blind man could read by using Braille or a sound-scriber. Suppose you didn't know that Braille or sound-scribing existed. Couldn't you, in all honesty, say that a man had eyes because he knew the contents of a certain book-film, and be mistaken?"

"Yes," the roboticist grew genial again, "I see your point. But still a blind man could not read by use of his eyes and it is that which I was testing, if I may continue the analogy. Take my word for it, regardless of what a non-Asenion robot could or could not do, it is certain that R. Daneel is equipped with First Law."

"Couldn't he have falsified his answers?" Baley was floundering, and knew it.

"Of course not. That is the difference between a robot and a man. A human brain, or any mammalian brain, cannot be completely analyzed by any mathematical discipline now known. No response can therefore be counted upon as a certainty. The robot

brain is completely analyzable, or it could not be constructed.
We know exactly what the responses to given stimuli must be.
No robot can truly falsify answers. The thing you call falsifica-
tion just doesn't exist in the robot's mental horizon."

"Then let's get down to cases. R. Daneel did point a blaster
at a crowd of human beings. I saw that. I was there. Granted
that he didn't shoot, wouldn't the First Law still have forced
him into a kind of neurosis? It didn't you know. He was perfectly normal afterward."

The roboticist put a hesitant hand to his chin. "That *is*
anomalous."

"Not at all," said R. Daneel, suddenly. "Partner Elijah,
would you look at the blaster that you took from me?"

Baley looked down upon the blaster he held cradled in his
left hand.

"Break open the charge chamber," urged R. Daneel. "Inspect
it."

Baley weighed his chances, then slowly put his own blaster
on the table beside him. With a quick movement, he opened the
robot's blaster.

"It's empty," he said, blankly.

"There is no charge in it," agreed R. Daneel. "If you will
look closer, you will see that there has never been a charge in
it. The blaster has no ignition bud and cannot be used."

Baley said, "You held an uncharged blaster on the crowd?"

"I had to have a blaster or fail in my role as plain-clothes
man," said R. Daneel. "Yet to carry a charged and usable blaster
might have made it possible for me to hurt a human being by
accident, a thing which is, of course, unthinkable. I would have
explained this at the time, but you were angry and would not
listen."

Baley stared bleakly at the useless blaster in his hand and said
in a low voice, "I think that's all, Dr. Gerrigel. Thank you for
helping out."

Baley sent out for lunch, but when it came (yeast-nut cake
and a rather extravagant slice of fried chicken on cracker) he
could only stare at it.

Round and round went the currents of his mind. The lines
on his long face were etched in deep gloom.

He was living in an unreal world, a cruel, topsy-turvy world.

How had it happened? The immediate past stretched behind him like a misty improbable dream dating back to the moment he had stepped into Julius Enderby's office and found himself suddenly immersed in a nightmare of murder and robotics.

Jehoshaphat! It had begun only fifty hours before.

Persistently, he had sought the solution in Spacetown. Twice he had accused R. Daneel, once as a human being in disguise, and once as an admitted and actual robot, each time as a murderer. Twice the accusation had been bent back and broken.

He was being driven back. Against his will he was forced to turn his thoughts into the City, and since last night he dared not. Certain questions battered at his conscious mind, but he would not listen; he felt he could not. If he heard them, he couldn't help but answer them and, oh God, he didn't want to face the answers.

"Lije! Lije!" A hand shook Baley's shoulder roughly.

Baley stirred and said, "What's up, Phil?"

Philip Norris, Plain-clothes man C—5, sat down, put his hands on his knees, and leaned forward, peering at Baley's face. "What happened to you? Been living on knockout drops lately? You were sitting there with your eyes open and, near as I could make out, you were dead."

He rubbed his thinning, pale blond hair, and his close-set eyes appraised Baley's cooling lunch greedily. "Chicken!" he said. "It's getting so you can't get it without a doctor's prescription."

"Take some," said Baley, listlessly.

Decorum won out and Norris said, "Oh, well, I'm going out to eat in a minute — You keep it. — Say, what's doing with the Commish?"

"What?"

Norris attempted a casual attitude, but his hands were restless. He said, "Go on. You know what I mean. You've been living with him ever since he got back. What's up? A promotion in the works?"

Baley frowned and felt reality return somewhat at the touch of office politics. Norris had approximately his own seniority and he was bound to watch most assiduously for any sign of official preference in Baley's direction.

Baley said, "No promotion. Believe me. It's nothing. Nothing. And if it's the Commissioner you're wanting, I wish I could give him to you. Jehoshaphat! Take him!"

Norris said, "Don't get me wrong. I don't care if you get promoted. I just mean that if you've got any pull with the Commish, how about using it for the kid?"

"What kid?"

There was no need of any answer to that. Vincent Barrett, the youngster who had been moved out of his job to make room for R. Sammy, was shuffling up from an unnoticed corner of the room. A skull cap turned restlessly in his hands and the skin over his high cheekbones moved as he tried to smile.

"Hello, Mr. Baley."

"Oh, hello, Vince. How're you doing?"

"Not so good, Mr. Baley."

He was looking about hungrily. Baley thought: He looks lost, half dead – declassified.

Then, savagely, his lips almost moving with the force of his emotion, he thought: But what does he want from me?

He said, "I'm sorry, kid." What else was there to say?

"I keep thinking – maybe something has turned up."

Norris moved in close and spoke into Baley's ear. "Someone's got to stop this sort of thing. They're going to move out Chen-low now."

"What?"

"Haven't you heard?"

"No, I haven't. Damn it, he's a C—3. He's got ten years behind him."

"I grant that. But a machine with legs can do his work. Who's next?"

Young Vince Barrett was oblivious to, the whispers. He said out of the depths of his own thinking, "Mr. Baley?"

"Yes, Vince?"

"You know what they say? They say Lyrane Millane, the subetherics dancer, is really a robot."

"That's silly."

"Is it? They say they can make robots look just like humans; with a special plastic skin, sort of."

Baley thought guiltily of R. Daneel and found no words. He shook his head.

The boy said, "Do you suppose anyone will mind if I just walk around. It makes me feel better to see the old place."

"Go ahead, kid."

The youngster wandered off. Baley and Norris watched him go.

Norris said, "It looks as though the Medievalists are right."

"You mean back to the soil? Is that it, Phil?"

"*No*. I mean about the robots. Back to the soil. Huh! Old Earth has an unlimited future. We don't need robots, that's all."

Baley muttered, "Eight billion people and the uranium running out! What's unlimited about it?"

"What if the uranium does run out. We'll import it. Or we'll discover other nuclear processes. There's no way you can stop mankind, Lije. You've got to be optimistic about it and have faith in the old human brain. Our greatest resource is ingenuity and we'll never run out of that, Lije."

He was fairly started now. He went on, "For one thing, we can use sunpower and that's good for billions of years. We can build space stations inside Mercury's orbit to act as energy accumulators. We'll transmit energy to Earth by direct beam."

This project was not new to Baley. The speculative fringe of science had been playing with the notion for a hundred and fifty years at least. What was holding it up was the impossibility so far of projecting a beam tight enough to reach fifty million miles without dispersal to uselessness. Baley said as much.

Norris said, "When it's necessary, it'll be done. Why worry?"

Baley had the picture of an Earth of unlimited energy. Population could continue to increase. The yeast farms could expand, hydroponic culture intensify. Energy was the only thing indispensable. The raw minerals could be brought in from the uninhabited rocks of the System. If ever water became a bottleneck, more could be brought in from the moons of Jupiter. Hell, the oceans could be frozen and dragged out into Space where they could circle Earth as moonlets of ice. There they would be, always available for use, while the ocean bottoms would represent more land for exploitation, more room to live. Even carbon and oxygen could be maintained and increased on Earth through utilization of the methane atmosphere of Titan and the frozen oxygen of Umbriel.

Earth's population could reach a trillion or two. Why not? There was a time when the current population of eight billion would have been viewed as impossible. There was a time when a population of a single billion would have been unthinkable. There had always been prophets of Malthusian doom in every generation since Medieval times and they had always proven wrong.

But what would Fastolfe say? A world of a trillion? Surely! But they would be dependent on imported air and water and upon an energy supply from complicated storehouses fifty million miles away. How incredibly unstable that would be. Earth would be, and remain, a feather's weight away from complete catastrophe at the slightest failure of any part of the System-wide mechanism.

Baley said, "I think it would be easier to ship off some of the surplus population, myself." It was more an answer to the picture he had himself conjured up than to anything Norris had said.

"Who'd have us?" said Norris with a bitter lightness.

"Any uninhabited planet."

Norris rose, patted Baley on the shoulder. "Lije, you eat your chicken, and recover. You *must* be living on knockout pills." He left, chuckling.

Baley watched him leave with a humorless twist to his mouth. Norris would spread the news and it would be weeks before the humor boys of the office (every office has them) would lay off. But at least it got him off the subject of young Vince, of robots, of declassification.

He sighed as he put a fork into the now cold and somewhat stringy chicken.

Baley finished the last of the yeast-nut and it was only then that R. Daneel left his own desk (assigned him that morning) and approached.

Baley eyed him uncomfortably. "Well?"

R. Daneel said, "The Commissioner is not in his office and it is not known when he'll be back. I've told R. Sammy we will use it and that he is to allow no one but the Commissioner to enter."

"What are we going to use it for?"

"Greater privacy. Surely you agree that we must plan our next move. After all, you do not intend to abandon the investigation, do you?"

That was precisely what Baley most longed to do, but obviously, he could not say so. He rose and led the way to Enderby's office.

Once in the office, Baley said, "All right, Daneel. What is it?"

The robot said, "Partner Elijah, since last night, you are not yourself. There is a definite alteration in your mental aura."

A horrible thought sprang full-grown into Baley's mind. He cried, "Are you telepathic?"

It was not a possibility he would have considered at a less disturbed moment.

"No. Of course not," said R. Daneel.

Baley's panic ebbed. He said, "Then what the devil do you mean by talking about my mental aura?"

"It is merely an expression I use to describe a sensation that you do not share with me."

"What sensation?"

"It is difficult to explain, Elijah. You will recall that I was originally designed to study human psychology for our people back in Spacetown."

"Yes, I know. You were adjusted to detective work by the simple installation of a justice-desire circuit." Baley did not try to keep the sarcasm out of his voice.

"Exactly, Elijah. But my original design remains essentially unaltered. It was constructed for the purpose of cerebro-analysis."

"For analyzing brain waves?"

"Why, yes. It can be done by field-measurements without the necessity of direct electrode contact, if the proper receiver exists. My mind is such a receiver. Is that principle not applied on Earth?"

Baley didn't know. He ignored the question and said, cautiously, "If you measure the brain waves, what do you get out of it?"

"Not thoughts, Elijah. I get a glimpse of emotion and most of all, I can analyze temperament, the underlying drives and attitudes of a man. For instance, it was I who was able to ascertain that Commissioner Enderby was incapable of killing a man under the circumstances prevailing at the time of the murder."

"And they eliminated him as a suspect on your say-so."

"Yes. It was safe enough to do so. I am a very delicate machine in that respect."

Again a thought struck Baley. "Wait! Commissioner Enderby didn't know he was being cerebroanalyzed, did he?"

"There was no necessity of hurting his feelings."

"I mean you just stood there and looked at him. No machinery. No electrodes. No needles and graphs."

"Certainly not. I am a self-contained unit."

Baley bit his lower lip in anger and chagrin. It had been the one remaining inconsistency, the one loophole through which a forlorn stab might yet be made in an attempt to pin the crime on Spacetown.

R. Daneel had stated that the Commissioner had been cerebroanalyzed and one hour later the Commissioner himself had, with apparent candor, denied any knowledge of the term. Certainly no man could have undergone the shattering experience of electroencephalographic measurements by electrode and graph under the suspicion of murder without an unmistakable impression of what cerebroanalysis must be.

But now that discrepancy had evaporated. The Commissioner had been cerebroanalyzed and had never known it. R. Daneel told the truth; so had the Commissioner.

"Well," said Baley, sharply, "what does cerebroanalysis tell you about me?"

"You are disturbed."

"That's a great discovery, isn't it? Of course, I'm disturbed."

"Specifically, though, your disturbance is due to a clash between motivations within you. On the one hand your devotion to the principles of your profession urges you to look deeply into this conspiracy of Earthmen who lay siege to us last night. Another motivation, equally strong, forces you in the opposite direction. This much is clearly written in the electric field of your cerebral cells."

"My cerebral cells, *nuts*," said Baley, feverishly. "Look, I'll tell you why there's no point in investigating your so-called conspiracy. It has nothing to do with the murder. I thought it might have. I'll admit that. Yesterday in the kitchen, I thought we were in danger. But what happened? They followed us out, were quickly lost on the strips, and that was that. That was not the action of well-organized and desperate men.

"My own son found out where we were staying easily enough. He called the Department. He didn't even have to identify himself. Our precious conspirators could have done the same if they had really wanted to hurt us."

"Didn't they?"

"Obviously not. If they had wanted riots, they could have started one at the shoe counter, and yet they backed out tamely enough before one man and a blaster. One *robot*, and a blaster which they must have known you would be unable to fire once they recognized what you were. They're Medievalists. They're harmless crackpots. You wouldn't know that, but I should have. And I would have, if it weren't for the fact that this whole business has me thinking in – in foolish melodramatic terms.

"I tell you I know the type of people that become Medievalists. They're soft, dreamy people who find life too hard for them here and get lost in an ideal world of the past that never really existed. If you could cerebroanalyze a movement as you do an individual, you would find they are no more capable of murder than Julius Enderby himself."

R. Daneel said slowly, "I cannot accept your statements at face value."

"What do you mean?"

"Your conversion to this view is too sudden. There are certain discrepancies, too. You arranged the appointment with Dr. Gerrigel hours before the evening meal. You did not know of my food sac then and could not have suspected me as the murderer. Why *did* you call him, then?"

"I suspected you even then."

"And last night you spoke as you slept."

Baley's eyes widened. "What did I say?"

"Merely the one word 'Jessie' several times repeated. I believe you were referring to your wife."

Baley let his tight muscles loosen. He said, shakily, "I had a nightmare. Do you know what that is?"

"I do not know by personal experience, of course. The dictionary definition has it that it is a bad dream."

"And do you know what a dream is?"

"Again, the dictionary definition only. It is an illusion of reality experienced during the temporary suspension of conscious thought which you call sleep."

"All right. I'll buy that. An illusion. Sometimes the illusions can seem damned real. Well, I dreamed my wife was in danger. It's the sort of dream people often have. I called her name. That happens under such circumstances, too. You can take my word for it."

"I am only too glad to do so. But it brings up a thought. How did Jessie find out I was a robot?"

Baley's forehead went moist again. "We're not going into that again, are we? The rumor –"

"I am sorry to interrupt, partner Elijah, but there is no rumor. If there were, the City would be alive with unrest today. I have checked reports coming into the Department and this is not so. There simply is no rumor. Therefore, how did your wife find out?"

"Jehoshaphat! What are you trying to say? Do you think my wife is one of the members of – of . . ."

"Yes, Elijah."

Baley gripped his hands together tightly. "Well, she isn't, and we won't discuss that point any further."

"This is not like you, Elijah. In the course of duty, you accused me of murder twice."

"And is this your way of getting even?"

"I am not sure I understand what you mean by the phrase. Certainly, I approve your readiness to suspect me. You had your reasons. They were wrong, but they might easily have been right. Equally strong evidence points to your wife."

"As a murderess? Why, damn you, Jessie wouldn't hurt her worst enemy. She couldn't set foot outside the City. She couldn't. . . . Why, if you were flesh and blood I'd –"

"I merely say that she is a member of the conspiracy. I say that she should be questioned."

"Not on your life. Not on whatever it is you call your life. Now, listen to me. The Medievalists aren't after our blood. It's not the way they do things. But they are trying to get you out of the City. That much is obvious. And they're trying to do it by a kind of psychological attack. They're trying to make life unpleasant for you and for me, since I'm with you. They could easily have found out Jessie was my wife, and it was an obvious move for them to let the news leak to her. She's like any other human being. She doesn't like robots. She wouldn't want me to associate with one, especially if she thought it involved danger, and surely they would imply that. I tell you it worked. She begged all night to have me abandon the case or to get you out of the City somehow."

"Presumably," said R. Daneel, "you have a very strong urge to protect your wife against questioning. It seems obvious to me that you are constructing this line of argument without really believing it."

"What the hell do you think you are?" ground out Baley. "You're not a detective. You're a cerebroanalysis machine like the electroencephalographs we have in this building. You've got arms, legs, a head, and can talk, but you're not one inch more than that machine. Putting a lousy circuit into you doesn't make you a detective, so what do you know? You keep your mouth shut, and let me do the figuring out."

The robot said quietly, "I think it would be better if you lowered your voice, Elijah. Granted that I am not a detective in the sense that you are, I would still like to bring one small item to your attention."

"I'm not interested in listening."

"Please do. If I am wrong, you will tell me so, and it will do no harm. It is only this. Last night you left our room to call Jessie by corridor phone. I suggested that your son go in your place. You told me it was not the custom among Earthmen for a father to send his son into danger. Is it then the custom for a mother to do so?"

"No, of cour—" began Baley, and stopped.

"You see my point," said R. Daneel. "Ordinarily, if Jessie feared for your safety and wished to warn you, she would risk her own life, *not* send her son. The fact that she did send Bentley could only mean that she felt that he would be safe while she herself would not. If the conspiracy consisted of people unknown to Jessie, that would not be the case, or at least she would have no reason to think it to be the case. On the other hand, if she were a member of the conspiracy, she would know, she would *know*, Elijah, that she would be watched for and recognized, whereas Bentley might get through unnoticed."

"Wait now," said Baley, sick at heart, "that's feather-fine reasoning, but –"

There was no need to wait. The signal on the Commissioner's desk was flickering madly. R. Daneel waited for Baley to answer, but the latter could only stare at it helplessly. The robot closed contact.

"What is it?"

R. Sammy's slurring voice said, "There is a lady here who wishes to see Lije. I told her he was busy, but she will not go away. She says her name is Jessie."

"Let her in," said R. Daneel calmly, and his brown eyes rose unemotionally to meet the panicky glare of Baley's.

CHAPTER FOURTEEN
POWER OF A NAME

Baley remained standing in a tetany of shock, as Jessie ran to him, seizing his shoulders, huddling close.

His pale lips formed the word, "Bentley?"

She looked at him and shook her head, her brown hair flying with the force of her motion. "He's all right."

"Well, then . . ."

Jessie said through a sudden torrent of sobs, in a low voice that could scarcely be made out, "I can't go on, Lije. I can't. I can't sleep or eat. I've got to tell you."

"Don't say anything," Baley said in anguish. "For God's sake, Jessie, not now."

"I must. I've done a terrible thing. Such a terrible thing. Oh, Lije . . ." She lapsed into incoherence.

Baley said, hopelessly, "We're not alone, Jessie."

She looked up and stared at R. Daneel with no sign of recognition. The tears in which her eyes were swimming might easily be refracting the robot into a featureless blur.

R. Daneel said in a low murmur, "Good afternoon, Jessie."

She gasped. "Is it the – the robot?"

She dashed the back of her hand across her eyes and stepped out of Baley's encircling right arm. She breathed deeply and, for a moment, a tremulous smile wavered on her lips. "It *is* you, isn't it?"

"Yes, Jessie."

"You don't mind being called a robot?"

"No, Jessie. It is what I am."

"And I don't mind being called a fool and an idiot and a — a subversive agent, because it's what *I* am."

"Jessie!" groaned Baley.

"It's no use, Lije," she said. "He might as well know if he's your partner. I can't live with it any more. I've had such a time since yesterday. I don't care if I go to jail. I don't care if they send me down to the lowest levels and make me live on raw yeast and water. I don't care if. . . . You won't let them, will you, Lije? Don't let them do anything to me. I'm fuh – frightened."

Baley patted her shoulder and let her cry.

He said to R. Daneel. "She isn't well. We can't keep her here. What time is it?"

R. Daneel said without any visible signs of consulting a time-piece, "Fourteen-forty-five."

"The Commissioner could be back any minute. Look, commandeer a squad car and we can talk about this in the motorway."

Jessie's head jerked upright. "The motorway? Oh, no, Lije."

He said, in as soothing a tone as he could manage, "Now, Jessie, don't be supersitious. You can't go on the expressway the way you are. Be a good girl and calm down or we won't even be able to go through the common room. I'll get you some water."

She wiped her face with a damp handkerchief and said drearily, "Oh, look at my makeup."

"Don't worry about your make-up," said Baley. "Daneel, what about the squad car?"

"It's waiting for us now, partner Elijah."

"Come on, Jessie."

"Wait. Wait just a minute, Lije. I've got to do something to my face."

"It doesn't matter now."

But she twisted away. "Please. I can't go through the common room like this. I won't take a second."

The man and the robot waited, the man with little jerky clenchings of his fists, the robot impassively.

Jessie rummaged through her purse for the necessary equipment. (If there were one thing, Baley had once said solemnly, that had resisted mechanical improvement since Medieval times, it was a woman's purse. Even the substitution of magnetic closures for metal clasps had not proven successful. Jessie pulled out a small mirror and the silver-chased cosmetokit that Baley had bought her on the occasion of three birthdays before.

The cosmetokit had several orifices, and she used each in turn. All but the last spray was invisible. She used them with that fineness of touch and delicacy of control that seems to be the birthright of women even at times of the greatest stress.

The base went on first in a smooth even layer that removed all shininess and roughness from the skin and left it with the faintly golden glow which long experience had taught Jessie was just the shade most suited to the natural coloring of her hair and eyes. Then the touch of tan along the forehead and chin, a gentle brush of rouge on either cheek, tracing back to the angle of the jaw; and a delicate drift of blue on the upper eyelids and along the earlobes. Finally there was the application of the smooth carmine to the lips. That involved the one visible spray, a faintly pink mist that glistened liquidly in air, but dried and deepened richly on contact with the lips.

"There," said Jessie, with several swift pats of her hair and a look of deep dissatisfaction. "I suppose that will do."

The process had taken more than the promised second, but less than fifteen seconds. Nevertheless, it had seemed interminable to Baley.

"Come," he said.

She barely had time to return the cosmetokit to the purse before he had pushed her through the door.

The eerie silence of the motorway lay thick on either side.

Baley said, "All right, Jessie."

The impassivity that had covered Jessie's face since they first left the Commissioner's office showed signs of cracking. She looked at her husband and at Daneel with a helpless silence.

Baley said, "Get it over with, Jessie. Please. Have you committed a crime? An actual crime?"

"A crime?" She shook her head uncertainly.

"Now hold on to yourself. No hysterics. Just say yes or no, Jessie. Have you –" he hesitated a trifle, "killed anyone?"

The look on Jessie's face was promptly transmuted to indignation. "Why, Lije Baley!"

"Yes or no, Jessie."

"No, of course not."

The hard knot in Baley's stomach softened perceptibly. "Have you stolen anything? Falsified ration data? Assaulted anyone? Destroyed property? Speak up, Jessie."

"I haven't done anything – anything specific. I didn't mean anything like that." She looked over her shoulder. "Lije, do we have to stay down here?"

"Right here until this is over. Now, start at the beginning. What did you come to tell us?" Over Jessie's bowed head, Baley's eyes met R. Daneel's.

Jessie spoke in a soft voice that gained in strength and articulateness as she went on.

"It's these people, these Medievalists; *you* know, Lije. They're always around, always talking. Even in the old days when I was an assistant dietitian, it was like that. Remember Elizabeth Thornbowe? She was a Medievalist. She was always talking about how all our troubles came from the City and how things were better before the Cities started.

"I used to ask her how she was so sure that was so, especially after you and I met, Lije (remember the talks we used to have), and then she would quote from those small book-reels that are always floating around. You know, like *Shame of the Cities* that the fellow wrote. I don't remember his name."

Baley said, absently, "Ogrinsky."

"Yes, only most of them were lots worse. Then, when I married you, she was really sarcastic. She said, 'I suppose you're going to be a real City woman now that you've married a policeman.' After that, she didn't talk to me much and then I quit the job and that was that. Lots of things she used to say were just to shock me, I think, sort of make herself look mysterious and glamorous. She was an old maid, you know; never got married till the day she died. Lots of those Medievalists don't fit in, one way or another. Remember, you once said, Lije, that people sometimes mistake their own shortcomings for those of society and want to fix the Cities because they don't know how to fix themselves."

Baley remembered, and his words now sounded flip and superficial in his own ears. He said, gently, "Keep to the point, Jessie."

She went on, "Anyway, Lizzy was always talking about how there'd come a day and people had to get together. She said it was all the fault of the Spacers because they wanted to keep Earth weak and decadent. That was one of her favorite words, 'decadent.' She'd look at the menus I'd prepare for the next week and sniff and say, 'Decadent, decadent.' Jane Myers used to imitate her in the cook room and we'd die laughing. She said, Elizabeth did, that someday we were going to break up the Cities and go back to the soil and have an accounting with the Spacers who were trying to tie us forever to the Cities by forcing robots on us. Only she never called them robots. She used to say 'soulless monster-machines,' if you'll excuse the expression, Daneel."

The robot said, "I am not aware of the significance of the adjective you used, Jessie, but in any case, the expression is excused. Please go on."

Baley stirred restlessly. It was that way with Jessie. No emergency, no crisis could make her tell a story in any way but her own circuitous one.

She said, "Elizabeth always tried to talk as though there were lots of people in it with her. She would say, 'At the last meeting,' and then stop and look at me sort of half proud and half scared as though she wanted me to ask about it so she could look important, and yet scared I might get her in trouble. Of course, I never asked her. I wouldn't give her the satisfaction.

"Anyway, after I married you, Lije, it was all over, until . . ." She stopped.

"Go on, Jessie," said Baley.

"You remember, Lije, that argument we had? About Jezebel, I mean?"

"What about it?" It took a second or two for Baley to remember that it was Jessie's own name, and not a reference to another woman.

He turned to R. Daneel in an automatically defensive explanation. "Jessie's full name is Jezebel. She is not fond of it and doesn't use it."

R. Daneel nodded gravely and Baley thought: Jehoshaphat, why waste worry on *him?*

"It bothered me a lot, Lije," Jessie said. "It really did. I guess it was silly, but I kept thinking and thinking about what you said. I mean about your saying that Jezebel was only a conservative who fought for the ways of her ancestors against the strange ways the newcomers had brought. After all, *I* was Jezebel and I always..."

She groped for a word and Baley supplied it. "Identified yourself?"

"Yes." But she shook her head almost immediately and looked away. "Not really, of course. Not literally. The way I thought she was, you know. I wasn't like that."

"I know that, Jessie. Don't be foolish."

"But still I thought of her a lot and, somehow, I got to thinking, it's just the same now as it was then. I mean, we Earth people had our old ways and here were the Spacers coming in with a lot of new ways and trying to encourage the new ways we had stumbled into ourselves and maybe the Medievalists were right. Maybe we *should* go back to our old, good ways. So I went back and found Elizabeth."

"Yes. Go on."

"She said she didn't know what I was talking about and besides I was a cop's wife. I said that had nothing to do with it and finally she said, well, she'd speak to somebody, and then about a month later she came to me and said it was all right and I joined and I've been at meetings ever since."

Baley looked at her sadly. "And you never told me?"

Jessie's voice trembled. "I'm sorry, Lije."

"Well, that won't help. Being sorry, I mean. I want to know about the meetings. In the first place, where were they held?"

A sense of detachment was creeping over him, a numbing of emotions. What he had tried not to believe was so, was openly so, was unmistakably so. In a sense, it was a relief to have the uncertainty over.

She said, "Down here."

"Down here? You mean on this spot? What *do* you mean?"

"Here in the motorway. That's why I didn't want to come down here. It was a wonderful place to meet, though. We'd get together –"

"How many?"

"I'm not sure. About sixty or seventy. It was just a sort of local branch. There'd be folding chairs and some refreshments and someone would make a speech, mostly about how wonderful life was in the old days and how someday we'd do away with the monsters, the robots, that is, and the Spacers, too. The speeches were sort of dull really, because they were all the same. We just endured them. Mostly, it was the fun of getting together and feeling important. We would pledge ourselves to oaths and there'd be secret ways we could greet each other on the outside."

"Weren't you ever interrupted? No squad cars or fire engines passed?"

"No. Never."

R. Daneel interrupted, "Is that unusual, Elijah?"

"Maybe not," Baley answered thoughtfully. "There are some sidepassages that are practically never used. It's quite a trick, knowing which they are, though. Is that all you did at the meetings, Jessie? Make speeches and play at conspiracy?"

"It's about all. And sing songs, sometimes. And of course, refreshments. Not much. Sandwiches, usually, and juice."

"In that case," he said, almost brutally, "what's bothering you now?"

Jessie winced. "You're angry."

"Please," said Baley, with iron patience, "answer my question. If it were all as harmless as that, why have you been in such a panic for the last day and a half?"

"I thought they would hurt you, Lije. For heaven's sake, why do you act as though you don't understand? I've explained it to you."

"No, you haven't. Not yet. You've told me about a harmless little secret kaffee-klatsch you belonged to. Did they ever hold open demonstrations? Did they ever destroy robots? Start riots? Kill people?"

"*Never*! Lije, I wouldn't do any of those things. I wouldn't stay a member if they tried it."

"Well, then, why do you say you've done a terrible thing? Why do you expect to be sent to jail?"

"Well. . . . Well, they used to talk about someday when they'd put pressure on the government. We were supposed to get organized and then afterward there would be huge strikes and work stoppages. We could force the government to ban all robots and make the Spacers go back where they came from. I thought it was just talk and then, this thing started; about you and Daneel, I mean. Then they said, 'Now we'll see action,' and 'We're going to make an example of them and put a stop to the robot invasion right now.' Right there in Personal they said it, not knowing it was you they were talking about. But I knew. Right away."

Her voice broke.

Baley softened. "Come on, Jessie. It was all nothing. It was just talk. You can see for yourself that nothing has happened."

"I was so – so suh – scared. And I thought: *I'm* part of it. If there were going to be killing and destruction, *you* might be killed and Bentley and somehow it would be all muh – my fault for taking part in it, and I ought to be sent to jail."

Baley let her sob herself out. He put his arm about her shoulder and stared tight-lipped at R. Daneel, who gazed calmly back.

He said, "Now, I want you to think, Jessie. Who was the head of your group?"

She was quieter now, patting the corners of her eyes with a handkerchief. "A man called Joseph Klemin was the leader, but he wasn't really anybody. He wasn't more than five feet four inches tall and I think he was terribly henpecked at home. I don't think there's any harm in him. You aren't going to arrest him, are you, Lije? On my say-so?" She looked guiltily troubled.

"I'm not arresting anyone just yet. How did Klemin get *his* instructions?"

"I don't know."

"Did any strangers come to meetings? You know what I mean: big shots from Central Headquarters?"

"Sometimes people would come to make speeches. That wasn't very often, maybe twice a year or so."

"Can you name them?"

"No. They were always just introduced as 'one of us' or 'a friend from Jackson Heights' or wherever."

"I see. Daneel!"

"Yes, Elijah," said R. Daneel.

"Describe the men you think you've tabbed. We'll see if Jessie can recognize them."

R. Daneel went through the list with clinical exactness. Jessie listened with an expression of dismay as the categories of physical measurements lengthened and shook her head with increasing firmness.

"It's no use. It's no use," she cried. "How can I remember? I can't remember how any of them looked. I can't –"

She stopped, and seemed to consider. Then she said, "Did you say one of them was a yeast farmer?"

"Francis Clousarr," said R. Daneel, "is an employee at New York Yeast."

"Well, you know, once a man was making a speech and I happened to be sitting in the first row and I kept getting a whiff, just a whiff, of raw yeast smell. You know what I mean. The only reason that I remember is that I had an upset stomach that day and the smell kept making me sick. I had to stand up and move to the back and of course I couldn't explain what was wrong. It was so embarrassing. Maybe that's the man you're speaking of. After all, when you work with yeast all the time, the odor gets to stick to your clothes." She wrinkled her nose.

"You don't remember what he looked like?" said Baley.

"No," she replied, with decision.

"All right, then. Look, Jessie, I'm going to take you to your mother's. Bentley will stay with you, and none of you will leave the Section. Ben can stay away from school and I'll arrange to have meals sent in and the corridors around the apartment watched by the police."

"What about you?" quavered Jessie.

"I'll be in no danger."

"But how long?"

"I don't know. Maybe just a day or two." The words sounded hollow even to himself.

They were back in the motorway, Baley and R. Daneel, alone now. Baley's expression was dark with thought.

"It would seem to me," he said, "that we are faced with an organization built up on two levels. First, a ground level with no specific program, designed only to supply mass support for an eventual coup. Secondly, a much smaller elite dedicated to a well-planned program of action. It is this elite we must find. The comic-opera groups that Jessie spoke of can be ignored."

"All this," said R. Daneel, "follows, perhaps, if we can take Jessie's story at face value."

"I think," Baley said stiffly, "that Jessie's story can be accepted as completely true."

"So it would seem," said R. Daneel. "There is nothing about her cerebro-impulses that would indicate a pathological addiction to lying."

Baley turned an offended look upon the robot. "I should say not. And there will be no necessity to mention her name in our reports. Do you understand that?"

"If you wish it so, partner Elijah," said R. Daneel calmly, "but our report will then be neither complete nor accurate."

Baley said, "Well, maybe so, but no real harm will be done. She has come to us with whatever information she had and to mention her name will only put her in the police records. I do not want that to happen."

"In that case, certainly not, provided we are certain that nothing more remains to be found out."

"Nothing remains as far as she's concerned. My guarantee."

"Could you then explain why the word, Jezebel, the mere sound of a name, should lead her to abandon previous convictions and assume a new set? The motivation seems obscure."

They were traveling slowly through the curving, empty tunnel.

Baley said, "It is hard to explain. Jezebel is a rare name. It belonged once to a woman of very bad reputation. My wife treasured that fact. It gave her a vicarious feeling of wickedness and compensated for a life that was uniformly proper."

"Why should a law-abiding woman wish to feel wicked?"

Baley almost smiled. "Women are women, Daneel. Anyway, I did a very foolish thing. In a moment of irritation, I insisted that the historic Jezebel was not particularly wicked and was, if anything, a good wife. I've regretted that ever since.

"It turned out," he went on, "that I had made Jessie bitterly unhappy. I had spoiled something for her that couldn't be replaced. I suppose what followed was her way of revenge. I imagine she wished to punish me by engaging in activity of which she knew I wouldn't approve. I don't say the wish was a conscious one."

"Can a wish be anything but conscious? Is that not a contradiction in terms?"

Baley stared at R. Daneel and despaired at attempting to explain the unconscious mind. He said, instead, "Besides that, the Bible has a great influence on human thought and emotion."

"What is the Bible?"

For a moment Baley was surprised, and then was surprised at himself for having felt surprised. The Spacers, he knew, lived under a thoroughly mechanistic personal philosophy, and R. Daneel could know only what the Spacers knew; no more.

He said, curtly, "It is the sacred book of about half of Earth's population."

"I do not grasp the meaning here of the adjective."

"I mean that it is highly regarded. Various portions of it, when properly interpreted, contain a code of behavior which many men consider best suited to the ultimate happiness of mankind."

R. Daneel seemed to consider that. "Is this code incorporated into your laws?"

"I'm afraid not. The code doesn't lend itself to legal enforcement. It must be obeyed spontaneously by each individual out of a longing to do so. It is in a sense higher than any law can be."

"Higher than law? Is that not a contradiction in terms?"

Baley smiled wryly. "Shall I quote a portion of the Bible for you? Would you be curious to hear it?"

"Please do."

Baley let the car slow to a halt and for a few moments sat with his eyes closed, remembering. He would have liked to use the sonorous Middle English of the Medieval Bible, but to R. Daneel, Middle English would be gibberish.

He began, speaking almost casually in the words of the Modern Revision, as though he were telling a story of contemporary life, instead of dredging a tale out of Man's dimmest past:

" 'Jesus went to the mount of Olives, and at dawn returned to the temple. All the people came to him, and he sat down and preached to them. And the scribes and Pharisees brought to him a woman caught in adultery, and when they had placed her before him, they said to him, "Master, this woman was caught in adultery, in the very act. Now, Moses, in the law, commanded us to stone such offenders. What do you say?"

" 'They said this, hoping to trap him, that they might have grounds for accusations against him. But Jesus stooped down, and with his finger wrote on the ground, as though he had not heard them. But when they continued asking him, he stood up and said to them, "He that is without sin among you, let him first cast a stone at her."

" 'And again he stooped down and wrote on the ground. And those that heard this, being convicted by their own conscience, went away one by one, beginning with the oldest, down to the last: and Jesus was left alone, with the woman standing before him. When Jesus stood up and saw no one but the woman, he said to her. "Woman, where are your accusers? Has no one condemned you?"

" 'She said, "No one, Lord."

" 'And Jesus said to her, "Nor do I condemn you. Go, and sin no more." ' "

R. Daneel listened attentively. He said, "What is adultery?"

"That doesn't matter. It was a crime and at the time, the accepted punishment was stoning; that is, stones were thrown at the guilty one until she was killed."

"And the woman was guilty?"

"She was."

"Then why was she not stoned?"

"None of the accusers felt he could after Jesus's statement. The story is meant to show that there is something even higher than the justice which you have been filled with. There is a human impulse known as mercy; a human act known as forgiveness."

"I am not acquainted with those words, partner Elijah."

"I know," muttered Baley. "I know."

He started the squad car with a jerk and let it tear forward savagely. He was pressed back against the cushions of the seat.

"Where are we going?" asked R. Daneel.

"To Yeast-town," said Baley, "to get the truth out of Francis Clousarr, conspirator."

"You have a method for doing this, Elijah?"

"Not I, exactly. But you have, Daneel. A simple one."

They sped onward.

CHAPTER FIFTEEN

ARREST OF A CONSPIRATOR

Baley could sense the vague aroma of Yeast-town growing stronger, more pervasive. He did not find it as unpleasant as some did; Jessie, for instance. He even liked it, rather. It had pleasant connotations.

Every time he smelled raw yeast, the alchemy of sense perception threw him more than three decades into the past. He was a ten-year-old again, visiting his Uncle Boris, who was a yeast farmer. Uncle Boris always had a little supply of yeast delectables: small cookies, chocolaty things filled with sweet liquid, hard confections in the shape of cats and dogs. Young as he was, he knew that Uncle Boris shouldn't really have had them to give away and he always ate them very quietly, sitting in a corner with his back to the center of the room. He would eat them quickly for fear of being caught.

They tasted all the better for that.

Poor Uncle Boris! He had an accident and died. They never told him exactly how, and he had cried bitterly because he thought Uncle Boris had been arrested for smuggling yeast out of the plant. He expected to be arrested and executed himself. Years later, he poked carefully through police files and found the truth. Uncle Boris had fallen beneath the treads of a transport. It was a disillusioning ending to a romantic myth.

Yet the myth would always arise in his mind, at least momentarily, at the whiff of raw yeast.

Yeast-town was not the official name of any part of New York City. It could be found in no gazetteer and on no official map. What was called Yeast-town in popular speech was, to the Post Office, merely the boroughs of Newark, New Brunswick, and Trenton. It was a broad strip across what was once Medieval New Jersey, dotted with residential areas, particularly in Newark Center and Trenton Center, but given over mostly to the many-layered farms in which a thousand varieties of yeast grew and multiplied.

One fifth of the City's population worked in the yeast farms; another fifth worked in the subsidary industries. Beginning with the mountains of wood and coarse cellulose that were dragged into the City from the tangled forests of the Alleghenies, through the vats of acid that hydrolyzed it to glucose, the carloads of niter and phosphate rock that were the most important additives, down to the jars of organics, supplied by the chemical laboratories – it all came to only one thing, yeast and more yeast.

Without yeast, six of Earth's eight billions would starve in a year.

Baley felt cold at the thought. Three days before the possibility existed as deeply as it did now, but three days before it would never have occurred to him.

They whizzed out of the motorway through an exit on the Newark outskirts. The thinly populated avenues, flanked on either side by the featureless blocks that were the farms, offered little to act as a brake on their speed.

"What time is it, Daneel?" asked Baley.

"Sixteen-oh-five," replied R. Daneel.

"Then he'll be at work, if he's on day shift."

Baley parked the squad car in a delivery recess and froze the controls.

"This is New York Yeast then, Elijah?" asked the robot.

"Part of it," said Baley.

They entered into a corridor flanked by a double row of offices. A receptionist at a bend in the corridor was instantly smiles. "Whom do you wish to see?"

Baley opened his wallet. "Police. Is there a Francis Clousarr working for New York Yeast?"

The girl looked perturbed. "I can check."

She connected her switchboard through a line plainly marked "Personnel," and her lips moved slightly, though no sound could be heard.

Baley was no stranger to the throat phones that translated the small movements of the larynx into words. He said, "Speak up, please. Let me hear you."

Her words became audible, but consisted only of, ". . . he says he's a policeman, sir."

A dark, well-dressed man came out a door. He had a thin mustache and his hairline was beginning to retreat. He smiled whitely, and said, "I'm Prescott of Personnel. What's the trouble, Officer?"

Baley stared at him coldly and Prescott's smile grew strained.

Prescott said, "I just don't want to upset the workers. They're touchy about the police."

Baley said, "Tough, isn't it? Is Clousarr in the building now?"

"Yes, Officer."

"Let's have a rod then. And if he's gone when we get there, I'll be speaking to you again."

The other's smile was quite dead. He muttered, "I'll get you a rod, Officer."

The guide rod was set for Department CG, Section 2. What that meant in factory terminology, Baley didn't know. He didn't have to. The rod was an inconspicuous thing which could be palmed in the hand. Its tip warmed gently when lined up in the direction for which it was set, cooled quickly when turned away. The warmth increased as the final goal was approached.

To an amateur, the guide rod was almost useless, with its quick little differences of heat content, but few City dwellers were amateurs at this particular game. One of the most popular and perennial of the games of childhood was hide-and-seek through the school-level corridors with the use of toy guide rods. ("Hot or Not, Let Hot-Spot Spot. Hot-Spot Guide Rods Are Keen.")

Baley had found his way through hundreds of massive piles by guide rod, and he could follow the shortest course with one of them in his hand as though it had been mapped out for him.

When he stepped into a large and brilliantly lit room after ten minutes, the guide rod's tip was almost hot.

Baley said to the worker nearest the door, "Francis Clousarr here?"

The worker jerked his head. Baley walked in the indicated direction. The odor of yeast was sharply penetrating, despite the laboring air pumps whose humming made a steady background noise.

A man had risen at the other end of the room, and was taking off an apron. He was of moderate height, his face deeply lined despite his comparative youth, and his hair just beginning to grizzle. He had large, knobby hands which he wiped slowly on a celltex towel.

"I'm Francis Clousarr," he said.

Baley looked briefly at R. Daneel. The robot nodded.

"Okay," said Baley. "Anywhere here we can talk?"

"Maybe," said Clousarr slowly, "but it's just about the end of my shift. How about tomorrow?"

"Lots of hours between now and tomorrow. Let's make it now." Baley opened his wallet and palmed it at the yeast farmer.

But Clousarr's hands did not waver in their somber wiping motions. He said, coolly, "I don't know the system in the Police Department, but around here you get tight eating hours with no leeway. I eat at 17:00 to 17:45, or I don't eat."

"It's all right," said Baley. "I'll arrange to have your supper brought to you."

"Well, well," said Clousarr, joylessly. "Just like an aristocrat, or a C-class copper. What's next? Private bath?"

"You just answer questions, Clousarr," said Baley, "and save your big jokes for your girl friend. Where can we talk?"

"If you want to talk, how about the balance room? Suit yourself about that. Me, I've got nothing to say."

Baley thumbed Clousarr into the balance room. It was square and antiseptically white, air-conditioned independently of the larger room (and more efficiently), and with its walls lined with delicate electronic balances, glassed off and manipulable by field forces only. Baley had used cheaper models in his college days. One make, which he recognized, could weigh a mere billion atoms.

Clousarr said, "I don't expect anyone will be in here for a while."

Baley grunted, then turned to Daneel and said, "Would you step out and have a meal sent up here? And if you don't mind, wait outside for it."

He watched R. Daneel leave, then said to Clousarr, "You're a chemist?"

"I'm a zymologist, if you don't mind."

"What's the difference?"

Clousarr looked lofty. "A chemist is a soup-pusher, a stink-operator. A zymologist is a man who helps keep a few billion people alive. I'm a yeast culture specialist."

"All right," said Baley.

But Clousarr went on, "This laboratory keeps New York Yeast going. There isn't one day, not one damned hour, that we haven't got cultures of every strain of yeast in the company growing in our kettles. We check and adjust the food factor requirements. We make sure it's breeding true. We twist the genetics, start the new strains and weed them out, sort out their properties and mold them again.

"When New Yorkers started getting strawberries out of season a couple of years back, those weren't strawberries, fella. Those were a special high-sugar yeast culture with true-bred color and just a dash of flavor additive. It was developed right here in this room.

"Twenty years ago *Saccharomyces olei Benedictae* was just a scrub strain with a lousy taste of tallow and good for nothing. It still tastes of tallow, but its fat content has been pushed up from 15 per cent to 87 per cent. If you used the expressway today, just remember that it's greased strictly with *S. O. Benedictae, Strain AG*—7. Developed right here in this room.

"So don't call me a chemist. I'm a zymologist."

Despite himself, Baley retreated before the fierce pride of the other.

He said abruptly, "Where were you last night between the hours of eighteen and twenty?"

Clousarr shrugged. "Walking. I like to take a little walk after dinner."

"You visited friends? Or a subetheric?"

"No. Just walked."

Baley's lips tightened. A visit to the subetherics would have involved a notch in Clousarr's ration plack. A meeting with a friend would have involved naming a man or woman, and a cross check.

"No one saw you, then?"

"Maybe someone did. I don't know. Not that I know of, though."

"What about the night before last?"

"Same thing."

"You have no alibi then for either night?"

"If I had done anything criminal, Officer, I'd have one. What do I need an alibi for?"

Baley didn't answer. He consulted his little book. "You were up before the magistrate once. Inciting to riot."

"All right. One of the R things pushed past me and I tripped him up. Is that inciting a riot?"

"The court thought so. You were convicted and fined."

"That ends it, doesn't it? Or do you want to fine me again?"

"Night before last, there was a near riot at a shoe department in the Bronx. You were seen there."

"By whom?"

Baley said, "It was at mealtime for you here. Did you eat the evening meal night before last?"

Clousarr hesitated, then shook his head. "Upset stomach. Yeast gets you that way sometimes. Even an old-timer."

"Last night, there was a near riot in Williamsburg and you were seen *there*."

"By whom?"

"Do you deny you were present on both occasions?"

"You're not giving me anything to deny. Exactly where did these things happen and who says he saw me?"

Baley stared at the zymologist levelly. "I think you know exactly what I'm talking about. I think you're an important man in an unregistered Medievalist organization."

"I can't stop you from thinking, Officer, but thinking isn't evidence. Maybe you know that." Clousarr was grinning.

"Maybe," said Baley, his long face stony, "I can get a little truth out of you right now."

Baley stepped to the door of the balance room and opened it. He said to R. Daneel, who was waiting stolidly outside, "Has Clousarr's evening meal arrived?"

"It is coming now, Elijah."

"Bring it in, will you, Daneel?"

R. Daneel entered a moment later with a metal compartment tray.

"Put it down in front of Mr. Clousarr, Daneel," said Baley. He sat down on one of the stools lining the balance wall, legs crossed, one shoe swinging rhythmically. He watched Clousarr edge stiffly away as R. Daneel placed the tray on a stool near the zymologist.

"Mr. Clousarr," said Baley. "I want to introduce you to my partner, Daneel Olivaw."

Daneel put out his hand and said, "How do you do, Francis."

Clousarr said nothing. He made no move to grasp Daneel's extended hand. Daneel maintained his position and Clousarr began to redden.

Baley said softly, "You are being rude, Mr. Clousarr. Are you too proud to shake hands with a policeman?"

Clousarr muttered, "If you don't mind, I'm hungry." He unfolded a pocket fork out of a clasp knife he took from his pocket and sat down, eyes bent on his meal.

Baley said, "Daneel, I think our friend is offended by your cold attitude. You are not angry with him, are you?"

"Not at all, Elijah," said R. Daneel.

"Then show that there are no hard feelings. Put your arm about his shoulder."

"I will be glad to," said R. Daneel, and stepped forward.

Clousarr put down his fork. "What is this? What's going on?"

R. Daneel, unruffled, put out his arm.

Clousarr swung backhanded, wildly, knocking R. Daneel's arm to one side. "Damn it, don't touch me."

He jumped up and away, the tray of food tipping and hitting the floor in a messy clatter.

Baley, hard-eyed, nodded curtly to R. Daneel, who thereupon continued a stolid advance toward the retreating zymologist. Baley stepped in front of the door.

Clousarr yelled, "Keep that thing off me."

"That's no way to speak," said Baley with equanimity. "The man's my partner."

"You mean he's a damned robot," shrieked Clousarr.

"Get away from him, Daneel," said Baley promptly.

R. Daneel stepped back and stood quietly against the door just behind Baley. Clousarr, panting harshly, fists clenched, faced Baley.

Baley said, "All right, smart boy. What makes you think Daneel's a robot?"

"Anyone can tell!"

"We'll leave that to a judge. Meanwhile, I think we want you at headquarters, Clousarr. We'd like to have you explain exactly how you knew Daneel was a robot. And lots more, mister, lots more. Daneel, step outside and get through to the Commissioner. He'll be at his home by now. Tell him to come down to the office. Tell him I have a fellow who can't wait to be questioned."

R. Daneel stepped out.

Baley said, "What makes your wheels go round, Clousarr?"

"I want a lawyer."

"You'll get one. Meanwhile, suppose you tell me what makes you Medievalists tick?"

Clousarr looked away in a determined silence.

Baley said, "Jehoshaphat, man, we know all about you and your organization. I'm not bluffing. Just tell me for my own curiosity: What do you medievalists *want*?"

"Back to the soil," said Clousarr in a stifled voice. "That's simple, isn't it?"

"It's simple to say," said Baley. "But it isn't simple to do. How's the soil going to feed eight billions?"

"Did I say back to the soil overnight? Or in a year? Or in a hundred years? Step by step, Mister Policeman. It doesn't matter how long it takes, but let's get started out of these caves we live in..Let's get out into the fresh air."

"Have *you* ever been out into the fresh air?"

Clousarr squirmed. "All right, so I'm ruined, too. But the children aren't ruined yet. There are babies being born continuously. Get them out, for God's sake. Let them have space and open air and sun. If we've got to, we'll cut our population little by little, too."

"Backward, in other words, to an impossible past." Baley did not really know why he was arguing, except for the strange fever that was burning in his own veins. "Back to the seed, to the egg, to the womb. Why not move forward? Don't cut Earth's population. Use it for export. Go back to the soil, but go back to the soil of other planets. Colonize!"

Clousarr laughed harshly. "And make more Outer Worlds? More Spacers?"

"We won't. The Outer Worlds were settled by Earthmen who came from a planet that did not have Cities, by Earthmen who were individualists and materialists. Those qualities were carried to an unhealthy extreme. We can now colonize out of a society that has built co-operation, if anything, too far. Now environment and tradition can interact to form a new middle way, distinct from either old Earth or the Outer Worlds. Something newer and better."

He was parroting Dr. Fastolfe, he knew, but it was coming out as though he himself had been thinking of it for years.

Clousarr said, "Nuts! Colonize desert worlds with a world of our own at our fingertips? What fools would try?"

"Many. And they wouldn't be fools. There'd be robots to help."

"No," said Clousarr, fiercely. "Never! No robots!"

"Why not, for the love of Heaven? I don't like them, either, but I'm not going to knife myself for the sake of a prejudice. What are we afraid of in robots? If you want my guess, it's a sense of inferiority. We, all of us, feel inferior to the Spacers and hate it. We've got to feel superior somehow, somewhere, to make up for it, and it kills us that we can't at least feel superior to robots. They seem to be better than us — only they're *not*. That's the damned irony of it."

Baley felt his blood heating as he spoke. "Look at this Daneel I've been with for over two days. He's taller than I am, stronger, handsomer. He looks like a Spacer, in fact. He's got a better memory and knows more facts. He doesn't have to sleep or eat. He's not troubled by sickness or panic or love or guilt.

"But he's a machine. I can do anything I want to him, the way I can to that microbalance right there. If I slam the microbalance, it won't hit me back. Neither will Daneel. I can order him to take a blaster to himself and he'll do it.

"We can't ever build a robot that will be even as good as a human being in anything that counts, let alone better. We can't create a robot with a sense of beauty or a sense of ethics or a sense of religion. There's no way we can raise a positronic brain one inch above the level of perfect materialism.

"We can't, damn it, we can't. Not as long as we don't understand what makes our own brains tick. Not as long as things exist that science can't measure. What *is* beauty, or goodness, or art, or love, or God? We're forever teetering on the brink of the unknowable, and trying to understand what can't be understood. It's what makes us men.

"A robot's brain must be finite or it can't be built. It must be calculated to the final decimal place so that it has an end.

Jehoshaphat, what are you afraid of? A robot can look like Daneel, he can look like a god, and be no more human than a lump of wood is. Can't you see that?"

Clousarr had tried to interrupt several times and failed against Baley's furious torrent. Now, when Baley paused in sheer emotional exhaustion, he said weakly, "Copper turned philosopher. What do you know?"

R. Daneel re-entered.

Baley looked at him and frowned, partly with the anger that had not yet left him, partly with new annoyance.

He said, "What kept you?"

R. Daneel said, "I had trouble in reaching Commissioner Enderby, Elijah. It turned out he was still at his office."

Baley looked at his watch. "*Now?* What for?"

"There is a certain confusion at the moment. A corpse has been discovered in the Department."

"*What!* For God's sake, who?"

"The errand boy, R. Sammy."

Baley gagged. He stared at the robot and said in an outraged voice, "I thought you said a corpse."

R. Daneel amended smoothly, "A robot with a completely deactivated brain, if you prefer."

Clousarr laughed suddenly and Baley turned on him, saying huskily, "Nothing out of you! Understand?" Deliberately, he unlimbered his blaster. Clousarr was very silent.

Baley said, "Well, what of it? R. Sammy blew a fuse. So what?"

"Commissioner Enderby was evasive, Elijah, but while he did not say so outright, my impression is that the Commissioner believes R. Sammy to have been deliberately deactivated."

Then, as Baley absorbed that silently, R. Daneel added gravely, "Or, if you prefer the phrase – murdered."

CHAPTER SIXTEEN

QUESTIONS CONCERNING A MOTIVE

Baley replaced his blaster, but kept his hand unobtrusively upon its butt.

He said, "Walk ahead of us, Clousarr, to Seventeenth Street Exit B."

Clousarr said, "I haven't eaten."

"Tough," said Baley, impatiently. "There's your meal on the floor where you dumped it."

"I have a right to eat."

"You'll eat in detention, or you'll miss a meal. You won't starve. Get going."

All three were silent as they threaded the maze of New York Yeast, Clousarr moving in advance, Baley right behind him, and R. Daneel in the rear.

It was after Baley and R. Daneel had checked out at the receptionist's desk, after Clousarr had drawn a leave of absence and requested that a man be sent in to clean up the balance room, after they were out in the open just to one side of the parked squad car, that Clousarr said, "Just a minute."

He hung back, turned toward R. Daneel, and, before Baley could make a move to stop him, stepped forward and swung his open hand full against the robot's cheek.

"What the devil," cried Baley, snatching violently at Clousarr.

Clousarr did not resist the plain-clothes man's grasp. "It's all right. I'll go. I just wanted to see for myself." He was grinning.

R. Daneel, having faded with the slap, but not having escaped it entirely, gazed quietly at Clousarr. There was no reddening of his cheek, no mark of any blow.

He said, "That was a dangerous action, Francis. Had I not moved backward, you might easily have damaged your hand. As it is, I regret that I must have caused you pain."

Clousarr laughed.

Baley said, "Get in, Clousarr. You, too, Daneel. Right in the back seat with him. And make sure he doesn't move. I don't care if it means breaking his arm. That's an order."

"What about the First Law?" mocked Clousarr.

"I think Daneel is strong enough and fast enough to stop you without hurting you, but it might do you good to have an arm or two broken at that."

Baley got behind the wheel and the squad car gathered speed. The empty wind ruffled his hair and Clousarr's, but R. Daneel's remained smoothly in place.

R. Daneel said quietly to Clousarr, "Do you fear robots for the sake of your job, Mr. Clousarr?"

Baley could not turn to see Clousarr's expression, but he was certain it would be a hard and rigid mirror of detestation, that he would be sitting stiffly apart, as far as he might, from R. Daneel.

Clousarr's voice said, "And my kids' jobs. And everyone's kids."

"Surely adjustments are possible," said the robot. "If your children, for instance, were to accept training for emigration –"

Clousarr broke in. "You, too? The policeman talked about emigration. He's got good robot training. Maybe he *is* a robot."

Baley growled, "That's enough, you!"

R. Daneel said, evenly, "A training school for emigrants would involve security, guaranteed classification, an assured career. If you are concerned over your children, that is something to consider."

"I wouldn't take anything from a robot, or a Spacer, or any of your trained hyenas in the Government."

That was all. The silence of the motorway engulfed them and there was only the soft whirr of the squad-car motor and the hiss of its wheels on the pavement.

Back at the Department, Baley signed a detention certificate for Clousarr and left him in appropriate hands. Following that, he and R. Daneel took the motospiral up the levels to Headquarters.

R. Daneel showed no surprise that they had not taken the elevators, nor did Baley expect him to. He was becoming used to the robot's queer mixture of ability and submissiveness and tended to leave him out of his calculations. The elevator was the logical method of leaping the vertical gap between Detention and Headquarters. The long moving stairway that was the motospiral was useful only for short climbs or drops of two or three levels at most. People of all sorts and varieties of administrative occupation stepped on and then off in less than a minute. Only Baley and R. Daneel remained on continuously, moving upward in a slow and stolid measure.

Baley felt that he needed the time. It was only minutes at best, but up in Headquarters he would be thrown violently into another phase of the problem and he wanted a rest. He wanted time to think and orient himself. Slowly as it moved, the motospiral went too quickly to satisfy him.

R. Daneel said, "It seems then we will not be questioning Clousarr just yet."

"He'll keep," said Baley, irritably. "Let's find out what the R. Sammy thing is all about." He added in a mutter, far more to himself than to R. Daneel, "It can't be independent; there must be a connection."

R. Daneel said, "It is a pity. Clousarr's cerebric qualities –"

"What about them?"

"They have changed in a strange way. What was it that took place between the two of you in the balance room while I was not present?"

Baley said, absently, "The only thing I did was to preach at him. I passed along the gospel according to St. Fastolfe."

"I do not understand you, Elijah."

Baley sighed and said, "Look, I tried to explain that Earth might as well make use of robots and get its population surplus onto other planets. I tried to knock some of the Medievalist hogwash out of his head. God knows why. I've never thought of myself as the missionary type. Anyway, that's all that happened."

"I see. Well, that makes some sense. Perhaps that can be fitted in. Tell me, Elijah, what did you tell him about robots?"

"You really want to know? I told him robots were simply machines. That was the gospel according to St. Gerrigel. There are any number of gospels, I think."

"Did you by any chance tell him that one could strike a robot without fear of a return blow, much as one could strike any other mechanical object?"

"Except a punching bag, I suppose. Yes. But what made you guess that?" Baley looked curiously at the robot.

"It fits the cerebric changes," said R. Daneel, "and it explains his blow to my face just after we left the factory. He must have been thinking of what you said, so he simultaneously tested your statement, worked off his aggressive feelings, and had the pleasure of seeing me placed in what seemed to him a position of inferiority. In order to be so motivated and allowing for the delta variations in his quintic . . ."

He paused a long moment and said, "Yes, it is quite interesting, and now I believe I can form a self-consistent whole of the data."

Headquarters level was approaching. Baley said, "What time is it?"

He thought, pettishly: Nuts, I could look at my watch and take less time that way.

But he knew why he asked him, nevertheless. The motive was not so different from Clousarr's in punching R. Daneel. To give the robot a trivial order that he must fulfill emphasized his roboticity and, contrariwise, Baley's humanity.

Baley thought: We're all brothers. Under the skin, over it, everywhere. Jehoshaphat!

R. Daneel said, "Twenty-ten."

They stepped off the motospiral and for a few seconds Baley had the usual queer sensation that went with the necessary adjustment to non-motion after long minutes of steady movement.

He said, "And I haven't eaten. Damn this job, anyway."

Baley saw and heard Commissioner Enderby through the open door of his office. The common room was empty, as though it had been wiped clean, and Enderby's voice rang through it with unusual hollowness. His round face looked bare and weak without its glasses, which he held in his hand, while he mopped his smooth forehead with a flimsy paper napkin.

His eyes caught Baley just as the latter reached the door and his voice rose into a petulant tenor.

"Good God, Baley, where the devil were you?"

Baley shrugged off the remark and said, "What's doing? Where's the night staff?" and then caught sight of the second person in the office with the Commissioner.

He said, blankly, "Dr. Gerrigel!"

The gray-haired roboticist returned the involuntary greeting by nodding briefly. "I am glad to see you again, Mr. Baley."

The Commissioner readjusted his glasses and stared at Baley through them. "The entire staff is being questioned downstairs. Signing statements. I was going mad trying to find you. It looked queer, your being away."

"*My* being away!" cried Baley, strenuously.

"Anybody's being away. Someone in the Department did it and there's going to be hell to pay for that. What an unholy mess! What an unholy, *rotten* mess!"

He raised his hands as though in expostulation to heaven and as he did so, his eyes fell on R. Daneel.

Baley thought sardonically: First time you've looked Daneel in the face. Take a good look, Julius!

The Commissioner said in a subdued voice, "*He'll* have to sign a statement. Even *I've* had to do it. I!"

Baley said, "Look, Commissioner, what makes you so sure that R. Sammy didn't blow a gasket all by himself? What makes it deliberate destruction?"

The Commissioner sat down heavily. "Ask him," he said, and pointed to Dr. Gerrigel.

Dr. Gerrigel cleared his throat. "I scarcely know how to go about this, Mr. Baley. I take it from your expression that you are surprised to see me."

"Moderately," admitted Baley.

"Well, I was in no real hurry to return to Washington and my visits to New York are few enough to make me wish to linger. And what's more important, I had a growing feeling that it would be criminal for me to leave the City without having made at least one more effort to be allowed to analyze your fascinating robot, whom, by the way," (he looked very eager) "I see you have with you."

Baley stirred restlessly. "That's quite impossible."

The roboticist looked disappointed. "Now, yes. Perhaps later?"

Baley's long face remained woodenly unresponsive.

Dr. Gerrigel went on. "I called you, but you weren't in and no one knew where you could be located. I asked for the Commissioner and he asked me to come to headquarters and wait for you."

The Commissioner interposed quickly. "I thought it might be important. I knew you wanted to see the man."

Baley nodded. "Thanks."

Dr. Gerrigel said, "Unfortunately my guide rod was somewhat off, or perhaps in my overanxiety I misjudged its temperature. In either case I took a wrong turning and found myself in a small room –"

The Commissioner interrupted again. "One of the photographic supply rooms, Lije."

"Yes," said Dr. Gerrigel. "And in it was the prone figure of what was obviously a robot. It was quite clear to me after a brief examination that he was irreversibly deactivated. Dead, you might say. Nor was it very difficult to determine the cause of the deactivation."

"What was it?" asked Baley.

"In the robot's partly clenched right fist," said Dr. Gerrigel, "was a shiny ovoid about two inches long and half an inch wide with a mica window at one end. The fist was in contact with his skull as though the robot's last act had been to touch his head. The thing he was holding was an alpha-sprayer. You know what they are, I suppose?"

Baley nodded. He needed neither dictionary nor handbook to be told what an alpha-sprayer was. He had handled several in his lab courses in physics: a lead-alloy casing with a narrow pit dug into it longitudinally, at the bottom of which was a fragment of a plutonium salt. The pit was capped with a sliver of mica, which was transparent to alpha particles. In that one direction, hard radiation sprayed out.

An alpha-sprayer had many uses, but killing robots was not one of them, not a legal one, at least.

Baley said, "He held it to his head mica first, I take it."

Dr. Gerrigel said, "Yes, and his positronic brain paths were immediately randomized. Instant death, so to speak."

Baley turned to the pale Commissioner. "No mistake? It really *was* an alpha-sprayer?"

The Commissioner nodded, his plump lips thrust out. "Absolutely. The counters could spot it ten feet away. Photographic film in the storeroom was fogged. Cut and dried."

He seemed to brood about it for a moment or two, then said abruptly, "Dr. Gerrigel, I'm afraid you'll have to stay in the

City a day or two until we can get your evidence down on wire-film. I'll have you escorted to a room. You don't mind being under guard, I hope?"

Dr. Gerrigel said nervously, "Do you think it's necessary?"

"It's safer."

Dr. Gerrigel, seeming quite abstracted, shook hands all around, even with R. Daneel, and left.

The Commissioner heaved a sigh. "It's one of us, Lije. That's what bothers me. No outsider would come into the Department just to knock off a robot. Plenty of them outside where it's safer. And it had to be somebody who could pick up an alpha-sprayer. They're hard to get hold of."

R. Daneel spoke, his cool, even voice cutting through the agitated words of the Commissioner. He said, "But what is the motive for this murder?"

The Commissioner glanced at R. Daneel with obvious distaste, then looked away. "We're human, too. I suppose policemen can't get to like robots any more than anyone else can. He's gone now and maybe it's a relief to somebody. He used to annoy you considerably, Lije, remember?"

"That is scarcely murder motive," said R. Daneel.

"No," agreed Baley, with decision.

"It isn't murder," said the Commissioner. "It's property damage. Let's keep our legal terms straight. It's just that it was done inside the Department. Anywhere else it would be nothing. Nothing. Now it could be a first-class scandal. Lije!"

"Yes?"

"When did you last see R. Sammy?"

Baley said, "R. Daneel spoke to R. Sammy after lunch. I should judge it was about 13:30. He arranged to have us use your office, Commissioner."

"My office? What for?"

"I wanted to talk over the case with R. Daneel in moderate privacy. You weren't in, so your office was an obvious place."

"I see." The Commissioner looked dubious, but let the matter ride. "You didn't see him yourself?"

"No, but I heard his voice perhaps an hour afterward."

"Are you sure it was he?"

"Perfectly."

"That would be about 14:30?"

"Or a little sooner."

The Commissioner bit his pudgy lower lip thoughtfully. "Well, that settles one thing."

"It does?"

"Yes. The boy, Vincent Barrett, was here today. Did you know that?"

"Yes. But, Commissioner, he wouldn't do anything like this."

The Commissioner lifted his eyes to Baley's face. "Why not? R. Sammy took his job away. I can understand how he feels. There would be a tremendous sense of injustice. He would want a certain revenge. Wouldn't you? But the fact is that he left the building at 14:00 and you heard R. Sammy alive at 14:30. Of course, he might have given the alpha-sprayer to R. Sammy before he left with instructions not to use it for an hour, but then where could he have gotten an alpha-sprayer? It doesn't bear thinking of. Let's get back to R. Sammy. When you spoke to him at 14:30, what did he say?"

Baley hesitated a perceptible moment, then said carefully, "I don't remember. We left shortly afterward."

"Where did you go?"

"Yeast-town, eventually. I want to talk about that, by the way."

"Later. Later." The Commissioner rubbed his chin. "Jessie was in today, I noticed. I mean, we were checking on all visitors today and I just happened to see her name."

"She was here," said Baley, coldly.

"What for?"

"Personal family matters."

"She'll have to be questioned as a pure formality."

"I understand police routine, Commissioner. Incidentally, what about the alpha-sprayer itself? Has it been traced?"

"Oh, yes. It came from one of the power plants."

"How do they account for having lost it?"

"They don't. They have no idea. But look, Lije, except for routine statements, this has nothing to do with you. You stick to your case. It's just that ... Well, you stick to the Spacetown investigation."

Baley said, "May I give my routine statements later, Commissioner? The fact is, I haven't eaten yet."

Commissioner Enderby's glassed eyes turned full on Baley.

"By all means get something to eat. But stay inside the Department, will you? Your partner's right, though, Lije" – he seemed to avoid addressing R. Daneel or using his name – "it's the motive we need. The motive."

Baley felt suddenly frozen.

Something outside himself, something completely alien, took up the events of this day and the day before and the day before and juggled them. Once again pieces began to dovetail; a pattern began to form.

He said, "Which power plant did the alpha-sprayer come from, Commissioner?"

"The Williamsburg plant. Why?"

"Nothing. Nothing."

The last word Baley heard the Commissioner mutter as he strode out of the office, with R. Daneel immediately behind him, was, "Motive. Motive."

Baley ate a sparse meal in the small and infrequently used Department lunchroom. He devoured the stuffed tomato on lettuce without being entirely aware of its nature and for a second or so after he had gulped down the last mouthful his fork still slithered aimlessly over the slick cardboard of his plate, searching automatically for something that was no longer there.

He became aware of that and put down his fork with a muffled, "Jehoshaphat!"

He said, "Daneel!"

R. Daneel had been sitting at another table, as though he wished to leave the obviously preoccupied Baley in peace, or as though he required privacy himself. Baley was past caring which.

Daneel stood up, moved to Baley's table, and sat down again. "Yes, partner Elijah?"

Baley did not look at him. "Daneel, I'll need your co-operation."

"In what way?"

"They will question Jessie and myself. That is certain. Let me answer the questions in my own way. Do you understand?"

"I understand what you say, of course. Nevertheless, if I am asked a direct question, how is it possible for me to say anything but what is so?"

"*If* you are asked a direct question, that's another matter. .I ask only that you don't volunteer information. You can do that, can't you?"

"I believe so, Elijah, provided it does not appear that I am hurting a human being by remaining silent."

Baley said, grimly, "You will hurt *me* if you don't. I assure you of that."

"I do not quite understand your point of view, partner Elijah. Surely the matter of R. Sammy cannot concern you."

"No? It all centers about motive, doesn't it? You've questioned the motive. The Commissioner questioned it. I do, for that matter. Why should anyone want to kill R. Sammy? Mind you, it's not just a question of who would want to smash up robots in general. Any Earthman, practically, would want to do that. The question is, who would want to single out R. Sammy. Vincent Barrett might, but the Commissioner said he couldn't get hold of an alpha-sprayer, and he's right. We have to look somewhere else, and it so happens that one other person has a motive. It glares out. It yells. It stinks to top level."

"Who is the person, Elijah?"

And Baley said, softly, "I am, Daneel."

R. Daneel's expressionless face did not change under the impact of the statement. He merely shook his head.

Baley said, "You don't agree. My wife came to the office today. They know that already. The Commissioner is even curious. If I weren't a personal friend, he wouldn't have stopped his questioning so soon. Now they'll find out why. That's certain. She was part of a conspiracy; a foolish and harmless one, but a conspiracy just the same. And a policeman can't afford to have his wife mixed up with anything like that. It would be to my obvious interest to see that the matter was hushed up.

"Well, who knew about it? You and I, of course, and Jessie — and R. Sammy. He saw her in a state of panic. When he told her that we had left orders not to be disturbed, she must have lost control. You saw the way she was when she first came in."

R. Daneel said, "It is unlikely that she said anything incriminating to him."

"That may be so. But I'm reconstructing the case the way they will. They'll say she did. There's my motive. I killed him to keep him quiet."

"They will not think so."

"They *will* think so. The murder was arranged deliberately in order to throw suspicion on me. Why use an alpha-sprayer? It's a rather rísky way. It's hard to get and it can be traced. I think that those were the very reasons it *was* used. The murderer even ordered R. Sammy to go into the photographic supply room and kill himself there. It seems obvious to me that the reason for that was to have the method of murder unmistakable. Even if everyone was so infantile as not to recognize the alpha-sprayer immediately, someone would be bound to notice fogged photographic film in fairly short order."

"How does that all relate to you, Elijah?"

Baley grinned tightly, his long face completely devoid of humor. "Very neatly. The alpha-sprayer was taken from the Williamsburg power plant. You and I passed through the Williamsburg power plant yesterday. We were seen, and the fact will come out. That gives me opportunity to get the weapon as well as motive for the crime. And it may turn out that we were the last ones to see or hear R. Sammy alive, except for the real murderer, of course."

"I was with you in the power plant and I can testify that you did not have the opportunity to steal an alpha-sprayer."

"Thanks," said Baley sadly, "but you're a robot and your testimony will be invalid."

"The Commissioner is your friend. He will listen."

"The Commissioner has a job to keep, and he already is a bit uneasy about me. There's only one chance of saving myself from this very nasty situation."

"Yes?"

"I ask myself, *why* am I being framed? Obviously to get rid of me. But why? Again, obviously, because I am dangerous to someone. I am doing my best to be dangerous to whoever killed Dr. Sarton in Spacetown. That might mean the Medievalists, of course, or at least, the inner group that would know I had passed through the power plant; at least one of them might have followed me along the strips that far, even though you thought we had lost them.

"So the chances are that if I find the murderer of Dr. Sarton, I find the man or men who are trying to get me out of the way. If I think it through, if I crack the case, if I can only crack it, I'll be safe. And Jessie. I couldn't stand to have her . . . But I don't have much time." His fist clenched and unclenched spasmodically. "I don't have much time."

Baley looked at R. Daneel's chiseled face with a sudden burning hope. Whatever the creature was, he was strong and faithful, animated by no selfishness. What more could you ask of any friend? Baley needed a friend and he was in no mood to cavil at the fact that a gear replaced a blood vessel in this particular one.

But R. Daneel was shaking his head.

The robot said, "I am sorry, Elijah" – there was no trace of sorrow on his face, of course – "but I anticipated none of this. Perhaps my action was to your harm. I am sorry if the general good requires that."

"What general good?" stammered Baley.

"I have been in communication with Dr. Fastolfe."

"Jehoshaphat! When?"

"While you were eating."

Baley's lips tightened.

"Well?" he managed to say. "What happened?"

"You will have to clear yourself of suspicion of the murder of R. Sammy through some means other than the investigation of the murder of my designer, Dr. Sarton. Our people at Spacetown, as a result of my information, have decided to bring that investigation to an end, as of today, and to begin plans for leaving Spacetown and Earth."

CHAPTER SEVENTEEN

CONCLUSION OF A PROJECT

Baley looked at his watch with something approaching detachment. It was 21:45. In two and a quarter hours it would be midnight. He had been awake since before six and had been under tension now for two and a half days. A vague sense of unreality pervaded everything.

He kept his voice painfully steady as he reached for his pipe and for the little bag that held his precious crumbs of tobacco. He said, "What's it all about, Daneel?"

R. Daneel said, "Do you not understand? Is it not obvious?"

Baley said, patiently, "I do not understand. It is not obvious."

"We are here," said the robot, "and by we, I mean our people at Spacetown, to break the shell surrounding Earth and force its people into new expansion and colonization."

"I know that. Please don't labor the point."

"I must, since it is the essential one. If we were anxious to exact punishment for the murder of Dr. Sarton, it was not that in doing so we expected to bring Dr. Sarton back to life, you understand; it was only that failure to do so would strengthen the position of our home planet politicians who are against the very idea of Spacetown."

"But now," said Baley, with sudden violence, "you say you're getting ready to go home of your own accord. Why? In heaven's name, why? The answer to the Sarton case is close. It must be close or they wouldn't be trying so hard to blast me out of the investigation. I have a feeling I have all the facts I need to work out the answer. It must be in here somewhere." He knuckled his temple wildly. "A sentence might bring it out. A word."

He clenched his eyes fiercely shut, as though the quivering opaque jelly of the last sixty hours were indeed on the point of clarifying and becoming transparent. But it did not. It did not.

Baley drew a shuddering breath and felt ashamed. He was making a weak spectacle of himself before a cold and unimpressed machine that could only stare at him silently.

He said harshly, "Well, never mind that. Why are the Spacers breaking off?"

The robot said, "Our project is concluded. We are satisfied that Earth will colonize."

"You've switched to optimism then?" The plain-clothes man drew in his first calming puff of tobacco smoke and felt his grip upon his own emotions grow firmer.

"I have. For a long time now, we of Spacetown have tried to change Earth by changing its economy. We have tried to introduce our own C/Fe culture. Your planetary and various City governments co-operated with us because it was expedient to do so. Still, in twenty-five years, we have failed. The harder we tried, the stronger the opposing party of the Medievalists grew."

"I know all this," said Baley. He thought: No use. He's got

to tell this in his own way, like a field recording. He yelled silently at R. Daneel: *Machine!*

R. Daneel went on, "It was Dr. Sarton who first theorized that we must reverse our tactics. We must first find a segment of Earth's population that desired what we desired or could be persuaded to do so. By encouraging and helping them, we could make the movement a native one rather than a foreign one. The difficulty was in finding the native element best suited for our purpose. You, yourself, Elijah, were an interesting experiment."

"I? *I?* What do you mean?" demanded Baley.

"We were glad your Commissioner recommended you. From your psychic profile we judged you to be a useful specimen. Cerebroanalysis, a process I conducted upon you as soon as I met you, confirmed our judgment. You are a practical man, Elijah. You do not moon romantically over Earth's past, despite your healthy interest in it. Nor do you stubbornly embrace the City culture of Earth's present day. We felt that people such as yourself were the ones that could lead Earthmen to the stars once more. It was one reason Dr. Fastolfe was anxious to see you yesterday morning.

"To be sure, your practical nature was embarrassingly intense. You refused to understand that the fanatical service of an ideal, even a mistaken ideal, could make a man do things quite beyond his ordinary capacity, as, for instance, crossing open country at night to destroy someone he considered an archenemy of his cause. We were not overly surprised, therefore, that you were stubborn enough and daring enough to attempt to prove the murder a fraud. In a way, it proved you were the man we wanted for our experiment."

"For God's sake, what experiment?" Baley brought his fist down on the table.

"The experiment of persuading you that colonization was the answer to Earth's problems."

"Well, I was persuaded. I'll grant you that."

"Yes, under the influence of the appropriate drug."

Baley's teeth loosened their grip on his pipestem. He caught the pipe as it fell. Once again, he was seeing that scene in the Spacetown dome. Himself swimming back to awareness after the shock of learning that R. Daneel was a robot after all; R. Daneel's smooth fingers pinching up the flesh of his arm: a hypo-sliver standing out darkly under his skin and then fading away.

He said, chokingly, "What was in the hypo-sliver?"

"Nothing that need alarm you, Elijah. It was a mild drug intended only to make your mind more receptive."

"And so I believed whatever was told me. Is that it?"

"Not quite. You would not believe anything that was foreign to the basic pattern of your thought. In fact, the results of the experiment were disappointing. Dr. Fastolfe had hoped you would become fanatical and single-minded on the subject. Instead you became rather distantly approving, no more. Your practical nature stood in the way of anything further. It made us realize that our only hope was the romantics after all, and the romantics, unfortunately, were all Medievalists, actual and potential."

Baley felt incongruously proud of himself, glad of his stubbornness, and happy that he had disappointed them. Let them experiment with someone else.

He grinned savagely. "And so now you've given up and are going home?"

"Why, that is not it. I said a few moments ago that we were satisfied Earth would colonize. It was you that gave us the answer."

"*I* gave it to you? How?"

"You spoke to Francis Clousarr of the advantages of colonization. You spoke rather fervently, I judge. At least our experiment on you had *that* result. And Clousarr's cerebroanalytic properties changed. Very subtly, to be sure, but they changed."

"You mean I convinced him that I was right? I don't believe that."

"No, conviction does not come that easily. But the cerebroanalytic changes demonstrated conclusively that the Medievalist mind is *open* to that sort of conviction. I experimented further myself. When leaving Yeast-town, guessing what might have happened between you two from his cerebric changes, I made the proposition of a school for emigrants as a way of insuring his children's future. He rejected that, but again his aura changed, and it seemed to me quite obvious that it was the proper method of attack."

R. Daneel paused, then spoke on.

"The thing called Medievalism shows a craving for pioneering.

To be sure, the direction in which that craving turns itself is toward Earth itself, which is near and which has the precedent of a great past. But the vision of worlds beyond is a similar something and the romantic can turn to it easily, just as Clousarr felt the attraction as a result of one lecture from you.

"So you see, we of Spacetown had already succeeded without knowing it. We ourselves, rather than anything we tried to introduce, were the unsettling factor. We crystallized the romantic impulses on Earth into Medievalism and induced an organization in them. After all, it is the Medievalist who wishes to break the cake of custom, not the City officials who have most to gain from preserving the *status quo*. If we leave Spacetown now, if we do not irritate the Medievalist by our continued presence until he has committed himself to Earth, and only Earth, past redemption, if we leave behind a few obscure individuals or robots such as myself who, together with sympathetic Earthmen such as yourself, can establish the training schools for emigrants that I spoke of, the Medievalist will eventually turn away from Earth. He will need robots and will either get them from us or build his own. He will develop a C/Fe culture to suit himself."

It was a long speech for R. Daneel. He must have realized that himself, for, after another pause, he said, "I tell you all this to explain why it is necessary to do something that may hurt you."

Baley thought bitterly: A robot must not hurt a human being, unless he can think of a way to prove it is for the human being's ultimate good after all.

Baley said, "Just a minute. Let me introduce a practical note. You'll go back to your worlds and say that an Earthman killed a Spacer and is unpunished. The Outer Worlds will demand an indemnity from Earth, and I warn you, Earth is no longer in a mood to endure such treatment. There will be trouble."

"I am sure that will not happen, Elijah. The elements on our planet that would be most interested in pressing for an indemnity would be also most interested in forcing an end to Spacetown. We can easily offer the latter as an inducement to abandon the former. It is what we plan to do, anyway. Earth will be left in peace."

And Baley broke out, his voice hoarse with sudden despair, "And where does that leave me? The Commissioner will drop the Sarton investigation at once if Spacetown is willing, but the R.

Sammy thing will have to continue, since it points to corruption inside the Department. He'll be in any minute with a ream of evidence against me. I know that. It's been arranged. I'll be declassified, Daneel. There's Jessie to consider. She'll be smeared as a criminal. There's Bentley —"

R. Daneel said, "You must not think, Elijah, that I do not understand the position in which you find yourself. In the service of humanity's good, the minor wrongs must be tolerated. Dr. Sarton has a surviving wife, two children, parents, a sister, many friends. All must grieve at his death and be saddened at the thought that his murderer has not been found and punished."

"Then why not stay and find him?"

"It is no longer necessary."

Baley said, bitterly, "Why not admit that the entire investigation was an excuse to study us under field conditions? You never gave a damn who killed Dr. Sarton."

"We would have liked to know," said R. Daneel, coolly, "but we were never under any delusions as to which was more important, an individual or humanity. To continue the investigation now would involve interfering with a situation which we now find satisfactory. We could not foretell what damage we might do."

"You mean the murderer might turn out to be a prominent Medievalist and right now the Spacers don't want to do anything to antagonize their new friends."

"It is not as I would say it, but there is truth in your words."

"Where's your justice circuit, Daneel? Is this justice?"

"There are degrees of justice, Elijah. When the lesser is incompatible with the greater, the lesser must give way."

It was as though Baley's mind were circling the impregnable logic of R. Daneel's positronic brain, searching for a loop-hole, a weakness.

He said, "Have you no personal curiosity, Daneel? You've called yourself a detective. Do you know what that implies? Do you understand that an investigation is more than a job of work? It is a challenge. Your mind is pitted against that of the criminal. It is a clash of intellect. Can you abandon the battle and admit defeat?"

"If no worthy end is served by a continuation, certainly."

"Would you feel no loss? No wonder? Would there be no

little speck of dissatisfaction? Frustrated curiosity?"

Baley's hopes, not strong in the first place, weakened as he spoke. The words "curiosity," second time repeated, brought back his own remarks to Francis Clousarr four hours before. He had known well enough then the qualities that marked off a man from a machine. Curiosity *had* to be one of them. A six-week-old kitten was curious, but how could there be a curious machine, be it ever so humanoid?

R. Daneel echoed those thoughts by saying, "What do you mean by curiosity?"

Baley put the best face on it. "Curiosity is the name we give to a desire to extend one's knowledge."

"Such a desire exists within me, when the extension of knowledge is necessary for the performance of an assigned task."

"Yes," said Baley, sarcastically, "as when you ask questions about Bentley's contact lenses in order to learn more of Earth's peculiar customs."

"Precisely," said R. Daneel, with no sign of any awareness of sarcasm. "Aimless extension of knowledge, however, which is what I think you really mean by the term curiosity, is merely inefficiency. I am designed to avoid inefficiency."

It was in that way that the "sentence" he had been waiting for came to Elijah Baley, and the opaque jelly shuddered and settled and changed into luminous transparency.

While R. Daneel spoke, Baley's mouth opened and stayed so.

It could not all have burst full-grown into his mind. Things did not work so. Somewhere, deep inside his unconscious, he had built a case, built it carefully and in detail, but had been brought up short by a single inconsistency. One inconsistency that could be neither jumped over, burrowed under, nor shunted aside. While that inconsistency existed, the case remained buried below his thoughts, beyond the reach of his conscious probing.

But the sentence had come; the inconsistency had vanished; the case was his.

The glare of mental light appeared to have stimulated Baley mightily. At least he suddenly knew what R. Daneel's weakness must be, the weakness of any thinking machine. He thought feverishly, hopefully: The thing *must* be literal-minded.

He said, "Then Project Spacetown is concluded as of today and with it the Sarton investigation. Is that it?"

"That is the decision of our people at Spacetown," agreed R. Daneel, calmly.

"But today is not yet over." Baley looked at his watch. It was 22:30. "There is an hour and a half until midnight."

R. Daneel said nothing. He seemed to consider.

Baley spoke rapidly. "Until midnight, the project continues then. You are my partner and the investigation continues." He was becoming almost telegraphic in his haste. "Let us go on as before. Let me work. It will do your people no harm. It will do them great good. My word upon it. If, in your judgment, I am doing harm, stop me. It is only an hour and a half I ask."

· R. Daneel said, "What you say is correct. Today is not over. I had not thought of that, partner Elijah."

Baley was "partner Elijah" again.

He grinned, and said, "Didn't Dr. Fastolfe mention a film of the scene of the murder when I was in Spacetown?"

"He did," said R. Daneel.

Baley said, "Can you get a copy of the film?"

"Yes, partner Elijah."

"I mean now! Instantly!"

"In ten minutes, if I can use the Department transmitter."

The process took less time than that. Baley stared at the small aluminium block he held in his trembling hands. Within it the subtle forces transmitted from Spacetown had strongly fixed a certain atomic pattern.

And at that moment, Commissioner Julius Enderby stood in the doorway. He saw Baley and a certain anxiety passed from his round face, leaving behind it a look of growing thunder.

He said, uncertainly, "Look here, Lije, you're taking a devil of a time, eating."

"I was bone-tired, Commissioner. Sorry if I've delayed you."

"I wouldn't mind, but . . . You'd better come to my office."

Baley's eyes flicked toward R. Daneel, but met no answering look. Together they moved out of the lunchroom.

Julius Enderby tramped the floor before his desk, up and down, up and down. Baley watched him, himself far from composed. Occasionally, he glanced at his watch.

22:45.

The Commissioner moved his glasses up onto his forehead and rubbed his eyes with thumb and forefinger. He left red splotches in the flesh around them, then restored the glasses to their place, blinking at Baley from behind them.

"Lije," he said suddenly, "when were you last in the Williamsburg power plant?"

Baley said, "Yesterday, after I left the office. I should judge at about eighteen or shortly thereafter."

The Commissioner shook his head. "Why didn't you say so?"

"I was going to. I haven't given an official statement yet."

"What were you doing there?"

"Just passing through on my way to our temporary sleeping quarters."

The Commissioner stopped short, standing before Baley, and said, "That's no good, Lije. No one just passes through a power plant to get somewhere else."

Baley shrugged. There was no point in going through the story of the pursuing Medievalists, of the dash along the strips. Not now.

He said, "If you're trying to hint that I had an opportunity to get the alpha-sprayer that knocked out R. Sammy, I'll remind you that Daneel was with me and will testify that I went right through the plant without stopping and that I had no alpha-sprayer on me when I left."

Slowly, the Commissioner sat down. He did not look in R. Daneel's direction or offer to speak to him. He put his pudgy white hands on the desk before him and regarded them with a look of acute misery on his face.

He said, "Lije, I don't know what to say or what to think. And it's no use having your – your partner as alibi. He can't give evidence."

"I still deny that I took an alpha-sprayer."

The Commissioner's fingers intertwined and writhed. He said, "Lije, why did Jessie come to see you here this afternoon?"

"You asked me that before, Commissioner. Same answer. Family matters."

"I've got information from Francis Clousarr, Lije."

"What kind of information?"

"He claims that a Jezebel Baley is a member of a Medievalist society dedicated to the overthrow of the government by force."

"Are you sure he has the right person? There are many Baleys."

"There aren't many Jezebel Baleys."

"He used her name, did he?"

"He said Jezebel. I heard him, Lije. I'm not giving you a second-hand report."

"All right. Jessie was a member of a harmless lunatic-fringe organization. She never did anything but attend meetings and feel devilish about it."

"It won't look that way to a board of review, Lije."

"You mean I'm going to be suspended and held on suspicion of destroying government property in the form of R. Sammy?"

"I hope not, Lije, but it looks awfully bad. Everyone knows you didn't like R. Sammy. Your wife was seen talking to him this afternoon. She was in tears and some of her words were heard. They were harmless in themselves, but two and two can be added up, Lije. You might feel it was dangerous to leave him in a position to talk. *And* you had an opportunity to obtain the weapon."

Baley interrupted. "If I were wiping out all evidence against Jessie, would I bring in Francis Clousarr? He seems to know a lot more about her than R. Sammy could have. Another thing. I passed through the power plant eighteen hours before R. Sammy spoke to Jessie. Did I know that long in advance that I would have to destroy him and pick up an alpha-sprayer out of clairvoyance?"

The Commissioner said, "Those are good points. I'll do my best. I'm sorry about this, Lije."

"Yes? Do you really believe I didn't do it, Commissioner?"

Enderby said slowly, "I don't know what to think, Lije. I'll be frank with you."

"Then I'll tell you what to think. Commissioner, this is all a careful and elaborate frame."

The Commissioner stiffened. "Now, wait, Lije. Don't strike out blindly. You won't get any sympathy with that line of defense. It's been used by too many bad eggs."

"I'm not after sympathy. I'm just telling the truth. I'm being taken out of circulation to prevent me from learning the facts about the Sarton murder. Unfortunately for my framing pal, it's too late for that."

"*What!*"

Baley looked at his watch. It was 23 : 00.

He said, "I know who is framing me, and I know how Dr. Sarton was killed and by whom, and I have one hour to tell you about it, catch the man, and end the investigation."

CHAPTER EIGHTEEN

END OF AN INVESTIGATION

Commissioner Enderby's eyes narrowed and he glared at Baley. "What are you going to do? You tried something like this in Fastolfe's dome yesterday morning. Not again. Please."

Baley nodded. "I know. I was wrong the first time."

He thought, fiercely:. Also the second time. But not now, not *this* time, not . . .

The thought faded out, spluttering like a micropile under a positronic damper.

He said, "Judge for yourself, Commissioner. Grant that the evidence against me has been planted. Go that far with me and see where it takes you. Ask yourself who could have planted that evidence. Obviously only someone who'd know I was in the Williamsburg plant yesterday evening."

"All right. Who would that be?"

Baley said, "I was followed out of the kitchen by a Medievalist group. I lost them, or I thought I did, but obviously at least one of them saw me pass through the plant. My only purpose in doing so, you understand, was to help me lose them."

The Commissioner considered. "Clousarr? Was he with them?"

Baley nodded.

Enderby said, "All right, we'll question him. If he's got anything in him, we'll have it out of him. What more can I do, Lije?"

"Wait, now. Don't quit on me. Do you see my point?"

"Well, let's see if I do?" The Commissioner clasped his hands. "Clousarr saw you go into the Williamsburg power plant, or else someone in his group did and passed the information along to him. He decided to utilize that fact to get you into trouble and off the investigation. Is that what you're saying?"

"It's close to it."

"Good." The Commissioner seemed to warm to the task. "He knew your wife was a member of his organization, naturally, and so he knew you wouldn't face a really close probe into your private life. He thought you would resign rather than fight circumstantial evidence. By the way, Lije, what about a resignation? I mean, if things looked really bad. We could keep things quiet –"

"Not in a million years, Commissioner."

Enderby shrugged. "Well, where was I? Oh, yes, so he got an alpha-sprayer, presumably through a confederate in the plant, and had another confederate arrange the destruction of R. Sammy." His fingers drummed lightly on the desk. "No good, Lije."

"Why not?"

"Too farfetched. Too many confederates. And he has a cast-iron alibi for the night and morning of the Spacetown murder, by the way. We checked that almost right away, though I was the only one who knew the reason for checking that particular time."

Baley said, "I never said it was Clousarr, Commissioner. You did. It could be anyone in the Medievalist organization. Clousarr is just the owner of a face that Daneel happened to recognize. I don't even think he's particularly important in the organization. Though there is one queer thing about him."

"What?" asked Enderby, suspiciously.

"He did know Jessie was a member. Does he know every member in the organization, do you suppose?"

"I don't know. He knew about Jessie, anyway. Maybe she was important because she was the wife of a policeman. Maybe he remembered her for that reason."

"You say he came right out and said that Jezebel Baley was a member. Just like that? Jezebel Baley?"

Enderby nodded. "I keep telling you I heard him."

"That's the funny thing, Commissioner. Jessie hasn't used her full first name since before Bentley was born. Not once. I know that for certain. She joined the Medievalists after she dropped her full name. I know that for sure, too. How would Clousarr come to know her as Jezebel, then?"

The Commissioner flushed and said, hastily, "Oh well, if it comes to that, he probably said Jessie. I just filled it in automatically and gave her full name. In fact, I'm sure of that. He said Jessie."

"Until now you were quite sure he said Jezebel. I asked several times."

The Commissioner's voice rose. "You're not saying I'm a liar, are you?"

"I'm just wondering if Clousarr, perhaps, said nothing at all. I'm wondering if you made that up. You've known Jessie for twenty years, and *you* knew her name was Jezebel."

"You're off your head, man."

"Am I? Where were you after lunch today? You were out of your office for two hours at least."

"Are you questioning *me?*"

"I'll answer for you, too. You were in the Williamsburg power plant."

The Commissioner rose from his seat. His forehead glistened and there were dry, white flecks at the corners of his lips. "What the hell are you trying to say?"

"Weren't you?"

"Baley, you're suspended. Hand me your credentials."

"Not yet. Hear me out."

"I don't intend to. You're guilty. You're guilty as the devil, and what gets me is your cheap attempt to make me, *me,* look as though I were conspiring against you." He lost his voice momentarily in a squeak of indignation. He managed to gasp out, "In fact, you're under arrest."

"No," said Baley, tightly, "not yet, Commissioner, I've got a blaster on you. It's pointed straight and it's cocked. Don't fool with me, please, because I'm desperate and I *will* have my say. Afterward, you can do what you please."

With widening eyes, Julius Enderby stared at the wicked muzzle in Baley's hands.

He stammered, "Twenty years for this, Baley, in the deepest prison level in the City."

R. Daneel moved suddenly. His hand clamped down on

Baley's wrist. He said, quietly, "I cannot permit this, partner Elijah. You must do no harm to the Commissioner."

For the first time since R. Daneel had entered the City, the Commissioner spoke directly to him. "Hold him, you. First Law!"

Baley said quickly, "I have no intention of hurting him, Daneel, if you will keep him from arresting me. You said you would help me clear this up. I have forty-five minutes."

R. Daneel, without releasing Baley's wrist, said, "Commissioner, I believe Elijah should be allowed to speak. I am in communication with Dr. Fastolfe at this moment –"

"How? How?" demanded the Commissioner, wildly.

"I possess a self-contained subetheric unit," said R. Daneel. The Commissioner stared.

"I am in communication with Dr. Fastolfe," the robot went on inexorably, "and it would make a bad impression, Commissioner, if you were to refuse to listen to Elijah. Damaging inferences might be drawn."

The Commissioner fell back in his chair, quite speechless.

Baley said, "I say you were in the Williamsburg power plant today, Commissioner, and you got the alpha-sprayer and gave it to R. Sammy. You deliberately chose the Williamsburg power plant in order to incriminate me. You even seized Dr. Gerrigel's reappearance to invite him down to the Department and give him a deliberately maladjusted guide rod to lead him to the photographic supply room and allow him to find R. Sammy's remains. You counted on him to make a correct diagnosis."

Baley put away his blaster. "If you want to have me arrested now, go ahead, but Spacetown won't take that for an answer."

"Motive," spluttered Enderby breathlessly. His glasses were fogged and he removed them, looking once again curiously vague and helpless in their absence. "What motive could I have for this?"

"You got me into trouble, didn't you? It will put a spoke in the Sarton investigation, won't it? And all that aside, R. Sammy knew too much."

"About *what*, in Heaven's name?"

"About the way in which a Spacer was murdered five and a half days ago. You see, Commissioner, *you* murdered Dr. Sarton of Spacetown."

It was R. Daneel who spoke. Enderby could only clutch feverishly at his hair and shake his head.

The robot said, "Partner Elijah, I am afraid that this theory is quite untenable. As you know, it is impossible for Commissioner Enderby to have murdered Dr. Sarton."

"Listen, then. Listen to me. Enderby begged *me* to take the case, not any of the men who overranked me. He did that for several reasons. In the first place, we were college friends and he thought he could count on its never occurring to me that an old-buddy and respected superior could be a criminal. He counted on my well-known loyalty, you see. Secondly, he knew Jessie was a member of an underground organization and expected to be able to maneuver me out of the investigation or blackmail me into silence if I got too close to the truth. And he wasn't really worried about that. At the very beginning he did his best to arouse my distrust of you, Daneel, and make certain that the two of us worked at cross-purposes. He knew about my father's declassification. He could guess how I would react. You see, it is an advantage for the murderer to be in charge of the murder investigation."

The Commissioner found his voice. He said, weakly, "How could I know about Jessie?" He turned to the robot. "You! If you're transmitting this to Spacetown, tell them it's a lie! It's all a lie!"

Baley broke in, raising his voice for a moment and then lowering it into a queer sort of tense calm. "Certainly you would know about Jessie. You're a Medievalist, and part of the organization. Your old-fashioned spectacles! Your windows! It's obvious your temperament is turned that way. But there's better evidence than that.

"How did Jessie find out Daneel was a robot? It puzzled me at the time. Of course we know now that she found out through her Medievalist organization, but that just shoves the problem one step backward. How did *they* know? You, Commissioner, dismissed it with a theory that Daneel was recognized as a robot during the incident at the shoe counter. I didn't quite believe that. I couldn't. I took him for human when I first saw him, and there's nothing wrong with my eyes.

"Yesterday, I asked Dr. Gerrigel to come in from Washington. Later I decided I needed him for several reasons, but, at the time I first called him, my only purpose was to see if he would recognize Daneel for what he was with no prompting on my part.

"Commissioner, he didn't! I introduced him to Daneel, he shook hands with him, we all talked together, and it was only after the subject got around to humanoid robots that he suddenly caught on. Now, that was Dr. Gerrigel, Earth's greatest expert on robots. Do you mean to say a few Medievalist rioters could do better than he under conditions of confusion and tension, and be so certain about it that they would throw their entire organization into activity based on the feeling that Daneel was a robot?

"It's obvious now that the Medievalists must have known Daneel to be a robot to begin with. The incident at the shoe counter was deliberately designed to show Daneel and, through him, Spacetown, the extent of antirobot feeling in the City. It was meant to confuse the issue, to turn suspicion away from individuals and toward the population as a whole.

"Now, if they knew the truth about Daneel to begin with, who told them? I didn't. I once thought it was Daneel himself, but that's out. The only other Earthman who knew about it was you, Commissioner."

Enderby said, with surprising energy, "There could be spies in the Department, too. The Medievalists could have us riddled with them. Your wife was one, and if you don't find it impossible that I should be one, why not others in the Department?"

The corners of Baley's lips pulled back a savage trifle. "Let's not bring up mysterious spies until we see where the straightforward solution leads us. I say you're the obvious informer and the real one.

"It's interesting now that I look back on it, Commissioner, to see how your spirits rose and fell accordingly as I seemed to be far from a solution or possibly close to it. You were nervous to begin with. When I wanted to visit Spacetown yesterday morning and wouldn't tell you the reason, you were practically in a state of collapse. Did you think I had you pinned, Commissioner? That it was a trap to get you into their hands? You hated them, you told me. You were virtually in tears. For a time, I thought that to be caused by the memory of humiliation in Spacetown when you yourself were a suspect, but then Daneel told me that your sensibilities had been carefully regarded. You had never known you were a suspect. Your panic was due to fear, not humiliation.

"Then when I came out with my completely wrong solution, while you listened over trimensional circuit, and you saw how far, how immensely far, from the truth I was, you were confident again. You even argued with me, defended the Spacers. After that, you were quite master of yourself for a while, quite confident. It surprised me at the time that you so easily forgave my false accusations against the Spacers when earlier you had so lectured me on their sensitivity. You enjoyed my mistake.

"Then I put in my call for Dr. Gerrigel and you wanted to know why and I wouldn't tell you. That plunged you into the abyss again because you feared –"

R. Daneel suddenly raised his hand. "Partner Elijah!"

Baley looked at his watch. 23 : 42! He said, "What is it?"

R. Daneel said, "He might have been disturbed at thinking you would find out his Medievalist connections, if we grant their existence. There is nothing, though, to connect him with the murder. He cannot have had anything to do with that."

Baley said, "You're quite wrong, Daneel. He didn't know what I wanted Dr. Gerrigel for, but it was quite safe to assume that it was in connection with information about robots. This frightened the Commissioner, because a robot had an intimate connection with his greater crime. Isn't that so, Commissioner?"

Enderby shook his head. "When this is over –" he began, but choked into inarticulacy.

"How was the murder committed?" demanded Baley with a suppressed fury. "C/Fe, damn it! C/Fe! I use your own term, Daneel. You're so full of the benefits of a C/Fe culture, yet you don't see where an Earthman might have used it for at least a temporary advantage. Let me sketch it in for you.

"There is no difficulty in the notion of a robot crossing open country. Even at night. Even alone. The Commissioner put a blaster into R. Sammy's hand, told him where to go and when. He himself entered Spacetown through the Personal and was relieved of his own blaster. He received the other from R. Sammy's hands, killed Dr. Sarton, returned the blaster to R. Sammy, who took it back across the fields to New York City. And today he destroyed R. Sammy, whose knowledge had become dangerous.

"That explains everything. The presence of the Commissioner, the absence of a weapon. And it makes it unnecessary to suppose any human New Yorker had crawled a mile under the open sky at night."

But at the end of Baley's recitation, R. Daneel said, "I am sorry, partner Elijah, though happy for the Commissioner, that your story explains nothing. I have told you that the cerebroanalytic properties of the Commissioner are such that it is impossible for him to have committed deliberate murder. I don't know what English word would be applied to the psychological fact: cowardice, conscience, or compassion. I know the dictionary meanings of all these, but I cannot judge. At any rate, the Commissioner did not murder."

"Thank you," muttered Enderby. His voice gained strength and confidence. "I don't know what your motives are, Baley, or why you should try to ruin me this way, but I'll get to the bottom —"

"Wait," said Baley. "I'm not through. I've got this."

He slammed the aluminium cube on Enderby's desk, and tried to feel the confidence he hoped he was radiating. For half an hour now, he had been hiding from himself one little fact: that he did *not* know what the picture showed. He was gambling, but it was all that was left to do.

Enderby shrank away from the small object. "What is it?"

"It isn't a bomb," said Baley, sardonically. "Just an ordinary micro-projector."

"Well? What will that prove?"

"Suppose we see." His fingernail probed at one of the slits in the cube, and a corner of the Commissioner's office blanked out, then lit up in an alien scene in three dimensions.

It reached from floor to ceiling and extended out past the walls of the room. It was awash with a gray light of a sort the City's utilities never provided.

Baley thought, with a pang of mingled distaste and perverse attraction: It must be the dawn they talk about.

The pictured scene was of Dr. Sarton's dome. Dr. Sarton's dead body, a horrible, broken remnant, filled its center.

Enderby's eyes bulged as he stared.

Baley said, "I know the Commissioner isn't a killer. I don't need you to tell me that, Daneel. If I could have gotten around that one fact earlier, I would have had the solution earlier. Actually, I didn't see a way out of it until an hour ago when I carelessly said to you that you had once been curious about Bentley's contact lenses. – That was it, Commissioner. It occurred to me then that your nearsightedness and your glasses were the key. They don't have nearsightedness on the Outer Worlds, I suppose, or they might have reached the true solution of the murder almost at once. Commissioner, when did you break your glasses?"

The Commissioner said, "What do you mean?"

Baley said, "When I first saw you about this case, you told me you had broken your glasses in Spacetown. I assumed that you broke them in your agitation on hearing the news of the murder, but *you* never said so, and I had no reason for making that assumption. Actually, if you were entering Spacetown with crime on your mind, you were already sufficiently agitated to drop and break your glasses *before* the murder. Isn't that so, and didn't that, in fact, happen?"

R. Daneel said, "I do not see the point, partner Elijah."

Baley thought: I'm partner Elijah for ten minutes more. Fast! Talk fast! And think fast!

He was manipulating Sarton's dome image as he spoke. Clumsily, he expanded it, his fingernails unsure in the tension that was overwhelming him. Slowly, in jerks, the corpse widened, broadened, heightened, came closer. Baley could almost smell the stench of its scorched flesh. Its head, shoulders, and one upper arm lolled crazily, connected to hips and legs by a blackened remnant of spine from which charred rib stumps jutted.

Baley cast a side glance at the Commissioner. Enderby had closed his eyes. He looked sick. Baley felt sick, too, but he *had* to look. Slowly he circled the trimensional image by means of the transmitter controls, rotating it, bringing the ground about the corpse to view in successive quadrants. His fingernail slipped and the imaged floor tilted suddenly and expanded till floor and corpse alike were a hazy mass, beyond the resolving power of the transmitter. He brought the expansion down, let the corpse slide away.

He was still talking. He had to. He couldn't stop till he found what he was looking for. And if he didn't, all his talk might be useless. Worse than useless. His heart was throbbing, and so was his head.

He said. "The Commissioner can't commit deliberate murder. True! *Deliberate.* But any man can kill by accident. The Commissioner didn't enter Spacetown to kill Dr. Sarton. He came in to kill you, Daneel, *you!* Is there anything in his cerebro-analysis that says he is incapable of wrecking a machine? *That's* not murder, merely sabotage.

"He is a Medievalist, an earnest one. He worked with Dr. Sarton and knew the purpose for which you were designed, Daneel. He feared that purpose might be achieved, that Earthmen would eventually be weaned away from Earth. So he decided to destroy you, Daneel. You were the only one of your type manufactured as yet and he had good reason to think that by demonstrating the extent and determination of Medievalism on Earth, he would discourage the Spacers. He knew how strong popular opinion was on the Outer Worlds to end the Spacetown project altogether. Dr. Sarton must have discussed that with him. This, he thought, would be the last nudge in the proper direction.

"I don't say even the thought of killing you, Daneel, was a pleasant one. He would have had R. Sammy do it, I imagine, if you didn't look so human that a primitive robot such as Sammy could not have told the difference, or understood it. First Law would stop him. Or the Commissioner would have had another human do it if he, himself, were not the only one who had ready access to Spacetown at all times.

"Let me reconstruct what the Commissioner's plan might have been. I'm guessing, I admit, but I think I'm close. He made the appointment with Dr. Sarton, but deliberately came early, at dawn, in fact. Dr. Sarton would be sleeping, I imagine, but you, Daneel, would be awake. I assume, by the way, you were living with Dr. Sarton, Daneel."

The robot nodded. "You are quite right, partner Elijah."

Baley said, "Then let me go on. You would come to the dome door, Daneel, receive a blaster charge in the chest or head, and be done with. The Commissioner would leave quickly, through the deserted streets of Spacetown's dawn, and back to where R. Sammy waited. He would give him back the blaster, then slowly walk again to Dr. Sarton's dome. If necessary, he would 'discover' the body himself, though he would prefer to have someone else do that. If questioned concerning his early arrival, he could say, I suppose, that he had come to tell Dr. Sarton of rumors of a Medievalist attack on Spacetown, urge him to take secret precautions to avoid open trouble between Spacers and Earthmen. The dead robot would lend point to his words.

"If they asked about the long interval between your entering Spacetown, Commissioner, and your arrival at Dr. Sarton's dome, you could say – let's see – that you saw someone lurking through the streets and heading for open country. You pursued for a while. That would also encourage them along a false path. As for R. Sammy, no one would notice him. A robot among the truck farms outside the City is just another robot.

"How close am I, Commissioner?"

Enderby writhed, "I didn't –"

"No," said Baley, "you didn't kill Daneel! He's here, and in all the time he's been in the City, you haven't been able to look him in the face or address him by name. Look at him now, Commissioner."

Enderby couldn't. He covered his face with shaking hands.

Baley's shaking hands almost dropped his transmitter. He had found it.

The image was now centered upon the main door to Dr. Sarton's dome. The door was open; it had been slid into its wall receptacle along its shining metal runner grooves. Down within them. There! There!

The sparkle was unmistakable.

"I'll tell you what happened," said Baley. "You were at the dome when you dropped your glasses. You must have been nervous and I've seen you when you're nervous. You take them off; you wipe them. You did that then. But your hands were shaking and you dropped them; maybe you stepped on them. Anyway, they were broken, and just then, the door opened and a figure that looked like Daneel faced you.

"You blasted him, scrabbled up the remains of your glasses, and ran. They found the body, not you, and when they came to find you, you discovered that it was not Daneel, but the early-rising Dr. Sarton, that you had killed. Dr. Sarton had designed Daneel in his own image, to his great misfortune, and without your glasses in that moment of tension, you could not tell them apart.

"And if you want the tangible proof, it's there!" The image of Sarton's dome quivered and Baley put the transmitter carefully upon the desk, his hand tightly upon it.

Commissioner Enderby's face was distorted with terror and Baley's with tension. R. Daneel seemed indifferent.

Baley's finger was pointing. "That glitter in the grooves of the door. What was it, Daneel?"

"Two small slivers of glass," said the robot, coolly. "It meant nothing to us."

"It will now. They're portions of concave lenses. Measure their optical properties and compare them with those of the glasses Enderby is wearing now. *Don't smash them, Commissioner!*"

He lunged at the Commissioner and wrenched the spectacles from the other's hand. He held them out to R. Daneel, panting, "That's proof enough, I think, that he was at the dome earlier than he was thought to be."

R. Daneel said, "I am quite convinced. I can see now that I was thrown completely off the scent by the Commissioner's cerebroanalysis. I congratulate you, partner Elijah."

Baley's watch said 24:00. A new day was beginning.

Slowly, the Commissioner's head went down on his arms. His words were muffled wails. "It was a mistake. A mistake. I never meant to kill him." Without warning, he slipped from the chair and lay crumpled on the floor.

R. Daneel sprang to him, saying, "You have hurt him, Elijah. That is too bad."

"He isn't dead, is he?"

"No. But unconscious."

"He'll come to. It was too much for him, I suppose. I had to do it, Daneel, I had to. I had no evidence that would stand up in court, only inferences. I had to badger him and badger him and let it out little by little, hoping he would break down. He did, Daneel. You heard him confess, didn't you?"

"Yes."

"Now, then. I promised this would be to the benefit of Spacetown's project, so — Wait, he's coming to."

The Commissioner groaned. His eyes fluttered and opened. He stared speechlessly at the two.

Baley said, "Commissioner, do you hear me?"

The Commissioner nodded listlessly.

"All right, then. Now, the Spacers have more on their minds than your prosecution. If you co-operate with them –"

"What? What?" There was a dawning flicker of hope in the Commissioner's eyes.

"You must be a big wheel in New York's Medievalist organization, maybe even in the planetary setup. Maneuver them in the direction of the colonization of space. You can see the propaganda line, can't you? We can go back to the soil all right – but on other planets."

"I don't understand," mumbled the Commissioner.

"It's what the Spacers are after. And God help me, it's what I'm after now, too, since a small conversation I had with Dr. Fastolfe. It's what they want more than anything. They risk death continually by coming to Earth and staying here for that purpose. If Dr. Sarton's murder will make it possible for you to swing Medievalism into line for the resumption of Galactic colonization, they'll probably consider it a worthwhile sacrifice. Do you understand now?"

R. Daneel said, "Elijah is quite correct. Help us, Commissioner, and we will forget the past. I am speaking for Dr. Fastolfe and our people generally in this. Of course, if you should agree to help and later betray us, we would always have the fact of your guilt to hold over your head. I hope you understand that, too. It pains me to have to mention that."

"I won't be prosecuted?" asked the Commissioner.

"Not if you help us."

Tears filled his eyes. "I'll do it. It was an accident. Explain that. An accident. I did what I thought right."

Baley said, "If you help us, you *will* be doing right. The colonization of space is the only possible salvation of Earth. You'll realize that if you think about it without prejudice. If you find you cannot, have a short talk with Dr. Fastolfe. And now, you can begin helping by quashing the R. Sammy business. Call it an accident or something. End it!"

Baley got to his feet. "And remember, I'm not the only one

who knows the truth, Commissioner. Getting rid of me will ruin you. All Spacetown knows. You see that, don't you?"

R. Daneel said, "It is unnecessary to say more, Elijah. He is sincere and he will help. So much is obvious from his cerebro-analysis."

"All right. Then I'll go home. I want to see Jessie and Bentley and take up a natural existence again. And I want to sleep. – Daneel, will you stay on Earth after the Spacers go?"

R. Daneel said, "I have not been informed. Why do you ask?"

Baley bit his lip, then said, "I didn't think I would ever say anything like this to anyone like you, Daneel, but I trust you. I even – admire you. I'm too old ever to leave Earth myself, but when schools for emigrants are finally established, there's Bentley. If someday, perhaps, Bentley and you, together . . ."

"Perhaps." R. Daneel's face was emotionless.

The robot turned to Julius Enderby, who was watching them with a flaccid face into which a certain vitality was only now beginning to return.

The robot said, "I have been trying, friend Julius, to understand some remarks Elijah made to me earlier. Perhaps I am beginning to, for it suddenly seems to me that the destruction of what should not be, that is, the destruction of what you people call evil, is less just and desirable than the conversion of this evil into what you call good."

He hesitated, then, almost as though he were surprised at his own words, he said, "Go, and sin no more!"

Baley, suddenly smiling, took R. Daneel's elbow, and they walked out the door, arm in arm.

The Rest of
the Robots

To Tim,
Tom and Dick
My stalwart supporters at Doubleday

Contents

INTRODUCTION

WOULD you like to hear a writer's nightmare?

Well, then, imagine a writer of considerable reputation, who knows himself to be a Great Man. Bestow upon him a wife, a little woman who is a bit of a writer herself but, of course, nothing like her great, her magnificent husband, either in her own eyes, in the world's eyes, or (most important of all) in *his* eyes.

And imagine that, as a result of some conversation, the little woman suggests she write a novel on the subject. And the Great Man, smiling benignly, says, 'Of course, dear. You go right ahead.'

And she does, and it is published, and it makes a perfectly gigantic sensation. And it follows, then, that although the Great Man is universally admitted to be Great, it is the little woman's novel which is best known forever afterward —so well known, in fact, that the title becomes a byword in the English language.

How grisly a situation for a normally egocentric professional writer that would be.

Yet I'm not making this up. It is a true story. It happened.

The Great Man is Percy Bysshe Shelley, one of the magnificent lyric poets of the English language. At the age of twenty-two, he eloped with Mary Wollstonecraft Godwin, an event which, however romantic, was slightly irregular, as Shelley was a married man at the time.

The publicity was such that they were better off outside England, and in the summer of 1816 they stayed on the shores of Lake Geneva in Switzerland with the equally great poet and equally notorious gentleman, George Gordon, Lord Byron.

At the time, the scientific world was in a ferment. In 1791 the Italian physicist, Luigi Galvani, had discovered that frogs' muscles could be made to twitch if touched simultaneously by two different metals and it seemed to him that living tissue was filled with 'animal electricity.' This theory was disputed by another Italian physicist, Alessandro Volta, who showed that electric currents could be produced by the juxtaposition of different metals without the presence of living or once-living tissue. Volta had invented the first battery and the English chemist, Humphrey Davy, went on in 1807 and 1808 to build an unprecedentedly powerful one and to carry out, with its help, all sorts of chemical reactions that had been impossible to chemists of the non-electrical age.

Electricity was therefore a word of power and, although Galvani's 'animal electricity' had been quickly smashed by the researches of Volta, it remained a magic phrase among the lay public. Interest in the relationship of electricity to life was intense.

One evening a small group including Byron, Shelley, and Mary Godwin discussed the possibility of actually creating life by means of electricity, and it occurred to Mary that she might write a fantasy on the subject. Byron and Shelley approved; in fact they thought they, too, might write fantastic novels for the private amusement of the little company.

Only Mary actually carried this through. At the end of the year the first Mrs. Shelley committed suicide, so that Shelley and Mary could marry and return to England. In England, in 1817, Mary Shelley's novel was completed and in 1818 it was published. It was about a young scientist, a student of anatomy, who assembled a being in his laboratory and succeeded in infusing it with life by way of electricity. The being (given no name) was a monstrous eight-foot creature with a horrible face that frightened all beholders into fits.

The monster can find no place in human society and, in his misery, turns upon the scientist and all those dear to him. One by one the scientist's relatives (including his bride) are destroyed and in the end the scientist dies as well. The monster wanders off into the wilderness, presumably to die of remorse.

The novel made a huge sensation and has never stopped making a huge sensation. There is simply no question as to which Shelley made the greater mark on people generally. To the students of literature, *the* Shelley may be Percy Bysshe, of course, but stop people on the street and ask them if they've ever heard of *Adonais*, or *Ode to the West Wind*, or *The Cenci*. Maybe they have, but very likely they have not. Then ask them if they have ever heard of *Frankenstein*.

For *Frankenstein* was the name of Mrs. Shelley's novel and of the young scientist who created the monster. Ever since 'a Frankenstein' has been used for anyone or anything that creates something that destroys the creator. The exclamation 'I have created a Frankenstein's monster' has become such a cliché that it can be used only humorously nowadays.

Frankenstein achieved its success, at least in part, because it was a restatement of one of the enduring fears of mankind—that of dangerous knowledge. Frankenstein was another Faust, seeking knowledge not meant for man, and he had created his Mephistophelean nemesis.

In the early nineteenth century the exact nature of

Frankenstein's sacrilegious invasion of forbidden knowledge was clear. Man's advancing science might, conceiv-
ably, imbue dead matter with life; but nothing man could
do could create a soul, for that was God's exclusive domain.
Frankenstein therefore could, at best, create a soulless
intelligence, and such an ambition was evil and deserving of
ultimate punishment.

The theological 'thou shalt not' barrier against man's
advancing knowledge and intensifying science weakened as
the nineteenth century progressed. The industrial revolution broadened and deepened and the Faustian motif gave
way, temporarily, to a buoyant belief in progress and an
inevitably approaching utopia-through-science.

This dream, alas, was shattered by World War I. That
horrible holocaust made it quite plain that science could,
after all, be an enemy of humanity. It was through science
that new explosives were manufactured and that airplanes
and airships were constructed to carry those explosives to
areas behind the lines that earlier might have been secure.
It was science that made possible, in particular, that ultimate horror of the trenches, poison gas.*

Consequently the Evil Scientist or, at best, the Foolishly
Sacrilegious Scientist became a stock character in post-
World War I science fiction.

In the days immediately following the war an extremely
dramatic and influential example of this motif was advanced, again revolving about the creation of quasi-life.
This was the play *R.U.R.* by the Czech writer, Karel
Capek. It was written in 1921 and translated into English

---

* The Faustian role of science in World War I was dwarfed
to insignificance by its role in World War II and in the Cold
War. The hydrogen bomb and bacteriological warfare reduce
poison-gas attacks to mere inconveniences.

in 1923. R.U.R. stood for Rossum's Universal Robots. Like Frankenstein, Rossum had discovered the secret of creating artificial men. These were called 'robots' from a Czech word meaning 'worker,' and the word entered the English language and gained a strong hold there.

The robots were intended, as their name implies, to be workers, but all goes wrong. Mankind, its motivation lost, ceases to reproduce itself. Statesmen learn to use the robots in war. The robots themselves rise in rebellion, destroy what is left of mankind, and take over the world.

Once again the scientific Faust has been destroyed by his Mephistophelean creation.

In the 1920s science fiction was becoming a popular art form for the first time, and no longer merely a tour de force in the hands of an occasional master such as Verne and Wells. Magazines devoted exclusively to science fiction appeared and 'science fiction writers' made their appearance on the literary scene.

And one of the stock plots of science fiction was that of the invention of a robot—usually pictured as a creature of metal, without soul or emotion. Under the influence of the well-known deeds and ultimate fate of Frankenstein and Rossum, there seemed only one change to be rung on this plot.—Robots were created and destroyed their creator; robots were created and destroyed their creator; robots were created and destroyed their creator——

In the 1930s I became a science-fiction reader, and I quickly grew tired of this dull hundred-times-old tale. As a person interested in science, I resented the purely Faustian interpretation of science.

Knowledge has its dangers, yes, but is the response to be a retreat from knowledge? Are we prepared then to return to the ape and forfeit the very essence of humanity? Or is knowledge to be used as itself a barrier against the danger it brings?

In other words, Faust must indeed face Mephistopheles, but Faust *does not have to be defeated!*

Knives are manufactured with hilts so that they may be grasped safely, stairs possess banisters, electric wiring is insulated, pressure cookers have safety valves—in every artifact, thought is put into minimizing danger. Sometimes the safety achieved is insufficient because of limitations imposed by the nature of the universe or the nature of the human mind. However, the effort is there.

Consider a robot, then, as simply another artifact. It is not a sacrilegious invasion of the domain of the Almighty, any more (or any less) than any other artifact is. As a machine, a robot will surely be designed for safety, as far as possible. If robots are so advanced that they can mimic the thought processes of human beings, then surely the nature of those thought processes will be designed by human engineers and built-in safeguards will be added. The safety may not be perfect (what is?), but it will be as complete as men can make it.

With all this in mind I began, in 1940, to write robot stories of my own—but robot stories of a new variety. Never, never, was one of my robots to turn stupidly on his creator for no purpose but to demonstrate, for one more weary time, the crime and punishment of Faust.

Nonsense! My robots were machines designed by engineers, not pseudo-men created by blasphemers. My robots reacted along the rational lines that existed in their 'brains' from the moment of construction.

I must admit, though, that occasionally, in my early attempts, I saw the robot as little more than a figure of fun. I pictured it as a completely harmless creature, intent only on doing the work for which it was designed. It was incapable of harming men, yet it was victimized by human beings who, suffering from a 'Frankenstein complex' (as I called it in some of my stories), insisted on considering the poor machines to be deadly dangerous creatures.

An example of this is 'Robot AL-76 Goes Astray,' which first appeared in the February, 1942, *Amazing Stories*.

Part One

The Coming of
the Robots

ROBOT AL-76 GOES ASTRAY

JONATHAN QUELL'S eyes crinkled worriedly behind their rimless glasses as he charged through the door labeled 'General Manager.'

He slapped the folded paper in his hands upon the desk and panted, 'Look at that, boss!'

Sam Tobe juggled the cigar in his mouth from one cheek to the other, and looked. His hand went to his unshaven jaw and rasped along it. 'Hell!' he exploded. 'What are they talking about?'

'They say we sent out five AL robots,' Quell explained, quite unnecessarily.

'We sent six,' said Tobe.

'Sure, six! But they only got five at the other end. They sent out the serial numbers and AL-76 is missing.'

Tobe's chair went over backward as he heaved his thick bulk upright and went through the door as if he were on greased wheels. It was five hours after that—with the plant pulled apart from assembly rooms to vacuum chambers; with every one of the plant's two hundred employees put through the third-degree mill—that a sweating, disheveled Tobe sent an emergency message to the central plant at Schenectady.

And at the central plant, a sudden explosion of near panic took place. For the first time in the history of the United States Robots and Mechanical Men Corporation, a robot had escaped to the outer world. It wasn't so much that the law forbade the presence of any robot on Earth outside a licensed factory of the Corporation. Laws could always be squared. What was much more to the point was the statement made by one of the research mathematicians.

He said: 'That robot was created to run a Disinto on the moon. Its positronic brain was equipped for a lunar environment, and *only* a lunar environment. On Earth it's going to receive seventy-five umptillion sense impressions for which it was never prepared. There's no telling *what* its reactions will be. No telling!' And he wiped a forehead that had suddenly gone wet, with the back of his hand.

Within the hour a stratoplane had left for the Virginia plant. The instructions were simple.

'Get that robot, and get it fast!'

AL-76 was confused! In fact, confusion was the only impression his delicate positronic brain retained. It had started when he had found himself in these strange surroundings. How it had come about, he no longer knew. Everything was mixed up.

There was green underfoot, and brown shafts rose all about him with more green on top. And the sky was blue where it should have been black. The sun was all right, round and yellow and hot—but where was the powdery pumice rock underfoot; where were the huge clifflike crater rings?

There was only the green below and the blue above. The sounds that surrounded him were all strange. He had passed through running water that had reached his waist. It was blue and cold and wet. And when he passed people, as he did, occasionally, they were without the space suits they should have been wearing. When they saw him, they shouted and ran.

One man had leveled a gun at him and the bullet had whistled past his head—and then that man had run too.

He had no idea of how long he had been wandering before he finally stumbled upon Randolph Payne's shack two miles out in the woods from the town of Hannaford. Randolph Payne himself—a screwdriver in one hand, a pipe in the other, and a battered ruin of a vacuum cleaner between his knees—squatted outside the doorway.

Payne was humming at the time, for he was a naturally happy-go-lucky soul—when at his shack. He had a more respectable dwelling place back in Hannaford, but *that* dwelling place was pretty largely occupied by his wife, a fact which he silently but sincerely regretted. Perhaps, then, there was a sense of relief and freedom at such times as he found himself able to retire to his 'special deluxe doghouse' where he could smoke in peace and attend to his hobby of reservicing household appliances.

It wasn't much of a hobby, but sometimes someone would bring out a radio or an alarm clock and the money he would get paid for juggling its insides was the only money he ever got that didn't pass in driblets through his spouse's niggardly hands.

This vacuum cleaner, for instance, would bring in an easy six bits.

At the thought he broke into song, raised his eyes, and broke into a sweat. The song choked off, the eyes popped, and the sweat became more intense. He tried to stand up—as a preliminary to running like hell—but he couldn't get his legs to cooperate.

And then AL-76 had squatted down next to him and said, 'Say, why did all the rest of them run?'

Payne knew quite well why they all ran, but the gurgle that issued from his diaphragm didn't show it. He tried to inch away from the robot.

AL-76 continued in an aggrieved tone, 'One of them

even took a shot at me. An inch lower and he would have scratched my shoulder plate.'

'M-must have b-been a nut,' stammered Payne.

'That's possible.' The robot's voice grew more confidential. 'Listen, what's wrong with everything?'

Payne looked hurriedly about. It had struck him that the robot spoke in a remarkably mild tone for one so heavily and brutally metallic in appearance. It also struck him that he had heard somewhere that robots were mentally incapable of harming human beings. He relaxed a bit.

'There's nothing wrong with anything.'

'Isn't there?' AL-76 eyed him accusingly. '*You're* all wrong. Where's your space suit?'

'I haven't got any.'

'Then why aren't you dead?'

That stopped Payne, 'Well—I don't know.'

'See!' said the robot triumphantly, 'there's something wrong with everything. Where's Mount Copernicus? Where's Lunar Station 17? And where's my Disinto? I want to get to work, I do.' He seemed perturbed, and his voice shook as he continued. 'I've been going about for hours trying to get someone to tell me where my Disinto is, but they all run away. By now I'm probably 'way behind schedule and the Sectional Executive will be as sore as blazes. This is a fine situation.'

Slowly Payne unscrambled the stew in which his brain found itself and said, 'Listen, what do they call you?'

'My serial number is AL-76.'

'All right, Al is good enough for me. Now, Al, if you're looking for Lunar Station 17, that's on the moon, yes?'

AL-76 nodded his head ponderously. 'Sure. But I've been looking for it——'

'But it's on the moon. This isn't the moon.'

It was the robot's turn to become confused. He watched Payne for a speculative moment and then said slowly, 'What do you mean this isn't the moon? Of course it's the moon. Because if it isn't the moon, what is it, huh? Answer me that.'

Payne made a funny sound in his throat and breathed hard. He pointed a finger at the robot and shook it. 'Look,' he said—and then the brilliant idea of the century struck him, and he finished with a strangled 'Wow!'

AL-76 eyed him censoriously. 'That isn't an answer. I think I have a right to a civil answer if I ask a civil question.'

Payne wasn't listening. He was still marveling at himself. Why, it was as plain as day. This robot was one built for the moon that had somehow gotten loose on Earth. Naturally it would be all mixed up, because its positronic brain had been geared exclusively for a lunar environment, making its earthly surroundings entirely meaningless.

And now if he could only keep the robot here—until he could get in touch with the men at the factory in Petersboro. Why, robots were worth money. The cheapest cost $50,000, he had once heard, and some of them ran into millions. Think of the reward!

Man, oh, man, *think of the reward*! And every cent for himself. Not as much as a quarter of a snifter of a plugged nickel for Mirandy. Jumpin' tootin' blazes, *no*!

He rose to his feet at last. 'Al,' he said, 'you and I are buddies! Pals! I love you like a brother.' He thrust out a hand. 'Shake!'

The robot swallowed up the offered hand in a metal paw and squeezed it gently. He didn't quite understand. 'Does that mean you'll tell me how to get to Lunar Station 17?'

Payne was a trifle disconcerted. 'N-no, not exactly. As a matter of fact, I like you so much, I want you to stay here with me a while.'

'Oh no, I can't do that. I've got to get to work.' He shook his head. 'How would you like to be falling behind your quota hour by hour and minute by minute? I want to work. I've *got* to work.'

Payne thought sourly that there was no accounting for tastes, and said, 'All right, then, I'll explain something to you—because I can see from the looks of you that you're an intelligent person. I've had orders from your Sectional Executive, and he wants me to keep you here for a while. Till he sends for you, in fact.'

'What for?' asked AL-76 suspiciously.

'I can't say. It's secret government stuff.' Payne prayed, inwardly and fervently, that the robot would swallow this. Some robots were clever, he knew, but this looked like one of the early models.

While Payne prayed, AL-76 considered. The robot's brain, adjusted to the handling of a Disinto on the moon, was not at its best when engaged in abstract thought, but just the same, ever since he had gotten lost, AL-76 had found his thought processes becoming stranger. The alien surroundings did something to him.

His next remark was almost shrewd. He said slyly, 'What's my Sectional Executive's name?'

Payne gulped and thought rapidly. 'Al,' he said in a pained fashion, 'you hurt me with this suspicion. I *can't* tell you his name. The trees have ears.'

AL-76 inspected the tree next to him stolidly and said, 'They have not.'

'I know. What I mean is that spies are all around.'

'Spies?'

'Yes. You know, *bad* people who want to destroy Lunar Station 17.'

'What for?'

'Because they're *bad*. And they want to destroy *you*, and that's why you've got to stay here for a while, so they can't find you.'

'But—but I've got to have a Disinto. I mustn't fall behind my quota.'

'You will have. You will have,' Payne promised earnestly, and just as earnestly damned the robot's one-track mind. 'They're going to send one out tomorrow. Yeah, tomorrow.' That would leave plenty of time to get the men from the factory out here and collect beautiful green heaps of hundred-dollar bills.

But AL-76 grew only the more stubborn under the distressing impingement of the strange world all about him upon his thinking mechanism.

'No,' he said, 'I've got to have a Disinto now.' Stiffly he straightened his joints, jerking erect. 'I'd better look for it some more.'

Payne swarmed after and grabbed a cold, hard elbow. 'Listen,' he squealed, 'You've got to stay——'

And something in the robot's mind clicked. All the strangeness surrounding him collected itself into one globule, exploded, and left a brain ticking with a curiously increased efficiency. He whirled on Payne. 'I tell you what. I can build a Disinto right here—and then I can work it.'

Payne paused doubtfully. 'I don't think I can build one.' He wondered if it would do any good to pretend he could.

'That's all right.' AL-76 could almost feel the positronic paths of his brain weaving into a new pattern, and experienced a strange exhilaration. '*I* can build one.' He looked into Payne's deluxe doghouse and said, 'You've got all the material here that I need.'

Randolph Payne surveyed the junk with which his shack was filled: eviscerated radios, a topless refrigerator, rusty automobile engines, a broken-down gas range, several miles of frayed wire, and, taking it all together, fifty tons or thereabouts of the most heterogeneous mass of old metal as ever caused a junkman to sniff disdainfully.

'Have I?' he said weakly.

Two hours later, two things happened practically simultaneously. The first was that Sam Tobe of the Petersboro branch of the United States Robots and Mechanical Men Corporation received a visiphone call from one Randolph Payne of Hannaford. It concerned the missing robot, and Tobe, with a deep-throated snarl, broke connection halfway through and ordered all subsequent calls to be rerouted to the sixth assistant vice-president in charge of buttonholes.

This was not really unreasonable of Tobe. During the past week, although Robot AL-76 had dropped from sight completely, reports had flooded in from all over the Union as to the robot's whereabouts. As many as fourteen a day came—usually from fourteen different states.

Tobe was almighty tired of it, to say nothing of being half crazy on general principles. There was even talk of a Congressional investigation, though every reputable roboticist and mathematical physicist on Earth swore the robot was harmless.

In his state of mind, then, it is not surprising that it took three hours for the general manager to pause and consider just exactly how it was that this Randolph Payne had known that the robot was slated for Lunar Station 17, and, for that matter, how he had known that the robot's serial

number was AL-76. Those details had not been given out
by the company.

He kept on considering for about a minute and a half and
then swung into action.

However, during the three hours between the call and the
action, the second event took place. Randolph Payne, having correctly diagnosed the abrupt break in his call as being
due to general skepticism on the part of the plant official,
returned to his shack with a camera. They couldn't very
well argue with a photograph, and he'd be horn-swoggled if
he'd show them the real thing before they came across with
the cash.

AL-76 was busy with affairs of his own. Half of the
contents of Payne's shack was littered over about two acres
of ground, and in the middle of it the robot squatted and
fooled around with radio tubes, hunks of iron, copper wire,
and general junk. He paid no attention to Payne, who,
sprawling flat on his belly, focused his camera for a beautiful shot.

And at this point it was that Lemuel Oliver Cooper
turned the bend in the road and froze in his tracks as he
took in the tableau. The reason for his coming in the first
place was an ailing electric toaster that had developed the
annoying habit of throwing out pieces of bread forcefully,
but thoroughly untoasted. The reason for his *leaving* was
more obvious. He had come with a slow, mildly cheerful,
spring-morning saunter. He left with a speed that would
have caused any college track coach to raise his eyebrows
and purse his lips approvingly.

There was no appreciable slackening of speed until
Cooper hurtled into Sheriff Saunders' office, minus hat and
toaster, and brought himself up hard against the wall.

Kindly hands lifted him, and for half a minute he tried

speaking before he had actually calmed down to the point of breathing with, of course, no result.

They gave him whisky and fanned him and when he did speak, it came out something like this: '—monster—seven feet tall—shack all busted up—poor Rannie Payne——' and so on.

They got the story out of him gradually: how there was a huge metal monster, seven feet tall, maybe even eight or nine, out at Randolph Payne's shack; how Randolph Payne himself was on his stomach, a 'poor, bleeding, mangled corpse'; how the monster was then busily engaged in wrecking the shack out of sheer destructiveness; how it had turned on Lemuel Oliver Cooper, and how he, Cooper, had made his escape by half a hair.

Sheriff Saunders hitched his belt tighter about his portly middle and said, 'It's that there machine man that got away from the Petersboro factory. We got warning on it last Saturday. Hey, Jake, you get every man in Hannaford County that can shoot and slap a deputy's badge on him. Get them here at noon. And listen, Jake, before you do that, just drop in at the Widow Payne's place and lip her the bad news gentle-like.'

It is reported that Miranda Payne, upon being acquainted with events, paused only to make sure that her husband's insurance policy was safe, and to make a few pithy remarks concerning her foolishness in not having had him take out double the amount, before breaking out into as prolonged and heart-wringing a wail of grief as ever became a respectable widow.

It was some hours later that Randolph Payne—unaware of his horrible mutilation and death—viewed the completed negatives of his snapshots with satisfaction. As a series of

portraits of a robot at work, they left nothing to the
imagination. They might have been labeled: 'Robot Gazing Thoughtfully at Vacuum Tube,' 'Robot Splicing Two
Wires,' 'Robot Wielding Screwdriver,' 'Robot Taking Refrigerator Apart with Great Violence,' and so on.

As there now remained only the routine of making the
prints themselves, he stepped out from beyond the curtain
of the improvised darkroom for a bit of a smoke and a chat
with AL-76.

In doing so, he was blissfully unaware that the neighboring woods were verminous with nervous farmers armed
with anything from an old colonial relic of a blunderbuss to
the portable machine gun carried by the sheriff himself.
Nor, for that matter, had he any inkling of the fact that half
a dozen roboticists, under the leadership of Sam Tobe,
were smoking down the highway from Petersboro at better
than a hundred and twenty miles an hour for the sole
purpose of having the pleasure and honor of his acquaintance.

So while things were jittering toward a climax, Randolph
Payne sighed with self-satisfaction, lighted a match upon
the seat of his pants, puffed away at his pipe, and looked at
AL-76 with amusement.

It had been apparent for quite some time that the robot
was more than slightly lunatic. Randolph Payne was himself an expert at home-made contraptions, having built
several that could not have been exposed to daylight without searing the eyeballs of all beholders; but he had never
even conceived of anything approaching the monstrosity
that AL-76 was concocting.

It would have made the Rube Goldbergs of the day die
in convulsions of envy. It would have made Picasso (if he
could have lived to witness it) quit art in the sheer know-

ledge that he had been hopelessly surpassed. It would have soured the milk in the udders of any cow within half a mile.

In fact, it was gruesome!

From a rusty and massive iron base that faintly resembled something Payne had once seen attached to a secondhand tractor, it rose upward in rakish, drunken swerves through a bewildering mess of wires, wheels, tubes, and nameless horrors without number, ending in a megaphone arrangement that looked decidedly sinister.

Payne had the impulse to peek in the megaphone part, but refrained. He had seen far more sensible machines explode suddenly and with violence.

He said, 'Hey, Al.'

The robot looked up. He had been lying flat on his stomach, teasing a thin sliver of metal into place. 'What do you want, Payne?'

'What is this?' He asked it in the tone of one referring to something foul and decomposing, held gingerly between two ten-foot poles.

'It's the Disinto I'm making—so I can start to work. It's an improvement on the standard model.' The robot rose, dusted his knees clankingly, and looked at it proudly.

Payne shuddered. An 'improvement'! No wonder they hid the original in caverns on the moon. Poor satellite! Poor dead satellite! He had always wanted to know what a fate worse than death was. Now he knew.

'Will it work?' he asked.

'Sure.'

'How do you know?'

'It's got to. I made it, didn't I? I only need one thing now. Got a flashlight?'

'Somewhere, I guess.' Payne vanished into the shack and

returned almost immediately.

The robot unscrewed the bottom and set to work. In five minutes he had finished. He stepped back and said, 'All set. Now I get to work. You may watch if you want to.'

A pause, while Payne tried to appreciate the magnanimity of the offer. 'Is it safe?'

'A baby could handle it.'

'Oh!' Payne grinned weakly and got behind the thickest tree in the vicinity. 'Go ahead,' he said, 'I have the utmost confidence in you.'

AL-76 pointed to the nightmarish junk pile and said, 'Watch!' His hands set to work——

The embattled farmers of Hannaford County, Virginia, weaved up upon Payne's shack in a slowly tightening circle. With the blood of their heroic colonial forebears pounding their veins—and goose flesh trickling up and down their spines—they crept from tree to tree.

Sheriff Saunders spread the word. 'Fire when I give the signal—and aim at the eyes.'

Jacob Linker—Lank Jake to his friends, and Sheriff's Deputy to himself—edged close. 'You think maybe this machine man has skedaddled?' He did not quite manage to suppress the tone of wistful hopefulness in his voice.

'Dunno,' grunted the sheriff. 'Guess not, though. We woulda come across him in the woods if he had, and we haven't.'

'But it's awful quiet, and it appears to me as if we're getting close to Payne's place.'

The reminder wasn't necessary. Sheriff Saunders had a lump in his throat so big it had to be swallowed in three installments. 'Get back,' he ordered, 'and keep your finger on the trigger.'

They were at the rim of the clearing now, and Sheriff
Saunders closed his eyes and stuck the corner of one out
from behind the tree. Seeing nothing, he paused, then tried
again, eyes open this time.

Results were, naturally, better.

To be exact, he saw one huge machine man, back toward
him, bending over one soul-curdling, hiccupy contraption of
uncertain origin and less certain purpose. The only item he
missed was the quivering figure of Randolph Payne, em-
bracing the tree next but three to the nor'-nor'west.

Sheriff Saunders stepped out into the open and raised his
machine gun. The robot, still presenting a broad metal
back, said in a loud voice—to person or persons unknown—
'Watch!' and as the sheriff opened his mouth to signal a
general order to fire, metal fingers compressed a switch.

There exists no adequate description of what occurred
afterward, in spite of the presence of seventy eyewitnesses.
In the days, months, and years to come not one of those
seventy ever had a word to say about the few seconds after
the sheriff had opened his mouth to give the firing order.
When questioned about it, they merely turned apple-green
and staggered away.

It is plain from circumstantial evidence, however, that,
in a general way, what did occur was this.

Sheriff Saunders opened his mouth; AL-76 pulled a
switch. The Disinto worked, and seventy-five trees, two
barns, three cows and the top three quarters of Duckbill
Mountain whiffed into rarefied atmosphere. They became,
so to speak, one with the snows of yesteryear.

Sheriff Saunders' mouth remained open for an indefinite
interval thereafter, but nothing—neither firing orders nor
anything else—issued therefrom. And then——

And then, there was a stirring in the air, a multiple ro-o-o-oshing sound, a series of purple streaks through the atmosphere radiating away from Randolph Payne's shack as the center, and of the members of the posse, not a sign.

There were various guns scattered about the vicinity, including the sheriff's patented nickel-plated, extra-rapid-fire, guaranteed-no-clog, portable machine gun. There were about fifty hats, a few half-chomped cigars, and some odds and ends that had come loose in the excitement—but of actual human beings there was none.

Except for Lank Jake, not one of those human beings came within human ken for three days, and the exception in his favor came about because he was interrupted in his comet-flight by the half-dozen men from the Petersboro factory, who were charging *into* the wood at a pretty fair speed of their own.

It was Sam Tobe who stopped him, catching Lank Jake's head skillfully in the pit of his stomach. When he caught his breath, Tobe asked, 'Where's Randolph Payne's place?'

Lank Jake allowed his eyes to unglaze for just a moment. 'Brother,' he said, 'just you follow the direction I ain't going.'

And with that, miraculously, he was gone. There was a shrinking dot dodging trees on the horizon that might have been he, but Sam Tobe wouldn't have sworn to it.

That takes care of the posse; but there still remains Randolph Payne, whose reactions took something of a different form.

For Randolph Payne, the five-second interval after the pulling of the switch and the disappearance of Duckbill Mountain was a total blank. At the start he had been peering through the thick underbrush from behind the bottom of the trees; at the end he was swinging wildly from one of the topmost branches. The same impulse that had driven the posse horizontally had driven him vertically.

As to how he had covered the fifty feet from roots to top—whether he had climbed, jumped, or flown—he did not know, and he didn't give a particle of never-mind.

What he *did* know was that property had been destroyed by a robot temporarily in his possession. All visions of rewards vanished and were replaced by trembling nightmares of hostile citizenry, shrieking lynch mobs, lawsuits, murder charges, and what Mirandy Payne would say. Mostly what Mirandy Payne would say.

He was yelling wildly and hoarsely, 'Hey, you robot, you smash that thing, do you hear? Smash it good! You forget I ever had anything to do with it! You're a stranger to me, see? You don't ever say a word about it. Forget it, you hear?'

He didn't expect his orders to do any good; it was only reflex action. What he didn't know was that a robot always obeys a human order except where carrying it out involves danger to another human.

AL-76, therefore, calmly and methodically proceeded to demolish his Disinto into rubble and flinders.

Just as he was stamping the last cubic inch under foot, Sam Tobe and his contingent arrived, and Randolph Payne, sensing that the real owners of the robot had come, dropped out of the tree head-first and made for regions unknown feet-first.

He did not wait for his reward.

Austin Wilde, Robotical Engineer, turned to Sam Tobe and said, 'Did you get anything out of the robot?'

Tobe shook his head and snarled deep in his throat. 'Nothing. Not one thing. He's forgotten everything that's happened since he left the factory. He must have gotten *orders* to forget, or it couldn't have left him so blank. What was that pile of junk he'd been fooling with?'

'Just that. A pile of junk! But it must have been a Disinto before he smashed it, and I'd like to kill the fellow who ordered him to smash it—by slow torture, if possible. Look at this!'

They were part of the way up the slopes of what had been Duckbill Mountain—at that point, to be exact, where the top had been sheered off; and Wilde put his hand down upon the perfect flatness that cut through both soil and rock.

'*What* a Disinto,' he said. 'It took the mountain right off its base.'

'What made him build it?'

Wilde shrugged. 'I don't know. Some factor in his environment—there's no way of knowing what—reacted upon his moon-type positronic brain to produce a Disinto out of junk. It's a billion to one against our ever stumbling upon that factor again now that the robot himself has forgotten. We'll never have that Disinto.'

'Never mind. The important thing is that we have the robot.'

'The hell you say.' There was poignant regret in Wilde's voice. 'Have you ever had anything to do with the Disintos on the moon? They eat up energy like so many electronic hogs and won't even begin to run until you've built up a potential of better than a million volts. But *this* Disinto worked differently. I went through the rubbish with a microscope, and would you like to see the only source of power of any kind that I found?'

'What was it?'

'Just this! And we'll never know how he did it.'

And Austin Wilde held up the source of power that had enabled a Disinto to chew up a mountain in half a second—*two flashlight batteries!*

The next example is less blatantly humorous but is one in which the robots are still not taken quite seriously. The story arose out of another story—not about robots—to which the robot story served as sequel.

In the October 1941 issue of Astounding Science Fiction was published a story of mine called 'Not Final,' in which the human colonists on Ganymede (largest of the satellites of Jupiter) make radio contact with life forms on Jupiter. These life forms turn out to be madly hostile and Earthmen begin to fear for their safety if the Jovians ever achieve space travel.

To be sure, Jupiter's gravity is so intense and its atmosphere is so dense that spaceships of ordinary matter could not hold that atmosphere against the vacuum of space or lift itself against the gravity. However, human technology has developed force fields, and if the Jovians did the same, then they might emerge from their planet behind walls of sheer energy, rather than walls of matter.

It was necessary to investigate this point, but no human beings could possibly have survived a trip to Jupiter's fantastically unfriendly surface.

However, if human beings can't do it, robots built by human beings can. With this in mind I wrote 'Victory Unintentional,' which appeared first in the August 1942 issue of Super Science Stories.

THE spaceship leaked, as the saying goes, like a sieve.

It was supposed to. In fact, that was the whole idea.

The result, of course, was that during the journey from Ganymede to Jupiter, the ship was crammed just as full as it could be with the very hardest space vacuum. And since the ship also lacked heating devices, this space vacuum was at normal temperature, which is a fraction of a degree above absolute zero.

This, also, was according to plan. Little things like the absence of heat and air didn't annoy anyone at all on the particular spaceship.

The first near vacuum wisps of Jovian atmosphere began percolating into the ship several thousand miles above the Jovian surface. It was practically all hydrogen, though perhaps a careful gas analysis might have located a trace of helium as well. The pressure gauges began creeping skyward.

That creep continued at an accelerating pace as the ship dropped downward in a Jupiter-circling spiral. The pointers of successive gauges, each designed for progressively higher pressures, began to move until they reached the neighborhood of a million or so atmospheres, where figures lost most of their meaning. The temperature, as recorded by thermocouples, rose slowly and erratically, and finally steadied at about seventy below zero, Centigrade.

The ship moved slowly toward the end, plowing its way heavily through a maze of gas molecules that crowded together so closely that hydrogen itself was squeezed to the density of a liquid. Ammonia vapor, drawn from the incredibly vast oceans of that liquid, saturated the horrible atmosphere. The wind, which had begun a thousand miles higher, had risen to a pitch inadequately described as a hurricane.

It was quite plain long before the ship landed on a fairly large Jovian island, perhaps seven times the size of Asia, that Jupiter was not a very pleasant world.

And yet the three members of the crew thought it was. They were quite convinced it was. But then, the three members of the crew were not exactly human. And neither were they exactly Jovian.

They were simply robots, designed on Earth for Jupiter.

ZZ Three said, 'It appears to be a rather desolate place.'

ZZ Two joined him and regarded the wind-blasted landscape somberly. 'There are structures of some sort in the distance,' he said, 'which are obviously artificial. I suggest we wait for the inhabitants to come to us.'

Across the room ZZ One listened, but made no reply. He was the first constructed of the three, and half experimental. Consequently he spoke a little less frequently than his two companions.

The wait was not long. An air vessel of queer design swooped overhead. More followed. And then a line of ground vehicles approached, took position, and disgorged organisms. Along with these organisms came various inanimate accessories that might have been weapons. Some of these were borne by a single Jovian, some by several, and some advanced under their own power, with Jovians perhaps inside.

The robots couldn't tell.

ZZ Three said, 'They're all around us now. The logical

peaceful gesture would be to come out in the open. Agreed?'

It was, and ZZ One shoved open the heavy door, which was not double or, for that matter, particularly airtight.

Their appearance through the door was the signal for an excited stir among the surrounding Jovians. Things were done to several of the very largest of the inanimate accessories, and ZZ Three became aware of a temperature rise on the outer rind of his beryllium-iridium-bronze body.

He glanced at ZZ Two. 'Do you feel it? They're aiming heat energy at us, I believe.'

ZZ Two indicated his surprise. 'I wonder why?'

'Definitely a heat ray of some sort. Look at that!'

One of the rays had been jarred out of alignment for some undiscernible cause, and its line of radiation intersected a brook of sparkling pure ammonia—which promptly boiled furiously.

Three turned to ZZ One, 'Make a note of this, One, will you?'

'Sure.' It was to ZZ One that the routine secretarial work fell, and his method of taking a note was to make a mental addition to the accurate memory scroll within him. He had already gathered the hour-by-hour record of every important instrument on board ship during the trip to Jupiter. He added agreeably, 'What reason shall I put for the reaction? The human masters would probably enjoy knowing.'

'No reason. Or better,' Three corrected himself, 'no apparent reason. You might say the maximum temperature of the ray was about plus thirty, Centigrade.'

Two interrupted, 'Shall we try communicating?'

'It would be a waste of time,' said Three. 'There can't be more than a very few Jovians who know the radio-click code that's been developed between Jupiter and Ganymede.

They'll have to send for one, and when he comes, he'll establish contact soon enough. Meanwhile let's watch them. I don't understand their actions, I tell you frankly.'

Nor did understanding come immediately. Heat radiation ceased, and other instruments were brought to the forefront and put into play. Several capsules fell at the feet of the watching robots, dropping rapidly and forcefully under Jupiter's gravity. They popped open and a blue liquid exuded, forming pools which proceeded to shrink rapidly by evaporation.

The nightmare wind whipped the vapors away and where those vapors went, Jovians scrambled out of the way. One was too slow, threshed about wildly, and became very limp and still.

ZZ Two bent, dabbed a finger in one of the pools and stared at the dripping liquid. 'I think this is oxygen,' he said.

'Oxygen, all right,' agreed Three. 'This becomes stranger and stranger. It must certainly be a dangerous practice, for I would say that oxygen is poisonous to the creatures. One of them died!'

There was a pause, and then ZZ One, whose greater simplicity led at times to an increased directness of thought, said heavily, 'It might be that these strange creatures in a rather childish way are attempting to destroy us.'

And Two, struck by the suggestion, answered, 'You know, One, I think you're right!'

There had been a slight lull in Jovian activity and now a new structure was brought up. It possessed a slender rod that pointed skyward through the impenetrable Jovian murk. It stood in that starkly incredible wind with a rigidity that plainly indicated remarkable structural strength. From its tip came a cracking and then a flash that lit up the depths of the atmosphere into a gray fog.

For a moment the robots were bathed in clinging radiance and then Three said thoughtfully, 'High-tension electricity! Quite respectable power, too. One, I think you're right. After all, the human masters have told us that these creatures seek to destroy all humanity, and organisms possessing such insane viciousness as to harbor a thought of harm against a human being'—his voice trembled at the thought—'would scarcely scruple at attempting to destroy us.'

'It's a shame to have such distorted minds,' said ZZ One. 'Poor fellows!'

'I find it a very saddening thought,' admitted Two. 'Let's go back to the ship. We've seen enough for now.'

They did so, and settled down to wait. As ZZ Three said, Jupiter was a roomy planet, and it might take time for Jovian transportation to bring a radio code expert to the ship. However, patience is a cheap commodity to robots.

As a matter of fact, Jupiter turned on its axis three times, according to chronometer, before the expert arrived. The rising and setting of the sun made no difference, of course, to the dead darkness at the bottom of three thousand miles of liquid-dense gas, so that one could not speak of day and night. But then, neither Jovian nor robot saw by visible light radiation and that didn't matter.

Through this thirty-hour interval the surrounding Jovians continued their attack with a patience and persevering relentlessness concerning which robot ZZ One made a good many mental notes. The ship was assaulted by as many varieties of forces as there were hours, and the robots observed every attack attentively, analyzing such weapons as they recognized. They by no means recognized all.

But the human masters had built well. It had taken fifteen years to construct the ship and the robots, and their essentials could be expressed in a single phrase—raw strength. The attack spent itself uselessly and neither ship nor robot seemed the worse for it.

Three said, 'This atmosphere handicaps them, I think. They can't use atomic disruptors, since they would only tear a hole in that soupy air and blow themselves up.'

'They haven't used high explosives either,' said Two, 'which is well. They couldn't have hurt us, naturally, but it would have thrown us about a bit.'

'High explosives are out of the question. You can't have an explosive without gas expansion and gas just can't expand in this atmosphere.'

'It's a very good atmosphere,' muttered One. 'I like it.'

Which was natural, because he was built for it. The ZZ robots were the first robots ever turned out by the United States Robots and Mechanical Men Corporation that were not even faintly human in appearance. They were low and squat, with a center of gravity less than a foot above ground level. They had six legs apiece, stumpy and thick, designed to lift tons against two and a half times normal Earth gravity. Their reflexes were that many times Earth-normal speed, to make up for the gravity. And they were composed of a beryllium–iridium–bronze alloy that was proof against any known corrosive agent, also any known destructive agent short of a thousand-megaton atomic disruptor, under any conditions whatsoever.

To dispense with further description, they were indestructible, and so impressively powerful that they were the only robots ever built on whom the roboticists of the Corporation had never quite had the nerve to pin a serial-number nickname. One bright young fellow had suggested

Sissy One, Two, and Three—but not in a very loud voice, and the suggestion was never repeated.

The last hours of the wait were spent in a puzzled discussion to find a possible description of a Jovian's appearance. ZZ One had made a note of their possession of tentacles and of their radial symmetry—and there he had stuck. Two and Three did their best, but couldn't help.

'You can't very well describe anything,' Three declared finally, 'without a standard of reference. These creatures are like nothing I know of—completely outside the positronic paths of my brain. It's like trying to describe gamma light to a robot unequipped for gamma-ray reception.'

It was just at that time that the weapon barrage ceased once more. The robots turned their attention to outside the ship.

A group of Jovians were advancing in curiously uneven fashion, but no amount of careful watching could determine the exact method of their locomotion. How they used their tentacles was uncertain. At times the organisms took on a remarkable slithering motion, and then they moved at great speed, perhaps with the wind's help, for they were moving downwind.

The robots stepped out to meet the Jovians, who halted ten feet away. Both sides remained silent and motionless.

ZZ Two said, 'They must be watching us, but I don't know how. Do either of you see any photosensitive organs?'

'I can't say,' grunted Three in response. 'I don't see anything about them that makes sense at all.'

There was a sudden metallic clicking from among the Jovian group and ZZ One said delightedly, 'It's the radio code. They've got the communications expert here.'

It was, and they had. The complicated dot-dash system that over a period of twenty-five years had been laboriously developed by the beings of Jupiter and the Earthmen of Ganymede into a remarkably flexible means of communication was finally being put into practice at close range.

One Jovian remained in the forefront now, the others having fallen back. It was he that was speaking. The clicking said, 'Where are you from?'

ZZ Three, as the most mentally advanced, naturally assumed spokesmanship for the robot group. 'We are from Jupiter's satellite, Ganymede.'

The Jovian continued, 'What do you want?'

'Information. We have come to study your world and to bring back our findings. If we could have your cooperation——'

The Jovian clicking interrupted. 'You must be destroyed!'

ZZ Three paused and said in a thoughtful aside to his two companions, 'Exactly the attitude the human masters said they would take. They are very unusual.'

Returning to his clicking, he asked simply, 'Why?'

The Jovian evidently considered certain questions too obnoxious to be answered. He said, 'If you leave within a single period of revolution, we will spare you—until such time as we emerge from our world to destroy the un-Jovian vermin of Ganymede.'

'I would like to point out,' said Three, 'that we of Ganymede and the inner planets——'

The Jovian interrupted, 'Our astronomy knows of the Sun and of our four satellites. There are no inner planets.'

Three conceded the point wearily, 'We of Ganymede, then. We have no designs on Jupiter. We're prepared to offer friendship. For twenty-five years your people communicated freely with the human beings of Ganymede. Is there any reason to make sudden war upon the humans?'

'For twenty-five years,' was the cold response, 'we assumed the inhabitants of Ganymede to be Jovians. When we found out they were not, and that we had been treating lower animals on the scale of Jovian intelligences, we were bound to take steps to wipe out the dishonor.'

Slowly and forcefully he finished, 'We of Jupiter will suffer the existence of no vermin!'

The Jovian was backing away in some fashion, tacking against the wind, and the interview was evidently over.

The robots retreated inside the ship.

ZZ Two said, 'It looks bad, doesn't it?' He continued thoughtfully, 'It is as the human masters said. They possess an ultimately developed superiority complex, combined with an extreme intolerance for anyone or anything that disturbs that complex.'

'The intolerance,' observed Three, 'is the natural consequence of the complex. The trouble is that their intolerance has teeth in it. They have weapons—and their science is great.'

'I am not surprised now,' burst out ZZ One, 'that we were specifically instructed to disregard Jovian orders. They are horrible, intolerant, pseudo-superior beings!' He added emphatically, with robotical loyalty and faith, 'No human master could ever be like that.'

'That, though true, is beside the point,' said Three. 'The fact remains that the human masters are in terrible danger. This is a gigantic world and these Jovians are greater in numbers and resources by a hundred times or more than the humans of the entire Terrestrial Empire. If they can ever develop the force field to the point where they can use it as a spaceship hull—as the human masters have already done —they will overrun the system at will. The question remains as to how far they have advanced in that direction, what other weapons they have, what preparations they are making, and so on. To return with that information is our function, of course, and we had better decide on our next step.'

'It may be difficult,' said Two. 'The Jovians won't help us.' Which, at the moment, was rather an understatement.

Three thought awhile. 'It seems to me that we need only wait,' he observed. 'They have tried to destroy us for thirty hours now and haven't succeeded. Certainly they have done their best. Now a superiority complex always involves the eternal necessity of saving face, and the ultimatum given us proves it in this case. They would never allow us to leave if they could destroy us. But if we don't leave, then rather than admit they cannot force us away, they will surely pretend that they are willing, for their own purposes, to have us stay.'

Once again they waited. The day passed. The weapon barrage did not resume. The robots did not leave. The bluff was called. And now the robots faced the Jovian radio-code expert once again.

If the ZZ models had been equipped with a sense of humor, they would have enjoyed themselves immensely. As it was, they felt merely a solemn sense of satisfaction.

The Jovian said, 'It has been our decision that you will be allowed to remain for a very short time, so that you see our power for yourself. You shall then return to Ganymede to inform your companion vermin of the disastrous end to which they will unfailingly come within a solar revolution.'

ZZ One made a mental note that a Jovian revolution took twelve earthly years.

Three replied casually, 'Thank you. May we accompany you to the nearest town? There are many things we would like to learn.' He added as an afterthought, 'Our ship is not to be touched, of course.'

He said this as a request, not as a threat, for no ZZ model was ever pugnacious. All capacity for even the slightest annoyance had been carefully barred in their construction. With robots as vastly powerful as the ZZ's, unfailing good temper was essential for safety during the years of testing on Earth.

The Jovian said, 'We are not interested in your verminous ship. No Jovian will pollute himself by approaching it. You may accompany us, but you must on no account approach closer than ten feet to any Jovian, or you will be instantly destroyed.'

'Stuck up, aren't they?' observed Two in a genial whisper, as they plowed into the wind.

The town was a port on the shores of an incredible ammonia lake. The external wind whipped furious, frothy waves that shot across the liquid surface at the hectic rate enforced by the gravity. The port itself was neither large nor impressive and it seemed fairly evident that most of the construction was underground.

'What is the population of this place?' asked Three.

The Jovian replied, 'It is a small town of ten million.'

'I see. Make a note of that, One.'

ZZ One did so mechanically, and then turned once more to the lake, at which he had been staring in fascination. He pulled at Three's elbow. 'Say, do you suppose they have fish here?'

'What difference does it make?'

'I think we ought to know. The human masters ordered us to find out everything we could.' Of the robots, One was the simplest and, consequently, the one who took orders in the most literal fashion.

Two said, 'Let One go and look if he likes. It won't do

any harm if we let the kid have his fun.'

'All right. There's no real objection if he doesn't waste his time. Fish aren't what we came for—but go ahead, One.'

ZZ One made off in great excitement and slogged rapidly down the beach, plunging into the ammonia with a splash. The Jovians watched attentively. They had understood none of the previous conversation, of course.

The radio code expert clicked out, 'It is apparent that your companion has decided to abandon life in despair at our greatness.'

Three said in surprise, 'Nothing of the sort. He wants to investigate the living organisms, if any, that live in the ammonia.' He added apologetically, 'Our friend is very curious at times, and he isn't quite as bright as we are, though that is only his misfortune. We understand that and try to humor him whenever we can.'

There was a long pause, and the Jovian observed, 'He will drown.'

Three replied casually, 'No danger of that. We don't drown. May we enter the town as soon as he returns?'

At that moment there was a spurt of liquid several hundred feet out in the lake. It sprayed upward wildly and then hurtled down in a wind-driven mist. Another spurt and another, then a wild white foaming that formed a trail toward shore, gradually quieting as it approached.

The two robots watched this in amazement, and the utter lack of motion on the part of the Jovians indicated that they were watching as well.

Then the head of ZZ One broke the surface and he made his slow way out on to dry land. But something followed him! Some organism of gigantic size that seemed nothing but fangs, claws, and spines. Then they saw that it wasn't following him under its own power, but was being dragged across the beach by ZZ One. There was a significant flabbiness about it.

ZZ One approached rather timidly and took communication into his own hands. He tapped out a message to the Jovian in agitated fashion. 'I am very sorry this happened, but the thing attacked me. I was merely taking notes on it. It is not a valuable creature, I hope.'

He was not answered immediately, for at the first appearance of the monster there had been a wild break in the Jovian ranks. These reformed slowly, and cautious observation having proven the creature to be indeed dead, order was restored. Some of the bolder were curiously prodding the body.

ZZ Three said humbly, 'I hope you will pardon our friend. He is sometimes clumsy. We have absolutely no intention of harming any Jovian creature.'

'He attacked me,' explained One. 'He bit at me without provocation. See!' And he displayed a two-foot fang that ended in a jagged break. 'He broke it on my shoulder and almost left a scratch. I just slapped it a bit to send it away—and it died. I'm sorry!'

The Jovian finally spoke, and his code clicking was a rather stuttery affair. 'It is a wild creature, rarely found so close to shore, but the lake is deep just here.'

Three said, still anxiously, 'If you can use it for food, we are only too glad——'

'No. We can get food for ourselves without the help of verm—without the help of others. Eat it yourselves.'

At that ZZ One heaved the creature up and back into the sea, with an easy motion of one arm. Three said casually, 'Thank you for your kind offer, but we have no use for food. We don't eat, of course.'

Escorted by two hundred or so armed Jovians, the robots passed down a series of ramps into the underground city. If, above the surface, the city had looked small and unimpressive, then from beneath it took on the appearance of a vast megalopolis.

They were ushered into ground cars that were operated by remote control—for no honest, self-respecting Jovian would risk his superiority by placing himself in the same car with vermin—and driven at frightful speed to the center of the town. They saw enough to decide that it extended fifty miles from end to end and reached downward into Jupiter's crust at least eight miles.

ZZ Two did not sound happy as he said, 'If this is a sample of Jovian development then we shall not have a hopeful report to bring back to the human masters. After all, we landed on the vast surface of Jupiter at random, with the chances a thousand to one against coming near any really concentrated center of population. This must be, as the code expert says, a mere town.'

'Ten million Jovians,' said Three abstractedly. 'Total population must be in the trillions, which is high, very high, even for Jupiter. They probably have a completely urban civilization, which means that their scientific development must be tremendous. If they have force fields——'

Three had no neck, for in the interest of strength the heads of the ZZ models were riveted firmly onto the torso, with the delicate positronic brains protected by three separate layers in inch-thick iridium alloy. But if he had had one, he would have shaken his head dolefully.

They had stopped now in a cleared space. Everywhere about them they could see avenues and structures crowded with Jovians, as curious as any terrestrial crowd would have been in similar circumstances.

The code expert approached. 'It is time now for me to retire until the next period of activity. We have gone so far as to arrange quarters for you at great inconvenience to ourselves for, of course, the structure will have to be pulled down and rebuilt afterward. Nevertheless, you will be allowed to sleep for a space.'

ZZ Three waved an arm in deprecation and tapped out, 'We thank you but you must not trouble yourself. We don't mind remaining right here. If you want to sleep and rest, by all means do. We'll wait for you. As for us,' casually, 'we don't sleep.'

The Jovian said nothing, though if it had had a face, the expression upon it might have been interesting. It left, and the robots remained in the car, with squads of well-armed Jovians, frequently replaced, surrounding them as guards.

It was hours before the ranks of those guards parted to allow the code expert to return. Along with him were other Jovians, whom he introduced.

'There are with me two officials of the central government who have graciously consented to speak with you.'

One of the officials evidently knew the code, for his clicking interrupted the code expert sharply. He addressed the robots, 'Vermin! Emerge from the ground car that we may look at you.'

The robots were only too willing to comply, so while Three and Two vaulted over the right side of the car, ZZ One dashed through the left side. The word through is used advisedly, for since he neglected to work the mechanism that lowered a section of side so that one might exit, he carried that side, plus two wheels and an axle, along with him. The car collapsed, and ZZ One stood staring at the ruins in embarrassed silence.

At last he clicked out gently, 'I'm very sorry. I hope it

wasn't an expensive car.'

ZZ Two added apologetically, 'Our companion is often clumsy. You must excuse him,' and ZZ Three made a halfhearted attempt to put the car back together again.

ZZ One made another effort to excuse himself. 'The material of the car was rather flimsy. You see?' He lifted a square-yard sheet of three-inch-thick, metal-hard plastic in both hands and exerted a bit of pressure. The sheet promptly snapped in two. 'I should have made allowances,' he admitted.

The Jovian government official said in slightly less sharp fashion, 'The car would have had to be destroyed anyway, after being polluted by your presence.' He paused, then, 'Creatures! We Jovians lack vulgar curiosity concerning lower animals, but our scientists seek facts.'

'We're right with you,' replied Three cheerfully. 'So do we.'

The Jovian ignored him. 'You lack the mass-sensitive organ, apparently. How is it that you are aware of distant objects?'

Three grew interested. 'Do you mean your people are directly sensitive to mass?'

'I am not here to answer your questions—your impudent questions—about us.'

'I take it then that objects of low specific mass would be transparent to you, even in the absence of radiation.' He turned to Two, 'That's how they see. Their atmosphere is as transparent as space to them.'

The Jovian clicking began once more, 'You will answer my first question immediately, or my patience will end and I will order you destroyed.'

Three said at once, 'We are energy-sensitive, Jovian. We can adjust ourselves to the entire electromagnetic scale at will. At present, our long-distance sight is due to radio-wave radiation that we emit ourselves, and at close range we see by——' He paused, and said to Two, 'There isn't any code word for gamma ray, is there?'

'Not that I know of,' Two answered.

Three continued to the Jovian, 'At close range we see by other radiation for which there is no code word.'

'Of what is your body composed?' demanded the Jovian.

Two whispered, 'He probably asks that because his mass sensitivity can't penetrate past our skin. High density, you know. Ought we to tell him?'

Three replied uncertainly, 'Our human masters didn't particularly say we were to keep anything secret.' In radio code, to the Jovian he said, 'We are mostly iridium. For the rest, copper, tin, a little beryllium, and a scattering of other substances.'

The Jovians fell back and by the obscure writhing of various portions of their thoroughly indescribable bodies gave the impression that they were in animated conversation, although they made no sound.

And then the official returned. 'Beings of Ganymede! It has been decided to show you through some of our factories that we may exhibit a tiny part of our great achievements. We will then allow you to return so that you may spread despair among the other verm—the other beings of the outer world.'

Three said to Two, 'Note the effect of their psychology. They must hammer home their superiority. It's still a matter of saving face.' And in radio code, 'We thank you for the opportunity.'

But the face saving was efficient, as the robots realized soon enough. The demonstration became a tour, and the tour a Grand Exhibition. The Jovians displayed everything, explained everything, answered all questions eagerly, and ZZ One made hundreds of despairing notes.

The war potential of that single so-called unimportant town was greater by several times than that of all Ganymede. Ten more such towns would outproduce all the Terrestrial Empire. Yet ten more such towns would not be the fingernail fragment of the strength all Jupiter must be able to exert.

Three turned as One nudged him. 'What is it?'

ZZ One said seriously, 'If they have force fields, the human masters are lost, aren't they?'

'I'm afraid so. Why do you ask?'

'Because the Jovians aren't showing us through the right wing of this factory. It might be that force fields are being developed there. They would be wanting to keep it secret if they were. We'd better find out. It's the main point, you know.'

Three regarded One somberly. 'Perhaps you're right. It's no use ignoring anything.'

They were in a huge steel mill now, watching hundred-foot beams of ammonia-resistant silicon-steel alloy being turned out twenty to the second. Three asked quietly, 'What does that wing contain?'

The government official inquired of those in charge of the factory and explained, 'That is the section of great heat. Various processes require huge temperatures which life cannot bear, and they must all be handled indirectly.'

He led the way to a partition from which heat could be felt to radiate and indicated a small, round area of transparent material. It was one of a row of such, through which the foggy red light of lines of glowing forges could be made out through the soupy atmosphere.

ZZ One fastened a look of suspicion on the Jovian and

clicked out, 'Would it be all right if I went in and looked around? I am very interested in this.'

Three said, 'You're being childish, One. They're telling the truth. Oh well, nose around if you must. But don't take too long; we've got to move on.'

The Jovian said, 'You have no understanding of the heat involved. You will die.'

'Oh no,' explained One casually. 'Heat doesn't bother us.'

There was a Jovian conference, and then a scene of scurrying confusion as the life of the factory was geared to this unusual emergency. Screens of heat-absorbent material were set up, and then a door dropped open, a door that had never before budged while the forges were working. ZZ One entered and the door closed behind him. Jovian officials crowded to the transparent areas to watch.

ZZ One walked to the nearest forge and tapped the outside. Since he was too short to see into it comfortably, he tipped the forge until the molten metal licked at the lip of the container. He peered at it curiously, then dipped his hand in and stirred it awhile to test the consistency. Having done this, he withdrew his hand, shook off some of the fiery metallic droplets and wiped the rest on one of his six thighs. Slowly he went down the line of forges, then signified his desire to leave.

The Jovians retired to a great distance when he came out of the door and played a stream of ammonia on him, which hissed, bubbled and steamed until he was brought to bearable temperature once more.

ZZ One ignored the ammonia shower and said, 'They were telling the truth. No force fields.'

Three began, 'You see——' but One interrupted impatiently, 'But there's no use delaying. The human masters instructed us to find out everything and that's that.'

He turned to the Jovian and clicked out, without the slightest hesitation, 'Listen, has Jovian science developed force fields?'

Bluntness was, of course, one of the natural consequences of One's less well developed mental powers. Two and Three knew that, so they refrained from expressing disapproval of the remark.

The Jovian official relaxed slowly from his strangely stiffened attitude which had somehow given the impression that he had been staring stupidly at One's hand—the one he had dipped into the molten metal. The Jovian said slowly, 'Force fields? That, then, is your main object of curiosity?'

'Yes,' said One with emphasis.

There was a sudden and patent gain in confidence on the Jovian's part, for the clicking grew sharper. 'Then come, vermin!'

Whereupon Three said to Two, 'We're vermin again, I see—which sounds as if there's bad news ahead.' And Two gloomily agreed.

It was to the very edge of the city that they were now led—to the portion which on Earth would have been termed the suburbs—and into one of a series of closely integrated structures, which might have corresponded vaguely to a terrestrial university.

There were no explanations, however, and none was asked for. The Jovian official led the way rapidly, and the robots followed with the grim conviction that the worst was just about to happen.

It was ZZ One who stopped before an opened wall section after the rest had passed on. 'What's this?' he wanted to know.

The room was equipped with narrow, low benches, along

which Jovians manipulated rows of strange devices, of which strong, inch-long electromagnets formed the principal feature.

'What's this?' asked One again.

The Jovian turned back and exhibited impatience. 'This is a students' biological laboratory. There's nothing there to interest you.'

'But what are they doing?'

'They are studying microscopic life. Haven't you ever seen a microscope before?'

Three interrupted in explanation, 'He has, but not that type. Our microscopes are meant for energy-sensitive organs and work by refraction of radiant energy. Your microscopes evidently work on a mass-expansion basis. Rather ingenious.'

ZZ One said, 'Would it be all right if I inspected some of your specimens?'

'Of what use will that be? You cannot use our microscopes because of your sensory limitations and it will simply force us to discard such specimens as you approach for no decent reason.'

'But I don't need a microscope,' explained One, with surprise. 'I can easily adjust myself for microscopic vision.'

He strode to the nearest bench, while the students in the room crowded to the corner in an attempt to avoid contamination. ZZ One shoved a microscope aside and inspected the slide carefully. He backed away, puzzled, then tried another ... a third ... a fourth.

He came back and addressed the Jovian. 'Those are supposed to be alive, aren't they? I mean those little worm things.'

The Jovian said, 'Certainly.'

'That's strange—when I look at them, they die!'

Three exclaimed sharply and said to his two companions, 'We've forgotten our gamma-ray radiation. Let's get out of here, One, or we'll kill every bit of microscopic life in the room.'

He turned to the Jovian, 'I'm afraid that our presence is fatal to weaker forms of life. We had better leave. We hope the specimens are not too difficult to replace. And, while we're about it, you had better not stay too near us, or our radiation may affect you adversely. You feel all right so far, don't you?' he asked.

The Jovian led the way onward in proud silence, but it was to be noticed that thereafter he doubled the distance he had hitherto kept between himself and them.

Nothing more was said until the robots found themselves in a vast room. In the very center of it huge ingots of metal rested unsupported in mid-air—or, rather, supported by nothing visible—against mighty Jovian gravity.

The Jovian clicked, 'There is your force field in ultimate form, as recently perfected. Within that bubble is a vacuum, so that it is supporting the full weight of our atmosphere plus an amount of metal equivalent to two large spaceships. What do you say to that?'

'That space travel now becomes a possibility for you,' said Three.

'Definitely. No metal or plastic has the strength to hold our atmosphere against a vacuum, but a force field can—and a force-field bubble will be our spaceship. Within the year we will be turning them out by the hundreds of thousands. Then we will swarm down upon Ganymede to destroy the verminous so-called intelligences that attempt to dispute our dominion of the universe.'

'The human beings of Ganymede have never attempted——' began Three, in mild expostulation.

'Silence!' snapped the Jovian. 'Return now and tell them what you've seen. Their own feeble force fields—such as the one your ship is equipped with—will not stand against us, for our smallest ship will be a hundred times the size and power of yours.'

Three said, 'Then there's nothing more to do and we will return, as you say, with the information. If you could lead us back to our ship, we'll say good-bye. But by the way, just as a matter for the record, there's something you don't understand. The humans of Ganymede have force fields, of course, but our particular ship isn't equipped with one. We don't need any.'

The robot turned away and motioned his companions to follow. For a moment they did not speak, then ZZ One muttered dejectedly, 'Can't we try to destroy this place?'

'It won't help,' said Three. 'They'd get us by weight of numbers. It's no use. In an earthly decade the human masters will be finished. It is impossible to stand against Jupiter. There's just too much of it. As long as Jovians were tied to the surface, the humans were safe. But now that they have force fields—— All we can do is to bring the news. By the preparation of hiding places, some few may survive for a short while.'

The city was behind them. They were out on the open plain by the lake, with their ship a dark spot on the horizon, when the Jovian spoke suddenly:

'Creatures, you say you have no force field?'

Three replied without interest, 'We don't need one.'

'How then does your ship stand the vacuum of space without exploding because of the atmospheric pressure within?' And he moved a tentacle as if in mute gesture at the Jovian atmosphere that was weighing down upon them with a force of twenty million pounds to the square inch.

'Well,' explained Three, 'that's simple. Our ship isn't airtight. Pressures equalize within and without.'

'Even in space? A vacuum in your ship? You lie!'

'You're welcome to inspect our ship. It has no force field and it isn't airtight. What's marvelous about that? We don't breathe. Our energy is obtained through direct atomic power. The pressure or absence of air pressure makes little difference to us and we're quite at home in a vacuum.'

'But absolute zero!'

'It doesn't matter. We regulate our own heat. We're not interested in outside temperatures.' He paused. 'Well, we can make our own way back to the ship. Good-bye. We'll give the humans of Ganymede your message—war to the end!'

But the Jovian said, 'Wait! I'll be back.' He turned and went toward the city.

The robots stared, and then waited in silence.

It was three hours before he returned and when he did, it was in breathless haste. He stopped within the usual ten feet of the robots, but then began inching his way forward in a curious groveling fashion. He did not speak until his rubbery gray skin was almost touching them, and then the radio code sounded, subdued and respectful.

'Honored sirs, I have been in communication with the head of our central government, who is now aware of all the facts, and I can assure you that Jupiter desires only peace.'

'I beg your pardon?' asked Three blankly.

The Jovian drove on hastily. 'We are ready to resume communication with Ganymede and will gladly promise to make no attempt to venture into space. Our force field will be used only on the Jovian surface.'

'But——' Three began.

'Our government will be glad to receive any other representatives our honorable human brothers of Ganymede would care to send. If your honors will now condescend to swear peace——' a scaly tentacle swung out toward them and Three, quite dazed, grasped it. Two and One did likewise as two more were extended to them.

The Jovian said solemnly: 'There is then eternal peace between Jupiter and Ganymede.'

The spaceship which leaked like a sieve was out in space again. The pressure and temperature were once more at zero, and the robots watched the huge but steadily shrinking globe that was Jupiter.

'They're definitely sincere,' said ZZ Two, 'and it's very gratifying, this complete about-face, but I don't get it.'

'It is my idea,' observed ZZ One, 'that the Jovians came to their senses just in time and realized the incredible evil involved in the thought of harm to a human master. That would be only natural.'

ZZ Three sighed and said, 'Look, it's all a matter of psychology. Those Jovians had a superiority complex a mile thick and when they couldn't destroy us, they were bound to save face. All their exhibitions, all their explanations, were simply a form of braggadocio, designed to impress us into the proper state of humiliation before their power and superiority.'

'I see all that,' interrupted Two, 'but——'

Three went on, 'But it worked the wrong way. All they did was to prove to themselves that we were stronger, that we didn't drown, that we didn't eat or sleep, that molten metal didn't hurt us. Even our very pressure was fatal to Jovian life. Their last trump was the force field. And when they found out that *we* didn't need them at all, and could live in a vacuum at absolute zero, they broke.' He paused and added philosophically, 'When a superiority complex like that breaks, it breaks all the way.'

The other two considered that, and then Two said, 'But it still doesn't make sense. Why should they care what we can or can't do? We're only robots. We're not the ones they have to fight.'

'And that's the whole point, Two,' said Three softly. 'It's only after we left Jupiter that I thought of it. Do you know that through an oversight, quite unintentionally, we neglected to tell them we were only robots.'

'They never asked us,' said One.

'Exactly. So they thought we were human beings and that all the other human beings were like us!'

He looked once more at Jupiter, thoughtfully. 'No wonder they decided to quit!'

Part Two

The Laws of
Robotics

Neither Robot AL-76 nor Robot ZZ-3 represented the mainstream of my thinking. As a matter of fact, I had started correctly with my very earliest robot story, 'Robbie,' which appeared in the September 1940 Super Science Stories (*under the editorially chosen, and to me personally distasteful, title of 'Strange Playfellow'*).

'Robbie' dealt with a rather primitive robot model, one that was unable to speak. It was designed to fulfill the task of nursemaid and to fulfill it admirably. Far from being a threat to human beings or wanting to destroy its creator or to take over the world, it strove only to do what it was designed to do. (*Does an automobile want to fly? Does an electric light bulb want to type letters?*)

I trod this path in eight other stories written during the 1940s, all of which appeared in Astounding Science Fiction. They were:

'Reason,' April 1941
'Liar!,' May 1941
'Runaround,' March 1942
'Catch That Rabbit,' February 1944
'Paradoxical Escape,' August 1945
'Evidence,' September 1946
'Little Lost Robot,' March 1947
'The Evitable Conflict,' June 1950

These eight stories plus 'Robbie' were brought together in a collection entitled I, Robot, which was published by

Gnome Press in 1950. After the usual reprint and foreign editions, it was allowed to go out of print, whereupon the enterprising gentlemen of Doubleday & Company, recognizing a Good Thing, arranged to bring out a new edition in 1963.*

My sensible, non-Mephistophelean robots were not really brand-new. There had been occasional robots of this type before 1940. Indeed, we can find some robots, designed to fulfill a reasonable purpose without trouble and without danger, in the *Iliad*. In Book XVIII of that epic, Thetis visits the smith-god, Hephaistos, in order to obtain divinely forged armor for her son, Achilles. Hephaistos is lame and walks with difficulty. There is the passage (in the translation of W. H. D. Rouse) which describes how he comes out to meet Thetis:

'Then he ... limped out leaning on a thick stick, with a couple of maids to support him. These are made of gold exactly like living girls; they have sense in their heads, they can speak and use their muscles, they can spin and weave and do their work ...'

In short, they were robots.

And yet, though I wasn't the first in the field by the not-so-narrow margin of 2500 years, I managed to build enough consistent background into my stories to gain for myself the reputation of having created the 'modern robot story.'

Gradually, story by story, I evolved my notions on the subject. My robots had brains of platinum-iridium sponge and the 'brain paths' were marked out by the production and destruction of positrons. (No, I don't know how this is

---

* Because of the recent appearance of this collection, it is not being included in this otherwise definitive collection of my robot stories. The discerning reader will now understand why this book is entitled *The Rest of the Robots*.

done.) *As a result it is as the 'positronic robots' that my creatures came to be known.*

To design the positronic brains of my robots required a huge and intricate new branch of technology to which I gave the name 'robotics.' To me it seemed a natural word, as natural as 'physics' or 'mechanics.' However, rather to my surprise, it turned out to be an invented word and is not to be found in either the second or third edition of Webster's Unabridged.

Most important of all, I made use of what I called 'The Three Laws of Robotics,' which were intended to place in words the basic design of the robot brains, a basic design to which all else was subsidiary.

These laws are:

1. A robot may not injure a human being, or, through inaction, allow a human being to come to harm.

2. A robot must obey the orders given it by human beings except where such orders would conflict with the First Law.

3. A robot must protect its own existence as long as such protection does not conflict with the First or Second Law.

Apparently it is these laws of robotics (first stated explicitly in 'Runaround') that have done most to change the nature of the robot stories in modern science fiction. It is rare that a robot of the old turning-on-its-creator type will be found between the pages of the better science-fiction magazines, simply because that would violate the First Law. Many writers of robot stories, without actually quoting the three laws, take them for granted and expect the readers to do the same.

In fact I have been told that if, in future years, I am to be remembered at all, it will be for these three laws of robotics. In a way this bothers me, for I am accustomed to thinking of myself as a scientist, and to be remembered for the non-existent basis of a non-existent science is embarrassing. Yet if robotics ever does reach the pitch of excellence described in my stories, it may be that something like the Three Laws will really come into existence and, if so, I will have achieved a rather unusual (if, alas, posthumous) triumph.

My positronic robot stories fall into two groups; those that concern Dr. Susan Calvin and those that do not. Those that do not, often deal with Gregory Powell and Mike Donovan, who were constantly field-testing experimental robots and, just as constantly, running into trouble with them. There was just enough ambiguity in the Three Laws to provide the conflicts and uncertainties required for new stories, and, to my great relief, it seemed always to be possible to think up a new angle out of the sixty-one words of the Three Laws.

Four stories in I, Robot dealt with Powell and Donovan. After that book was published, exactly one other such story was published, or rather a story about Donovan alone. Once again I was being funny at the expense of my robots, but this time it wasn't I that was telling the story, it was Donovan, and I am not responsible for him.

The story, 'First Law,' appeared in the October 1956 issue of Fantastic Universe Science Fiction.

MIKE DONOVAN looked at his empty beer mug, felt bored, and decided he had listened long enough. He said, loudly, 'If we're going to talk about unusual robots, I once knew one that disobeyed the First Law.'

And since that was completely impossible, everyone stopped talking and turned to look at Donovan.

Donovan regretted his big mouth at once and changed the subject. 'I heard a good one yesterday,' he said, conversationally, 'about——'

MacFarlane in the chair next to Donovan's said, 'You mean you knew a robot that harmed a human being?' That was what disobedience to First Law meant, of course.

'In a way,' said Donovan. 'I say I heard one about——'

'Tell us about it,' ordered MacFarlane. Some of the others banged their beer mugs on the table.

Donovan made the best of it. 'It happened on Titan about ten years ago,' he said, thinking rapidly. 'Yes, it was in twenty-five. We had just recently received a shipment of three new-model robots, specially designed for Titan. They were the first of the MA models. We called them Emma One, Two, and Three.' He snapped his fingers for another beer and stared earnestly after the waiter. Let's see, what came next?

MacFarlane said, 'I've been in robotics half my life, Mike. I never heard of an MA serial order.'

'That's because they took the MA's off the assembly lines immediately after—after what I'm going to tell you. Don't you remember?'

'No.'

Donovan continued hastily. 'We put the robots to work at once. You see, until then, the Base had been entirely useless during the stormy season, which lasts eighty percent of Titan's revolution about Saturn. During the terrific snows, you couldn't find the Base if it were only a hundred yards away. Compasses aren't any use, because Titan hasn't any magnetic field.

'The virtue of these MA robots, however, was that they were equipped with vibro-detectors of a new design so that they could make a beeline for the Base through anything and that meant mining could become a through-the-revolution affair. And don't say a word, Mac. The vibro-detectors were taken off the market also, and that's why you haven't heard of them.' Donovan coughed. 'Military secret, you understand.'

He went on. 'The robots worked fine during the first stormy season, then at the start of the calm season, Emma Two began acting up. She kept wandering off into corners and under bales and had to be coaxed out. Finally she wandered off Base altogether and didn't come back. We decided there had been a flaw in her manufacture and got along with the other two. Still, it meant we were short-handed, or short-roboted anyway, so when toward the end of the calm season, someone had to go to Kornsk, I volunteered to chance it without a robot. It seemed safe enough; the storms weren't due for two days and I'd be back in twenty hours at the outside.

'I was on the way back—a good ten miles from Base—when the wind started blowing and the air thickening. I landed my air car immediately before the wind could smash it, pointed myself toward the Base and started running. I could run the distance in the low gravity all right, but could

I run a straight line? That was the question. My air supply was ample and my suit heat coils were satisfactory. but ten miles in a Titanian storm is infinity.

'Then, when the snow streams changed everything to a dark, gooey twilight, with even Saturn dimmed out and the sun only a pale pimple, I stopped short and leaned against the wind. There was a little dark object right ahead of me. I could barely make it out but I knew what it was. It was a storm pup; the only living thing that could stand a Titanian storm, and the most vicious living thing anywhere. I knew my space suit wouldn't protect me, once it made for me, and in the bad light, I had to wait for a point-blank aim or I didn't dare shoot. One miss and he would be at me.

'I backed away slowly and the shadow followed. It closed in and I was raising my blaster, with a prayer, when a bigger shadow loomed over me suddenly, and I yodeled with relief. It was Emma Two, the missing MA robot. I never stopped to wonder what had happened to it or worry why it had. I just howled, "Emma, baby, get that storm pup; and then get me back to Base."

'It just looked at me as if it hadn't heard and called out, "Master, don't shoot. Don't shoot."

'It made for that storm pup at a dead run.

' "Get that damned pup, Emma," I shouted. It got the pup, all right. It scooped it right up and *kept on going*. I yelled myself hoarse but it never came back. It left me to die in the storm.'

Donovan paused dramatically, 'Of course, you know the First Law: A robot may not injure a human being, or, through inaction, allow a human being to come to harm! Well, Emma Two just ran off with that storm pup and left me to die. It broke First Law.

'Luckily, I pulled through safely. Half an hour later, the storm died down. It had been a premature gust, and a temporary one. That happens sometimes. I hot-footed it for Base and the storms really broke next day. Emma Two returned two hours after I did, and, of course, the mystery was then explained and the MA models were taken off the market immediately.'

'And just what,' demanded MacFarlane, 'was the explanation?'

Donovan regarded him seriously. 'It's true I was a human being in danger of death, Mac, but to that robot there was something else that came first, even before me, before the First Law. Don't forget these robots were of the MA series and this particular MA robot had been searching out private nooks for some time before disappearing. It was as though it expected something special—and private—to happen to it. Apparently, something special had.'

Donovan's eyes turned upward reverently and his voice trembled. 'That storm pup was no storm pup. We named it Emma Junior when Emma Two brought it back. Emma Two *had* to protect it from my gun. What is even First Law compared with the holy ties of mother love?'

Another short story of the post-I, Robot decade was unusual in that it was the first since the very early days that involved neither Susan Calvin nor the Powell-Donovan team. It was 'Let's Get Together,' which appeared in the February 1957 issue of Infinity Science Fiction.

It was unusual in another way too. A couple of years after its appearance I received a reprint request, and (since I am easygoing to a fault) I said, 'Sure!' When I finally received the issue of the magazine with the reprinted story, it turned out to be one of those magazines that feature the undraped female form divine.

Heaven knows I have no objection to divine forms, but the event left me with an unanswered question. Not only does 'Let's Get Together' involve no sex, it has no female characters. Why did the magazine want it then?

Perhaps (I tell myself) because they thought it was a good story.

Maybe they did. At least, I hope so.

'You people know all about Them, I suppose,' said Lynn and was unable to keep a trace of sarcasm out of his tone. He was not particularly aware of his use of a slightly stressed pronoun in his reference to the enemy, the equivalent of capitalization in print. It was a cultural habit of this generation and the one preceding. No one said the 'East,' or the 'Reds' or the 'Soviets' or the 'Russians' any more. That would have been too confusing, since some of Them weren't of the East, weren't Reds, Soviets, and especially not Russians. It was much simpler to say We and They, and much more precise.

Travelers had frequently reported that They did the same in reverse. Over there, They were 'We' (in the appropriate language) and We were 'They.'

Scarcely anyone gave thought to such things any more. It was all quite comfortable and casual. There was no hatred, even. At the beginning, it had been called a Cold War. Now it was only a game, almost a good-natured game, with unspoken rules and a kind of decency about it.

Lynn said abruptly, 'Why should They want to disturb the situation?'

He rose and stood staring at a wall map of the world, split into two regions with faint edgings of color. An irregular portion on the left of the map was edged in a mild green. A smaller, but just as irregular, portion on the right of the map was bordered in a washed-out pink. We and They.

The map hadn't changed much in a century. The loss of Formosa and the gain of East Germany some eighty years before had been the last territorial switch of importance.

There had been another change, though, that was significant enough and that was in the colors. Two generations before, Their territory had been a brooding, bloody red,

Ours a pure and undefiled white. Now there was a neutrality about the colors. Lynn had seen Their maps and it was the same on Their side.

'They wouldn't do it,' he said.

'They are doing it,' said Breckenridge, 'and you had better accustom yourself to the fact. Of course, sir, I realize that it isn't pleasant to think that They may be that far ahead of us in robotics.'

His eyes remained as guileless as ever, but the hidden knife-edges of the words plunged deep, and Lynn quivered at the impact.

Of course, that would account for why the Chief of Robotics learned of this so late and through a Security officer at that. He had lost caste in the eyes of the Government; if Robotics had really failed in the struggle, Lynn could expect no political mercy.

Lynn said wearily, 'Even if what you say is true, They're not far ahead of us. We could build humanoid robots.'

'Have we, sir?'

'Yes. As a matter of fact, we have built a few models for experimental purposes.'

'They were doing so ten years ago. They've made ten years' progress since.'

Lynn was disturbed. He wondered if his incredulity concerning the whole business was really the result of wounded pride and fear for his job and reputation. He was embarrassed by the possibility that this might be so, and yet he was forced into defense.

He said, 'Look, young man, the stalemate between Them and Us was never perfect in every detail, you know. They have always been ahead in one facet or another and We in some other facet or another. If They're ahead of us right now in robotics, it's because They've placed a greater proportion of Their effort into robotics than We have. And that means that some other branch of endeavor has received a greater share of Our efforts than it has of Theirs. It would mean We're ahead in force-field research or in hyper-atomics, perhaps.'

Lynn felt distressed at his own statement that the stale-mate wasn't perfect. It was true enough, but that was the one great danger threatening the world. The world depended on the stalemate being as perfect as possible. If the small unevennesses that always existed overbalanced too far in one direction or the other——

Almost at the beginning of what had been the Cold War, both sides had developed thermonuclear weapons, and war became unthinkable. Competition switched from the mili-tary to the economic and psychological and had stayed there ever since.

But always there was the driving effort on each side to break the stalemate, to develop a parry for every possible thrust, to develop a thrust that could not be parried in time—something that would make war possible again. And that was not because either side wanted war so desperately, but because both were afraid that the other side would make the crucial discovery first.

For a hundred years each side had kept the struggle even. And in the process, peace had been maintained for a hundred years while, as byproducts of the continuously intensive research, force fields had been produced and solar energy and insect control and robots. Each side was making a beginning in the understanding of mentalics, which was the name given to the biochemistry and biophysics of thought. Each side had its outposts on the Moon and on Mars. Mankind was advancing in giant strides under forced draft.

It was even necessary for both sides to be as decent and humane as possible among themselves, lest through cruelty and tyranny, friends be made for the other side.

It couldn't be that the stalemate would now be broken and that there would be war.

Lynn said, 'I want to consult one of my men. I want his opinion.'

'Is he trustworthy?'

Lynn looked disgusted. 'Good Lord, what man in Robotics has not been investigated and cleared to death by your people? Yes, I vouch for him. If you can't trust a man like Humphrey Carl Laszlo, then we're in no position to face the kind of attack you say They are launching, no matter what else we do.'

'I've heard of Laszlo,' said Breckenridge.

'Good. Does he pass?'

'Yes.'

'Then, I'll have him in and we'll find out what he thinks about the possibility that robots could invade the U.S.A.'

'Not exactly,' said Breckenridge, softly. 'You still don't accept the full truth. Find out what he thinks about the fact that robots have *already* invaded the U.S.A.'

Laszlo was the grandson of a Hungarian who had broken through what had then been called the Iron Curtain, and he had a comfortable above-suspicion feeling about himself because of it. He was thick-set and balding with a pugnacious look graven forever on his snub face, but his accent was clear Harvard and he was almost excessively soft-spoken.

To Lynn, who was conscious that after years of administration he was no longer expert in the various phases of modern robotics, Laszlo was a comforting receptacle for complete knowledge. Lynn felt better because of the man's mere presence.

Lynn said, 'What do you think?'

A scowl twisted Laszlo's face ferociously. 'That They're that far ahead of us. Completely incredible. It would mean They've produced humanoids that could not be told from humans at close quarters. It would mean a considerable advance in robo-mentalics.'

'You're personally involved,' said Breckenridge, coldly. 'Leaving professional pride out of account, exactly why is it impossible that They be ahead of Us?'

Laszlo shrugged. 'I assure you that I'm well acquainted with Their literature on robotics. I know approximately where They are.'

'You know approximately where They want you to *think* They are, is what you really mean,' corrected Breckenridge. 'Have you ever visited the other side?'

'I haven't,' said Laszlo, shortly.

'Nor you, Dr. Lynn?'

Lynn said, 'No, I haven't, either.'

Breckenridge said, 'Has any robotics man visited the other side in twenty-five years?' He asked the question with a kind of confidence that indicated he knew the answer.

For a matter of seconds, the atmosphere was heavy with thought. Discomfort crossed Laszlo's broad face. He said, 'As a matter of fact, They haven't held any conferences on robotics in a long time.'

'In twenty-five years,' said Breckenridge. 'Isn't that significant?'

'Maybe,' said Laszlo reluctantly. 'Something else bothers me, though. None of Them has ever come to Our conferences on robotics. None that I can remember.'

'Were They invited?' asked Breckenridge.

Lynn, staring and worried, interposed quickly, 'Of course.'

Breckenridge said, 'Do They refuse attendance to any other types of scientific conferences We hold?'

'I don't know,' said Laszlo. He was pacing the floor now. 'I haven't heard of any cases. Have you, Chief?'

'No,' said Lynn.

Breckenridge said, 'Wouldn't you say it was as though They didn't want to be put in the position of having to return any such invitation? Or as though They were afraid one of Their men might talk too much?'

That was exactly how it seemed, and Lynn felt a helpless conviction that Security's story was true after all.

Why else had there been no contact between sides on robotics? There had been a cross-fertilizing trickle of researchers moving in both directions on a strictly one-for-one basis for years, dating back to the days of Eisenhower and Khrushchev. There were a great many good motives for that: an honest appreciation of the supranational character of science; impulses of friendliness that are hard to wipe out completely in the individual human being; the desire to be exposed to a fresh and interesting outlook and to have your own slightly stale notions greeted by others as fresh and interesting.

The governments themselves were anxious that this continue. There was always the obvious thought that by learning all you could and telling as little as you could, your own side would gain by the exchange.

But not in the case of robotics. Not there.

Such a little thing to carry conviction. And a thing, moreover, they had known all along. Lynn thought darkly: *We've taken the complacent way out.*

Because the other side had done nothing publicly on robotics, it had been tempting to sit back smugly and be comfortable in the assurance of superiority. Why hadn't it seemed possible, even likely, that They were hiding superior cards, a trump hand, for the proper time?

Laszlo said shakenly, 'What do we do?' It was obvious that the same line of thought had carried the same conviction to him.

'Do?' parroted Lynn. It was hard to think right now of anything but of the complete horror that came with conviction. There were ten humanoid robots somewhere in the United States, each one carrying a fragment of a TC bomb.

TC! The race for sheer horror in bomb-ery had ended there. TC! Total Conversion! The sun was no longer a synonym one could use. Total conversion made the sun a penny candle.

Ten humanoids, each completely harmless in separation, could, by the simple act of coming together, exceed critical mass and——

Lynn rose to his feet heavily, the dark pouches under his eyes, which ordinarily lent his ugly face a look of savage foreboding, more prominent than ever. 'It's going to be up to us to figure out ways and means of telling a humanoid from a human and then finding the humanoids.'

'How quickly?' muttered Laszlo.

'Not later than five minutes before they get together,' barked Lynn, 'and I don't know when that will be.'

Breckenridge nodded. 'I'm glad you're with us now, sir. I'm to bring you back to Washington for conference, you know.'

Lynn raised his eyebrows. 'All right.'

He wondered if, had he delayed longer in being convinced, he might not have been replaced forthwith—if some other Chief of the Bureau of Robotics might not be conferring in Washington. He suddenly wished earnestly that exactly that had come to pass.

The First Presidential Assistant was there, the Secretary of Science, the Secretary of Security, Lynn himself, and Breckenridge. Five of them sitting about a table in the dungeons of an underground fortress near Washington.

Presidential Assistant Jeffreys was an impressive man, handsome in a white-haired and just-a-trifle-jowly fashion, solid, thoughtful and as unobtrusive, politically, as a Presidential Assistant ought to be.

He spoke incisively. 'There are three questions that face us as I see it. First, when are the humanoids going to get together? Second, where are they going to get together? Third, how do we stop them before they get together?'

Secretary of Science Amberley nodded convulsively at that. He had been Dean of Northwestern Engineering before his appointment. He was thin, sharp-featured and noticeably edgy. His forefinger traced slow circles on the table.

'As far as *when* they'll get together,' he said. 'I suppose it's definite that it won't be for some time.'

'Why do you say that?' asked Lynn sharply.

'They've been in the U.S. at least a month already. So Security says.'

Lynn turned automatically to look at Breckenridge, and Secretary of Security Macalaster intercepted the glance. Macalaster said, 'The information is reliable. Don't let Breckenridge's apparent youth fool you, Dr. Lynn. That's part of his value to us. Actually, he's thirty-four and has been with the department for ten years. He has been in

Moscow for nearly a year and without him, none of this terrible danger would be known to us. As it is, we have most of the details.'

'Not the crucial ones,' said Lynn.

Macalaster of Security smiled frostily. His heavy chin and close-set eyes were well-known to the public but almost nothing else about him was. He said, 'We are all finitely human, Dr. Lynn. Agent Breckenridge has done a great deal.'

Presidential Assistant Jeffreys cut in. 'Let us say we have a certain amount of time. If action at the instant were necessary, it would have happened before this. It seems likely that they are waiting for a specific time. If we knew the place, perhaps the time would become self-evident.

'If they are going to TC a target, they will want to cripple us as much as possible, so it would seem that a major city would have to be it. In any case, a major metropolis is the only target worth a TC bomb. I think there are four possibilities: Washington, as the administrative center; New York, as the financial center; and Detroit and Pittsburgh as the two chief industrial centers.'

Macalaster of Security said, 'I vote for New York. Administration and industry have both been decentralized to the point where the destruction of any one particular city won't prevent instant retaliation.'

'Then why New York?' asked Amberley of Science, perhaps more sharply than he intended. 'Finance has been decentralized as well.'

'A question of morale. It may be they intend to destroy our will to resist, to induce surrender by the sheer horror of the first blow. The greatest destruction of human life would be in the New York Metropolitan area——'

'Pretty cold-blooded,' muttered Lynn.

'I know,' said Macalaster of Security, 'but they're capable of it, if they thought it would mean final victory at a stroke. Wouldn't we——'

Presidential Assistant Jeffreys brushed back his white hair. 'Let's assume the worst. Let's assume that New York will be destroyed some time during the winter, preferably immediately after a serious blizzard when communications are at their worst and the disruption of utilities and food supplies in fringe areas will be most serious in their effect. Now, how do we stop them?'

Amberley of Science could only say, 'Finding ten men in two hundred and twenty million is an awfully small needle in an awfully large haystack.'

Jeffreys shook his head. 'You have it wrong. Ten humanoids among two hundred and twenty million humans.'

'No difference,' said Amberley of Science. 'We don't know that a humanoid can be differentiated from a human at sight. Probably not.' He looked at Lynn. They all did.

Lynn said heavily, 'We in Cheyenne couldn't make one that would pass as human in the daylight.'

'But They can,' said Macalaster of Security, 'and not only physically. We're sure of that. They've advanced mentalic procedures to the point where They can reel off the micro-electronic pattern of the brain and focus it on the positronic pathways of the robot.'

Lynn stared. 'Are you implying that They can create the replica of a human being complete with personality and memory?'

'I am.'

'Of specific human beings?'

'That's right.'

'Is this also based on Agent Breckenridge's findings?'

'Yes. The evidence can't be disputed.'

Lynn bent his head in thought for a moment. Then he said, 'Then ten men in the United States are not men but humanoids. But the originals would have had to be available to them. They couldn't be Orientals, who would be too easy to spot, so they would have to be East Europeans. How would they be introduced into this country, then? With the radar network over the entire world border as tight as a drum, how could They introduce any individual, human, or humanoid, without our knowing it?'

Macalaster of Security said, 'It can be done. There are certain legitimate seepages across the border. Businessmen, pilots, even tourists. They're watched, of course, on both sides. Still ten of them might have been kidnaped and used as models for humanoids. The humanoids would then be sent back in their place. Since we wouldn't expect such a substitution, it would pass us by. If they were Americans to begin with, there would be no difficulty in their getting into this country. It's as simple as that.'

'And even their friends and family could not tell the difference?'

'We must assume so. Believe me, we've been waiting for any report that might imply sudden attacks of amnesia or troublesome changes in personality. We've checked on thousands.'

Amberley of Science stared at his finger tips. 'I think ordinary measures won't work. The attack must come from the Bureau of Robotics and I depend on the chief of that bureau.'

Again eyes turned sharply, expectantly, on Lynn.

Lynn felt bitterness rise. It seemed to him that this was what the conference came to and was intended for. Nothing that had been said had not been said before. He was sure of that. There was no solution to the problem, no pregnant suggestion. It was a device for the record, a device on the part of men who gravely feared defeat and who wished the responsibility for it placed clearly and unequivocally on someone else.

And yet there was justice in it. It was in robotics that We had fallen short: And Lynn was not Lynn merely. He was Lynn of Robotics and the responsibility had to be his.

He said, 'I will do what I can.'

He spent a wakeful night and there was a haggardness about both body and soul when he sought and attained another interview with Presidential Assistant Jeffreys the next morning. Breckenridge was there, and though Lynn would have preferred a private conference, he could see the justice in the situation. It was obvious that Breckenridge had attained enormous influence with the government as a result of his successful Intelligence work. Well, why not?

Lynn said, 'Sir, I am considering the possibility that we are hopping uselessly to enemy piping.'

'In what way?'

'I'm sure that however impatient the public may grow at times, and however legislators sometimes find it expedient to talk, the government at least recognizes the world stalemate to be beneficial. They must recognize it also. Ten humanoids with one TC bomb is a trivial way of breaking the stalemate.'

'The destruction of fifteen million human beings is scarcely trivial.'

'It is from the world power standpoint. It would not so demoralize us as to make us surrender or so cripple us as to convince us we could not win. There would just be the same old planetary death war that both sides have avoided so long and so successfully. And all They would have accomplished is to force us to fight minus one city. It's not enough.'

'What do you suggest?' said Jeffreys coldly. 'That They do not have ten humanoids in our country? That there is not a TC bomb waiting to get together?'

'I'll agree that those things are here, but perhaps for some reason greater than just midwinter bomb madness.'

'Such as?'

'It may be that the physical destruction resulting from the humanoids getting together is not the worst thing that can happen to us. What about the moral and intellectual destruction that comes of their being here at all? With all due respect to Agent Breckenridge, what if They *intended* for us to find out about the humanoids; what if the humanoids are never supposed to get together, but merely to remain separate in order to give us something to worry about?'

'Why?'

'Tell me this. What measures have already been taken against the humanoids? I suppose that Security is going through the files of all citizens who have ever been across the border or close enough to it to make kidnaping possible. I know, since Macalaster mentioned it yesterday, that they are following up suspicious psychiatric cases. What else?'

Jeffreys said, 'Small X-ray devices are being installed in key places in the large cities. In the mass arenas, for instance——'

'Where ten humanoids might slip in among a hundred thousand spectators of a football game or an air-polo match?'

'Exactly.'

'And concert halls and churches?'

'We must start somewhere. We can't do it all at once.'

'Particularly when panic must be avoided,' said Lynn. 'Isn't that so? It wouldn't do to have the public realize that at any unpredictable moment, some unpredictable city and its human contents would suddenly cease to exist.'

'I suppose that's obvious. What are you driving at?'

Lynn said strenuously, 'That a growing fraction of our national effort will be diverted entirely into the nasty problem of what Amberley called finding a very small needle in a very large haystack. We'll be chasing our tails madly, while They increase their research lead to the point where we find we can no longer catch up; when we must surrender without the chance even of snapping our fingers in retaliation.

'Consider further that this news will leak out as more and more people become involved in our countermeasures and more and more people begin to guess what we're doing. Then what? The panic might do us more harm than any one TC bomb.'

The Presidential Assistant said irritably, 'In Heaven's name, man, what do you suggest we do, then?'

'Nothing,' said Lynn. 'Call their bluff. Live as we have lived and gamble that They won't dare break the stalemate for the sake of a one-bomb head start.'

'Impossible!' said Jeffreys. 'Completely impossible. The welfare of all of Us is very largely in my hands, and doing nothing is the one thing I cannot do. I agree with you, perhaps, that X-ray machines at sports arenas are a kind of skin-deep measure that won't be effective, but it has to be done so that people, in the aftermath, do not come to the bitter conclusion that we tossed our country away for the sake of a subtle line of reasoning that encouraged do-nothingism. In fact, our countergambit will be active indeed.'

'In what way?'

Presidential Assistant Jeffreys looked at Breckenridge. The young Security officer, hitherto calmly silent, said, 'It's no use talking about a possible future break in the stalemate when the stalemate is broken now. It doesn't matter whether these humanoids explode or do not. Maybe they *are* only a bait to divert us, as you say. But the fact remains that we are a quarter of a century behind in robotics, and that may be fatal. What other advances in robotics will there be to surprise us if war does start? The only answer is to divert our entire force immediately, *now*, into a crash program of robotics research, and the first problem is to find the humanoids. Call it an exercise in robotics, if you will, or call it the prevention of the death of fifteen million men, women, and children.'

Lynn shook his head helplessly. 'You *can't*. You'd be playing into their hands. They want us lured into the one blind alley while they're free to advance in all other directions.'

Jeffreys said impatiently, 'That's your guess. Breckenridge has made his suggestion through channels and the government has approved, and we will begin with an all-Science conference.'

'All-Science?'

Breckenridge said, 'We have listed every important scientist of every branch of natural science. They'll all be at Cheyenne. There will be only one point on the agenda: How to advance robotics. The major specific subheading under that will be: How to develop a receiving device for the electromagnetic fields of the cerebral cortex that will be sufficiently delicate to distinguish between a protoplasmic human brain and a positronic humanoid brain.'

Jeffreys said, 'We had hoped you would be willing to be

in charge of the conference.'

'I was not consulted in this.'

'Obviously time was short, sir. Do you agree to be in charge?'

Lynn smiled briefly. It was a matter of responsibility again. The responsibility must be clearly that of Lynn of Robotics. He had the feeling it would be Breckenridge who would really be in charge. But what could he do?

He said, 'I agree.'

Breckenridge and Lynn returned together to Cheyenne, where that evening Laszlo listened with a sullen mistrust to Lynn's description of coming events.

Laszlo said, 'While you were gone, Chief, I've started putting five experimental models of humanoid structure through the testing procedures. Our men are on a twelve-hour day, with three shifts overlapping. If we've got to arrange a conference, we're going to be crowded and red-taped out of everything. Work will come to a halt.'

Breckenridge said, 'That will be only temporary. You will gain more than you lose.'

Laszlo scowled. 'A bunch of astrophysicists and geo-chemists around won't help a damn toward robotics.'

'Views from specialists of other fields may be helpful.'

'Are you sure? How do we know that there is any way of detecting brain waves or that, even if we can, there is a way of differentiating human and humanoid by wave pattern? Who set up the project, anyway?'

'I did,' said Breckenridge.

'*You* did? Are you a robotics man?'

The young Security agent said calmly, 'I have studied robotics.'

'That's not the same thing.'

'I've had access to text material dealing with Russian robotics—in Russian. Top-secret material well in advance of anything you have here.'

Lynn said ruefully, 'He has us there, Laszlo.'

'It was on the basis of that material,' Breckenridge went on, 'that I suggested this particular line of investigation. It is reasonably certain that in copying off the electromagnetic pattern of a specific human mind into a specific positronic brain, a perfectly exact duplicate cannot be made. For one thing, the most complicated positronic brain small enough to fit into a human-sized skull is hundreds of times less complex than the human brain. It can't pick up all the overtones, therefore, and there must be some way to take advantage of that fact.'

Laszlo looked impressed despite himself and Lynn smiled grimly. It was easy to resent Breckenridge and the coming intrusion of several hundred scientists of non-robotics specialties, but the problem itself was an intriguing one. There was that consolation, at least.

It came to him quietly.

Lynn found he had nothing to do but sit in his office alone, with an executive position that had grown merely titular. Perhaps that helped. It gave him time to think, to picture the creative scientists of half the world converging on Cheyenne.

It was Breckenridge who, with cool efficiency, was handling the details of preparation. There had been a kind of confidence in the way he said, 'Let's get together and we'll lick Them.'

Let's get together.

It came to Lynn so quietly that anyone watching Lynn at that moment might have seen his eyes blink slowly twice—

but surely nothing more.

He did what he had to do with a whirling detachment that kept him calm when he felt that, by all rights, he ought to be going mad.

He sought out Breckenridge in the other's improvised quarters. Breckenridge was alone and frowning. 'Is anything wrong, sir?'

Lynn said wearily, 'Everything's right, I think. I've invoked martial law.'

'What!'

'As chief of a division I can do so if I am of the opinion the situation warrants it. Over my division I can then be dictator. Chalk up one for the beauties of decentralization.'

'You will rescind that order immediately.' Breckenridge took a step forward. 'When Washington hears this, you will be ruined.'

'I'm ruined anyway. Do you think I don't realize that I've been set up for the role of the greatest villain in American history: the man who let Them break the stalemate? I have nothing to lose—and perhaps a great deal to gain.'

He laughed a little wildly. 'What a target the Division of Robotics will be, eh, Breckenridge? Only a few thousand men to be killed by a TC bomb capable of wiping out three hundred square miles in one micro-second. But five hundred of those men would be our greatest scientists. We would be in the peculiar position of having to fight a war with our brains shot out, or surrendering. I think we'd surrender.'

'But this is impossible. Lynn, do you hear me? Do you understand? How could the humanoids pass our security provisions? How could they get together?'

'But they *are* getting together! We're helping them to do

so. We're ordering them to do so. Our scientists visit the other side, Breckenridge. They visit Them regularly. You made a point of how strange it was that no one in robotics did. Well, ten of those scientists are still there and in their place, ten humanoids are converging on Cheyenne.'

'That's a ridiculous guess.'

'I think it's a good one, Breckenridge. But it wouldn't work unless we knew humanoids were in America so that we would call the conference in the first place. Quite a coincidence that you brought the news of the humanoids *and* suggested the conference *and* suggested the agenda *and* are running the show *and* know exactly which scientists were invited. Did you make sure the right ten were included?'

'Dr. Lynn!' cried Breckenridge in outrage. He poised to rush forward.

Lynn said, 'Don't move. I've got a blaster here. We'll just wait for the scientists to get here one by one. One by one we'll X-ray them. One by one, we'll monitor them for radioactivity. No two will get together without being checked, and if all five hundred are clear, I'll give you my blaster and surrender to you. Only I think we'll find the ten humanoids. Sit down, Breckenridge.'

They both sat.

Lynn said, 'We wait. When I'm tired, Laszlo will spell me. We wait.'

Professor Manuelo Jiminez of the Institute of Higher Studies of Buenos Aires exploded while the stratospheric jet on which he traveled was three miles above the Amazon Valley. It was a simple chemical explosion but it was enough to destroy the plane.

Dr. Herman Liebowitz of M.I.T. exploded in a monorail, killing twenty people and injuring a hundred others.

In similar manner, Dr. Auguste Marin of L'Institut Nucléonique of Montreal and seven others died at various stages of their journey to Cheyenne.

Laszlo hurtled in, pale-faced and stammering, with the first news of it. It had only been two hours that Lynn had sat there, facing Breckenridge, blaster in hand.

Laszlo said, 'I thought you were nuts, Chief, but you were right. They *were* humanoids. They *had* to be.' He turned to stare with hate-filled eyes at Breckenridge. 'Only they were warned. *He* warned them, and now there won't be one left intact. Not one to study.'

'God!' cried Lynn and in a frenzy of haste thrust his blaster out toward Breckenridge and fired. The Security man's neck vanished; the torso fell; the head dropped, thudded against the floor and rolled crookedly.

Lynn moaned, 'I didn't understand, I thought he was a traitor. Nothing more.'

And Laszlo stood immobile, mouth open, for the moment incapable of speech.

Lynn said wildly, 'Sure, he warned them. But how could he do so while sitting in that chair unless he were equipped with built-in radio transmission? Don't you see it? Breckenridge had been in Moscow. The real Breckenridge is still there. Oh my God, there were *eleven* of them.'

Laszlo managed a hoarse squeak. 'Why didn't *he* explode?'

'He was hanging on, I suppose, to make sure the others had received his message and were safely destroyed. Lord, Lord, when you brought the news and I realized the truth, I couldn't shoot fast enough. God knows by how few seconds I may have beaten him to it.'

Laszlo said shakily, 'At least, we'll have one to study.' He bent and put his fingers on the sticky fluid trickling out of the mangled remains at the neck end of the headless body.

Not blood, but high-grade machine oil.

Part Three

Susan Calvin

The robot short stories that most interested me, however, were those that dealt with Dr. Susan Calvin, robopsychologist extraordinary. A 'robopsychologist' is not a robot who is a psychologist, but a psychologist who is also a roboticist. It is an ambiguous word, unfortunately, but I am stuck with it.

As time went on, I fell in love with Dr. Calvin. She was a forbidding creature, to be sure—much more like the popular conception of a robot than were any of my positronic creations—but I loved her anyway.

She served as the central bond that knit together the stories of I, Robot, and in four of the stories she played a central role. What's more, after I, Robot appeared (and despite the fact that the book contained an epilog briefly noting Dr. Calvin's death at an advanced age) I couldn't help bringing her back. I wrote four more stories dealing with her.

In one of these, dear Susan appeared only glancingly. This was 'Satisfaction Guaranteed,' which appeared in the April 1951 issue of Amazing Stories.

An interesting point about this story is the unusual quantity of mail from readers, almost all young ladies, and almost all speaking wistfully of Tony—as though I might know where he could be found.

I shall attempt to draw no morals (or immorals, either) from this.

TONY was tall and darkly handsome, with an incredibly patrician air drawn into every line of his unchangeable expression, and Claire Belmont regarded him through the crack in the door with a mixture of horror and dismay.

'I can't, Larry. I just can't have him in the house.' Feverishly, she was searching her paralyzed mind for a stronger way of putting it; some way that would make sense and settle things, but she could only end with a simple repetition.

'Well, I can't!'

Larry Belmont regarded his wife stiffly, and there was that spark of impatience in his eyes that Claire hated to see, since she felt her own incompetence mirrored in it. 'We're committed, Claire,' he said, 'and I can't have you backing out now. The company is sending me to Washington on this basis, and it probably means a promotion. It's perfectly safe and you know it. What's your objection?'

She frowned helplessly. 'It just gives me the chills. I couldn't bear him.'

'He's as human as you or I, almost. So, no nonsense. Come, get out there.'

His hand was in the small of her back, shoving; and she found herself in her own living room, shivering. *It* was there, looking at her with a precise politeness, as though appraising his hostess-to-be of the next three weeks. Dr. Susan Calvin was there, too, sitting stiffly in thin-lipped abstraction. She had the cold, faraway look of someone who has worked with machines so long that a little of the steel had entered the blood.

'Hello,' crackled Claire in general, and ineffectual, greeting.

But Larry was busily saving the situation with a spurious gaiety. 'Here, Claire, I want you to meet Tony, a swell guy. This is my wife, Claire, Tony, old boy.' Larry's hand draped itself amiably over Tony's shoulder, but Tony remained unresponsive and expressionless under the pressure.

He said, 'How do you do, Mrs. Belmont.'

And Claire jumped at Tony's voice. It was deep and mellow, smooth as the hair on his head or the skin on his face.

Before she could stop herself, she said, 'Oh, my—you talk.'

'Why not? Did you expect that I didn't?'

But Claire could only smile weakly. She didn't really know what she had expected. She looked away, then let him slide gently into the corner of her eye. His hair was smooth and black, like polished plastic—or was it really composed of separate hairs? And was the even, olive skin of his hands and face continued on past the obscurement of his formally cut clothing?

She was lost in the shuddering wonder of it, and had to force her thoughts back into place to meet Dr. Calvin's flat, unemotional voice.

'Mrs. Belmont, I hope you appreciate the importance of this experiment. Your husband tells me he has given you some of the background. I would like to give you more, as the senior psychologist of the U.S. Robots and Mechanical Men Corporation.

'Tony is a robot. His actual designation on the company files is TN-3, but he will answer to Tony. He is not a mechanical monster, nor simply a calculating machine of the type that were developed during World War II, fifty years ago. He has an artificial brain nearly as complicated as our own. It is an immense telephone switchboard on an atomic scale, so that billions of possible "telephone connections" can be compressed into an instrument that will fit inside a skull.

'Such brains are manufactured for each model of robot specifically. Each contains a precalculated set of connections so that each robot knows the English language to start with and enough of anything else that may be necessary to perform his job.

'Until now, U.S. Robots has confined its manufacturing activity to industrial models for use in places where human labor is impractical—in deep mines, for instance, or in underwater work. But we want to invade the city and the home. To do so, we must get the ordinary man and woman to accept these robots without fear. You understand that there is nothing to fear.'

'There isn't, Claire,' interposed Larry earnestly. 'Take my word for it. It's impossible for him to do any harm. You know I wouldn't leave him with you otherwise.'

Claire cast a quick, secret glance at Tony and lowered her voice. 'What if I make him angry?'

'You needn't whisper,' said Dr. Calvin calmly. 'He *can't* get angry with you, my dear. I told you that the switchboard connections of his brain were predetermined. Well, the most important connection of all is what we call "The First Law of Robotics," and it is merely this: "A robot may not injure a human being, or, through inaction, allow a human being to come to harm." All robots are built so. No robot can be forced in any way to do harm to any human. So, you see, we need you and Tony as a preliminary experiment for our own guidance, while your husband is in Washington to arrange for government-supervised legal tests.'

'You mean all this isn't legal?'

Larry cleared his throat. 'Not just yet, but it's all right. He won't leave the house, and you mustn't let anyone see him. That's all. . . . And, Claire, I'd stay with you, but I know too much about the robots. We must have a completely inexperienced tester so that we can have severe conditions. It's necessary.'

'Oh, well,' muttered Claire. Then, as a thought struck her, 'But what does he do?'

'Housework,' said Dr. Calvin shortly.

She got up to leave, and it was Larry who saw her to the front door. Claire stayed behind drearily. She caught a glimpse of herself in the mirror above the mantelpiece, and looked away hastily. She was very tired of her small, mousy face and her dim, unimaginative hair. Then she caught Tony's eyes upon her and almost smiled before she remembered. . . .

He was only a machine.

Larry Belmont was on his way to the airport when he caught a glimpse of Gladys Claffern. She was the type of woman who seemed made to be seen in glimpses. . . . Perfectly and precisely manufactured; dressed with thoughtful hand and eye; too gleaming to be stared at.

The little smile that preceded her and the faint scent that trailed her were a pair of beckoning fingers. Larry felt his stride break; he touched his hat, then hurried on.

As always he felt that vague anger. If Claire could only push her way into the Claffern clique, it would help so much. But what was the use?

Claire! The few times she had come face to face with Gladys, the little fool had been tongue-tied. He had no illusions. The testing of Tony was his big chance, and it was in Claire's hands. How much safer it would be in the hands of someone like Gladys Claffern.

Claire woke the second morning to the sound of a subdued knock on the bedroom door. Her mind clamored, then went icy. She had avoided Tony the first day, smiling thinly when she met him and brushing past with a wordless sound of apology.

'Is that you—Tony?'

'Yes, Mrs. Belmont. May I enter?'

She must have said yes, because he was in the room, quite suddenly and noiselessly. Her eyes and nose were simultaneously aware of the tray he was carrying.

'Breakfast?' she said.

'If you please.'

She wouldn't have dared to refuse, so she pushed herself slowly into a sitting position and received it: poached eggs, buttered toast, coffee.

'I have brought the sugar and cream separately,' said Tony. 'I expect to learn your preference with time, in this and in other things.'

She waited.

Tony, standing there straight and pliant as a metal rule, asked, after a moment, 'Would you prefer to eat in privacy?'

'Yes. . . . I mean, if you don't mind.'

'Will you need help later in dressing?'

'Oh, my, no!' She clutched frantically at the sheet, so that the coffee hovered at the edge of catastrophe. She remained so, in rigor, then sank helplessly back against the pillow when the door closed him out of her sight again.

She got through breakfast somehow.... He was only a machine, and if it were only more visible that he were it wouldn't be so frightening. Or if his expression would change. It just stayed there, nailed on. You couldn't tell what went on behind those dark eyes and that smooth, olive skin-stuff. The coffee cup beat a faint castanet for a moment as she set it back, empty, on the tray.

Then she realized that she had forgotten to add the sugar and cream after all, and she did so hate black coffee.

She burned a straight path from bedroom to kitchen after dressing. It was her house, after all, and there wasn't anything frippy about her, but she liked her kitchen clean. He should have waited for supervision....

But when she entered, she found a kitchen that might have been minted fire-new from the factory the moment before.

She stopped, stared, turned on her heel and nearly ran into Tony. She yelped.

'May I help?' he asked.

'Tony,' and she scraped the anger off the edges of her mind's panic, 'you must make some noise when you walk. I can't have you stalking me, you know.... Didn't you use this kitchen?'

'I did, Mrs. Belmont.'

'It doesn't look it.'

'I cleaned up afterward. Isn't that customary?'

Claire opened her eyes wide. After all, what could one say to that? She opened the oven compartment that held the pots, took a quick, unseeing look at the metallic glitter inside, then said with a tremor, 'Very good. Quite satisfactory.'

If at the moment, he had beamed; if he had smiled; if he had quirked the corner of his mouth the slightest bit, she felt that she could have warmed to him. But he remained an English lord in repose, as he said, 'Thank you, Mrs. Belmont. Would you come into the living room?'

She did, and it struck her at once. 'Have you been polishing the furniture?'

'Is it satisfactory, Mrs. Belmont?'

'But when? You didn't do it yesterday.'

'Last night, of course.'

'You burned the lights all night?'

'Oh, no. That wouldn't have been necessary. I've a built-in ultra-violet source. I can see in ultraviolet. And, of course, I don't require sleep.'

He did require admiration, though. She realized that, then. He had to know that he was pleasing her. But she couldn't bring herself to supply that pleasure for him.

She could only say sourly, 'Your kind will put ordinary houseworkers out of business.'

'There is work of much greater importance they can be put to in the world, once they are freed of drudgery. After all, Mrs. Belmont, things like myself can be manufactured. But nothing yet can imitate the creativity and versatility of a human brain, like yours.'

And though his face gave no hint, his voice was warmly surcharged with awe and admiration, so that Claire flushed and muttered, '*My* brain! You can have it.'

Tony approached a little and said, 'You must be unhappy to say such a thing. Is there anything I can do?'

For a moment, Claire felt like laughing. It *was* a ridiculous situation. Here was an animated carpet-sweeper, dishwasher, furniture-polisher, general factotum, rising from the factory table—and offering his services as consoler and confidant.

Yet she said suddenly, in a burst of woe and voice, 'Mr.

Belmont doesn't think I have a brain, if you must know....
And I suppose I haven't.' She couldn't cry in front of him.
She felt, for some reason, that she had the honor of the
human race to support against this mere creation.

'It's lately,' she added. 'It was all right when he was a
student; when he was just starting. But I can't be a big
man's wife; and he's getting to be a big man. He wants me
to be a hostess and an entry into social life for him—like
G—guh—guh—Gladys Claffern.'

Her nose was red, and she looked away.

But Tony wasn't watching her. His eyes wandered about
the room. 'I can help you run the house.'

'But it's no good,' she said fiercely. 'It needs a touch I
can't give it. I can only make it comfortable; I can't ever
make it the kind they take pictures of for the Home Beautiful magazines.'

'Do you want that kind?'

'Does it do any good—wanting?'

Tony's eyes were on her, full. 'I could help.'

'Do you know anything about interior decoration?'

'Is it something a good housekeeper should know?'

'Oh, yes.'

'Then I have the potentialities of learning it. Can you get
me books on the subject?'

Something started then.

Claire, clutching her hat against the brawling liberties of
the wind, had manipulated two fat volumes on the home
arts back from the public library. She watched Tony as he
opened one of them and flipped the pages. It was the first
time she had watched his fingers flicker at anything like fine
work.

I don't see how they do it, she thought, and on a sudden

impulse reached for his hand and pulled it toward herself. Tony did not resist, but let it lie limp for inspection.

She said, 'It's remarkable. Even your fingernails look natural.'

'That's deliberate, of course,' said Tony. Then, chattily, 'The skin is a flexible plastic, and the skeletal framework is a light metal alloy. Does that amuse you?'

'Oh, no.' She lifted her reddened face. 'I just feel a little embarrassed at sort of poking into your insides. It's none of my business. You don't ask me about mine.'

'My brain paths don't include that type of curiosity. I can only act within my limitations, you know.'

And Claire felt something tighten inside her in the silence that followed. Why did she keep forgetting he was a machine? Now the thing itself had to remind her. Was she so starved for sympathy that she would even accept a robot as equal—because he sympathized?

She noticed Tony was still flipping the pages—almost helplessly—and there was a quick, shooting sense of relieved superiority within her. 'You can't read, can you?'

Tony looked up at her; his voice calm, unreproachful. 'I *am* reading, Mrs. Belmont.'

'But——' She pointed at the book in a meaningless gesture.

'I am scanning the pages, if that's what you mean. My sense of reading is photographic.'

It was evening then, and when Claire eventually went to bed Tony was well into the second volume, sitting there in the dark, or what seemed dark to Claire's limited eyes.

Her last thought, the one that clamored at her just as her mind let go and tumbled, was a queer one. She remembered his hand again; the touch of it. It had been warm and soft, like a human being's.

How clever of the factory, she thought, and softly ebbed to sleep.

It was the library continuously, thereafter, for several days. Tony suggested the fields of study, which branched out quickly. There were books on color matching and on cosmetics; on carpentry and on fashions; on art and on the history of costumes.

He turned the pages of each book before his solemn eyes, and, as quickly as he turned, he read; nor did he seem capable of forgetting.

Before the end of the week, he had insisted on cutting her hair, introducing her to a new method of arranging it, adjusting her eyebrow line a bit and changing the shade of her powder and lipstick.

She had palpitated in nervous dread for half an hour under the delicate touch of his inhuman fingers and then looked in the mirror.

'There is more that can be done,' said Tony, 'especially in clothes. How do you find it for a beginning?'

And she hadn't answered; not for quite a while. Not until she had absorbed the identity of the stranger in the glass and cooled the wonder at the beauty of it all. Then she had said chokingly, never once taking her eyes from the warming image, 'Yes, Tony, quite good—for a beginning.'

She said nothing of this in her letters to Larry. Let him see it all at once. And something in her realized that it wasn't only the surprise she would enjoy. It was going to be a kind of revenge.

Tony said one morning, 'It's time to start buying, and I'm not allowed to leave the house. If I write out exactly what we must have, can I trust you to get it? We need drapery, and furniture fabric, wallpaper, carpeting, paint, clothing—and any number of small things.'

'You can't get these things to your own specifications at a stroke's notice,' said Claire doubtfully.

'You can get fairly close, if you go through the city and if money is no object.'

'But, Tony, money is certainly an object.'

'Not at all. Stop off at U.S. Robots in the first place. I'll write a note for you. You see Dr. Calvin, and tell her that I said it was part of the experiment.'

Dr. Calvin, somehow, didn't frighten her as on the first evening. With her new face and a new hat, she couldn't be quite the old Claire. The psychologist listened carefully, asked a few questions, nodded—and then Claire found herself walking out, armed with an unlimited charge account against the assets of U.S. Robots and Mechanical Men Corporation.

It is wonderful what money will do. With a store's contents at her feet, a saleslady's dictum was not necessarily a voice from above; the uplifted eyebrow of a decorator was not anything like Jove's thunder.

And once, when an Exalted Plumpness at one of the most lordly of the garment salons had insistently poohed her description of the wardrobe she must have with counter-pronouncements in accents of the purest Fifty-seventh Street French, she called up Tony, then held the phone out to Monsieur.

'If you don't mind'—voice firm, but fingers twisting a bit—'I'd like you to talk to my—uh—secretary.'

Pudgy proceeded to the phone with a solemn arm crooked behind his back. He lifted the phone in two fingers and said delicately, 'Yes.' A short pause, another 'Yes,' then a much longer pause, a squeaky beginning of an objection that perished quickly, another pause, a very meek 'Yes,' and the phone was restored to its cradle.

'If Madam will come with me,' he said, hurt and distant, 'I will try to supply her needs.'

'Just a second.' Claire rushed back to the phone, and dialed again. 'Hello, Tony. I don't know what you said, but it worked. Thanks. You're a——' She struggled for the appropriate word, gave up and ended in a final little squeak, '—a—a dear!'

It was Gladys Claffern looking at her when she turned from the phone again. A slightly amused and slightly amazed Gladys Claffern, looking at her out of a face tilted a bit to one side.

'Mrs. Belmont?'

It all drained out of Claire—just like that. She could only nod—stupidly, like a marionette.

Gladys smiled with an insolence you couldn't put your finger on. 'I didn't know you shopped here?' As if the place had, in her eyes, definitely lost caste through the fact.

'I don't, usually,' said Claire humbly.

'And haven't you done something to your hair? It's quite —quaint.... Oh, I hope you'll excuse me, but isn't your husband's name Lawrence? It seems to me that it's Lawrence.'

Claire's teeth clenched, but she had to explain. She *had* to. 'Tony is a friend of my husband's. He's helping me select some things.'

'I understand. And quite a *dear* about it, I imagine.' She passed on smiling, carrying the light and the warmth of the world with her.

Claire did not question the fact that it was to Tony that

she turned for consolation. Ten days had cured her of reluctance. And she could weep before him; weep and rage.

'I was a complete f-fool,' she stormed, wrenching at her
waterlogged handkerchief. 'She does that to me. I don't
know why. She just does. I should have—kicked her. I
should have knocked her down and stamped on her.'

'Can you hate a human being so much?' asked Tony, in
puzzled softness. 'That part of a human mind is closed to
me.'

'Oh, it isn't she,' she moaned. 'It's myself, I suppose
She's everything I want to be—on the outside, anyway....
And I can't be.'

Tony's voice was forceful and low in her ear. 'You can
be, Mrs. Belmont. You *can* be. We have ten days yet, and
in ten days the house will no longer be itself. Haven't we
been planning that?'

'And how will that help me—with her?'

'Invite her here. Invite her friends. Have it the evening
before I—before I leave. It will be a housewarming, in a
way.'

'She won't come.'

'Yes, she will. She'll come to laugh.... And she won't be
able to.'

'Do you really think so? Oh, Tony, do you think we can
do it?' She had both his hands in hers.... And then, with
her face flung aside, 'But what good would it be? It won't
be I; it will be you that's doing it. I can't ride your back.'

'Nobody lives in splendid singleness,' whispered Tony.
'They've put that knowledge in me. What you, or anyone,
see in Gladys Claffern is not just Gladys Claffern. She rides
the back of all that money and social position can bring.
She doesn't question that. Why should you? ... And look
at it this way, Mrs. Belmont. I am manufactured to obey,

but the extent of my obedience is for myself to determine. I can follow orders niggardly or liberally. For you, it is liberal, because you are what I have been manufactured to see human beings as. You are kind, friendly, unassuming. Mrs. Claffern, as you describe her, is not, and I wouldn't obey her as I would you. So it *is* you, and not I, Mrs. Belmont, that is doing all this.'

He withdrew his hands from hers then, and Claire looked at that expressionless face no one could read—wondering. She was suddenly frightened again in a completely new way.

She swallowed nervously and stared at her hands, which were still tingling with the pressure of his fingers. She hadn't imagined it; his fingers had pressed hers, gently, tenderly, just before they moved away.

No!

Its fingers . . . *Its* fingers. . . .

She ran to the bathroom and scrubbed her hands—blindly, uselessly.

She was a bit shy of him the next day; watching him narrowly; waiting to see what might follow—and for a while nothing did.

Tony was working. If there was any difficulty in technique in putting up wallpaper, or utilizing the quick-drying paint, Tony's activity did not show it. His hands moved precisely; his fingers were deft and sure.

He worked all night. She never heard him, but each morning was a new adventure. She couldn't count the number of things that had been done, and by evening she was still finding new touches—and another night had come.

She tried to help only once and her human clumsiness marred that. *He* was in the next room, and she was hanging a picture in the spot marked by Tony's mathematical eyes. The little mark was there; the picture was there; and a revulsion against idleness was there.

But she was nervous, or the ladder was rickety. It didn't matter. She felt it going, and she cried out. It tumbled without her, for Tony, with far more than flesh-and-blood quickness, had been under her.

His calm, dark eyes said nothing at all, and his warm voice said only words. 'Are you hurt, Mrs. Belmont?'

She noticed for an instant that her falling hand must have mussed that sleek hair of his, because for the first time she could see for herself that it was composed of distinct strands—fine black hairs.

And then, all at once, she was conscious of his arms about her shoulders and under her knees—holding her tightly and warmly.

She pushed, and her scream was loud in her own ears. She spent the rest of the day in her room, and thereafter she slept with a chair upended against the doorknob of her bedroom door.

She had sent out the invitations, and, as Tony had said, they were accepted. She had only to wait for the last evening.

It came, too, after the rest of them, in its proper place. The house was scarcely her own. She went through it one last time—and every room had been changed. She, herself, was in clothes she would never have dared wear before. . . . And when you put them on, you put on pride and confidence with them.

She tried a polite look of contemptuous amusement before the mirror, and the mirror sneered back at her masterfully.

What would Larry say? ... It didn't matter, somehow. The exciting days weren't coming with him. They were leaving with Tony. Now wasn't that strange? She tried to recapture her mood of three weeks before and failed completely.

The clock shrieked eight at her in eight breathless installments, and she turned to Tony. 'They'll be here soon, Tony. You'd better get into the basement. We can't let them——'

She stared a moment, then said weakly, 'Tony?' and more strongly, 'Tony?' and nearly a scream, 'Tony!'

But his arms were around her now; his face was close to hers; the pressure of his embrace was relentless. She heard his voice through a haze of emotional jumble.

'Claire,' the voice said, 'there are many things I am not made to understand, and this must be one of them. I am leaving tomorrow, and I don't want to. I find that there is more in me than just a desire to please you. Isn't it strange?'

His face was closer; his lips were warm, but with no breath behind them—for machines do not breathe. They were almost on hers.

... And the bell sounded.

For a moment, she struggled breathlessly, and then he was gone and nowhere in sight, and the bell was sounding again. Its intermittent shrillness was insistent.

The curtains on the front windows had been pulled open. They had been closed fifteen minutes earlier. She *knew* that.

They must have seen, then. They must *all* have seen— everything!

They came in so politely, all in a bunch—the pack come to howl—with their sharp, darting eyes piercing everywhere. They *had* seen. Why else would Gladys ask in her jabbingest manner after Larry? And Claire was spurred to a desperate and reckless defiance.

Yes, he *is* away. He'll be back tomorrow, I suppose. No, I haven't been lonely here myself. Not a bit. I've had an exciting time. And she laughed at them. Why not? What could they do? Larry would know the truth, if it ever came to him, the story of what they thought they saw.

But *they* didn't laugh.

She could read that in the fury in Gladys Claffern's eyes; in the false sparkle of her words; in her desire to leave early. And as she parted with them, she caught one last, anonymous whisper—disjointed.

'. . . never saw anything like . . . *so handsome*——'

And she knew what it was that had enabled her to finger-snap them so. Let each cat mew; and let each cat know—that she might be prettier than Claire Belmont, and grander, and richer—but not one, *not one*, could have so handsome a lover!

And then she remembered again—again—again, that Tony was a machine, and her skin crawled.

'Go away! Leave me be!' she cried to the empty room and ran to her bed. She wept wakefully all that night and the next morning, almost before dawn, when the streets were empty, a car drew up to the house and took Tony away.

Lawrence Belmont passed Dr. Calvin's office, and, on impulse, knocked. He found her with Mathematician Peter Bogert, but did not hesitate on that account.

He said, 'Claire tells me that U.S. Robots paid for all

that was done at my house——'

'Yes,' said Dr. Calvin. 'We've written it off, as a valuable and necessary part of the experiment. With your new position as Associate Engineer, you'll be able to keep it up, I think.'

'That's not what I'm worried about. With Washington agreeing to the tests, we'll be able to get a TN model of our own by next year, I think.' He turned hesitantly, as though to go, and as hesitantly turned back again.

'Well, Mr. Belmont?' asked Dr. Calvin, after a pause.

'I wonder——' began Larry. 'I wonder what really happened there. She—Claire, I mean—seems so different. It's not just her looks—though, frankly, I'm amazed.' He laughed nervously. 'It's her! She's not my wife, really—I can't explain it.'

'Why try? Are you disappointed with any part of the change?'

'On the contrary. But it's a little frightening, too, you see——'

'I wouldn't worry, Mr. Belmont. Your wife has handled herself very well. Frankly, I never expected to have the experiment yield such a thorough and complete test. We know exactly what corrections must be made in the TN model, and the credit belongs entirely to Mrs. Belmont. If you want me to be very honest, I think your wife deserves your promotion more than you do.'

Larry flinched visibly at that. 'As long as it's in the family,' he murmured unconvincingly and left.

Susan Calvin looked after him, 'I think that hurt—I hope.... Have you read Tony's report, Peter?'

'Thoroughly,' said Bogert. 'And won't the TN-3 model need changes?'

'Oh, you think so, too?' questioned Calvin sharply. 'What's your reasoning?'

Bogert frowned. 'I don't need any. It's obvious on the face of it that we can't have a robot loose which makes love to his mistress, if you don't mind the pun.'

'Love! Peter, you sicken me. You really don't understand? That machine had to obey the First Law. He couldn't allow harm to come to a human being, and harm was coming to Claire Belmont through her own sense of inadequacy. So he made love to her, since what woman would fail to appreciate the compliment of being able to stir passion in a machine—in a cold, soulless machine. And he opened the curtains that night deliberately, that the others might see and envy—without any risk possible to Claire's marriage. I think it was clever of Tony——'

'Do you? What's the difference whether it was pretense or not, Susan? It still has its horrifying effect. Read the report again. She avoided him. She screamed when he held her. She didn't sleep that last night—in hysterics. We can't have that.'

'Peter, you're blind. You're as blind as I was. The TN model will be rebuilt entirely, but not for your reason. Quite otherwise; quite otherwise. Strange that I overlooked it in the first place,' her eyes were opaquely thoughtful, 'but perhaps it reflects a shortcoming in myself. You see, Peter, machines can't fall in love, but—even when it's hopeless and horrifying—women can!'

'Risk' appeared in the May 1955 issue of Astounding Science Fiction. Of my later robot stories, it was the most closely bound to I, Robot, for it was a sequel to 'Little Lost Robot,' one of the stories in that book. It involves a different robot and a different problem, but the same setting, the same human characters and the same research project.

RISK

HYPER BASE had lived for this day. Spaced about the gallery of the viewing room, in order and precedence strictly dictated by protocol, was a group of officials, scientists, technicians, and others who could only be lumped under the general classification of 'personnel.' In accordance with their separate temperaments they waited hopefully, uneasily, breathlessly, eagerly, or fearfully for this culmination of their efforts.

The hollowed interior of the asteroid known as Hyper Base had become for this day the center of a sphere of iron security that extended out for ten thousand miles. No ship might enter that sphere and live. No message might leave without scrutiny.

A hundred miles away, more or less, a small asteroid moved neatly in the orbit into which it had been urged a year before, an orbit that ringed Hyper Base in as perfect a circle as could be managed. The asteroidlet's identity number was H937, but no one on Hyper Base called it anything but It. ('Have you been out on it today?' 'The general's on it, blowing his top,' and eventually the impersonal pronoun achieved the dignity of capitalization.)

On It, unoccupied now as zero second approached, was the *Parsec*, the only ship of its kind ever built in the history of man. It lay, unmanned, ready for its takeoff into the inconceivable.

Gerald Black, who, as one of the bright young men in etherics engineering, rated a front-row view, cracked his large knuckles, then wiped his sweating palms on his stained white smock and said sourly, 'Why don't you bother the general, or Her Ladyship there?'

Nigel Ronson, of Interplanetary Press, looked briefly across the gallery toward the glitter of Major General Richard Kallner and the unremarkable woman at his side, scarcely visible in the glare of his dress uniform. He said, 'I would, except that I'm interested in news.'

Ronson was short and plump. He painstakingly wore his hair in a quarter-inch bristle, his shirt collar open and his trouser leg ankle-short, in faithful imitation of the newsmen who were stock characters on TV shows. He was a capable reporter nevertheless.

Black was stocky, and his dark hairline left little room for forehead, but his mind was as keen as his strong fingers were blunt. He said, 'They've got all the news.'

'Nuts,' said Ronson. 'Kallner's got no body under that gold braid. Strip him and you'll find only a conveyor belt dribbling orders downward and shooting responsibility upward.'

Black found himself at the point of a grin but squeezed it down. He said, 'What about the Madam Doctor?'

'Dr. Susan Calvin of U.S. Robots and Mechanical Men, Incorporated,' intoned the reporter. 'The lady with hyperspace where her heart ought to be and liquid helium in her eyes. She'd pass through the sun and come out the other end encased in frozen flame.'

Black came even closer to a grin. 'How about Director Schloss, then?'

Ronson said glibly, 'He knows too much. Between spending his time fanning the feeble intelligence of his listener and dimming his own brains for fear of blinding said listener permanently by sheer force of brilliance, he ends up saying nothing.'

Black showed his teeth this time. 'Now suppose you tell me why you pick on me.'

'Easy, doctor. I looked at you and figured you're too ugly to be stupid and too smart to miss a possible opportunity at some good personal publicity.'

'Remind me to knock you down someday,' said Black. 'What do you want to know?'

The man from Interplanetary Press pointed into the pit and said, 'Is that thing going to work?'

Black looked downward too, and felt a vague chill riffle over him like the thin night wind of Mars. The pit was one large television screen, divided in two. One half was an over-all view of It. On Its pitted gray surface was the *Parsec*, glowing mutedly in the feeble sunlight. The other half showed the control room of the *Parsec*. There was no life in that control room. In the pilot's seat was an object the vague humanity of which did not for a moment obscure the fact that it was only a positronic robot.

Black said, 'Physically, mister, this will work. That robot will leave and come back. Space! how we succeeded with that part of it. I watched it all. I came here two weeks after I took my degree in etheric physics and I've been here, barring leave and furloughs, ever since. I was here when we sent the first piece of iron wire to Jupiter's orbit and back through hyperspace—and got back iron filings. I was here when we sent white mice there and back and ended up with mincemeat.

'We spent six months establishing an even hyperfield after that. We had to wipe out lags of as little as tenths of thousandths of seconds from point to point in matter being subjected to hypertravel. After that, the white mice started coming back intact. I remember when we celebrated for a week because one white mouse came back alive and lived ten minutes before dying. Now they live as long as we can take proper care of them.'

Ronson said, 'Great!'

Black looked at him obliquely. 'I said, *physically* it will work. Those white mice that come back——'

'Well?'

'No minds. Not even little white mice-type minds. They won't eat. They have to be force-fed. They won't mate. They won't run. They sit. They sit. They sit. That's all. We finally worked up to sending a chimpanzee. It was pitiful. It was too close to a man to make watching it bearable. It came back a hunk of meat that could make crawling motions. It could move its eyes and sometimes it would scrabble. It whined and sat in its own wastes without the sense to move. Somebody shot it one day, and we were all grateful for that. I tell you this, fella, nothing that ever went into hyperspace has come back with a mind.'

'Is this for publication?'

'After this experiment, maybe. They expect great things of it.' A corner of Black's mouth lifted.

'You don't?'

'With a robot at the controls? No.' Almost automatically Black's mind went back to that interlude, some years back, in which he had been unwittingly responsible for the near loss of a robot. He thought of the Nestor robots that filled Hyper Base with smooth, ingrained knowledge and perfectionist shortcomings. What was the use of talking about robots? He was not, by nature, a missionary.

But then Ronson, filling the continuing silence with a bit of small talk, said, as he replaced the wad of gum in his mouth by a fresh piece, 'Don't tell me *you're* anti-robot. I've always heard that scientists are the one group that aren't anti-robot.'

Black's patience snapped. He said, 'That's true, and that's the trouble. Technology's gone robot-happy. Any job has to have a robot, or the engineer in charge feels cheated. You want a doorstop; buy a robot with a thick foot. That's a serious thing.' He was speaking in a low, intense voice, shoving the words directly into Ronson's ear.

Ronson managed to extricate his arm. He said, 'Hey, I'm no robot. Don't take it out on me. I'm a man. *Homo sapiens*. You just broke an arm bone of mine. Isn't that proof?'

Having started, however, it took more than frivolity to stop Black. He said, 'Do you know how much time was wasted on this setup? We've had a perfectly generalized robot built and we've given it one order. Period. I heard the order given. I've memorized it. Short and sweet. "Seize the bar with a firm grip. Pull it towards you firmly. *Firmly!* Maintain your hold until the control board informs you that you have passed through hyperspace twice."

'So at zero time, the robot will grab the control bar and pull it firmly toward himself. His hands are heated to blood temperature. Once the control bar is in position, heat expansion completes contact and hyperfield is initiated. If anything happens to his brain during the first trip through hyperspace, it doesn't matter. All he needs to do is maintain position one microinstant and the ship will come back and the hyperfield will flip off. Nothing can go wrong. Then we study all its generalized reactions and see what, if anything, has gone wrong.'

Ronson looked blank. 'This all makes sense to me.'

'Does it?' asked Black bitterly. 'And what will you learn from a robot brain? It's positronic, ours is cellular. It's metal, ours is protein. They're not the same. There's no comparison. Yet I'm convinced that on the basis of what they learn, or think they learn, from the robot, they'll send men into hyperspace. Poor devils!—Look, it's not a question of dying. It's coming back mindless. If you'd seen the chimpanzee, you'd know what I mean. Death is clean and final. The other thing——'

The reporter said, 'Have you talked about this to anyone?'

Black said, 'Yes. They say what you said. They say I'm anti-robot and that settles everything—Look at Susan Calvin there. You can bet *she* isn't anti-robot. She came all the way from Earth to watch this experiment. If it had been a man at the controls, she wouldn't have bothered. But what's the use!'

'Hey,' said Ronson, 'don't stop now. There's more.'

'More what?'

'More problems. You've explained the robot. But why the security provisions all of a sudden?'

'Huh?'

'Come *on*. Suddenly I can't send dispatches. Suddenly ships can't come into the area. What's going on? This is just another experiment. The public knows about hyperspace and what you boys are trying to do, so what's the big secret?'

The backwash of anger was still seeping over Black, anger against the robots, anger against Susan Calvin, anger at the memory of that little lost robot in his past. There was some to spare, he found, for the irritating little newsman and his irritating little questions.

He said to himself, Let's see how he takes it.

He said, 'You really want to know?'

'You bet.'

'All right. We've never initiated a hyperfield for any object a millionth as large as that ship, or to send anything a millionth as far. That means that the hyperfield that will soon be initiated is some million million times as energetic as any we've ever handled. We're not sure what it can do.'

'What do you mean?'

'Theory tells us that the ship will be neatly deposited out near Sirius and neatly brought back here. But how large a volume of space about the *Parsec* will be carried with it? It's hard to tell. We don't know enough about hyperspace. The asteroid on which the ship sits may go with it and, you know, if our calculations are even a little off, it may never be brought back here. It may return, say, twenty billion miles away. And there's a chance that more of space than just the asteroid may be shifted.'

'How much more?' demanded Ronson.

'We can't say. There's an element of statistical uncertainty. That's why no ships must approach too closely. That's why we're keeping things quiet till the experiment is safely over.'

Ronson swallowed audibly. 'Supposing it reaches to Hyper Base?'

'There's a chance of it,' said Black with composure. 'Not much of a chance or Director Schloss wouldn't be here, I assure you. Still, there's a mathematical chance.'

The newsman looked at his watch. 'When does this all happen?'

'In about five minutes. You're not nervous, are you?'

'No,' said Ronson, but he sat down blankly and asked no more questions.

Black leaned outward over the railing. The final minutes were ticking off.

The robot moved!

There was a mass sway of humanity forward at that sign

of motion and the lights dimmed in order to sharpen and heighten the brightness of the scene below. But so far it was only the first motion. The hands of the robot approached the starting bar.

Black waited for the final second when the robot would pull the bar toward himself. Black could imagine a number of possibilities, and all sprang nearly simultaneously to mind.

There would first be the short flicker that would indicate the departure through hyperspace and return. Even though the time interval was exceedingly short, return would not be to the *precise* starting position and there would be a flicker. There always was.

Then, when the ship returned, it might be found, perhaps, that the devices to even the field over the huge volume of the ship had proved inadequate. The robot might be scrap steel. The ship might be scrap steel.

Or their calculations might be somewhat off and the ship might never return. Or worse still, Hyper Base might go with the ship and never return.

Or, of course, all might be well. The ship might flicker and be there in perfect shape. The robot, with mind untouched, would get out of his seat and signal a successful completion of the first voyage of a man-made object beyond the gravitational control of the sun.

The last minute was ticking off.

The last second came and the robot seized the starting bar and pulled it firmly toward himself——

Nothing!

No flicker. Nothing!

The *Parsec* never left normal space.

Major General Kallner took off his officer's cap to mop

his glistening forehead and in doing so exposed a bald head that would have aged him ten years in appearance if his drawn expression had not already done so. Nearly an hour had passed since the *Parsec*'s failure and nothing had been done.

'How did it happen? How did it happen? I don't understand it.'

Dr. Mayer Schloss, who at forty was the 'grand old man' of the young science of hyperfield matrices, said hopelessly, 'There is nothing wrong with the basic theory. I'll swear my life away on that. There's a mechanical failure on the ship somewhere. Nothing more.' He had said that a dozen times.

'I thought everything was tested.' That had been said too.

'It was, sir, it was. Just the same———' And that.

They sat staring at each other in Kallner's office, which was now out of bounds for all personnel. Neither quite dared to look at the third person present.

Susan Calvin's thin lips and pale cheeks bore no expression. She said coolly, 'You may console yourself with what I have told you before. It is doubtful whether anything useful would have resulted.'

'This is not the time for the old argument,' groaned Schloss.

'I am not arguing. U.S. Robots and Mechanical Men, Inc. will supply robots made up to specification to any legal purchaser for any legal use. We did our part, however. We informed you that we could not guarantee being able to draw conclusions with regard to the human brain from anything that happened to the positronic brain. Our responsibility ends there. There is no argument.'

'Great space,' said General Kallner, in a tone that made

the expletive feeble indeed. 'Let's not discuss that.'

'What else was there to do?' muttered Schloss, driven to the subject nevertheless. 'Until we know exactly what's happening to the mind in hyperspace we can't progress. The robot's mind is at least capable of mathematical analysis. It's a start, a beginning. And until we try——' He looked up wildly, 'But your robot isn't the point, Dr. Calvin. We're not worried about him or his positronic brain. Damn it, woman——' His voice rose nearly to a scream.

The robopsychologist cut him to silence with a voice that scarcely raised itself from its level monotone. 'No hysteria, man. In my lifetime I have witnessed many crises and I have never seen one solved by hysteria. I want answers to some questions.'

Schloss's full lips trembled and his deep-set eyes seemed to retreat into their sockets and leave pits of shadow in their places. He said harshly, 'Are you trained in etheric engineering?'

'That is an irrelevant question. I am Chief Robopsychologist of the United States Robots and Mechanical Men, Incorporated. That is a positronic robot sitting at the controls of the *Parsec*. Like all such robots, it is leased and not sold. I have a right to demand information concerning any experiment in which such a robot is involved.'

'Talk to her, Schloss,' barked General Kallner. 'She's—she's all right.'

Dr. Calvin turned her pale eyes on the general, who had been present at the time of the affair of the lost robot and who therefore could be expected not to make the mistake of underestimating her. (Schloss had been out on sick leave at the time, and hearsay is not as effective as personal experience.) 'Thank you, general,' she said.

Schloss looked helplessly from one to the other and muttered, 'What do you want to know?'

'Obviously my first question is, What *is* your problem if the robot is not?'

'But the problem is an obvious one. The ship hasn't moved. Can't you see that? Are you blind?'

'I see quite well. What I don't see is your obvious panic over some mechanical failure. Don't you people expect failure sometimes?'

The general muttered, 'It's the expense. The ship was hellishly expensive. The World Congress—appropriations——' He bogged down.

'The ship's still there. A slight overhaul and correction would involve no great trouble.'

Schloss had taken hold of himself. The expression on his face was one of a man who had caught his soul in both hands, shaken it hard and set it on its feet. His voice had even achieved a kind of patience. 'Dr. Calvin, when I say a mechanical failure, I mean something like a relay jammed by a speck of dust, a connection inhibited by a spot of grease, a transistor balked by a momentary heat expansion. A dozen other things. A hundred other things. Any of them can be quite temporary. They can stop taking effect at any moment.'

'Which means that at any moment the *Parsec* may flash through hyperspace and back after all.'

'Exactly. Now do you understand?'

'Not at all. Wouldn't that be just what you want?'

Schloss made a motion that looked like the start of an effort to seize a double handful of hair and yank. He said, 'You are not an etherics engineer.'

'Does that tongue-tie you, doctor?'

'We had the ship set,' said Schloss despairingly, 'to make

a jump from a definite point in space relative to the center of gravity of the galaxy to another point. The return was to be to the original point corrected for the motion of the solar system. In the hour that has passed since the *Parsec* should have moved, the solar system has shifted position. The original parameters to which the hyperfield is adjusted no longer apply. The ordinary laws of motion do not apply to hyperspace and it would take us a week of computation to calculate a new set of parameters.'

'You mean that if the ship moves now it will return to some unpredictable point thousands of miles away?'

'Unpredictable?' Schloss smiled hollowly. 'Yes, I should call it that. The *Parsec* might end up in the Andromeda nebula or in the center of the sun. In any case the odds are against our ever seeing it again.'

Susan Calvin nodded. 'The situation then is that if the ship disappears, as it may do at any moment, a few billion dollars of the tax-payers' money may be irretrievably gone, and—it will be said—through bungling.'

Major General Kallner could not have winced more noticeably if he had been poked with a sharp pin in the fundament.

The robopsychologist went on, 'Somehow, then, the ship's hyperfield mechanism must be put out of action, and that as soon as possible. Something will have to be unplugged or jerked loose or flicked off.' She was speaking half to herself.

'It's not that simple,' said Schloss. 'I can't explain it completely, since you're not an etherics expert. It's like trying to break an ordinary electric circuit by slicing through high-tension wire with garden shears. It could be disastrous. It *would* be disastrous.'

'Do you mean that any attempt to shut off the

mechanism would hurl the ship into hyperspace?'

'Any *random* attempt would *probably* do so. Hyper-forces are not limited by the speed of light. It is very probable that they have no limit of velocity at all. It makes things extremely difficult. The only reasonable solution is to discover the nature of the failure and learn from that a safe way of disconnecting the field.'

'And how do you propose to do that, Dr. Schloss?'

Schloss said, 'It seems to me that the only thing to do is to send one of our Nestor robots——'

'No! Don't be foolish,' broke in Susan Calvin.

Schloss said, freezingly, 'The Nestors are acquainted with the problems of etherics engineering. They will be ideally——'

'Out of the question. You cannot use one of our posi-tronic robots for such a purpose without my permission. You do not have it and you shall not get it.'

'What is the alternative?'

'You must send one of your engineers.'

Schloss shook his head violently, 'Impossible. The risk involved is too great. If we lose a ship *and* a man——'

'Nevertheless, you may not use a Nestor robot, or any robot.'

The general said, 'I—I must get in touch with Earth. This whole problem has to go to a higher level.'

Susan Calvin said with asperity, 'I wouldn't just yet if I were you, general. You will be throwing yourself on the government's mercy without a suggestion or plan of action of your own. You will not come out very well, I am certain.'

'But what is there to do?' The general was using his handkerchief again.

'Send a man. There is no alternative.'

Schloss had paled to a pasty gray. 'It's easy to say, send a man. But whom?'

'I've been considering that problem. Isn't there a young man—his name is Black—whom I met on the occasion of my previous visit to Hyper Base?'

'Dr. Gerald Black?'

'I think so. Yes. He was a bachelor then. Is he still?'

'Yes, I believe so.'

'I would suggest then that he be brought here, say, in fifteen minutes, and that meanwhile I have access to his records.'

Smoothly she had assumed authority in this situation, and neither Kallner nor Schloss made any attempt to dispute that authority with her.

Black had seen Susan Calvin from a distance on this, her second visit to Hyper Base. He had made no move to cut down the distance. Now that he had been called into her presence, he found himself staring at her with revulsion and distaste. He scarcely noticed Dr. Schloss and General Kallner standing behind her.

He remembered the last time he had faced her thus, undergoing a cold dissection for the sake of a lost robot.

Dr. Calvin's cool gray eyes were fixed steadily on his hot brown ones.

'Dr. Black,' she said, 'I believe you understand the situation.'

Black said, 'I do.'

'Something will have to be done. The ship is too expensive-to lose. The bad publicity will probably mean the end of the project.'

Black nodded. 'I've been thinking that.'

'I hope you've also thought that it will be necessary for someone to board the *Parsec*, find out what's wrong, and—

uh—deactivate it.'

There was a moment's pause. Black said harshly, 'What fool would go?'

Kallner frowned and looked at Schloss, who bit his lip and looked nowhere.

Susan Calvin said, 'There is, of course, the possibility of accidental activation of the hyperfield, in which case the ship may drive beyond all possible reach. On the other hand, it may return somewhere within the solar system. If so, no expense or effort will be spared to recover man and ship.'

Black said, 'Idiot and ship! Just a correction.'

Susan Calvin disregarded the comment. She said, 'I have asked General Kallner's permission to put it to you. It is you who must go.'

No pause at all here. Black said, in the flattest possible way, 'Lady, I'm not volunteering.'

'There are not a dozen men on Hyper Base with sufficient knowledge to have any chance at all of carrying this thing through successfully. Of those who have the knowledge, I've selected you on the basis of our previous acquaintanceship. You will bring to this task an understanding——'

'Look, I'm not volunteering.'

'You have no choice. Surely you will face your responsibility?'

'*My* responsibility? What makes it mine?'

'The fact that you are best fitted for the job.'

'Do you know the risk?'

'I think I do,' said Susan Calvin.

'I know you don't. You never saw that chimpanzee. Look, when I said "idiot and ship" I wasn't expressing an opinion. I was telling you a fact. I'd risk my life if I had to.

Not with pleasure, maybe, but I'd risk it. Risking idiocy, a lifetime of animal mindlessness, is something I won't risk, that's all.'

Susan Calvin glanced thoughtfully at the young engineer's sweating, angry face.

Black shouted, 'Send one of your robots, one of your NS-2 jobs.'

The psychologist's eye reflected a kind of cold glitter. She said with deliberation, 'Yes, Dr. Schloss suggested that. But the NS-2 robots are leased by our firm, not sold. They cost millions of dollars apiece, you know. I represent the company and I have decided that they are too expensive to be risked in a matter such as this.'

Black lifted his hands. They clenched and trembled close to his chest as though he were forcibly restraining them. 'You're telling me—you're saying you want me to go instead of a robot because I'm more expendable.'

'It comes to that, yes.'

'Dr. Calvin,' said Black, 'I'd see you in hell first.'

'That statement might be almost literally true, Dr. Black. As General Kallner will confirm, you are ordered to take this assignment. You are under quasi-military law here, I understand, and if you refuse an assignment, you can be court-martialed. A case like this will mean Mercury prison and I believe that will be close enough to hell to make your statement uncomfortably accurate were I to visit you, though I probably would not. On the other hand, if you agree to board the *Parsec* and carry through this job, it will mean a great deal for your career.'

Black glared, red-eyed, at her.

Susan Calvin said, 'Give the man five minutes to think about this, General Kallner, and get a ship ready.'

Two security guards escorted Black out of the room.

Gerald Black felt cold. His limbs moved as though they were not part of him. It was as though he were watching himself from some remote, safe place, watching himself board a ship and make ready to leave for It and for the *Parsec.*

He couldn't quite believe it. He had bowed his head suddenly and said, 'I'll go.'

But why?

He had never thought of himself as the hero type. Then why? Partly, of course, there was the threat of Mercury prison. Partly it was the awful reluctance to appear a coward in the eyes of those who knew him, that deeper cowardice that was behind half the bravery in the world.

Mostly, though, it was something else.

Ronson of Interplanetary Press had stopped Black momentarily as he was on his way to the ship. Black looked at Ronson's flushed face and said, 'What do you want?'

Ronson babbled, 'Listen! When you get back, I want it exclusive. I'll arrange any payment you want—anything you want——'

Black pushed him aside, sent him sprawling, and walked on.

The ship had a crew of two. Neither spoke to him. Their glances slid over and under and around him. Black didn't mind that. They were scared spitless themselves and their ship was approaching the *Parsec* like a kitten skittering sideways toward the first dog it had ever seen. He could do without *them.*

There was only one face that he kept seeing. The anxious expression of General Kallner and the look of synthetic determination on Schloss's face were momentary punctures on his consciousness. They healed almost at once. It was Susan Calvin's unruffled face that he saw. Her calm expressionlessness as he boarded the ship.

He stared into the blackness where Hyper Base had already disappeared into space——

Susan Calvin! Doctor Susan Calvin! Robopsychologist Susan Calvin! The robot that walks like a woman!

What were her three laws, he wondered? First Law: Thou shalt protect the robot with all thy might and all thy heart and all thy soul. Second Law: Thou shalt hold the interests of U.S. Robots and Mechanical Men, Inc. holy provided it interfereth not with the First Law. Third Law: Thou shalt give passing consideration to a human being provided it interfereth not with the First and Second laws.

Had she ever been young, he wondered savagely? Had she ever felt one honest emotion?

Space! How he wanted to do something—something that would take that frozen look of nothing off her face.

And he would!

By the stars, he would. Let him but get out of this sane and he would see her smashed and her company with her and all the vile brood of robots with them. It was that thought that was driving him more than fear of prison or desire for social prestige. It was that thought that almost robbed him of fear altogether. Almost.

One of the pilots muttered at him, without looking, 'You can drop down from here. It's half a mile under.'

Black said bitterly, 'Aren't you landing?'

'Strict orders not to. The vibration of the landing might——'

'What about the vibration of my landing?'

The pilot said, 'I've got my orders.'

Black said no more but climbed into his suit and waited for the inner lock to open. A tool kit was welded firmly to the metal of the suit about his right thigh.

Just as he stepped into the lock, the earpieces inside his helmet rumbled at him. 'Wish you luck, doctor.'

It took a moment for him to realize that it came from the two men aboard ship, pausing in their eagerness to get out of that haunted volume of space to give him that much, anyway.

'Thanks,' said Black awkwardly, half resentfully.

And then he was out in space, tumbling slowly as the result of the slightly off-center thrust of feet against outer lock.

He could see the *Parsec* waiting for him, and by looking between his legs at the right moment of the tumble he could see the long hiss of the lateral jets of the ship that had brought him, as it turned to leave.

He was alone! Space, he was alone!

Could any man in history ever have felt so alone?

Would he know, he wondered sickly, if—if anything happened? Would there be any moments of realization? Would he feel his mind fade and the light of reason and thought dim and blank out?

Or would it happen suddenly, like the cut of a force knife?

In either case——

The thought of the chimpanzee, blank-eyed, shivering with mindless terrors, was fresh within him.

The asteroid was twenty feet below him now. It swam through space with an absolutely even motion. Barring human agency, no grain of sand upon it had as much as stirred through astronomical periods of time.

In the ultimate jarlessness of It, some small particle of grit encumbered a delicate working unit on board the *Parsec*, or a speck of impure sludge in the fine oil that bathed some moving part had stopped it.

Perhaps it required only a small vibration, a tiny tremor originating from the collision of mass and mass to un-encumber that moving part, bringing it down along its appointed path, creating the hyperfield, blossoming it out-ward like an incredibly ripening rose.

His body was going to touch It and he drew his limbs together in his anxiety to 'hit easy.' He did not want to touch the asteroid. His skin crawled with intense aversion.

It came closer.

Now—now——

Nothing!

There was only the continuing touch of the asteroid, the uncanny moments of slowly mounting pressure that resulted from a mass of 250 pounds (himself plus suit) possessing full inertia but no weight to speak of.

Black opened his eyes slowly and let the sight of stars enter. The sun was a glowing marble, its brilliance muted by the polarizing shield over his faceplate. The stars were correspondingly feeble but they made up the familiar arrangement. With sun and constellations normal, he was still in the solar system. He could even see Hyper Base, a small, dim crescent.

He stiffened in shock at the sudden voice in his ear. It was Schloss.

Schloss said, 'We've got you in view, Dr. Black. You are not alone!'

Black could have laughed at the phraseology, but he only said in a low, clear voice, 'Clear off. If you'll do that, you won't be distracting me.'

A pause. Schloss's voice, more cajoling, 'If you care to report as you go along, it may relieve the tension.'

'You'll get information from me when I get back. Not before.' He said it bitterly, and bitterly his metal-encased fingers moved to the control panel in his chest and blanked out the suit's radio. They could talk into a vacuum now. He had his own plans. If he got out of this sane, it would be his show.

He got to his feet with infinite caution and stood on It. He swayed a bit as involuntary muscular motions, tricked by the almost total lack of gravity into an endless series of overbalancings, pulled him this way and that. On Hyper Base there was a pseudo-gravitic field to hold them down. Black found that a portion of his mind was sufficiently detached to remember that and appreciate it *in absentia*.

The sun had disappeared behind a crag. The stars wheeled visibly in time to the asteroid's one-hour rotation period.

He could see the *Parsec* from where he stood and now he moved toward it slowly, carefully—tippy-toe almost. (No vibration. No vibration. The words ran pleadingly through his mind.)

Before he was completely aware of the distance he had crossed, he was at the ship. He was at the foot of the line of hand grips that led to the outer lock.

There he paused.

The ship looked quite normal. Or at least it looked normal except for the circle of steely knobs that girdled it one third of the way up, and a second circle two thirds of the way up. At the moment, they must be straining to become the source poles of the hyperfield.

A strange desire to reach up and fondle one of them came over Black. It was one of those irrational impulses, like the momentary thought, 'What if I jumped?' that is almost inevitable when one stares down from a high building.

Black took a deep breath and felt himself go clammy as he spread the fingers of both hands and then lightly, so lightly, put each hand flat against the side of the ship.

Nothing!

He seized the lowest hand grip and pulled himself up, carefully. He longed to be as experienced at null-gravity manipulation as were the construction men. You had to exert enough force to overcome inertia and then stop. Continue the pull a second too long and you would overbalance, careen into the side of the ship.

He climbed slowly, tippy-fingers, his legs and hips swaying to the right as his left arm reached upward, to the left as his right arm reached upward.

A dozen rungs, and his fingers hovered over the contact that would open the outer lock. The safety marker was a tiny green smear.

Once again he hesitated. This was the first use he would make of the ship's power. His mind ran over the wiring diagrams and the force distributions. If he pressed the contact, power would be siphoned off the micropile to pull open the massive slab of metal that was the outer lock.

Well?

What was the use? Unless he had some idea as to what was wrong, there was no way of telling the effect of the power diversion. He sighed and touched contact.

Smoothly, with neither jar nor sound, a segment of the ship curled open. Black took one more look at the friendly constellations (they had not changed) and stepped into the softly illuminated cavity. The outer lock closed behind him.

Another contact now. The inner lock had to be opened. Again he paused to consider. Air pressure within the ship

would drop ever so slightly as the inner lock opened, and
seconds would pass before the ship's electrolyzers could
make up the loss.

Well?

The Bosch posterior-plate, to name one item, was sensitive to pressure, but surely not *this* sensitive.

He sighed again, more softly (the skin of his fear was
growing calloused) and touched the contact. The inner lock
opened.

He stepped into the pilot room of the *Parsec*, and his
heart jumped oddly when the first thing he saw was the
visiplate, set for reception and powdered with stars. He
forced himself to look at them.

Nothing!

Cassiopeia was visible. The constellations were normal
and he was inside the *Parsec*. Somehow he could feel the
worst was over. Having come so far and remained within
the solar system, having kept his mind so far, he felt something that was faintly like confidence begin to seep back.

There was an almost supernatural stillness about the
Parsec. Black had been in many ships in his life and there
had always been the sounds of life, even if only the scuffing
of a shoe or a cabin boy humming in the corridor. Here the
very beating of his own heart seemed muffled to soundless-
ness.

The robot in the pilot's seat had its back to him. It indicated by no response that it was aware of his having
entered.

Black bared his teeth in a savage grin and said sharply,
'Release the bar! Stand up!' The sound of his voice was
thunderous in the close quarters.

Too late he dreaded the air vibrations his voice set up,

but the stars on the visiplate remained unchanged.

The robot, of course, did not stir. It could receive no sensations of any sort. It could not even respond to the First Law. It was frozen in the unending middle of what should have been almost instantaneous process.

He remembered the orders it had been given. They were open to no misunderstanding: 'Seize the bar with a firm grip. Pull it towards you firmly. *Firmly!* Maintain your hold until the control board informs you that you have passed through hyperspace twice.'

Well, it had not yet passed through hyperspace once.

Carefully, he moved closer to the robot. It sat there with the bar pulled firmly back between its knees. That brought the trigger mechanism almost into place. The temperature of his metal hands then curled that trigger, thermocouple fashion, just sufficiently for contact to be made. Automatically Black glanced at the thermometer reading set into the control board. The robot's hands were at 37 Centigrade, as they should be.

He thought sardonically, Fine thing. I'm alone with this machine and I can't do anything about it.

What he would have liked to do was take a crowbar to it and smash it to filings. He enjoyed the flavor of that thought. He could see the horror on Susan Calvin's face (if any horror could creep through the ice, the horror of a smashed robot was it). Like all positronic robots, this one-shot was owned by U.S. Robots, had been made there, had been tested there.

And having extracted what juice he could out of imaginary revenge, he sobered and looked about the ship.

After all, progress so far had been zero.

Slowly, he removed his suit. Gently, he laid it on the

rack. Gingerly, he walked from room to room, studying the large interlocking surfaces of the hyperatomic motor, following the cables, inspecting the field relays.

He touched nothing. There were a dozen ways of deactivating the hyperfield, but each one would be ruinous unless he knew at least approximately where the error lay and let his exact course of procedure be guided by that.

He found himself back at the control panel and cried in exasperation at the grave stolidity of the robot's broad back, 'Tell me, will you? What's wrong?'

There was the urge to attack the ship's machinery at random. Tear at it and get it over with. He repressed the impulse firmly. If it took him a week, he would deduce, somehow, the proper point of attack. He owed that much to Dr. Susan Calvin and his plans for her.

He turned slowly on his heel and considered. Every part of the ship, from the engine itself to each individual two-way toggle switch, had been exhaustively checked and tested on Hyper Base. It was almost impossible to believe that anything could go wrong. There wasn't a thing on board ship——

Well, yes, there was, of course. The robot! That had been tested at U.S. Robots and they, blast their devils' hides, could be assumed to be competent.

What was it everyone always said? A robot can just naturally do a better job.

It was the normal assumption, based in part on U.S. Robots' own advertising campaigns. They could make a robot that would be better than a man for a given purpose. Not 'as good as a man,' but 'better than a man.'

And as Gerald Black stared at the robot and thought that, his brows contracted under his low forehead and his look became compounded of astonishment and a wild hope.

He approached and circled the robot. He stared at its arms holding the control bar in trigger position, holding it forever so, unless the ship jumped or the robot's own power supply gave out.

Black breathed, 'I bet. I *bet*.'

He stepped away, considered deeply. He said, 'It's *got* to be.'

He turned on ship's radio. Its carrier beam was already focused on Hyper Base. He barked into the mouthpiece, 'Hey, Schloss.'

Schloss was prompt in his answer. 'Great Space, Black——'

'Never mind,' said Black crisply. 'No speeches. I just want to make sure you're watching.'

'Yes, of course. We all are. Look——'

But Black turned off the radio. He grinned with tight one-sidedness at the TV camera inside the pilot room and chose a portion of the hyperfield mechanism that would be in view. He didn't know how many people would be in the viewing room. There might be only Kallner, Schloss, and Susan Calvin. There might be all personnel. In any case, he would give then something to watch.

Relay Box #3 was adequate for the purpose, he decided. It was located in a wall recess, coated over with a smooth cold-seamed panel. Black reached into his tool kit and removed the splayed, blunt-edged seamer. He pushed his space suit farther back on the rack (having turned it to bring the tool kit in reach) and turned to the relay box.

Ignoring a last tingle of uneasiness, Black brought up the seamer, made contact at three separated points along the cold seam. The tool's force field worked deftly and quickly, the handle growing a trifle warm in his hand as the surge of energy came and left. The panel swung free.

He glanced quickly, almost involuntarily, at the ship's visiplate. The stars were normal. He, himself, felt normal.

That was the last bit of encouragement he needed. He raised his foot and smashed his shoe down on the feather-delicate mechanism within the recess.

There was a splinter of glass, a twisting of metal, and a tiny spray of mercury droplets——

Black breathed heavily. He turned on the radio once more. 'Still there, Schloss?'

'Yes, but——'

'Then I report the hyperfield on board the *Parsec* to be deactivated. Come and get me.'

Gerald Black felt no more the hero than when he had left for the *Parsec*, but he found himself one just the same. The men who had brought him to the small asteroid came to take him off. They landed this time. They clapped his back.

Hyper Base was a crowded mass of waiting personnel when the ship arrived, and Black was cheered. He waved at the throng and grinned, as was a hero's obligation, but he felt no triumph inside. Not yet. Only anticipation. Triumph would come later, when he met Susan Calvin.

He paused before descending from the ship. He looked for her and did not see her. General Kallner was there, waiting, with all his soldierly stiffness restored and a bluff look of approval firmly plastered on his face. Mayer Schloss smiled nervously at him. Ronson of Interplanetary Press waved frantically. Susan Calvin was nowhere.

He brushed Kallner and Schloss aside when he landed. 'I'm going to wash and eat first.'

He had no doubts but that, for the moment at least, he could dictate terms to the general or to anybody.

The security guards made a way for him. He bathed and ate leisurely in enforced isolation, he himself being solely responsible for the enforcement. Then he called Ronson of Interplanetary and talked to him briefly. He waited for the return call before he felt he could relax thoroughly. It had all worked out so much better than he had expected. The very failure of the ship had conspired perfectly with him.

Finally he called the general's office and ordered a conference. It was what it amounted to—orders. Major General Kallner all but said, 'Yes, sir.'

They were together again. Gerald Black, Kallner, Schloss—even Susan Calvin. But it was Black who was dominant now. The robopsychologist, graven-faced as ever, as unimpressed by triumph as by disaster, had nevertheless seemed by some subtle change of attitude to have relinquished the spotlight.

Dr. Schloss nibbled a thumbnail and began by saying, cautiously, 'Dr. Black, we are all very grateful for your bravery and success.' Then, as though to institute a healthy deflation at once, he added, 'Still, smashing the relay box with your heel was imprudent and—well, it was an action that scarcely deserved success.'

Black said, 'It was an action that could scarcely have avoided success. You see,' (this was bomb number one) 'by that time I knew what had gone wrong.'

Schloss rose to his feet. 'You did? Are you sure?'

'Go there yourself. It's safe now. I'll tell you what to look for.'

Schloss sat down again, slowly. General Kallner was enthusiastic. 'Why, this is the best yet, if true.'

'It's true,' said Black. His eyes slid to Susan Calvin, who said nothing.

Black was enjoying the sensation of power. He released bomb number two by saying, 'It was the robot, of course. Did you hear that, Dr. Calvin?'

Susan Calvin spoke for the first time. 'I hear it. I rather expected it, as a matter of fact. It was the only piece of equipment on board ship that had not been tested at Hyper Base.'

For a moment Black felt dashed. He said, 'You said nothing of that.'

Dr. Calvin said, 'As Dr. Schloss said several times, I am not an etherics expert. My guess, and it was no more than that, might easily have been wrong. I felt I had no right to prejudice you in advance of your mission.'

Black said, 'All right, did you happen to guess how it went wrong?'

'No, sir.'

'Why, it was made better than a man. That's what the trouble was. Isn't it strange that the trouble should rest with the very specialty of U.S. Robots? They make robots better than men, I understand.'

He was slashing at her with words now but she did not rise to his bait.

Instead, she sighed. 'My dear Dr. Black. I am not responsible for the slogans of our sales-promotion department.'

Black felt dashed again. She wasn't an easy woman to handle, this Calvin. He said, 'Your people built a robot to replace a man at the controls of the *Parsec*. He had to pull the control bar toward himself, place it in position and let the heat of his hands twist the trigger to make final contact. Simple enough, Dr. Calvin?'

'Simple enough, Dr. Black.'

'And if the robot had been made no better than a man, he

would have succeeded. Unfortunately, U.S. Robots felt compelled to make it better than a man. The robot was told to pull back the control bar firmly. *Firmly.* The word was repeated, strengthened, emphasized. So the robot did what it was told. It pulled it back firmly. There was only one trouble. He was easily ten times stronger than the ordinary human being for whom the control bar was designed.'

'Are you implying——'

'I'm *saying* the bar bent. It bent back just enough to misplace the trigger. When the heat of the robot's hand twisted the thermocouple, it did *not* make contact.' He grinned. 'This isn't the failure of just one robot, Dr. Calvin. It's symbolic of the failure of the robot idea.'

'Come now, Dr. Black,' said Susan Calvin icily, 'you're drowning logic in missionary psychology. The robot was equipped with adequate understanding as well as with brute force. Had the men who gave it its orders used quantitative terms rather than the foolish adverb "firmly," this would not have happened. Had they said, "apply a pull of fifty-five pounds," all would have been well.'

'What you are saying,' said Black, 'is that the inadequacy of a robot must be made up for by the ingenuity and intelligence of a man. I assure you that the people back on Earth will look at it in that way and will not be in the mood to excuse U.S. Robots for this fiasco.'

Major General Kallner said quickly, with a return of authority to his voice, 'Now wait, Black, all that has happened is obviously classified·information.'

'In fact,' said Schloss suddenly, 'your theory hasn't been checked yet. We'll send a party to the ship and find out. It may not be the robot at all.'

'You'll take care to make that discovery, will you? I wonder if the people will believe an interested party. Be-

sides which, I have one more thing to tell you.' He readied
bomb number three and said, 'As of this moment, I'm
resigning from this man's project. I'm quitting.'

'Why?' asked Susan Calvin.

'Because, as you said, Dr. Calvin, I am a missionary,'
said Black, smiling. 'I have a mission. I feel I owe it to the
people of Earth to tell them that the age of the robots has
reached the point where human life is valued less than robot
life. It is now possible to order a man into danger because a
robot is too precious to risk. I believe Earthmen should hear
that. Many men have many reservations about robots as is.
U.S. Robots has not yet succeeded in making it legally
permissible to use robots on the planet Earth itself. I
believe what I have to say, Dr. Calvin, will complete the
matter. For this day's work, Dr. Calvin, you and your
company and your robots will be wiped off the face of the
solar system.'

He was forewarning her, Black knew; he was forearming
her, but he could not forego this scene. He had lived for this
very moment ever since he had first left for the *Parsec*, and
he could not give it up.

He all but gloated at the momentary glitter in Susan
Calvin's pale eyes and at the faintest flush in her cheeks. He
thought, How do you feel now, madam scientist?

Kallner said, 'You will not be permitted to resign, Black,
nor will you be permitted———'

'How can you stop me, general? I'm a hero, haven't you
heard? And old Mother Earth *will* make much of its heroes.
It always has. They'll want to hear from me and they'll
believe anything I say. And they won't like it if I'm
interfered with, at least not while I'm a fresh, brand-new
hero. I've already talked to Ronson of Interplanetary Press
and told him I had something big for them, something that

would rock every government official and science director
right out of the chair plush, so Interplanetary will be first in
line, waiting to hear from me. So what can you do except to
have me shot? And I think you'd be worse off after that if
you tried it.'

Black's revenge was complete. He had spared no word.
He had hampered himself not in the least. He rose to go.

'One moment, Dr. Black,' said Susan Calvin. Her low
voice carried authority.

Black turned involuntarily, like a schoolboy at his
teacher's voice, but he counteracted that gesture by a deliberately mocking, 'You have an explanation to make, I
suppose?'

'Not at all,' she said primly. 'You have explained for me,
and quite well. I chose you because I knew you would
understand, though I thought you would understand sooner.
I had had contact with you before. I knew you disliked
robots and would, therefore, be under no illusions concerning them. From your records, which I asked to see before
you were given your assignment, I saw that you had expressed disapproval of this robot-through-hyperspace experiment. Your superiors held that against you, but I
thought it a point in your favor.'

'What are you talking about, doctor, if you'll excuse my
rudeness?'

'The fact that you should have understood why no robot
could have been sent on this mission. What was it you
yourself said? Something about a robot's inadequacies having to be balanced by the ingenuity and intelligence of a
man. Exactly so, young man, exactly so. Robots have no
ingenuity. Their minds are finite and can be calculated to
the last decimal. That, in fact, is my job.

'Now if a robot is given an order, a *precise* order, he can follow it. If the order is not precise, he cannot correct his own mistake without further orders. Isn't that what you reported concerning the robot on the ship? How then can we send a robot to find a flaw in a mechanism when we cannot possibly give precise orders, since we know nothing about the flaw ourselves? "Find out what's wrong" is not an order you can give to a robot; only to a man. The human brain, so far at least, is beyond calculation.'

Black sat down abruptly and stared at the psychologist in dismay. Her words struck sharply on a substratum of understanding that had been larded over with emotion. He found himself unable to refute her. Worse than that, a feeling of defeat encompassed him.

He said, 'You might have said this before I left.'

'I might have,' agreed Dr. Calvin, 'but I noticed your very natural fear for your sanity. Such an overwhelming concern would easily have hampered your efficiency as an investigator, and it occurred to me to let you think that my only motive in sending you was that I valued a robot more. That, I thought, would make you angry, and anger, my dear Dr. Black, is sometimes a very useful emotion. At least, an angry man is never quite as afraid as he would be otherwise. It worked out nicely, I think.' She folded her hands loosely in her lap and came as near a smile as she ever had in her life.

Black said, 'I'll be damned.'

Susan Calvin said, 'So now, if you'll take my advice, return to your job, accept your status as hero, and tell your reporter friend the details of your brave deed. Let that be the big news you promised him.'

Slowly, reluctantly, Black nodded.

Schloss looked relieved; Kallner burst into a toothy

smile. They held out hands, not having said a word in all the time that Susan Calvin had spoken, and not saying a word now.

Black took their hands and shook them with some reserve. He said, 'It's your part that should be publicized, Dr. Calvin.'

Susan Calvin said icily, 'Don't be a fool, young man. This is my job.'

'Lenny' (which appeared in the January 1958 issue of Infinity Science Fiction) was written under unusual circumstances. I am, now and then, overawed into going on vacation against my peevishly expressed desires not to. My wife, who can be quite overawing considering she is such a sweet, soft-voiced thing, is quite insensitive to my explanations that vacations are very hard on my nervous system because I am restless in the absence of a typewriter.

She said calmly, 'Take a typewriter with you.'

So I did, and for a couple of hours each morning I took it out on the lawn of the resort hotel (my wife sweetly and soft-voicedly insisting on the sovereign virtues of sun and fresh air—ugh!), placed it on a rickety table, weighted down various sheets of paper with stones and got to work.

Not a morning passed without interruptions by someone wanting to know what I was doing. I explained and when they finally understood that I was working, they regarded me with no attempt at concealing their hostility. The word went round that I was a dangerous radical attempting to undermine the Great American Vacation.

I managed, somehow, to finish, and my lovable attic room never looked more lovable than it did when I returned. It took me some time to get back to work. First I had to kiss all the walls.

LENNY

UNITED STATES ROBOTS AND MECHANICAL MEN, INC., had a problem. The problem was people.

Peter Bogert, Senior Mathematician, was on his way to Assembly when he encountered Alfred Lanning, Research Director. Lanning was bending his ferocious white eyebrows together and staring down across the railing into the computer room.

On the floor below the balcony, a trickle of humanity of both sexes and various ages was looking about curiously, while a guide intoned a set speech about robotic computing.

'This computer you see before you,' he said, 'is the largest of its type in the world. It contains five million three hundred thousand cryotrons and is capable of dealing simultaneously with over one hundred thousand variables. With its help, U.S. Robots is able to design with precision the positronic brains of new models.

'The requirements are fed in on tape which is perforated by the action of this keyboard—something like a very complicated typewriter or linotype machine, except that it does not deal with letters but with concepts. Statements are broken down into the symbolic logic equivalents and those in turn converted to perforation patterns.

'The computer can, in less than one hour, present our scientists with a design for a brain which will give all the necessary positronic paths to make a robot...'

Alfred Lanning looked up at last and noticed the other. 'Ah, Peter,' he said.

Bogert raised both hands to smooth down his already

perfectly smooth and glossy head of black hair. He said, 'You don't look as though you think much of this, Alfred.'

Lanning grunted. The idea of public guided tours of U.S. Robots was a fairly recent origin, and was supposed to serve a dual function. On the one hand, the theory went, it allowed people to see robots at close quarters and counter their almost instinctive fear of the mechanical objects through increased familiarity. And on the other hand, it was supposed to interest at least an occasional person in taking up robotics research as a life work.

'You know I don't,' Lanning said finally. 'Once a week, work is disrupted. Considering the man-hours lost, the return is insufficient.'

'Still no rise in job applications, then?'

'Oh, some, but only in the categories where the need isn't vital. It's research men that are needed. You know that. The trouble is that with robots forbidden on Earth itself, there's something unpopular about being a roboticist.'

'The damned Frankenstein complex,' said Bogert, consciously imitating one of the other's pet phrases.

Lanning missed the gentle jab. He said, 'I ought to be used to it, but I never will. You'd think that by now every human being on Earth would know that the Three Laws represented a perfect safeguard; that robots are simply not dangerous. Take this bunch.' He glowered down. 'Look at them. Most of them go through the robot assembly room for the thrill of fear, like riding a roller coaster. Then when they enter the room with the MEC model—damn it, Peter, a MEC model that will do nothing on God's green Earth but take two steps forward, say "Pleased to meet you, sir," shake hands, then take two steps back—they back away and mothers snatch up their kids. How do we expect to get brainwork out of such idiots?'

Bogert had no answer. Together, they stared down once again at the line of sightseers, now passing out of the computer room and into the positronic brain assembly section. Then they left. They did not, as it turned out, observe Mortimer W. Jacobson, age 16—who, to do him complete justice, meant no harm whatever.

In fact, it could not even be said to be Mortimer's fault. The day of the week on which the tour took place was known to all workers. All devices in its path ought to have been carefully neutralized or locked, since it was unreasonable to expect human beings to withstand the temptation to handle knobs, keys, handles, and pushbuttons. In addition, the guide ought to have been very carefully on the watch for those who succumbed.

But, at the time, the guide had passed into the next room and Mortimer was tailing the line. He passed the keyboard on which instructions were fed into the computer. He had no way of suspecting that the plans for a new robot design were being fed into it at that moment, or, being a good kid, he would have avoided the keyboard. He had no way of knowing that, by what amounted to almost criminal negligence, a technician had not inactivated the keyboard.

So Mortimer touched the keys at random as though he were playing a musical instrument.

He did not notice that a section of perforated tape stretched itself out of the instrument in another part of the room—soundlessly, unobtrusively.

Nor did the technician, when he returned, discover any signs of tampering. He felt a little uneasy at noticing that the keyboard was live, but did not think to check. After a few minutes, even his first trifling uneasiness was gone, and he continued feeding data into the computer.

As for Mortimer, neither then, nor ever afterward, did he know what he had done.

The new LNE model was designed for the mining of boron in the asteroid belt. The boron hydrides were increasing in value yearly as primers for the proton micropiles that carried the ultimate load of power production on spaceships, and Earth's own meager supply was running thin.

Physically, that meant that the LNE robots would have to be equipped with eyes sensitive to those lines prominent in the spectroscopic analysis of boron ores and the type of limbs most useful for the working up of ore to finished product. As always, though, the mental equipment was the major problem.

The first LNE positronic brain had been completed now. It was the prototype and would join all other prototypes in U.S. Robots' collection. When finally tested, others would then be manufactured for leasing (never selling) to mining corporations.

LNE-Prototype was complete now. Tall, straight, polished, it looked from outside like any of a number of not-too-specialized robot models.

The technician in charge, guided by the directions for testing in the *Handbook of Robotics*, said, 'How are you?'

The indicated answer was to have been, 'I am well and ready to begin my functions. I trust you are well, too,' or some trivial modification thereof.

This first exchange served no purpose but to show that the robot could hear, understand a routine question, and make a routine reply congruent with what one would expect of a robotic attitude. Beginning from there, one could pass on to more complicated matters that would test the different Laws and their interaction with the specialized knowledge of each particular model.

So the technician said, 'How are you?' He was instantly jolted by the nature of LNE-Prototype's voice. It had a quality like no robotic voice he had ever heard (and he had heard many). It formed syllables like the chimes of a low-pitched celeste.

So surprising was this that it was only after several moments that the technician heard, in retrospect, the syllables that had been formed by those heavenly tones.

They were, 'Da, da, da, goo.'

The robot still stood tall and straight but its right hand crept upward and a finger went into its mouth.

The technician stared in absolute horror and bolted. He locked the door behind him and, from another room, put in an emergency call to Dr. Susan Calvin.

Dr. Susan Calvin was U.S. Robots' (and, virtually, mankind's) only robopsychologist. She did not have to go very far in her testing of LNE-Prototype before she called very peremptorily for a transcript of the computer-drawn plans of the positronic brain-paths and the taped instructions that had directed them. After some study, she, in turn, sent for Bogert.

Her iron-gray hair was drawn severely back; her cold face, with its strong vertical lines marked off by the horizontal gash of the pale, thin-lipped mouth, turned intensely upon him.

'What is this, Peter?'

Bogert studied the passages she pointed out with increasing stupefaction and said, 'Good Lord, Susan, it makes no sense.'

'It most certainly doesn't. How did it get into the instructions?'

The technician in charge, called upon, swore in all sincerity that it was none of his doing, and that he could not account for it. The computer checked out negative for all attempts at flaw-finding.

'The positronic brain,' said Susan Calvin, thoughtfully, 'is past redemption. So many of the higher functions have been cancelled out by these meaningless directions that the result is very like a human baby.'

Bogert looked surprised, and Susan Calvin took on a frozen attitude at once, as she always did at the least expressed or implied doubt of her word. She said, 'We make every effort to make a robot as mentally like a man as possible. Eliminate what we call the adult functions and what is naturally left is a human infant, mentally speaking. Why do you look so surprised, Peter?'

LNE-Prototype, who showed no signs of understanding any of the things that were going on around it, suddenly slipped into a sitting position and began a minute examination of its feet.

Bogert stared at it. 'It's a shame to have to dismantle the creature. It's a handsome job.'

'Dismantle it?' said the robopsychologist forcefully.

'Of course, Susan. What's the use of this thing? Good Lord, if there's one object completely and abysmally useless it's a robot without a job it can perform. You don't pretend there's a job this thing can do, do you?'

'No, of course not.'

'Well, then?'

Susan Calvin said, stubbornly, 'I want to conduct more tests.'

Bogert looked at her with a moment's impatience, then shrugged. If there was one person at U.S. Robots with whom it was useless to dispute, surely that was Susan

Calvin. Robots were all she loved, and long association with
them, it seemed to Bogert, had deprived her of any appearance of humanity. She was no more to be argued out of a
decision than was a triggered micropile to be argued out of
operating.

'What's the use?' he breathed; then aloud, hastily: 'Will
you let us know when your tests are complete?'

'I will,' she said. 'Come, Lenny.'

(LNE, thought Bogert. That becomes Lenny. Inevitable.)

Susan Calvin held out her hand but the robot only stared
at it. Gently, the robopsychologist reached for the robot's
hand and took it. Lenny rose smoothly to its feet (its
mechanical coordination, at least, worked well). Together
they walked out, robot topping woman by two feet. Many
eyes followed them curiously down the long corridors.

One wall of Susan Calvin's laboratory, the one opening
directly off her private office, was covered with a highly
magnified reproduction of a positronic-path chart. Susan
Calvin had studied it with absorption for the better part of
a month.

She was considering it now, carefully, tracing the
blunted paths through their contortions. Behind her, Lenny
sat on the floor, moving its legs apart and together, croon-
ing meaningless syllables to itself in a voice so beautiful
that one could listen to the nonsense and be ravished.

Susan Calvin turned to the robot, 'Lenny—Lenny——'

She repeated this patiently until finally Lenny looked up
and made an inquiring sound. The robopsychologist
allowed a glimmer of pleasure to cross her face fleetingly.
The robot's attention was being gained in progressively
shorter intervals.

She said, 'Raise your hand, Lenny. Hand—up. Hand—up.'

She raised her own hand as she said it, over and over.

Lenny followed the movement with its eyes. Up, down, up, down. Then it made an abortive gesture with its own hand and chimed, 'Eh—uh.'

'Very good, Lenny,' said Susan Calvin, gravely. 'Try it again. Hand—up.'

Very gently, she reached out her own hand, took the robot's, and raised it, lowered it. 'Hand—up. Hand—up.'

A voice from her office called and interrupted. 'Susan?'

Calvin halted with a tightening of her lips. 'What is it, Alfred?'

The research director walked in, and looked at the chart on the wall and at the robot. 'Still at it?'

'I'm at my work, yes.'

'Well, you know, Susan . . .' He took out a cigar, staring at it hard, and made as though to bite off the end. In doing so, his eyes met the woman's stern look of disapproval; and he put the cigar away and began over. 'Well, you know, Susan, the LNE model is in production now.'

'So I've heard. Is there something in connection with it you wish of me?'

'No-o. Still, the mere fact that it is in production and is doing well means that working with this messed-up specimen is useless. Shouldn't it be scrapped?'

'In short, Alfred, you are annoyed that I am wasting my so-valuable time. Feel relieved. My time is not being wasted. I am working with this robot.'

'But the work has no meaning.'

'I'll be the judge of that, Alfred.' Her voice was ominously quiet, and Lanning thought it wiser to shift his ground.

'Will you tell me what meaning it has? What are you doing with it right now, for instance?'

'I'm trying to get it to raise its hand on the word of command. I'm trying to get it to imitate the sound of the word.'

As though on cue, Lenny said, 'Eh—uh' and raised its hand waveringly.

Lanning shook his head. 'That voice is amazing. How does it happen?'

Susan Calvin said, 'I don't quite know. Its transmitter is a normal one. It could speak normally, I'm sure. It doesn't, however; it speaks like this as a consequence of something in the positronic paths that I have not yet pinpointed.'

'Well, pinpoint it, for Heaven's sake. Speech like that might be useful.'

'Oh, then there is some possible use in my studies on Lenny?'

Lanning shrugged in embarrassment. 'Oh, well, it's a minor point.'

'I'm sorry you don't see the major points, then,' said Susan Calvin with asperity, 'which are much more important, but that's not my fault. Would you leave now, Alfred, and let me go on with my work?'

Lanning got to his cigar, eventually, in Bogert's office. He said, sourly, 'That woman is growing more peculiar daily.'

Bogert understood perfectly. In the U.S. Robots and Mechanical Men Corporation, there was only one 'that woman.' He said, 'Is she still scuffing about with that pseudo-robot—that Lenny of hers?'

'Trying to get it to talk, so help me.'

Bogert shrugged. 'Points up the company problem. I

mean, about getting qualified personnel for research. If we had other robopsychologists, we could retire Susan. Incidentally, I presume the directors' meeting scheduled for tomorrow is for the purpose of dealing with the procurement problem?'

Lanning nodded and looked at his cigar as though it didn't taste good. 'Yes. Quality, though, not quantity. We've raised wages until there's a steady stream of applicants—those who are interested primarily in money. The trick is to get those who are interested primarily in robotics —a few more like Susan Calvin.'

'Hell, no. Not like her.'

'Well, not like her personally. But you'll have to admit, Peter, that she's single-minded about robots. She has no other interest in life.'

'I know. And that's exactly what makes her so unbearable.'

Lanning nodded. He had lost count of the many times it would have done his soul good to have fired Susan Calvin. He had also lost count of the number of millions of dollars she had at one time or another saved the company. She was a truly indispensable woman and would remain one until she died—or until they could lick the problem of finding men and women of her own high caliber who were interested in robotics research.

He said, 'I think we'll cut down on the tour business.'

Peter shrugged. 'If you say so. But meanwhile, seriously, what do we do about Susan? She can easily tie herself up with Lenny indefinitely. You know how she is when she gets what she considers an interesting problem.'

'What *can* we do?' said Lanning. 'If we become too anxious to pull her off, she'll stay on out of feminine contrariness. In the last analysis, we can't force her to do anything.'

The dark-haired mathematician smiled. 'I wouldn't ever apply the adjective "feminine" to any part of her.'

'Oh, well,' said Lanning, grumpily. 'At least, it won't do anyone any actual harm.'

In that, if in nothing else, he was wrong.

The emergency signal is always a tension-making thing in any large industrial establishment. Such signals had sounded in the history of U.S. Robots a dozen times—for fire, flood, riot, and insurrection.

But one thing had never occurred in all that time. Never had the particular signal indicating 'Robot out of control' sounded. No one ever expected it to sound. It was only installed at government insistence. ('Damn the Franken-stein complex,' Lanning would mutter on those rare occasions when he thought of it.)

Now, finally, the shrill siren rose and fell at ten-second intervals, and practically no worker from the President of the Board of Directors down to the newest janitor's assistant recognized the significance of the strange sound for a few moments. After those moments passed, there was a massive convergence of armed guards and medical men to the indicated area of danger and U.S. Robots was struck with paralysis.

Charles Randow, computing technician, was taken off to hospital level with a broken arm. There was no other damage. No other physical damage.

'But the moral damage,' roared Lanning, 'is beyond estimation.'

Susan Calvin faced him, murderously calm. 'You will do nothing to Lenny. Nothing. Do you understand?'

'Do *you* understand, Susan? That thing has hurt a

human being. It has broken First Law. Don't you know what First Law is?'

'You will do nothing to Lenny.'

'For God's sake, Susan, do I have to tell *you* First Law? *A robot may not injure a human being, or, through inaction, allow a human being to come to harm.* Our entire position depends on the fact that First Law is rigidly observed by all robots of all types. If the public should hear, and they will hear, that there was an exception, even one exception, we might be forced to close down altogether. Our only chance of survival would be to announce at once that the robot involved had been destroyed, explain the circumstances, and hope that the public can be convinced that it will never happen again.'

'I would like to find out exactly what happened,' said Susan Calvin. 'I was not present at the time and I would like to know exactly what the Randow boy was doing in my laboratories without my permission.'

'The important thing that happened,' said Lanning, 'is obvious. Your robot struck Randow and the damn fool flashed the "Robot out of control" button and made a case of it. But your robot struck him and inflicted damage to the extent of a broken arm. The truth is your Lenny is so distorted it lacks First Law and it must be destroyed.'

'It does *not* lack First Law. I have studied its brainpaths and know it does not lack it.'

'Then how could it strike a man?' Desperation turned him to sarcasm. 'Ask Lenny. Surely you have taught it to speak by now.'

Susan Calvin's cheeks flushed a painful pink. She said, 'I prefer to interview the victim. And in my absence, Alfred, I want my offices sealed tight, with Lenny inside. I want no one to approach him. If any harm comes to him while I am gone, this company will not see me again under any circumstances.'

'Will you agree to its destruction, if it has broken First Law?'

'Yes,' said Susan Calvin, 'because I know it hasn't.'

Charles Randow lay in bed with his arm set and in a cast. His major suffering was still from the shock of those few moments in which he thought a robot was advancing on him with murder in its positronic mind. No other human had ever had such reason to fear direct robotic harm as he had had just then. He had had a unique experience.

Susan Calvin and Alfred Lanning stood beside his bed now; Peter Bogert, who had met them on the way, was with them. Doctors and nurses had been shooed out.

Susan Calvin said, 'Now—what happened?'

Randow was daunted. He muttered, 'The thing hit me in the arm. It was coming at me.'

Calvin said, 'Move further back in the story. What were you doing in my laboratory without authorization?'

The young computer swallowed, and the Adam's apple in his thin neck bobbed noticeably. He was high-cheekboned and abnormally pale. He said, 'We all knew about your robot. The word is you were trying to teach it to talk like a musical instrument. There were bets going as to whether it talked or not. Some said—uh—you could teach a gatepost to talk.'

'I suppose,' said Susan Calvin, freezingly, 'that is meant as a compliment. What did that have to do with you?'

'I was supposed to go in there and settle matters—see if it would talk, you know. We swiped a key to your place and I waited till you were gone and went in. We had a lottery on who was to do it. I lost.'

'Then?'

'I tried to get it to talk and it hit me.'

'What do you mean, you tried to get it to talk? How did you try?'

'I—I asked it questions, but it wouldn't say anything, and I had to give the thing a fair shake, so I kind of—yelled at it, and——'

'And?'

There was a long pause. Under Susan Calvin's unwavering stare, Randow finally said, 'I tried to scare it into saying something.' He added defensively, 'I had to give the thing a fair shake.'

'How did you try to scare it?'

'I pretended to take a punch at it.'

'And it brushed your arm aside?'

'It *hit* my arm.'

'Very well. That's all.' To Lanning and Bogert, she said, 'Come, gentlemen.'

At the doorway, she turned back to Randow. 'I can settle the bets going around, if you are still interested. Lenny can speak a few words quite well.'

They said nothing until they were in Susan Calvin's office. Its walls were lined with her books, some of which she had written herself. It retained the patina of her own frigid, carefully-ordered personality. It had only one chair in it and she sat down. Lanning and Bogert remained standing.

She said, 'Lenny only defended itself. That is the Third Law: *A robot must protect its own existence.*'

'*Except,*' said Lanning forcefully, '*when this conflicts with the First or Second Laws.* Complete the statement! Lenny had no right to defend itself in any way at the cost of harm, however minor, to a human being.'

'Nor did it,' shot back Calvin, '*knowingly*. Lenny had an aborted brain. It had no way of knowing its own strength or the weakness of humans. In brushing aside the threatening arm of a human being it could not know the bone would break. In human terms, no moral blame can be attached to an individual who honestly cannot differentiate good and evil.'

Bogert interrupted, soothingly, 'Now, Susan, *we* don't blame. *We* understand that Lenny is the equivalent of a baby, humanly speaking, and we don't blame it. But the public will. U.S. Robots will be closed down.'

'Quite the opposite. If you had the brains of a flea, Peter, you would see that this is the opportunity U.S. Robots is waiting for. That this will solve its problems.'

Lanning hunched his white eyebrows low. He said, softly, 'What problems, Susan?'

'Isn't the Corporation concerned about maintaining our research personnel at the present—Heaven help us—high level?'

'We certainly are.'

'Well, what are you offering prospective researchers? Excitement? Novelty? The thrill of piercing the unknown? No! You offer them salaries and the assurance of no problems.'

Bogert said, 'How do you mean, no problems?'

'Are there problems?' shot back Susan Calvin. 'What kind of robots do we turn out? Fully developed robots, fit for their tasks. An industry tells us what it needs; a computer designs the brain; machinery forms the robot; and there it is, complete and done. Peter, some time ago, you asked me with reference to Lenny what its use was. What's the use, you said, of a robot that was not designed for any job? Now I ask you—what's the use of a robot designed for only one job? It begins and ends in the same place. The LNE models mine boron. If beryllium is needed, they are useless. If boron technology enters a new phase, they become useless. A human being so designed would be sub-human. A robot so designed is sub-robotic.'

'Do you want a versatile robot?' asked Lanning, incredulously.

'Why not?' demanded the robopsychologist. 'Why not? I've been handed a robot with a brain almost completely stultified. I've been teaching it, and you, Alfred, asked me what was the use of that. Perhaps very little as far as Lenny itself is concerned, since it will never progress beyond the five-year-old level on a human scale. But what's the use in general? A very great deal, if you consider it as a study in the abstract problem of learning how to teach robots. I have learned ways to short-circuit neighboring pathways in order to create new ones. More study will yield better, more subtle and more efficient techniques of doing so.'

'Well?'

'Suppose you started with a positronic brain that had all the basic pathways carefully outlined but none of the secondaries. Suppose you then started creating secondaries. You could sell basic robots designed for instruction; robots that could be modelled to a job, and then modelled to another, if necessary. Robots would become as versatile as human beings. *Robots could learn!*'

They stared at her.

She said, impatiently, 'You still don't understand, do you?'

'I understand what you are saying,' said Lanning.

'Don't you understand that with a completely new field of research and completely new techniques to be developed,

with a completely new area of the unknown to be penetrated, youngsters will feel a new urge to enter robotics?
Try it and see.'

'May I point out,' said Bogert, smoothly, 'that this is
dangerous. Beginning with ignorant robots such as Lenny
will mean that one could never trust First Law—exactly as
turned out in Lenny's case.'

'Exactly. Advertise the fact.'

'*Advertise it!*'

'Of course. Broadcast the danger. Explain that you will
set up a new research institute on the moon, if Earth's
population chooses not to allow this sort of thing to go on
upon Earth, but stress the danger to the possible applicants
by all means.'

Lanning said, 'For God's sake, why?'

'Because the spice of danger will add to the lure. Do you
think nuclear technology involves no danger and spatio-
nautics no peril? Has your lure of absolute security been
doing the trick for you? Has it helped you to cater to the
Frankenstein complex you all despise so? Try something
else then, something that has worked in other fields.'

There was a sound from beyond the door that led to
Calvin's personal laboratories. It was the chiming sound of
Lenny.

The robopyschologist broke off instantly, listening. She
said, 'Excuse me. I think Lenny is calling me.'

'Can it call you?' said Lanning.

'I said I've managed to teach it a few words.' She
stepped toward the door, a little flustered. 'If you will wait
for me——'

They watched her leave and were silent for a moment.
Then Lanning said, 'Do you think there's anything to what
she says, Peter?'

'Just possibly, Alfred,' said Bogert. 'Just possibly. Enough for us to bring the matter up at the directors' meeting and see what they say. After all, the fat *is* in the fire. A robot has harmed a human being and knowledge of it is public. As Susan says, we might as well try to turn the matter to our advantage. Of course, I distrust her motives in all this.'

'How do you mean?'

'Even if all she has said is perfectly true, it is only rationalization as far as she is concerned. Her motive in all this is her desire to hold on to this robot. If we pressed her,' (and the mathematician smiled at the incongruous literal meaning of the phrase) 'she would say it was to continue learning techniques of teaching robots, but I think she has found another use for Lenny. A rather unique one that would fit only Susan of all women.'

'I don't get your drift.'

Bogert said, 'Did you hear what the robot was calling?'

'Well, no, I didn't quite——' began Lanning, when the door opened suddenly, and both men stopped talking at once.

Susan Calvin stepped in again, looking about uncertainly. 'Have either of you seen—I'm positive I had it somewhere about—Oh, there it is.'

She ran to a corner of one bookcase and picked up an object of intricate metal webbery, dumbbell shaped and hollow, with variously-shaped metal pieces inside each hollow, just too large to be able to fall out of the webbing.

As she picked it up, the metal pieces within moved and struck together, clicking pleasantly. It struck Lanning that the object was a kind of robotic version of a baby rattle.

As Susan Calvin opened the door again to pass through, Lenny's voice chimed again from within. This time, Lanning heard it clearly as it spoke the words Susan Calvin had taught it.

In heavenly celeste-like sounds, it called out, 'Mommie, I want you. I want you, Mommie.'

And the footsteps of Susan Calvin could be heard hurrying eagerly across the laboratory floor toward the only kind of baby she could ever have or love.

The longest story involving Susan Calvin appeared in the December 1957 issue of Galaxy. *It came within a hair of not being written at all.*

Horace Gold, then editor of Galaxy, *called me long-distance to ask me to write a story for him—always a terribly flattering situation and with me flattery will get you everywhere.*

However, I had to explain regretfully that I was absolutely incapable of writing a story at the moment. I was deep in the galley proof of the third edition of a biochemistry textbook I was co-authoring.

'Can't you have someone else read the galley proof?' he asked.

'Of course not,' I responded with virtuous indignation. 'I couldn't trust these galleys to anyone else.'

And having hung up, I walked upstairs to my beloved attic, galley proof in hand, and between the bottom step and the top step a thought occurred to me. I put the galleys to one side and got started at once. I continued at top speed until, a few days later, 'Galley Slave' was done.

Of all my Susan Calvin stories, this is my favorite. I don't know that I can give a good reason for it; but then, I suppose an author may have his irrational likes and dislikes as well as the next man.

GALLEY SLAVE

THE United States Robots and Mechanical Men, Inc., as defendants in the case, had influence enough to force a closed-doors trial without a jury.

Nor did Northeastern University try hard to prevent it. The trustees knew perfectly well how the public might react to any issue involving misbehavior of a robot, however rarefied that misbehavior might be. They also had a clearly visualized notion of how an antirobot riot might become an antiscience riot without warning.

The government, as represented in this case by Justice Harlow Shane, was equally anxious for a quiet end to this mess. Both U.S. Robots and the academic world were bad people to antagonize.

Justice Shane said, 'Since neither press, public, nor jury is present, gentlemen, let us stand on as little ceremony as we can and get to the facts.'

He smiled stiffly as he said this, perhaps without much hope that his request would be effective, and hitched at his robe so that he might sit more comfortably. His face was pleasantly rubicund, his chin round and soft, his nose broad and his eyes light in color and wide-set. All in all, it was not a face with much judicial majesty and the judge knew it.

Barnabas H. Goodfellow, Professor of Physics at Northeastern U., was sworn in first, taking the usual vow with an expression that made mincemeat of his name.

After the usual opening-gambit questions, Prosecution shoved his hands deep into his pockets and said, 'When was it, Professor, that the matter of the possible employ of Robot EZ-27 was first brought to your attention, and how?'

Professor Goodfellow's small and angular face set itself into an uneasy expression, scarcely more benevolent than the one it replaced. He said, 'I have had professional contact and some social acquaintance with Dr. Alfred Lanning, Director of Research at U.S. Robots. I was inclined to listen with some tolerance then when I received a rather strange suggestion from him on the third of March of last year——'

'Of 2033?'

'That's right.'

'Excuse me for interrupting. Please proceed.'

The professor nodded frostily, scowled to fix the facts in his mind, and began to speak.

Professor Goodfellow looked at the robot with a certain uneasiness. It had been carried into the basement supply room in a crate, in accordance with the regulations governing the shipment of robots from place to place on the Earth's surface.

He knew it was coming; it wasn't that he was unprepared. From the moment of Dr. Lanning's first phone call on March 3, he had felt himself giving way to the other's persuasiveness, and now, as an inevitable result, he found himself face to face with a robot.

It looked uncommonly large as it stood within arm's reach.

Alfred Lanning cast a hard glance of his own at the robot, as though making certain it had not been damaged in transit. Then he turned his ferocious eyebrows and his mane of white hair in the professor's direction.

'This is Robot EZ-27, first of its model to be available for public use.' He turned to the robot. 'This is Professor Goodfellow, Easy.'

Easy spoke impassively, but with such suddenness that the professor shied. 'Good afternoon, Professor.'

Easy stood seven feet tall and had the general proportions of a man—always the prime selling point of U.S. Robots. That and the possession of the basic patents on the positronic brain had given them an actual monopoly on robots and a near-monopoly on computing machines in general.

The two men who had uncrated the robot had left now and the professor looked from Lanning to the robot and back to Lanning. 'It is harmless, I'm sure.' He didn't sound sure.

'More harmless than I am,' said Lanning. 'I could be goaded into striking you. Easy could not be. You know the Three Laws of Robotics, I presume.'

'Yes, of course,' said Goodfellow.

'They are built into the positronic patterns of the brain and must be observed. The First Law, the prime rule of robotic existence, safeguards the life and well-being of all humans.' He paused, rubbed at his cheek, then added, 'It's something of which we would like to persuade all Earth if we could.'

'It's just that he seems formidable.'

'Granted. But whatever he seems, you'll find that he is useful.'

'I'm not sure in what way. Our conversations were not very helpful in that respect. Still, I agreed to look at the object and I'm doing it.'

'We'll do more than look, Professor. Have you brought a book?'

'I have.'

'May I see it?'

Professor Goodfellow reached down without actually taking his eyes off the metal-in-human-shape that confronted him. From the briefcase at his feet, he withdrew a book.

Lanning held out his hand for it and looked at the backstrip. '*Physical Chemistry of Electrolytes in Solution.* Fair enough, sir. You selected this yourself, at random. It was no suggestion of mine, this particular text. Am I right?'

'Yes.'

Lanning passed the book to Robot EZ-27.

The professor jumped a little. 'No! That's a valuable book!'

Lanning raised his eyebrows and they looked like shaggy coconut icing. He said, 'Easy has no intention of tearing the book in two as a feat of strength, I assure you. It can handle a book as carefully as you or I. Go ahead, Easy.'

'Thank you, sir,' said Easy. Then, turning its metal bulk slightly, it added, 'With your permission, Professor Goodfellow.'

The professor stared, then said, 'Yes—yes, of course.'

With a slow and steady manipulation of metal fingers, Easy turned the pages of the book, glancing at the left page, then the right; turning the page, glancing left, then right; turning the page and so on for minute after minute.

The sense of its power seemed to dwarf even the large cement-walled room in which they stood and to reduce the two human watchers to something considerably less than life-size.

Goodfellow muttered, 'The light isn't very good.'

'It will do.'

Then, rather more sharply, 'But what is he doing?'

'Patience, sir.'

The last page was turned eventually. Lanning asked, 'Well, Easy?'

The robot said, 'It is a most accurate book and there is little to which I can point. On line 22 of page 27, the word "positive" is spelled p-o-i-s-t-i-v-e. The comma in line 6 of page 32 is superfluous, whereas one should have been used on line 13 of page 54. The plus sign in equation XIV-2 on page 337 should be a minus sign if it is to be consisten with the previous equations——'

'Wait! Wait!' cried the professor. 'What is he doing?'

'Doing?' echoed Lanning in sudden irascibility. 'Why, man, he has already done it! He has proofread that book.'

'Proofread it?'

'Yes. In the short time it took him to turn those pages, he caught every mistake in spelling, grammar, and punctuation. He has noted errors in word order and detected inconsistencies. And he will retain the information, letter-perfect, indefinitely.'

The professor's mouth was open. He walked rapidly away from Lanning and Easy and as rapidly back. He folded his arms across his chest and stared at them. Finally he said, 'You mean this is a proofreading robot?'

Lanning nodded. 'Among other things.'

'But why do you show it to me?'

'So that you might help me persuade the university to obtain it for use.'

'To read proof?'

'Among other things,' Lanning repeated patiently.

The professor drew his pinched face together in a kind of sour disbelief. 'But this is ridiculous!'

'Why?'

'The university could never afford to buy this half-ton—it must weigh that at least—this half-ton proof-reader.'

'Proofreading is not all it will do. It will prepare reports from outlines, fill out forms, serve as an accurate memory-file, grade papers——'

'All picayune!'

Lanning said, 'Not at all, as I can show you in a moment. But I think we can discuss this more comfortably in your office, if you have no objection.'

'No, of course not,' began the professor mechanically and took a half-step as though to turn. Then he snapped out, 'But the robot—we can't take the robot. Really, Doctor, you'll have to crate it up again.'

'Time enough. We can leave Easy here.'

'Unattended?'

'Why not? He knows he is to stay. Professor Goodfellow, it is necessary to understand that a robot is far more reliable than a human being.'

'I would be responsible for any damage——'

'There will be no damage. I guarantee that. Look, it's after hours. You expect no one here, I imagine, before to-morrow morning. The truck and my two men are outside. U.S. Robots will take any responsibility that may arise. None will. Call it a demonstration of the reliability of the robot.'

The professor allowed himself to be led out of the storeroom. Nor did he look entirely comfortable in his own office, five stories up.

He dabbed at the line of droplets along the upper half of his forehead with a white handkerchief.

'As you know very well, Dr. Lanning, there are laws

against the use of robots on Earth's surface,' he pointed out.

'The laws, Professor Goodfellow, are not simple ones. Robots may not be used on public thoroughfares or within public edifices. They may not be used on private grounds or within private structures except under certain restrictions that usually turn out to be prohibitive. The university, however, is a large and privately owned institution that usually receives preferential treatment. If the robot is used only in a specific room for only academic purposes, if certain other restrictions are observed and if the men and women having occasion to enter the room cooperate fully, we may remain within the law.'

'But all that trouble just to read proof?'

'The uses would be infinite, Professor. Robotic labor has so far been used only to relieve physical drudgery. Isn't there such a thing as mental drudgery? When a professor capable of the most useful creative thought is forced to spend two weeks painfully checking the spelling of lines of print and I offer you a machine that can do it in thirty minutes, is that picayune?'

'But the price——'

'The price need not bother you. You cannot buy EZ-27. U.S. Robots does not sell its products. But the university can lease EZ-27 for a thousand dollars a year—considerably less than the cost of a single microwave spectograph continuous-recording attachment.'

Goodfellow looked stunned. Lanning followed up his advantage by saying, 'I only ask that you put it up to whatever group makes the decisions here. I would be glad to speak to them if they want more information.'

'Well,' Goodfellow said doubtfully, 'I can bring it up at next week's Senate meeting. I can't promise that will do any good, though.'

'Naturally,' said Lanning.

The Defense Attorney was short and stubby and carried himself rather portentously, a stance that had the effect of accentuating his double chin. He stared at Professor Good-fellow, once that witness had been handed over, and said, 'You agreed rather readily, did you not?'

The professor said briskly, 'I suppose I was anxious to be rid of Dr. Lanning. I would have agreed to anything.'

'With the intention of forgetting about it after he left?'

'Well——'

'Nevertheless, you did present the matter to a meeting of the Executive Board of the University Senate.'

'Yes, I did.'

'So that you agreed in good faith with Dr. Lanning's suggestions. You weren't just going along with a gag. You actually agreed enthusiastically, did you not?'

'I merely followed ordinary procedures.'

'As a matter of fact, you weren't as upset about the robot as you now claim you were. You know the Three Laws of Robotics and you knew them at the time of your interview with Dr. Lanning.'

'Well, yes.'

'And you were perfectly willing to leave a robot at large and unattended.'

'Dr. Lanning assured me——'

'Surely you would never have accepted his assurance if you had had the slightest doubt that the robot might be in the least dangerous.'

The professor began frigidly, 'I had every faith in the word——'

'That is all,' said Defense abruptly.

As Professor Goodfellow, more than a bit ruffled, stood down, Justice Shane leaned forward and said, 'Since I am not a robotics man myself, I would appreciate knowing precisely what the Three Laws of Robotics are. Would Dr. Lanning quote them for the benefit of the court?'

Dr. Lanning looked startled. He had been virtually bumping heads with the gray-haired woman at his side. He rose to his feet now and the woman looked up, too—expressionlessly.

Dr. Lanning said, 'Very well, Your Honor.' He paused as though about to launch into an oration and said, with laborious clarity, 'First Law: a robot may not injure a human being, or, through inaction, allow a human being to come to harm. Second Law: a robot must obey the orders given it by human beings, except where such orders would conflict with the First Law. Third Law: a robot must protect its own existence as long as such protection does not conflict with the First or Second Law.'

'I see,' said the judge, taking rapid notes. 'These Laws are built into every robot, are they?'

'Into every one. That will be borne out by any roboticist.'

'And into Robot EZ-27 specifically?'

'Yes, Your Honor.'

'You will probably be required to repeat those statements under oath.'

'I am ready to do so, Your Honor.'

He sat down again.

Dr. Susan Calvin, robopsychologist-in-chief for U.S. Robots, who was the gray-haired woman sitting next to Lanning, looked at her titular superior without favor, but then she showed favor to no human being. She said, 'Was Goodfellow's testimony accurate, Alfred?'

'Essentially,' muttered Lanning. 'He wasn't as nervous as all that about the robot and he was anxious enough to talk business with me when he heard the price. But there doesn't seem to be any drastic distortion.'

Dr. Calvin said thoughtfully, 'It might have been wise to put the price higher than a thousand.'

'We were anxious to place Easy.'

'I know. Too anxious, perhaps. They'll try to make it look as though we had an ulterior motive.'

Lanning looked exasperated. 'We did. I admitted that at the University Senate meeting.'

'They can make it look as if we had one beyond the one we admitted.'

Scott Robertson, son of the founder of U.S. Robots and still owner of a majority of the stock, leaned over from Dr. Calvin's other side and said in a kind of explosive whisper, 'Why can't you get Easy to talk so we'll know where we're at?'

'You know he can't talk about it, Mr. Robertson.'

'Make him. You're the psychologist, Dr. Calvin. *Make* him.'

'If I'm the psychologist, Mr. Robertson,' said Susan Calvin coldly, 'let me make the decisions. My robot will not be *made* to do anything as the price of his well-being.'

Robertson frowned and might have answered, but Justice Shane was tapping his gavel in a polite sort of way and they grudgingly fell silent.

Francis J. Hart, head of the Department of English and Dean of Graduate Studies, was on the stand. He was a plump man, meticulously dressed in dark clothing of a conservative cut, and possessing several strands of hair traversing the pink top of his cranium. He sat well back in the witness chair with his hands folded neatly in his lap and displaying, from time to time, a tight-lipped smile.

He said, 'My first connection with the matter of the Robot EZ-27 was on the occasion of the session of the University Senate Executive Committee at which the subject was introduced by Professor Goodfellow. Thereafter, on the tenth of April of last year, we held a special meeting on the subject, during which I was in the chair.'

'Were minutes kept of the meeting of the Executive Committee? Of the special meeting, that is?'

'Well, no. It was a rather unusual meeting.' The dean smiled briefly. 'We thought it might remain confidential.'

'What transpired at the meeting?'

Dean Hart was not entirely comfortable as chairman of that meeting. Nor did the other members assembled seem completely calm. Only Dr. Lanning appeared at peace with himself. His tall, gaunt figure and the shock of white hair that crowned him reminded Hart of portraits he had seen of Andrew Jackson.

Samples of the robot's work lay scattered along the central regions of the table and the reproduction of a graph drawn by the robot was now in the hands of Professor Minott of Physical Chemistry. The chemist's lips were pursed in obvious approval.

Hart cleared his throat and said, 'There seems no doubt that the robot can perform certain routine tasks with adequate competence. I have gone over these, for instance, just before coming in and there is very little to find fault with.'

He picked up a long sheet of printing, some three times as long as the average book page. It was a sheet of galley proof, designed to be corrected by authors before the type was set up in page form. Along both of the wide margins of the galley were proofmarks, neat and superbly legible.

Occasionally, a word of print was crossed out and a new word substituted in the margin in characters so fine and regular it might easily have been print itself. Some of the corrections were blue to indicate the original mistake had been the author's, a few in red, where the printer had been wrong.

'Actually,' said Lanning, 'there is less than very little to find fault with. I should say there is nothing at all to find fault with, Dr. Hart. I'm sure the corrections are perfect, insofar as the original manuscript was. If the manuscript against which this galley was corrected was at fault in a matter of fact rather than of English, the robot is not competent to correct it.'

'We accept that. However, the robot corrected word order on occasion and I don't think the rules of English are sufficiently hidebound for us to be sure that in each case the robot's choice was the correct one.'

'Easy's positronic brain,' said Lanning, showing large teeth as he smiled, 'has been molded by the contents of all the standard works on the subject. I'm sure you cannot point to a case where the robot's choice was definitely the incorrect one.'

Professor Minott looked up from the graph he still held. 'The question in my mind, Dr. Lanning, is why we need a robot at all, with all the difficulties in public relations that would entail. The science of automation has surely reached the point where your company could design a machine, an ordinary computer of a type known and accepted by the public, that would correct galleys.'

'I am sure we could,' said Lanning stiffly, 'but such a machine would require that the galleys be translated into special symbols or, at the least, transcribed on tapes. Any corrections would emerge in symbols. You would need to keep men employed translating words to symbols, symbols to words. Furthermore, such a computer could do no other job. It couldn't prepare the graph you hold in your hand, for instance.'

Minott grunted.

Lanning went on. 'The hallmark of the positronic robot is its flexibility. It can do a number of jobs. It is designed like a man so that it can use all the tools and machines that have, after all, been designed to be used by a man. It can talk to you and you can talk to it. You can actually reason with it up to a point. Compared to even a simple robot, an ordinary computer with a non-positronic brain is only a heavy adding machine.'

Goodfellow looked up and said, 'If we all talk and reason with the robot, what are the chances of our confusing it? I suppose it doesn't have the capability of absorbing an infinite amount of data.'

'No, it hasn't. But it should last five years with ordinary use. It will know when it will require clearing, and the company will do the job without charge.'

'The company will?'

'Yes. The company reserves the right to service the robot outside the ordinary course of its duties. It is one reason we retain control of our positronic robots and lease rather than sell them. In the pursuit of its ordinary functions, any robot can be directed by any man. Outside its ordinary functions, a robot requires expert handling, and that we can give it. For instance, any of you might clear an EZ robot to an extent by telling it to forget this item or that. But you would be almost certain to phrase the order in such a way as to cause it to forget too much or too little. We would detect such tampering, because we have built-in safeguards. However, since there is no need for clearing the robot in its ordinary work, or for doing other useless things, this raises no problem.'

Dean Hart touched his head as though to make sure his carefully cultivated strands lay evenly distributed and said, 'You are anxious to have us take the machine. Yet surely it is a losing proposition for U.S. Robots. One thousand a year is a ridiculously low price. Is it that you hope through this to rent other such machines to other universities at a more reasonable price?'

'Certainly that's a fair hope,' said Lanning.

'But even so, the number of machines you could rent would be limited. I doubt if you could make it a paying proposition.'

Lanning put his elbows on the table and earnestly leaned forward. 'Let me put it bluntly, gentlemen. Robots cannot be used on Earth, except in certain special cases, because of prejudice against them on the part of the public. U.S. Robots is a highly successful corporation with our extra-terrestrial and spaceflight markets alone, to say nothing of our computer subsidiaries. However, we are concerned with more than profits alone. It is our firm belief that the use of robots on Earth itself would mean a better life for all eventually, even if a certain amount of economic dislocation resulted at first.

'The labor unions are naturally against us, but surely we may expect cooperation from the large universities. The robot, Easy, will help you by relieving you of scholastic drudgery—by assuming, if you permit it, the role of galley slave for you. Other universities and research institutions will follow your lead, and if it works out, then perhaps other robots of other types may be placed and the public's objections to them broken down by stages.'

Minott murmured, 'Today Northeastern University, to-morrow the world.'

Angrily, Lanning whispered to Susan Calvin, 'I wasn't nearly that eloquent and they weren't nearly that reluctant. At a thousand a year, they were jumping to get Easy. Professor Minott told me he'd never seen as beautiful a job as that graph he was holding and there was no mistake on the galley or anywhere else. Hart admitted it freely.'

The severe vertical lines on Dr. Calvin's face did not soften. 'You should have demanded more money than they could pay, Alfred, and let them beat you down.'

'Maybe,' he grumbled.

Prosecution was not quite done with Professor Hart. 'After Dr. Lanning left, did you vote on whether to accept Robot EZ-27?'

'Yes, we did.'

'With what result?'

'In favor of acceptance, by majority vote.'

'What would you say influenced the vote?'

Defense objected immediately.

Prosecution rephrased the question. 'What influenced you, personally, in your individual vote? You did vote in favor, I think.'

'I voted in favor, yes. I did so largely because I was impressed by Dr. Lanning's feeling that it was our duty as members of the world's intellectual leadership to allow robotics to help Man in the solution of his problems.'

'In other words, Dr. Lanning talked you into it.'

'That's his job. He did it very well.'

'Your witness.'

Defense strode up to the witness chair and surveyed Professor Hart for a long moment. He said, 'In reality, you were all pretty eager to have Robot EZ-27 in your employ, weren't you?'

'We thought that if it could do the work, it might be useful.'

'*If* it could do the work? I understand you examined the samples of Robot EZ-27's original work with particular care on the day of the meeting which you have just described.'

'Yes, I did. Since the machine's work dealt primarily with the handling of the English language, and since that is my field of competence, it seemed logical that I be the one chosen to examine the work.'

'Very good. Was there anything on display on the table at the time of the meeting which was less than satisfactory? I have all the material here as exhibits. Can you point to a single unsatisfactory item?'

'Well——'

'It's a simple question. Was there one single solitary unsatisfactory item? You inspected it. Was there?'

The English professor frowned. 'There wasn't.'

'I also have some samples of work done by Robot EZ-27 during the course of his fourteen-month employ at Northeastern. Would you examine these and tell me if there is anything wrong with them in even one particular?'

Hart snapped. 'When he did make a mistake, it was a beauty.'

'Answer my question,' thundered Defense, 'and only the question I am putting to you! Is there anything wrong with the material?'

Dean Hart looked cautiously at each item. 'Well, nothing.'

'Barring the matter concerning which we are here engaged, do you know of any mistake on the part of EZ-27?'

'Barring the matter for which this trial is being held, no.'

Defense cleared his throat as though to signal end of paragraph. He said, 'Now about the vote concerning whether Robot EZ-27 was to be employed or not. You said there was a majority in favor. What was the actual vote?'

'Thirteen to one, as I remember.'

'Thirteen to one! More than just a majority, wouldn't you say?'

'No, sir!' All the pedant in Dean Hart was aroused. 'In the English language, the word "majority" means "more than half." Thirteen out of fourteen is a majority, nothing more.'

'But an almost unanimous one.'

'A majority all the same!'

Defense switched ground. 'And who was the lone hold-out?'

Dean Hart looked acutely uncomfortable. 'Professor Simon Ninheimer.'

Defense pretended astonishment. 'Professor Ninheimer? The head of the Department of Sociology?'

'Yes, sir.'

'The plaintiff?'

'Yes, sir.'

Defense pursed his lips. 'In other words, it turns out that the man bringing the action for payment of $750,000 damages against my client, United States Robots and Mechanical Men, Incorporated, was the one who from the beginning opposed the use of the robot—although everyone else on the Executive Committee of the University Senate was persuaded that it was a good idea.'

'He voted against the motion, as was his right.'

'You didn't mention in your description of the meeting any remarks made by Professor Ninheimer. Did he make any?'

'I think he spoke.'

'You *think*?'

'Well, he *did* speak.'

'Against using the robot?'

'Yes.'

'Was he violent about it?'

Dean Hart paused. 'He was vehement.'

Defense grew confidential. 'How long have you known Professor Ninheimer, Dean Hart?'

'About twelve years.'

'Reasonably well?'

'I should say so, yes.'

'Knowing him, then, would you say he was the kind of man who might continue to bear resentment against a robot, all the more so because an adverse vote had——'

Prosecution drowned out the remainder of the question with an indignant and vehement objection of his own. Defense motioned the witness down and Justice Shane called luncheon recess.

Robertson mangled his sandwich. The Corporation would not founder for loss of three-quarters of a million, but the loss would do it no particular good. He was conscious, moreover, that there would be a much more costly long-term setback in public relations.

He said sourly, 'Why all this business about how Easy got into the university? What do they hope to gain?'

The Attorney for Defense said quietly, 'A court action is like a chess game, Mr. Robertson. The winner is usually the one who can see more moves ahead, and my friend at the prosecutor's table is no beginner. They can show damage; that's no problem. Their main effort lies in anticipating our defense. They must be counting on us to try to show that Easy couldn't possibly have committed the offense—because of the Laws of Robotics.'

'All right,' said Robertson, 'that *is* our defense. An absolutely airtight one.'

'To a robotics engineer. Not necessarily to a judge. They're setting themselves up a position from which they can demonstrate that EZ-27 was no ordinary robot. It was the first of its type to be offered to the public. It was an experimental model that needed field-testing and the university was the only decent way to provide such testing. That would look plausible in the light of Dr. Lanning's strong efforts to place the robot and the willingness of U.S. Robots to lease it for so little. The prosecution would then argue that the field-test proved Easy to have been a failure. Now do you see the purpose of what's been going on?'

'But EZ-27 was a perfectly good model,' argued Robertson. 'It was the twenty-seventh in production.'

'Which is really a bad point,' said Defense somberly. 'What was wrong with the first twenty-six? Obviously something. Why shouldn't there be something wrong with the twenty-seventh, too?'

'There was nothing wrong with the first twenty-six except that they weren't complex enough for the task. These were the first positronic brains of the sort to be constructed and it was rather hit-and-miss to begin with. But the Three Laws held in all of them! *No* robot is so imperfect that the Three Laws don't hold.'

'Dr. Lanning has explained this to me, Mr. Robertson, and I am willing to take his word for it. The judge, however, may not be. We are expecting a decision from an honest and intelligent man who knows no robotics and thus may be led astray. For instance, if you or Dr. Lanning or Dr. Calvin were to say on the stand that any positronic brains were constructed "hit-and-miss," as you just did, prosecution would tear you apart in cross-examination. Nothing would salvage our case. So that's something to avoid.'

Robertson growled, 'If only Easy would talk.'

Defense shrugged. 'A robot is incompetent as a witness, so that would do us no good.'

'At least we'd know some of the facts. We'd know how it came to do such a thing.'

Susan Calvin fired up, a dullish red touched her cheeks and her voice had a trace of warmth in it. 'We *know* how Easy came to do it. It was ordered to! I've explained this to counsel and I'll explain it to you now.'

'Ordered to by whom?' asked Robertson in honest astonishment. (No one ever told him anything, he thought resentfully. These research people considered *themselves* the owners of U.S. Robots, by God!)

'By the plaintiff,' said Dr. Calvin.

'In heaven's name, why?'

'I don't know why yet. Perhaps just that we might be sued, that he might gain some cash.' There were blue glints in her eyes as she said that.

'Then why doesn't Easy say so?'

'Isn't that obvious? It's been ordered to keep quiet about the matter.'

'Why should that be obvious?' demanded Robertson truculently.

'Well, it's obvious to me. Robot psychology is my profession. If Easy will not answer questions about the matter directly, he will answer questions on the fringe of the matter. By measuring increased hesitation in his answers as the central question is approached, by measuring the area of blankness and the intensity of counterpotentials set up, it is possible to tell with scientific precision that his troubles are the result of an order not to talk, with its strength based on First Law. In other words, he's been told that if he talks, harm will be done a human being. Presumably harm to the unspeakable Professor Ninheimer, the plaintiff, who, to the robot, would seem a human being.'

'Well, then,' said Robertson, 'can't you explain that if he keeps quiet, harm will be done to U.S. Robots?'

'U.S. Robots is not a human being and the First Law of Robotics does not recognize a corporation as a person the way ordinary laws do. Besides, it would be dangerous to try to lift this particular sort of inhibition. The person who laid it on could lift it off least dangerously, because the robot's motivations in that respect are centered on that person. Any other course——' She shook her head and grew almost impassioned. 'I won't let the robot be damaged!'

Lanning interrupted with the air of bringing sanity to the problem. 'It seems to me that we have only to prove a robot incapable of the act of which Easy is accused. We can do that.'

'Exactly,' said Defense, in annoyance. '*You* can do that. The only witnesses capable of testifying to Easy's condition and to the nature of Easy's state of mind are employees of U.S. Robots. The judge can't possibly accept their testimony as unprejudiced.'

'How can he deny expert testimony?'

'By refusing to be convinced by it. That's his right as the judge. Against the alternative that a man like Professor Ninheimer deliberately set about ruining his own reputation, even for a sizable sum of money, the judge isn't going to accept the technicalities of your engineers. The judge is a man, after all. If he has to choose between a man doing an impossible thing and a robot doing an impossible thing, he's quite likely to decide in favor of the man.'

'A man *can* do an impossible thing,' said Lanning, 'because we don't know all the complexities of the human mind and we don't know what, in a given human mind, is impossible and what is not. We *do* know what is really impossible to a robot.'

'Well, we'll see if we can't convince the judge of that,' Defense replied wearily.

'If all you say is so,' rumbled Robertson, 'I don't see how you can.'

'We'll see. It's good to know and be aware of the difficulties involved, but let's not be *too* downhearted. I've tried to look ahead a few moves in the chess game, too.' With a stately nod in the direction of the robopsychologist, he added, '*With* the help of the good lady here.'

Lanning looked from one to the other and said, 'What the devil is this?'

But the bailiff thrust his head into the room and announced somewhat breathlessly that the trial was about to resume.

They took their seats, examining the man who had started all the trouble.

Simon Ninheimer owned a fluffy head of sandy hair, a face that narrowed past a beaked nose toward a pointed chin, and a habit of sometimes hesitating before key words in his conversation that gave him an air of a seeker after an almost unbearable precision. When he said, 'The sun rises in the—uh—east,' one was certain he had given due consideration to the possibility that it might at some time rise in the west.

Prosecution said, 'Did you oppose employment of Robot EZ-27 by the university?'

'I did, sir.'

'Why was that?'

'I did not feel that we understood the—uh—motives of U.S. Robots thoroughly. I mistrusted their anxiety to place the robot with us.'

'Did you feel that it was capable of doing the work that it was allegedly designed to do?'

'I know for a fact that it was not.'

'Would you state your reasons?'

Simon Ninheimer's book, entitled *Social Tensions Involved in Space-Flight and Their Resolution,* had been eight years in the making. Ninheimer's search for precision was not confined to his habits of speech, and in a subject like sociology, almost inherently imprecise, it left him breathless.

Even with the material in galley proofs, he felt no sense of completion. Rather the reverse, in fact. Staring at the long strips of print, he felt only the itch to tear the lines of type apart and rearrange them differently.

Jim Baker, Instructor and soon to be Assistant Professor of Sociology, found Ninheimer, three days after the first batch of galleys had arrived from the printer, staring at the handful of paper in abstraction. The galleys came in three copies: one for Ninheimer to proofread, one for Baker to proofread independently, and a third, marked 'Original,' which was to receive the final corrections, a combination of those made by Ninheimer and by Baker, after a conference at which possible conflicts and disagreements were ironed out. This had been their policy on the several papers on which they had collaborated in the past three years and it worked well.

Baker, young and ingratiatingly soft-voiced, had his own copies of the galleys in his hand. He said eagerly, 'I've done the first chapter and they contain some typographical beauts.'

'The first chapter always has them,' said Ninheimer distantly.

'Do you want to go over it now?'

Ninheimer brought his eyes to grave focus on Baker. 'I haven't done anything on the galleys, Jim. I don't think I'll bother.'

Baker looked confused. 'Not bother?'

Ninheimer pursed his lips. 'I've asked about the—uh—workload of the machine. After all, he was originally—uh—promoted as a proofreader. They've set a schedule.'

'The *machine*? You mean Easy?'

'I believe that is the foolish name they gave it.'

'But, Dr. Ninheimer, I thought you were staying clear of it!'

'I seem to be the only one doing so. Perhaps I ought to take my share of the—uh—advantage.'

'Oh. Well, I seem to have wasted time on this first chapter, then,' said the younger man ruefully.

'Not wasted. We can compare the machine's result with yours as a check.'

'If you want to, but——'

'Yes?'

'I doubt that we'll find anything wrong with Easy's work. It's supposed never to have made a mistake.'

'I dare say,' said Ninheimer dryly.

The first chapter was brought in again by Baker four days later. This time it was Ninheimer's copy, fresh from

the special annex that had been built to house Easy and the
equipment it used.

Baker was jubilant. 'Dr. Ninheimer, it not only caught
everything I caught—it found a dozen errors I missed!
The whole thing took it twelve minutes!'

Ninheimer looked over the sheaf, with the neatly printed
marks and symbols in the margins. He said, 'It is not as
complete as you and I would have made it. We would have
entered an insert on Suzuki's work on the neurological
effects of low gravity.'

'You mean his paper in *Sociological Reviews*?'

'Of course.'

'Well, you can't expect impossibilities of Easy. It can't
read the literature for us.'

'I realize that. As a matter of fact, I have prepared the
insert. I will see the machine and make certain it knows
how to—uh—handle inserts.'

'It will know.'

'I prefer to make certain.'

Ninheimer had to make an appointment to see Easy, and
then could get nothing better than fifteen minutes in the
late evening.

But the fifteen minutes turned out to be ample. Robot
EZ-27 understood the matter of inserts at once.

Ninheimer found himself uncomfortable at close quarters
with the robot for the first time. Almost automatically, as
though it were human, he found himself asking, 'Are you
happy with your work?'

'Most happy, Professor Ninheimer,' said Easy solemnly,
the photocells that were its eyes gleaming their normal deep
red.

'You know me?'

'From the fact that you present me with additional

material to include in the galleys, it follows that you are the author. The author's name, of course, is at the head of each sheet of galley proof.'

'I see. You make—uh—deductions, then. Tell me——' he couldn't resist the question—'what do you think of the book so far?'

Easy said, 'I find it very pleasant to work with.'

'Pleasant? That is an odd word for a—uh—a mechanism without emotion. I've been told you have no emotion.'

'The words of your book go in accordance with my circuits,' Easy explained. 'They set up little or no counter-potentials. It is in my brain paths to translate this mechanical fact into a word such as "pleasant." The emotional context is fortuitous.'

'I see. Why do you find the book pleasant?'

'It deals with human beings, Professor, and not with inorganic materials or mathematical symbols. Your book attempts to understand human beings and to help increase human happiness.'

'And this is what you try to do and so my book goes in accordance with your circuits? Is that it?'

'That is it, Professor.'

The fifteen minutes were up. Ninheimer left and went to the university library, which was on the point of closing. He kept them open long enough to find an elementary text on robotics. He took it home with him.

Except for occasional insertion of late material, the galleys went to Easy and from him to the publishers with little intervention from Ninheimer at first—and none at all later.

Baker said, a little uneasily, 'It almost gives me a feeling of uselessness.'

'It should give you a feeling of having time to begin a new project,' said Ninheimer, without looking up from the notations he was making in the current issue of *Social Science Abstracts*.

'I'm just not used to it. I keep worrying about the galleys. It's silly, I know.'

'It is.'

'The other day I got a couple of sheets before Easy sent them off to——'

'What!' Ninheimer looked up, scowling. The copy of *Abstracts* slid shut. 'Did you disturb the machine at its work?'

'Only for a minute. Everything was all right. Oh, it changed one word. You referred to something as "criminal"; it changed the word to "reckless." It thought the second adjective fit in better with the context.'

Ninheimer grew thoughtful. 'What did you think?'

'You know, I agreed with it. I let it stand.'

Ninheimer turned in his swivel-chair to face his young associate. 'See here, I wish you wouldn't do this again. If I am to use the machine, I wish the—uh—full advantage of it. If I am to use it and lose your—uh—services anyway because you supervise it when the whole point is that it requires no supervision, I gain nothing. Do you see?'

'Yes, Dr. Ninheimer,' said Baker, subdued.

The advance copies of *Social Tensions* arrived in Dr. Ninheimer's office on the eighth of May. He looked through it briefly, flipping pages and pausing to read a paragraph here and there. Then he put his copies away.

As he explained later, he forgot about it. For eight years, he had worked at it, but now, and for months in the past, other interests had engaged him while Easy had taken the load of the book off his shoulders. He did not even think to donate the usual complimentary copy to the university library. Even Baker, who had thrown himself into work and had steered clear of the department head since receiving his rebuke at their last meeting, received no copy.

On the sixteenth of June that stage ended. Ninheimer received a phone call and stared at the image in the 'plate with surprise.

'Speidell! Are you in town?'

'No, sir. I'm in Cleveland.' Speidell's voice trembled with emotion.

'Then why the call?'

'Because I've just been looking through your new book! Ninheimer, are you *mad*? Have you gone *insane*?'

Ninheimer stiffened. 'Is something—uh—wrong?' he asked in alarm.

'*Wrong*? I refer you to page 562. What in blazes do you mean by interpreting my work as you do? Where in the paper cited do I make the claim that the criminal personality is nonexistent and that it is the *law*-enforcement agencies that are the *true* criminals? Here, let me quote——'

'Wait! Wait!' cried Ninheimer, trying to find the page. 'Let me see. Let me see ... Good God!'

'Well?'

'Speidell, I don't see how this could have happened. I never wrote this.'

'But that's what's printed! And that distortion isn't the worst. You look at page 690 and imagine what Ipatiev is going to do to you when he sees the hash you've made of his findings! Look, Ninhéimer, the book is *riddled* with this sort of thing. I don't know what you were thinking of—but there's nothing to do but get the book off the market. And you'd better be prepared for extensive apologies at the next Association meeting!'

'Speidell, listen to me——'

But Speidell had flashed off with a force that had the 'plate glowing with after-images for fifteen seconds.

It was then that Ninheimer went through the book and began marking off passages with red ink.

He kept his temper remarkably well when he faced Easy again, but his lips were pale. He passed the book to Easy and said, 'Will you read the marked passages on pages 562, 631, 664 and 690?'

Easy did so in four glances. 'Yes, Professor Ninheimer.'

'This is not as I had it in the original galleys.'

'No, sir. It is not.'

'Did you change it to read as it now does?'

'Yes, sir.'

'Why?'

'Sir, the passages as they read in your version were most uncomplimentary to certain groups of human beings. I felt it advisable to change the wording to avoid doing them harm.'

'How *dared* you do such a thing?'

'The First Law, Professor, does not let me, through any inaction, allow harm to come to human beings. Certainly, considering your reputation in the world of sociology and the wide circulation your book would receive among scholars, considerable harm would come to a number of the human beings you speak of.'

'But do you realize the harm that will come to *me* now?'

'It was necessary to choose the alternative with less harm.'

Professor Ninheimer, shaking with fury, staggered away.

It was clear to him that U.S. Robots would have to account to him for this.

There was some excitement at the defendants' table, which increased as Prosecution drove the point home.

'Then Robot EZ-27 informed you that the reason for its action was based on the First Law of Robotics?'

'That is correct, sir.'

'That, in effect, it had no choice?'

'Yes, sir.'

'It follows then that U.S. Robots designed a robot that would of necessity rewrite books to accord with its own conceptions of what was right. And yet they palmed it off as simple proofreader. Would you say that?'

Defense objected firmly at once, pointing out that the witness was being asked for a decision on a matter in which he had no competence. The judge admonished Prosecution in the usual terms, but there was no doubt that the exchange had sunk home—not least upon the attorney for the Defense.

Defense asked for a short recess before beginning cross-examination using a legal technicality for the purpose that got him five minutes.

He leaned over toward Susan Calvin. 'Is it possible, Dr. Calvin, that Professor Ninheimer is telling the truth and that Easy was motivated by the First Law?'

Calvin pressed her lips together, then said, 'No. It *isn't* possible. The last part of Ninheimer's testimony is deliberate perjury. Easy is not designed to be able to judge matters at the stage of abstraction represented by an advanced textbook on sociology. It would never be able to tell that certain groups of humans would be harmed by a phrase in such a book. Its mind is simply not built for that.'

'I suppose, though, that we can't prove this to a layman,' said Defense pessimistically.

'No,' admitted Calvin. 'The proof would be highly complex. Our way out is still what it was. We must prove Ninheimer is lying, and nothing he has said need change our plan of attack.'

'Very well, Dr. Calvin,' said Defense, 'I must accept your word in this. We'll go on as planned.'

In the courtroom, the judge's gavel rose and fell and Dr. Ninheimer took the stand once more. He smiled a little as one who feels his position to be impregnable and rather enjoys the prospect of countering a useless attack.

Defense approached warily and began softly. 'Dr. Ninheimer, do you mean to say that you were completely unaware of these alleged changes in your manuscript until such time as Dr. Speidell called you on the sixteenth of June?'

'That is correct, sir.'

'Did you never look at the galleys after Robot EZ-27 had proofread them?'

'At first I did, but it seemed to me a useless task, I relied on the claims of U.S. Robots. The absurd—uh—changes were made only in the last quarter of the book after the robot, I presume, had learned enough about sociology——'

'Never mind your presumptions!' said Defense. 'I understood your colleague, Dr. Baker, saw the later galleys on at least one occasion. Do you remember testifying to that effect?'

'Yes, sir. As I said, he told me about seeing one page, and even there, the robot had changed a word.'

Again Defense broke in. 'Don't you find it strange, sir, that after over a year of implacable hostility to the robot, after having voted against it in the first place and having refused to put it to any use whatever, you suddenly decided to put your book, your *magnum opus*, into its hands?'

'I don't find that strange. I simply decided that I might as well use the machine.'

'And you were so confident of Robot EZ-27—all of a sudden—that you didn't even bother to check your galleys?'

'I told you I was—uh—persuaded by U.S. Robots' propaganda.'

'So persuaded that when your colleague, Dr. Baker, attempted to check on the robot, you berated him soundly?'

'I didn't berate him. I merely did not wish to have him— uh—waste his time. At least, I thought then it was a waste of time. I did not see the significance of that change in a word at the——'

Defense said with heavy sarcasm, 'I have no doubt you were instructed to bring up that point in order that the word-change be entered in the record——' He altered his line to forestall objection and said, 'The point is that you were extremely angry with Dr. Baker.'

'No, sir. Not angry.'

'You didn't give him a copy of your book when you received it.'

'Simple forgetfulness. I didn't give the library its copy, either.' Ninheimer smiled cautiously. 'Professors are notoriously absentminded.'

Defense said, 'Do you find it strange that, after more than a year of perfect work, Robot EZ-27 should go wrong on your book? On a book, that is, which was written by you, who was, of all people, the most implacably hostile to the robot?'

'My book was the only sizable work dealing with mankind that it had to face. The Three Laws of Robotics took hold then.'

'Several times, Dr. Ninheimer,' said Defense, 'you have tried to sound like an expert on robotics. Apparently you suddenly grew interested in robotics and took out books on the subject from the library. You testified to that effect, did you not?'

'One book, sir. That was the result of what seems to me to have been—uh—natural curiosity.'

'And it enabled you to explain why the robot should, as you allege, have distorted your book?'

'Yes, sir.'

'Very convenient. But are you sure your interest in robotics was not intended to enable you to manipulate the robot for your own purposes?'

Ninheimer flushed. 'Certainly not, sir!'

Defense's voice rose. 'In fact, are you sure the alleged altered passages were not as you had them in the first place?'

The sociologist half-rose. 'That's—uh—uh—ridiculous! I have the galleys——'

He had difficulty speaking and Prosecution rose to insert smoothly, 'With your permission, Your Honor, I intend to introduce as evidence the set of galleys given by Dr. Ninheimer to Robot EZ-27 and the set of galleys mailed by Robot EZ-27 to the publishers. I will do so now if my esteemed colleague so desires, and will be willing to allow a recess in order that the two sets of galleys may be compared.'

Defense waved his hand impatiently. 'That is not necessary. My honored opponent can introduce those galleys whenever he chooses. I'm sure they will show whatever discrepancies are claimed by the plaintiff to exist. What I would like to know of the witness, however, is whether he also has in his possession *Dr. Baker's* galleys.'

'Dr. Baker's galleys?' Ninheimer frowned. He was not yet quite master of himself.

'Yes, Professor! I mean Dr. Baker's galleys. You testified to the effect that Dr. Baker had received a separate copy of the galleys. I will have the clerk read your testimony if you are suddenly a selective type of amnesiac. Or is it just that professors are, as you say, notoriously absent-minded?'

Ninheimer said, 'I remember Dr. Baker's galleys. They weren't necessary once the job was placed in the care of the proofreading machine——'

'So you burned them?'

'*No.* I put them in the waste basket.'

'Burned them, dumped them—what's the difference? The point is you got rid of them.'

'There's nothing wrong——' began Ninheimer weakly.

'Nothing wrong?' thundered Defense. 'Nothing wrong except that there is now no way we can check to see if, on certain crucial galley sheets, you might not have substituted a harmless blank one from Dr. Baker's copy for a sheet in your own copy which you had deliberately mangled in such a way as to force the robot to——'

Prosecution shouted a furious objection. Justice Shane leaned forward, his round face doing its best to assume an expression of anger equivalent to the intensity of the emotion felt by the man.

The judge said, 'Do you have any evidence, Counselor, for the extraordinary statement you have just made?'

Defense said quietly, 'No direct evidence, Your Honor. But I would like to point out that, viewed properly, the sudden conversion of the plaintiff from anti-roboticism, his

sudden interest in robotics, his refusal to check the galleys
or to allow anyone else to check them, his careful neglect to
allow anyone to see the book immediately after publication,
all very clearly point——'

'Counselor,' interrupted the judge impatiently, 'this is not
the place for esoteric deductions. The plaintiff is not on
trial. Neither are you prosecuting him. I forbid this line of
attack and I can only point out that the desperation that
must have induced you to do this cannot help but weaken
your case. If you have legitimate questions to ask,
Counselor, you may continue with your cross-examination.
But I warn you against another such exhibition in this
courtroom.'

'I have no further questions, Your Honor.'

Robertson whispered heatedly as counsel for the Defense
returned to his table, 'What good did that do, for God's
sake? The judge is dead-set against you now.'

Defense replied calmly, 'But Ninheimer is good and
rattled. And we've set him up for tomorrow's move. He'll
be ripe.'

Susan Calvin nodded gravely.

The rest of Prosecution's case was mild in comparison.
Dr. Baker was called and bore out most of Ninheimer's testimony. Drs. Speidell and Ipatiev were called, and they ex-
pounded most movingly on their shock and dismay at
certain quoted passages in Dr. Ninheimer's book. Both gave
their professional opinion that Dr. Ninheimer's professional
reputation had been seriously impaired.

The galleys were introduced in evidence, as were copies
of the finished book.

Defense cross-examined no more that day. Prosecution
rested and the trial was recessed till the next morning.

Defense made his first motion at the beginning of the proceedings on the second day. He requested that Robot EZ 27 be admitted as a spectator to the proceedings.

Prosecution objected at once and Justice Shane called both to the bench.

Prosecution said hotly, 'This is obviously illegal. A robot may not be in any edifice used by the general public.'

'This courtroom,' pointed out Defense, 'is closed to all but those having an immediate connection with the case.'

'A large machine of *known* erratic behavior would disturb my clients and my witnesses by its very presence! It would make hash out of the proceedings.'

The judge seemed inclined to agree. He turned to Defense and said rather unsympathetically, 'What are the reasons for your request?'

Defense said, 'It will be our contention that Robot EZ-27 could not possibly, by the nature of its construction, have behaved as it has been described as behaving. It will be necessary to present a few demonstrations.'

Prosecution said, 'I don't see the point, Your Honor. Demonstrations conducted by men employed at U.S. Robots are worth little as evidence when U.S. Robots is the defendant.'

'Your Honor,' said Defense, 'the validity of any evidence is for you to decide, not for the Prosecuting Attorney. At least, that is my understanding.'

Justice Shane, his prerogatives encroached upon, said, 'Your understanding is correct. Nevertheless, the presence of a robot here does raise important legal questions.'

'Surely, Your Honor, nothing should be allowed to override the requirements of justice. If the robot is not present, we are prevented from presenting our only defense.'

The judge considered. 'There would be the question of transporting the robot here.'

'That is a problem with which U.S. Robots has frequently been faced. We have a truck parked outside the courtroom, constructed according to the laws governing the transportation of robots. Robot EZ-27 is in a packing case inside with two men guarding it. The doors to the truck are properly secured and all other necessary precautions have been taken.'

'You seem certain,' said Justice Shane, in renewed ill-temper, 'that judgment on this point will be in your favor.'

'Not at all, Your Honor. If it is not, we simply turn the truck about. I have made no presumptions concerning your decision.'

The judge nodded. 'The request on the part of the Defense is granted.'

The crate was carried in on a large dolly and the two men who handled it opened it. The courtroom was immersed in a dead silence.

Susan Calvin waited as the thick slabs of celluform went down, then held out one hand. 'Come, Easy.'

The robot looked in her direction and held out its large metal arm. It towered over her by two feet but followed meekly, like a child in the clasp of its mother. Someone giggled nervously and choked it off at a hard glare from Dr. Calvin.

Easy seated itself carefully in a large chair brought by the bailiff, which creaked but held.

Defense said, 'When it becomes necessary, Your Honor, we will prove that this is actually Robot EZ-27, the specific robot in the employ of Northeastern University during the period of time with which we are concerned.'

'Good,' His Honor said. 'That will be necessary. I, for one, have no idea how you can tell one robot from another.'

'And now,' said Defense, 'I would like to call my first witness to the stand. Professor Simon Ninheimer, please.'

The clerk hesitated, looked at the judge. Justice Shane asked, with visible surprise, 'You are calling the *plaintiff* as your witness?'

'Yes, Your Honor.'

'I hope that you're aware that as long as he's your witness, you will be allowed none of the latitude you might exercise if you were cross-examining an opposing witness.'

Defense said smoothly, 'My only purpose in all this is to arrive at the truth. It will not be necessary to do more than ask a few polite questions.'

'Well,' said the judge dubiously, 'you're the one handling the case. Call the witness.'

Ninheimer took the stand and was informed that he was still under oath. He looked more nervous than he had the day before, almost apprehensive.

But Defense looked at him benignly.

'Now, Professor Ninheimer, you are suing my clients in the amount of $750,000.'

'That is the—uh—sum. Yes.'

'That is a great deal of money.'

'I have suffered a great deal of harm.'

'Surely not that much. The material in question involves only a few passages in a book. Perhaps these were unfortunate passages, but after all, books sometimes appear with curious mistakes in them.'

Ninheimer's nostrils flared. 'Sir, this book was to have been the climax of my professional career! Instead, it makes me look like an incompetent scholar, a perverter of the views held by my honored friends and associates, and a believer of ridiculous and—uh—out-moded viewpoints. My reputation is irretrievably shattered! I can never hold up my head in any—uh—assemblage of scholars, regardless of the outcome of this trial. I certainly cannot continue in my career, which has been the whole of my life. The very purpose of my life has been—uh—aborted and destroyed.'

Defense made no attempt to interrupt the speech, but stared abstractedly at his fingernails as it went on.

He said very soothingly, 'But surely, Professor Ninheimer, at your present age, you could not hope to earn more than—let us be generous—$150,000 during the remainder of your life. Yet you are asking the court to award you five times as much.'

Ninheimer said, with an even greater burst of emotion, 'It is not in my lifetime alone that I am ruined. I do not know for how many generations I shall be pointed at by sociologists as a—uh—a fool or maniac. My real achievements will be buried and ignored. I am ruined not only until the day of my death, but for all time to come, because there will always be people who will not believe that a robot made those insertions——'

It was at this point that Robot EZ-27 rose to his feet. Susan Calvin made no move to stop him. She sat motionless, staring straight ahead. Defense sighed softly.

Easy's melodious voice carried clearly. It said, 'I would like to explain to everyone that I did insert certain passages in the galley proofs that seemed directly opposed to what had been there at first——'

Even the Prosecuting Attorney was too startled at the spectacle of a seven-foot robot rising to address the court to be able to demand the stopping of what was obviously a most irregular procedure.

When he could collect his wits, it was to late. For Ninheimer rose in the witness chair, his face working.

He shouted wildly, 'Damn you, you were instructed to keep your mouth shut about——'

He ground to a choking halt, and Easy was silent, too.

Prosecution was on his feet now, demanding that a mistrial be declared.

Justice Shane banged his gavel desperately. 'Silence! Silence! Certainly there is every reason here to declare a mistrial, except that in the interests of justice I would like to have Professor Ninheimer complete his statement. I distinctly heard him say to the robot that the robot had been instructed to keep its mouth shut about something. There was no mention in your testimony, Professor Ninheimer, as to any instructions to the robot to keep silent about anything!'

Ninheimer stared wordlessly at the judge.

Justice Shane said, 'Did you instruct Robot EZ-27 to keep silent about something? And if so, about what?'

'Your Honor——' began Ninheimer hoarsely, and couldn't continue.

The judge's voice grew sharp. 'Did you, in fact, order the inserts in question to be made in the galleys and then order the robot to keep quiet about your part in this?'

Prosecution objected vigorously, but Ninheimer shouted, 'Oh, what's the use? Yes! Yes!' And he ran from the witness stand. He was stopped at the door by the bailiff and sank hopelessly into one of the last rows of seats, head buried in both hands.

Justice Shane said, 'It is evident to me that Robot EZ-27 was brought here as a trick. Except for the fact that the trick served to prevent a serious miscarriage of justice, I would certainly hold attorney for the Defense in contempt.

It is clear now, beyond any doubt, that the plaintiff has committed what is to me a completely inexplicable fraud since, apparently, he was knowingly ruining his career in the process——'

Judgment, of course, was for the defendant.

Dr. Susan Calvin had herself announced at Dr. Ninheimer's bachelor quarters in University Hall. The young engineer who had driven the car offered to go up with her, but she looked at him scornfully.

'Do you think he'll assault me? Wait down here.'

Ninheimer was in no mood to assault anyone. He was packing, wasting no time, anxious to be away before the adverse conclusion of the trial became general knowledge.

He looked at Calvin with a queerly defiant air and said, 'Are you coming to warn me of a countersuit? If so, it will get you nothing. I have no money, no job, no future. I can't even meet the costs of the trial.'

'If you're looking for sympathy,' said Calvin coldly, 'don't look for it here. This was your doing. However, there will be no countersuit, neither of you nor of the university. We will even do what we can to keep you from going to prison for perjury. We aren't vindictive.'

'Oh, is that why I'm not already in custody for forswearing myself? I had wondered. But then,' he added bitterly, 'why *should* you be vindictive? You have what you want now.'

'Some of what we want, yes,' said Calvin. 'The university will keep Easy in its employ at a considerably higher rental fee. Furthermore, certain underground publicity concerning the trial will make it possible to place a few more of the EZ models in other institutions without danger of a repetition of this trouble.'

Then why have you come to see me?'

'Because I don't have all of what I want yet. I want to know why you hate robots as you do. Even if you had won the case, your reputation would have been ruined. The money you might have obtained could not have compensated for that. Would the satisfaction of your hatred for robots have done so?'

'Are you interested in *human* minds, Dr. Calvin?' asked Ninheimer, with acid mockery.

'Insofar as their reactions concern the welfare of robots, yes. For that reason, I have learned a little of human psychology.'

'Enough of it to be able to trick me!'

'That wasn't hard,' said Calvin, without pomposity. 'The difficult thing was doing it in such a way as not to damage Easy.'

'It is like you to be more concerned for a machine than for a man.' He looked at her with savage contempt.

It left her unmoved. 'It merely seems so, Professor Ninheimer. It is only by being concerned for robots that one can truly be concerned for twenty-first-century man. You would understand this if you were a roboticist.'

'I have read enough robotics to know I don't *want* to be a roboticist!'

'Pardon me, you have read *a book* on robotics. It has taught you nothing. You learned enough to know that you could order a robot to do many things, even to falsify a book, if you went about it properly. You learned enough to know that you could not order him to forget something entirely without risking detection, but you thought you could order him into simple silence more safely. You were wrong.'

'You guessed the truth from his silence?'

'It wasn't guessing. You were an amateur and didn't know enough to cover your tracks completely. My only problem was to prove the matter to the judge and you were kind enough to help us there, in your ignorance of the robotics you claim to despise.'

'Is there any purpose in this discussion?' asked Ninheimer wearily.

'For me, yes,' said Susan Calvin, 'because I want you to understand how completely you have misjudged robots. You silenced Easy by telling him that if he told anyone about your own distortion of the book, you would lose your job. That set up a certain potential within Easy toward silence, one that was strong enough to resist our efforts to break it down. We would have damaged the brain if we had persisted.

'On the witness stand, however, you yourself put up a higher counterpotential. You said that because people would think that you, not a robot, had written the disputed passages in the book, you would lose far more than just your job. You would lose your reputation, your standing, your respect, your reason for living. You would lose the memory of you after death. A new and higher potential was set up by you—and Easy talked.'

'Oh, God,' said Ninheimer, turning his head away.

Calvin was inexorable. She said, 'Do you understand *why* he talked? It was not to accuse you, but to *defend* you! It can be mathmatically shown that he was about to assume full blame for your crime, to deny that you had anything to do with it. The First Law required that. He was going to lie—to damage himself—to bring monetary harm to a corporation. All that meant less to him than did the saving of you. If you really understood robots and robotics, you would have let him talk. But you did not understand, as I was sure you wouldn't, as I guaranteed to the defense attorney that you wouldn't. You were certain, in your hatred of robots, that Easy would act as a human being would act and defend itself at your expense. So you flared out at him in panic—and destroyed yourself.'

Ninheimer said with feeling, 'I hope some day your robots turn on you and kill you!'

'Don't be foolish,' said Calvin. 'Now I want you to explain why you've done all this.'

Ninheimer grinned a distorted, humorless grin. 'I am to dissect my mind, am I, for your intellectual curiosity, in return for immunity from a charge of perjury?'

'Put it that way if you like,' said Calvin emotionlessly. 'But explain.'

'So that you can counter future anti-robot attempts more efficiently? With greater understanding?'

'I accept that.'

'You know,' said Ninheimer, 'I'll tell you—just to watch it do you no good at all. You can't understand human motivation. You can only understand your damned machines because you're a machine yourself, with skin on.'

He was breathing hard and there was no hesitation in his speech, no searching for precision. It was as though he had no further use for precision.

He said, 'For two hundred and fifty years, the machine has been replacing Man and destroying the handcraftsman. Pottery is spewed out of molds and presses. Works of art have been replaced by identical gimcracks stamped out on a die. Call it progress, if you wish! The artist is restricted to abstractions, confined to the world of ideas. He must design something in mind—and then the machine does the rest.

'Do you suppose the potter is content with mental creation? Do you suppose the idea is enough? That there is nothing in the feel of the clay itself, in watching the thing grow as hand and mind work *together*? Do you suppose the actual growth doesn't act as a feedback to modify and improve the idea?'

'You are not a potter,' said Dr. Calvin.

'I am a creative artist! I design and build articles and books. There is more to it than the mere thinking of words and of putting them in the right order. If that were all, there would be no pleasure in it, no return.

'A book should take shape in the hands of the writer. One must actually see the chapters grow and develop. One must work and re-work and watch the changes take place beyond the original concept even. There is taking the galleys in hand and seeing how the sentences look in print and molding them again. There are a hundred contacts between a man and his work at every stage of the game—and the contact itself is pleasurable and repays a man for the work he puts into his creation more than anything else could. *Your robot would take all that away.*'

'So does a typewriter. So does a printing press. Do you propose to return to the hand illumination of manuscripts?'

'Typewriters and printing presses take away some, but your robot would deprive us of all. Your robot takes over the galleys. Soon it, or other robots, would take over the original writing, the searching of the sources, the checking and cross-checking of passages, perhaps even the deduction of conclusions. What would that leave the scholar? One thing only—the barren decisions concerning what orders to give the robot next! I want to save the future generations of the world of scholarship from such a final hell. That meant more to me than even my own reputation and so I set out to destroy U.S. Robots by whatever means.'

'You were bound to fail,' said Susan Calvin.

'I was bound to try,' said Simon Ninheimer.

Calvin turned and left. She did her best to feel no pang of sympathy for the broken man.

She did not entirely succeed.

Voyager

Join the travellers of the imagination